All the Beauty
of the Sun

The Boy I Love Trilogy

The Boy I Love
All the Beauty of the Sun
Paper Moon

Say You Love Me

The Good Father

All the Beauty
of the Sun

MARION HUSBAND

Published by Accent Press Ltd – 2012

ISBN 9781908262011

Printed and bound by CPI Group (UK) Ltd, Croydon, CR0 4YY

Cover design by Sarah Ann Davies

All the Beauty of the Sun

O, how this spring of love resembleth
The uncertain glory of an April day,
Which now shows all the beauty of the sun,
And by and by a cloud takes all away.

William Shakespeare, *The Two Gentlemen of Verona*,
Act 1, Scene 3

November 1924

MY DEAR PAUL,

In the pub this evening, a man died. I knew him, a little; he was a man I didn't care for, a braggart; I think he would sometimes beat his wife. Now he is dead, dropped to the pub's bare boards, his beer spilt around him. The other drinkers said that it was a good way to go – the very best way, in fact – fast: one moment happy – content, at least – the next quite dead and gone. Fred, the landlord, asked me to say something over the corpse, and I obliged; just a few words – you could probably recite something like them yourself – such words we have all invented.

Why should I start a letter to you like this? I imagine you reading these lines in your sunny courtyard by the fountain you told me about, but transported by my words to dull, cold England, to a backstreet in London, to a public house where only old men drink. You will kneel beside me, beside the old man's dead body, and catch my eye as I finish my made-up blessing; you will smile that smile you use when you remember how sad and ridiculous the world is, that look in your eye like a lifeline you throw me when I'm drowning. Later, we would walk back to my rooms, we would drink each other's health and not talk of anything at all, not death, not drowning, not even simply getting on with life. You would only tell me about Tangiers, the fountain where the sparrows bathe and the orange tree you inexpertly tend. You would tell me a joke, the one about the corporal and the can-can girl, or the one about the priest who stopped being a priest but couldn't stop *being* a priest.

1

How is dear Patrick? How is your work? The painting of the little Arab boy you sent me hangs above my fireplace but it occurred to me that it should have a much wider audience. I have heard of a man who is about to open an art gallery. His name is Lawrence Hawker – should I show him the portrait? Would you come back to England to exhibit your work? You would be the toast of the London art world, I am sure, and how proud I would be to introduce you as my friend. There is also someone I would very much like you to meet; her name is Ann and she is young and very lovely – perhaps much too young and lovely for me, but all the same, all the same, she is kind and bright and lively and she makes me feel as if I have woken up from a fitful sleep into a sunny day. There now; I am becoming poetical, a sign of something, perhaps.

I know you may not want to come home to England, I know there are difficulties, but I do so feel that your work *needs* to be seen here. You write that you are continuing to work on the soldier portraits – I'm sorry, I don't know what else to call them – the war pictures? – and perhaps an exhibition of these would be timely; there are memorials being built to the dead, but they are so clean and tidy, so stone cold. What else can we do to honour our lost friends?

It goes without writing that it would be wonderful to see you – and Patrick – again. You will write that I should travel to Morocco to see you, that I should be brave, *goodbye Piccadilly, farewell Leicester Square* and all that. I have a small store of bravery I am saving for a rainy day and perhaps when that day comes I shall pack up and head for your sunny shore. But in the meantime, do consider sending your pictures to this Hawker fellow. Cause a stir; *make* them sit up and take notice.

With all my very best wishes to you and of course to Patrick,

Matthew

Chapter One

WATCHING ANN BRUSH HER hair, Edmund had the idea that he should ask her how he compared with the other men she slept with. Did she like him more? Was he in some way better or worse? Clumsier perhaps? Or more tender, energetic, desirable? He wondered if he really, truly wanted to know, because of course, no one asked such questions, no one with any pride, or any sense at all of conviction. Lawrence Hawker, for example, would never be so crass. Hawker was older, a careless, sophisticated man, someone who, in Edmund's heart of hearts, he thought of as one of the grown-ups.

Edmund knew he should, conventionally, be jealous of his rival; but jealousy would make him unconventional within their tight little circle. Besides, Hawker and he weren't rivals: Ann slept with them both, and he suspected that Hawker cared even less about this than he did. All the same, Edmund would like to know if she cared more or less about him. He supposed he wanted to know that at least. At least he would like to know that he made some impression, some *something*.

Lying on his back in her bed, his hands clasped beneath his head, the sheet crumpled beneath his body, he laughed because there was something absurd in all this that he hadn't realised until now; he had been taking promiscuity seriously when perhaps he should have thought of it as a parlour game: *bed-hopping – the winner the first to finish with his pride intact.*

Ann turned from the mirror above the fireplace to frown at him, hairbrush poised mid-stroke. Blonde hairs curled from the bristles, bright in the lamplight. She was naked and her skin was pale and quite perfect, wondrously so. No wonder Joseph Day

3

wanted to paint her so often; they all did, but it was only Day who was skilled enough, whose finished results Ann decided were worth the uncomfortable, boring hours of modelling.

Turning back to the mirror she asked, 'What are you laughing at?'

He wondered how she might react to his questions, *Who do you prefer, Lawrence Hawker or me? Which of us thrills you most?* He might ask if she had slept with his friend Andrew, too – although he suspected Andrew was queer. He thought of Andrew, decided it would be best not to think about him, not now, but when he was alone, perhaps. For now he imagined asking her, *Am I different in any way?* She would laugh; he imagined she would say, 'Silly boy!' But all the same, the thought of differences could not be unthought; he knew that he would return to these differences, worry them over and over; he knew that this worrying could overwhelm him.

The bedcovers were in deep folds at his groin and he pulled them up to his chin, cold suddenly. Her scent lingered on the sheet, warm and touching like cheap violet sweets; earlier he had noticed a blood stain on the side where she slept and had been reassured even as a part of him wanted her to be pregnant, that part that was irrational and boorish and as desperate to be confirmed as virile as any man who had ever lived. But that part of him seemed particularly unconvincing, an under-rehearsed act he was performing for a knowing, critical audience. Besides, paternity couldn't be assured, of course; also there was the used johnnie flaccid on the floor beside the bed; he was always very careful, very afraid of disease. 'VD kills in a particularly nasty way,' his father had told him, and he should know, the great doctor having witnessed such deaths. Edmund remembered the rest of this lecture from his father as particularly oblique, even by his father's standard, how he had talked about how he must be sure of himself and not go rushing at windmills. He had been sixteen at the time, his virginity still shaming. Perhaps his father had sensed this shame, although he didn't like to think so.

Ann picked up her knickers from the floor and began to dress. Her room was on the second floor above a pawn shop and was just big enough for the bed and a chest of drawers and a

4

chair strewn with her clothes. A midnight-blue party dress hung from the picture rail beside a pale lemon blouse with a pussy-cat bow and jagged sweat marks under the arms. Face powder dusted the chest of drawers, where an unscrewed lipstick lay beside the crumbling square of mascara he had seen her spit into to moisten the blackness for the spiky brush. A crumbed plate and tea-stained cup, an empty milk bottle and an ashtray were lined up on the windowsill. Her shoes were everywhere: separated, upside down, small hazards of pointed heels and trailing laces. A stocking dangled limply from the bedstead, still holding the shape of her leg and foot, the toe stiffening a little; as she sat on the bed to roll up its pair she said, 'Get dressed or we'll be late. I don't want to be late for Lawrence.'

'No, of course you don't.'

She glanced at him, perhaps suspecting his jealousy, if indeed he *was* jealous. She looked away again, paying attention to her suspenders. 'I promised Lawrence I wouldn't be late – this is an important night for the gallery.'

'Whatever time we turn up, we'll be first. I'll be surprised if the others even bother.'

'Andrew's going – he's told everyone they should see this artist's pictures.'

He snorted: how like Andrew to be so impressionable; he had his fancies, his enthusiasms that he would quickly forget. Next week there would be someone else to rave about. The thought of Andrew's excited gushing made him close his eyes in despair.

Ann patted his leg beneath the sheet. 'Come on. Don't look so glum. You laugh for no reason and then you look glum like this,' – she pulled a face.

She stood up and returned to the mirror to pin up her hair, humming tunelessly under her breath. Occasionally she sang snatches from a repertoire of music-hall songs – songs that even he, sheltered middle-class boy that he was, recognised as full of double entendre. *Dirty girl,* he thought, as he often did. The kind of girl he couldn't take home to his mother, the kind of girl a man practised on – as if anyone needed to practise. Perhaps he did. Perhaps the more he practised the more he would straighten

5

himself out. He was using her – the thought had occurred to him before, of course. But didn't everyone use everyone? Agitated, he tossed aside the bed covers and gathered his clothes. Ann went to the window and drew the curtains. The clock on her mantelpiece chimed the hour; the coals on her fire shifted and caved in. Outside a drunk warbled a song he was sure Ann would know. Edmund pulled on his trousers and tucked in his shirt; he buttoned his flies and fastened his collar and noticed a stain on his frayed cuff. He found his tie draped in a pleasingly louche manner on the end of the bed and put it on. Ann straightened the knot, standing back to regard him quizzically.

'Don't be sad,' she said.

'I'm not.'

She put on her coat, handed him his, held out his scarf, all the while watching him as though she was nursery nurse to his wayward child. Ready, she unlocked the door and stepped out into the dank, dark little passageway, preceding him down the steep flight of stairs.

He was sad, despite his protestation. Yet he knew there was no reason for his sadness. Until the idea he'd had about questioning Ann over how he compared with Lawrence Hawker, he'd been fine, but a feeling of melancholy had crept over him, a feeling he knew had been lying in wait for him for a little time now, only foiled by drink and sex. In the King's Head last night he, Andrew and Day had drunk until Susie would no longer serve them, and then they had staggered to Andrew's rooms and seen off a bottle of port. Port, for Christ's sake, inducing the most savage hangover he'd had for a while. That morning, as he and Barnes had opened the bookshop where he worked, Barnes had wrinkled his nose. 'You smell like my old Aunt Florrie on Christmas night.' Stepping closer he made a show of sniffing him. 'You should wash more, nice boy like you, frequent a decent barber.'

He had instinctively rubbed his chin; it wouldn't have been the first time he'd forgotten to shave. Barnes pulled up the blinds on the front windows and Edmund had stepped back from the sunlight, wincing. 'Bitten by the vampire, were we?'

Barnes had said; then in his ordinarily weary voice added, 'Go and make the tea. There are some aspirin behind the caddy.'

Walking along Percy Street, Ann's arm through his, Edmund thought that perhaps sad was not the word for his mood; rather he was disappointed; rather he had walked into a brick wall behind which lay all his hopes and ambitions, everything he had once fondly hoped he would be. If he stepped back and jumped as high as he could, he could just about see over this wall, catch tantalizing glimpses of a life he might lead if only he wasn't so damnably lazy, if only he gave up his job at the bookshop and got down to some serious work.

Serious work. This was his father's expression, the two words always shackled together like prisoners on a chain gang. Serious work was cutting open bodies, delving about in their insides, stitching them back up restored, more often than not. Serious work was not painting, not unless he was deathly intense about it, prepared to work and work and work and still get nowhere, never catching up with the little talent he supposed he had. Seriously, he should paint and do nothing else, caught up in a maniacal mindfulness, not eating, not sleeping, fractured from the ordinary, a transcendental life.

Such seriousness seemed preposterous to him. Slowly Edmund had come to realise that he was possessed of a clerk's self-conscious heart. There were times when he could even bring himself to feel content working in the bookshop, the slow hours ticking by in steady, companionable quiet. He liked the smell of the books, particularly the old, next-to-worthless ones, those they left out in boxes on the pavement in front of the window, their spines fading without the protection of lost dust jackets. He liked the pathos of those books and their forgotten authors, those many who had tried and not quite failed; he knew he couldn't work in an art gallery, where that same, soft feeling would be unbearable.

Like it or not, however, he couldn't entirely escape into the bookshop and pretend he had never had an ambition. He knew those who did work and work and didn't give up in a fit of horrible self-awareness and pique: Andrew, who had actually sold some of his seascapes; he knew, in a way, Day, who would probably be famous some day, if he didn't kill himself first. And of course, he knew Ann, their muse. He was surprised when she decided she would like to go to bed with him, but her enthusiasm for his body did help to relieve the depleting ennui that lately he couldn't shake off, even if afterwards he was pestered by questions and doubts.

He was aware of Ann's arm through his, her warm, vital closeness. She walked quickly, easily matching his pace, although she was so much shorter. She'd once laughed, 'Don't I look like the scullery maid out with the young master?' He was six foot three inches and broad shouldered. As blond as her, he looked younger than his years, and as she was older than he was, he knew that she didn't take him seriously. There, that word again. Andrew, Day, and all his other friends were serious. He was not.

They turned into a street where once-grand houses had been converted into flats: the cold, damp basements for the poorest; the larger, drafty rooms with their cracked window panes and bare, creaking floorboards for those who were a little less desperate. When he had first left home, he had lived on this street, in a room he thought must have been the maid's in better times: cramped beneath its sloping ceiling it was certainly like the maids' rooms in his parents' house. His window had looked out over rooftops; if he craned his neck, he could see the dome of St Paul's. Through the gaps in the floorboards he could eavesdrop on his downstairs neighbours – Russian Jews, whose exoticness made him feel as though he had arrived at a place even further away from home than they were.

As they passed his old flat, and he looked up at the attic window to see if there was a light, Ann squeezed his arm. 'This artist – Lawrence said his work is all about the war.'

There was no light; he imagined that the attic room – where he had once, with such hope and enthusiasm, painted the rain-darkened view of roofs – was unoccupied, settling even further into disrepair. There would be dead flies on the sills, the undisturbed dust no longer agitating in the deep shaft of light that fell at noon across the sagging bed. There would be a stronger smell of damp, more evidence of mice and a colder draught beneath the door. Perhaps he could go back there, start again as if the last year had never even begun; as if he was still that enthusiastic boy, the money his father had given him for this *experiment* miraculously unspent, his naivety still happily in place.

As if he could be that time traveller, he promised himself he would work; he would put his weight behind breaking the stubbornly unyielding shell of his talent. But he remembered that the money was spent; he remembered the bookshop, its easy cosiness; he thought about his new room, its tidiness because he had realised he couldn't pretend to be a man who didn't care about a certain level of comfort and order; he recalled how cold and lonely, how *untypical* of him, that first little flat had been.

Cautiously Ann persisted, 'This artist. His name is Paul Harris – he fought during the war, Lawrence told me. That's what he paints – the war. Battle scenes. Dead soldiers.'

He glanced down at her, her head at the level of his heart, her face turned up to his, her cheeks pink from the cold. In a certain light she could look very young, younger than he was. He would paint her like this; recreate these exact circumstances – close to her, looking down at her as she looked up at him – to capture her vulnerability, her occasional, surprising shyness of him. The portrait would catch only a moment of truthfulness, such a fleeting moment it would hardly be true at all. He put his arms around her, pulling her close so that he wouldn't have to see how anxious she looked.

'I heard the paintings were controversial.'

She pushed away from him. '*Controversial*? What if we can't look?'

He sighed, feeling large and foolish and shallow – the worst of these feelings because he knew he would be able to look, to be critical or envious or dismissive – any of his usual responses – but he would *look*. He couldn't be afraid all the time, or made to feel grief whenever it was expected. He cleared his throat and felt larger and more foolish still. 'Shall we not go?'

'I have to go.'

'Then we'll go together,' he said, remembering that of

course she had to be there – Lawrence Hawker was expecting her. He pulled her arm through his again, patting her hand, ashamed of his cowardly resignation. 'Best foot forward?'

She laughed as though he wasn't quite right in the head. 'Left right, left right?'

'Indeed.' He had patted her hand, and now this gesture seemed to him to have struck the wrong note: it was too comradely, too affectionate, he supposed, and it came to him that perhaps affection was all he felt. He had the urge to say that he didn't care to be one among others, just to hear her reaction, but such grandstanding would only be part of that act he seemed intent on performing, and in truth her reaction meant little to him – he had an idea that she was acting a part, too, and there was comfort in this idea: he couldn't hurt her, just as she couldn't hurt him.

Chapter Two

IN THE PYTHON ART Gallery, Paul Harris felt for Patrick's letter in his pocket in the vain hope that his proximity to it, and by extension to Patrick, might help him overcome his nervousness. He felt that if he really concentrated he would be able to read the words by touch, all those closely packed, heavily indented words that were so surprisingly fluent. *My darling Paul, You have no idea how much I will miss you. All I can do is pray that you keep safe. I'm scared because I can't help believing that England is the most bloody rotten, most dangerous country in the world for you to be in. I should be there, with you, protecting you.*

The letter had been in his suitcase, tucked beneath underwear so that he'd find it quickly. He had put it to one side, unopened for a few hours, wondering whether he should open it at all. He could imagine what Pat would write. And, when he finally tore it from its envelope, he found that he was right, and that the letter did make him feel useless and weak. The letter had actually made him shake, confirming Patrick's worst beliefs: he wasn't fit to be away from him; he was defenceless without the big man, always had been; nothing but trouble ever came from being apart from him.

In his head he had a cartoon image of himself cowering behind Patrick, peeping out as Pat shielded him from truncheon-waving policemen. He should draw this cartoon and stick it to their bedroom mirror at home – wouldn't it make them both laugh? Wouldn't it dispel some of the tension between them? He fingered the letter, feeling the raggedly torn envelope – he had been in such a hurry to open it, once he had decided to, to have confirmation that Patrick missed him.

Perhaps that was why he had shook, because he was afraid he might not miss him, afraid that Pat had come to realise how weary he had become of shielding him; he might have written, *Perhaps you should stay in England – I know how much you miss it.*

He hadn't missed the miserable greyness of an English spring. He had forgotten how cold May in England could be, even wearing the heavy clothes Patrick had packed for him. Wool socks, long johns, vests, the kind of clothes he had almost forgotten about wearing, clothes that took him back immediately to England even as he watched Patrick fold them into the case. In the heat of their bedroom, he couldn't imagine holding these garments against his skin, let alone putting them on. Patrick had turned to him from shoving cashmere socks into the heavy brogues he had already packed. 'You should be doing this. I'm not your batman.'

'If you gave me the chance …'

But that was just it: Patrick took over and steered him through his alien life. He had become his dependent. With Patrick, he didn't have to stop being the kind of man who shook.

Through the gallery's brightly lit window, Paul saw that the rain had begun to come down in earnest. Beside him Lawrence Hawker sighed heavily. 'I hope the weather won't stop them coming.'

Paul turned to him. 'I'm sure it won't.' At once this sounded immodest, and he smiled uneasily. So far this evening all he had felt was this unease, a horrible, twisting nervousness that had meant he couldn't eat but had only smoked even more than he normally did so that he was down to his last cigarette, one he was saving with twitchy fidgetiness. He had a strong suspicion that no one would turn up, rain or no rain.

Paul cleared his throat. 'Lawrence, thank you for everything – for all this.'

'Nonsense. Hopefully we'll both make a bit of money out of this lot, eh?'

He was so business-like, this man, making him grateful that he wasn't what he had feared a gallery owner might be:

unbusiness-like, fey, *queer,* he supposed. 'If he is like us, don't fuck him,' Patrick had said.

'Do you have any faith in me?'

'Honestly?'

No, not honestly. He glanced at Lawrence, guessed he was about the same age as him, reasonably handsome in an unmistakably not-like-us way. He was very similar to a few of his fellow officers during the war, clipped and precise and so confident that even the youngest, greenest of them could make him feel gauche. That was how he felt now, and his paintings, hanging on the walls all around him, well lit, carefully ordered, reinforced this feeling, reinforced his nervousness, that sense that he might vomit at any moment. All of the paintings, without exception, were terrible, embarrassing: he should have burnt them all. Worse than embarrassing, they were impertinent, a slap in the face. Not for the first time that day, from the moment he had seen the paintings gathered together in this way, he felt like hiding in his hotel room until he could board the first boat back to Patrick.

Lawrence said, 'How do you feel?'

'Fine.' He cleared his throat again, longing for a cigarette. 'Fine.'

'Scotch? I'm having one. Steady the old nerves before the off, what?'

'No, thank you.'

'Sure?'

'Yes – thanks anyway.'

Hawker slapped his back. 'Don't look so bloody terrified! It'll be fine. I keep the drink in the back office. I've brandy, gin – sure I can't tempt you, old man?'

'Sure.'

When Hawker had gone to fetch his drink, Paul went to the window and looked out on to the street. He had passed a pub on the way from his hotel, and he imagined going there now. The King's Head – he had noticed its portrait of a flamboyant Charles II hanging above the door – would be busy, the kind of pub where the appearance of a stranger wouldn't cause a sudden, surly silence. The air would be pleasantly thick with

13

cigarette smoke; there would be a coal fire and not too dim, not too bright lamp light; there would be decent beer and a whisky chaser and cigarettes sold behind the bar. He could smoke and drink alone and untroubled and not think about Patrick or this exhibition or Hawker with his *old man* condescension. He would only think about being back in England, away from the relentless Moroccan sun. He would take time to consider if the homesickness for England he had tried to ignore for the last year had really let up now and if it had, then what was the feeling that had replaced it – this churning, restless anxiety?

He stared out of the window at the rain. He wouldn't mind so much if it kept people away; it would even be a relief. He thought about his portrait of Corporal Cooper – although no one except him knew that it was Cooper, that cheery, hapless boy who had served alongside him for two years until the summer of 1918. He had painted Cooper hunched over the task of writing a letter home, frowning in concentration as though each word was a trouble to him. He had painted Cooper because he remembered how the boy had looked up as he passed by, saying, 'What should I write to me Mam, sir?'

A man beside Cooper had laughed. 'Wish you were here?'

Paul remembered how he had stopped at the place in the trench where Cooper and a small group of men had hunkered down around a brazier, and how Cooper had looked up at him hopefully, as though he might know of something appropriate to write to a mother, words that wouldn't worry her or make her feel as though she was being lied to, cheerful, ordinary words that would ignore the war and remember some happy time – a Christmas or summer holiday – or look forward to such times to come. But Paul had found himself saying, 'Do you want me to write the letter for you, Cooper?'

'Yes, sir, if you wouldn't mind, sir.'

The others had laughed as Paul had taken the writing paper and pencil from him and sketched a cartoon of Cooper chewing a pencil, deep in thought. *The spit of him*, one of the others had called the drawing, and Cooper had grinned, bashful and delighted.

Staring out of the gallery window, Paul remembered the

14

sweet, lousy smell of those men – his own smell at the time – how they held out their grimy, mittened hands to the brazier's warmth and how their laughter followed him along the sandbagged trench. A still, cold, cloudless afternoon in early winter and quiet, not much doing, time enough to write letters and surprise the men with his odd little talent for caricature. Walking through that trench, bowed a little to keep his head well below the sandbags, he'd had an idea of using his talent, that if he survived he would make a record of the war that included men like Cooper struggling to reply to a mother's anxious letters, and there would be no pity or sentiment, there would only be the truth.

The truth. Should that have a capital T? Cooper's portrait was hanging behind him and he couldn't bear to turn around and look at it; he had failed. Somehow, disastrously, he had failed, and the portrait of Cooper was as sentimental as anything on the lid of a chocolate box. Cooper was too pretty, his expression too wistful: sentiment had crept in, despite his best efforts; he should try for a living illustrating greeting cards or advertisements for soap because all the paintings in this series he privately thought of as *Letters Home* had this same mawkish softness.

Only his portrait of Patrick had any merit at all. Patrick, on their bed at home, naked but for a sheet strategically draped at his groin – Pat had insisted on this modesty. Patrick, gazing back at him frankly and not uncritically. Paul was pleased at least by how he had managed to capture this tension between them, as if Patrick was about to say that he could always leave if he was so unhappy: *Go back to England, Paul, see how you get on without me.*

Lawrence Hawker came back, sipping at a large glass of Scotch. Raising the glass, he nodded towards a group of people approaching the gallery's door. 'Here they come. Looks as though we're on.' He grinned at him. 'All right?'

Yes, he was all right: he was home; Hawker had liked his work enough to show it and there were people coming through the door to see it. The rain was letting up and the evening sky was turning pink and gold as the sun set. He would buck up, behave; there would be no more maudlin self-pity. Besides, a handsome boy was coming through the door, catching his eye and smiling at him politely before turning his attention back to the girl he was with. Tall, blond, powerfully built, he would be the evening's interest; having someone to look at, however discreetly, always helped an evening along. He heard the boy laugh the confident, privileged laugh of a well-off, well-mannered Englishman, and he smiled to himself. He was home.

Chapter Three

JOSEPH DAY GROANED. 'ANN, sweetheart, tell me again what you see in that bloody English bastard?'

'Is he a bloody bastard?'

'Yes.' He groaned again. 'Oh Annie … come back with me tonight.'

'No, not tonight.'

Ahead of them, Edmund walked with Andrew in animated conversation. She heard Andrew laugh. Edmund had a knack of making others laugh: no one was immune to his charm, his easy light-heartedness, no one except Joseph, who believed that Edmund had robbed him of her. As if she didn't have any say in it, as if Edmund had come along and told him, *It's my turn, now.* In a way, that's just what he had done: he only pretended to be shambolic, pretended to follow her lead, pretended to be flattered. Actually, Edmund was what he was: an educated boy who had an unassailable belief in his own entitlement. Really, she should hate him.

Joseph grabbed her arm, stopping her. 'Ann – I can't work without you, you know that. I'm going mad here … The thought of you and him –'

'He's my bit of fun, that's all.'

'Why do you have to be such a slut?' Joseph tightened his grip on her arm, pulling her to him. 'Fun! If you want fun –'

'Fun?' Edmund had turned back and stood in front of them. He said, 'Perhaps I want some fun, Day.' His voice was hard; this voice of his: she realised it was why she wanted him. Then, in the easy, soft voice he used more often, Edmund said, 'Let her go, Joseph, there's a good fellow.'

'Piss off.'

17

She shook off Joseph's grasp. 'Shall we just go to this exhibition and look at the pictures?'

'Well, I think that's a jolly good idea, don't you, Joseph?'

Joseph glared at him. If they were to fight over her she couldn't predict who might come out on top. Joseph would cheat, she suspected; Edmund would treat it as a joke. She imagined him dusting off his jacket and smoothing back his hair, smiling even as he wiped the blood from his nose before holding out his hand for Joseph to shake. He should care about something, she thought suddenly, something more than himself.

Joseph pushed past him, breaking into an odd little jog to catch up with Andrew, who had sensibly walked on. Raising his eyebrows, Edmund smiled at her. 'A bit of fun, eh?'

'And aren't you relieved?'

He lit a cigarette, shaking out the match and tossing it down into the gutter. 'I'm relieved that I'm good for something.'

'Have I hurt your feelings?'

He laughed. 'Terribly. Anyway, fun is fun, isn't it? Unless it's an Irish euphemism I'm not familiar with?' He held out his hand to her and she imagined it bloody from the fight so that she hesitated a moment before taking it. Such large hands he had, capable and safe. As though he sensed her hesitation, he raised his eyebrows again, smiling a little as he asked, 'Are we friends?'

When she nodded he squeezed her hand, saying, 'All right, let's get out of this rain.'

When they reached the gallery, Joseph and Andrew were already inside. The place was crowded, a small scrum of bodies in the doorway, waiting for a little floor space to clear before they could go in.

A man approached them. 'Is this the Python Gallery?' He squinted up at the sign above the door. 'Ah yes. I see that it is …'

Edmund laughed, turning to her. '*Python?* Bloody silly name, isn't it?'

'Lawrence likes it.' She looked to the man who seemed as hesitant to go inside as Edmund was. 'Have you come to see the new exhibition?'

'Yes,' he glanced through the gallery's window, then back to her. 'Yes,' he repeated. 'I know the artist. Actually, he's my son.'

He's my son, George Harris thought, and I should be proud of him. I should have been here as they opened the doors, steadying his nerves – he had no doubt Paul would be nervous, although he would hide his nervousness well. Instead he had hung back in his hotel room, deciding whether he should go to the opening – if that was what they called such events – at all.

He *was* proud of him. He had always been proud of him. He remembered the day Paul joined the army; he could have wept with fear, but he was still proud. During the war, he had looked back on that pride with contempt, wondering at his own idiocy. He should have locked Paul away or else he should have taken him to one side and told him he knew his secret: *tell them you're homosexual, and they won't have you.* Oh yes, of course he should have said such a thing. Only shame had held him back. So, he would rather see his son killed than openly acknowledge what he was.

The irony was, he didn't mind about his homosexuality, not at least as he supposed some fathers would mind. He had guessed what Paul was when he was still a small child; it seemed that for most of Paul's life he had watched him too closely, looking for signs that would confirm his suspicions; he suspected that this watching had made him love Paul too carefully, wrongly, perhaps, as though Paul was never a child, only this man in the making.

As he was dying George's own father had said, 'Paul's different, like me.'

He knew his father had thought this deathbed confession, veiled as it was, would shock him. His father believed he was blind to *differences,* just as his father had been blind to George's awareness. But George hadn't been able to bring himself to pretend surprise, or even disguise his weariness, because by then he felt he owed his father nothing; and so he had said only, 'Yes, Dad. I know.'

Still, his father had seemed to want to make more of it, seeming to gather all his strength to search his face, to say at last, 'I'm sorry.'

George had wondered what he was apologising for: everything, perhaps, or nothing except this awkward moment. Impotently he'd said, 'Can't be helped.'

His father had laughed, done with the play-acting, only to struggle to catch his breath so that George had hoisted him up the bed, fussing with his pillows, earning himself a feeble slap on the wrist. He suspected that his father thought he lacked sensitivity – he suspected that all queer men thought this about normal men; it was their brand of arrogance, George thought, and Paul was just as affected by it.

The girl he had met on the street outside the gallery had been kind to him, although he had been embarrassed at the way he'd blurted out that the artist was his son, as though he was showing off. She and her amused-looking companion had introduced him to their friends and all the time the girl – Ann – looked around the room for the gallery's owner, craning her neck and standing on tip-toe in an attempt to see over the heads of the many people standing around. 'Lawrence will know where your son is, Dr Harris, if only I can find him …'

George hadn't yet looked at the paintings, not properly; too many people crowded around each picture and the place was full of their soft, thoughtful murmurings. He heard one man say, 'Stunning. Quite stunning. Oh yes, of course it's quite shocking, too …' The man laughed in response to something George didn't catch. 'Yes! No, I quite agree. One wouldn't want it actually hanging on one's *drawing-room* wall.'

The girl glanced at him, smiling sympathetically – the man's voice had been loud enough for everyone to hear. He smiled back at her, awkward now because he didn't feel as though he deserved this sympathy; he barely knew how he felt that his son had, so unexpectedly, turned into the kind of man who could inspire such talk. And these people were artists; he couldn't think of a single thing to say to them that wouldn't mark him out as a philistine. The girl was dressed rather oddly, a mismatch of jumble-sale clothes – he guessed her coat was once a man's, cut down to size – a bohemian stylishness that made him feel even more uncomfortable. She was, however, very lovely, albeit with the frail kind of beauty of someone half-famished; but she was also a little flushed, a little manic, and he wondered if perhaps she was consumptive; for all this he found it hard not to keep looking at her, professional interest vying with admiration. Her companion – lover, no doubt – watched him, still with that amused public-school-boy expression on his face, as though a provincial, middle-aged doctor was something of a joke in such a setting.

But the public school boy, Edmund, surprised him by saying gently, 'It's an awfully good turn-out. Tremendous. You must be extraordinarily proud.'

'Yes. Of course.' Even to his own ears he sounded off-hand. More than anything he wanted to get away from them to find Paul. He had imagined that he would walk in and Paul would be right there, as if he had been expecting him. He had imagined that they would look at his paintings together, alone, and that he would say the right things about them, although he had no idea what made him think he could. He had even imagined that his son would be pleased to see him; even that he could persuade him to come home. Idiotic, really. Even so, he hadn't imagined that there would be no sign of him, and that he would be pitied by a group of strangers who glanced at each other as though they didn't quite believe he was who he said he was.

But then, rather too brightly, the girl said, 'There's Lawrence!' She slipped past him, edging her way through the press of bodies until she reached a young man who grinned delightedly at her. George watched as this man kissed her cheeks; he heard him say, 'Darling girl!' And then, as he peered in his direction, 'Really? Paul never mentioned … No, I'm not sure where he's got to – circulating? God knows he should be – everyone wants to talk to him. The pictures have all been sold.'

George found himself face to face with this man, Lawrence, his hand shaken vigorously. And then Paul's voice behind him said, 'Dad,' and he was turning around, afraid of the emotions that surged against his heart.

* * *

21

Edmund sat across the restaurant table from the artist himself. Beside him sat Ann, who sat beside the artist's father, a man she had taken under her wing from the moment she set eyes on him, which was like her, of course – she never could resist lame ducks. The rest of their party, Lawrence Hawker, Day, Andrew, another artist he hadn't met before, sat further down the table strewn with empty wine bottles. He hadn't drunk very much; he should have, because he felt dull and churlish, and the wine would have helped him out of this shaming mood. He wondered if he was jealous of this artist's success, but also of his talent. He probed this idea as he might a rotten tooth, testing its painfulness, and decided that no, he wasn't jealous; he hadn't liked his paintings, in fact, had loathed them. He could see that they were technically good. He could also see that they were manipulative, and was surprised that it seemed no one else agreed with him.

The artist – whom he had heard Lawrence call Paul, but who signed his pictures *Francis Law* – hadn't drunk much either, as far as Edmund had noticed. He smoked endlessly, that was where he had disappeared to during the exhibition – to buy cigarettes. He had hardly eaten and, for a man who'd had such a successful evening, he seemed only exhausted. Edmund found himself watching him, wanting to figure him out as he would want to figure out any artist who had even this type of success. He must have made his watching too obvious because Paul – or Francis, or whatever his name was – looked up at him from flicking his cigarette ash into the ashtray and smiled wryly.

'All right,' Paul said, 'what conclusion have you reached?'

Embarrassed at being caught out, Edmund said, 'Sorry.'

'It's all right. You've had a rotten evening.'

'Have I?'

'I would like to slash the paintings, too.'

'They don't belong to you any more. Besides, that's just vanity.'

'You're right. And it was a foolish, vain thing to say, although it's true. I would like to take them all back and say that it was a bad mistake and that I'm sorry.' He looked down at his cigarette, rolling it around the rim of the ashtray. 'Christ.

Listen, don't mind me. They sold, that's an end to it.' He met his gaze. 'Did you hate them?'

Edmund thought about lying politely and then said, 'Yes, I'm afraid I did.'

'Why?'

'If you want to take them back, apologise for them, then I think you know why.' He marvelled at the pompousness in his voice – as if he knew what he was talking about – remembering how he had stood for a while in front of a painting of a soldier reading a letter as next to him another soldier slept, curled up like a small child, fully dressed even down to his boots, his face troubled, as though flinching through bad dreams. A lamp gave out a noxious yellow light; the reading soldier was smiling, an unexpectedly sweet, contented smile.

Edmund had wondered if this was the worst of the pictures or the best, his mood becoming ever sourer as he looked at it: wasn't this the worst kind of sentimental rubbish? Wasn't it made even more sentimental by the horror of some of the other pictures surrounding it? But he had gone on gazing at the picture, at that smile half covered by the boy's hand as though attempting to hide a private happiness. He thought that the boy could have been his brother Neville reading a letter he himself had sent. His brother might have smiled like that, despite everything … But it was sentimental to think so, and to be manipulated in such a way … No, he loathed that painting even more than he loathed the others.

Surprised by the anger he felt, Edmund said, 'I can't say you're not talented.'

The artist laughed. 'Thanks. I can't say that's not a compliment. I used to paint birds. The first picture I sold I called *Sparrows at the Drinking Fountain*. I should have stuck with birds, eh?' He held out his hand across the table. 'We weren't introduced. Paul Harris.'

'Edmund Coulson.'

'Are you an artist, Edmund?'

'No.'

Next to him, Ann said, 'He is, Paul. He's a wonderful artist.' She glanced at him. 'But he's given up. Like this –' she

23

dropped her head to the table as though exhausted, groaning a little – 'oh, it's too hard, too hard!' Raising her head again she said, 'He just won't try any more.'

'Won't I?'

She mimicked him, her voice gruff. He knew that she was drunk, that he should laugh, really, and not be hurt at all. She was gazing at him, her face hectic with colour. She looked angry enough to make even more of a fool of him, but it seemed that she realised she had gone too far because she looked down at the glass of wine in her hand. Quietly, she said, 'I don't think people should give up, that's all.'

He had never told her that he had given up; he wanted her to think that he could begin again at any time and that this inactivity was just a breathing space, a gearing up to some great work he was planning. But she had seen through him, of course, and now all he wanted was to get away from her. She represented a nonsense idea he had about himself, one that he should absolutely discard. He stood up so suddenly that his chair toppled over, and in a moment he was out on the street, struggling to light a cigarette as the matches broke in his fingers.

He smoked the cigarette but still couldn't face going back inside. He would smoke another to give himself more time. About to strike a match, a voice beside him said, 'Here.' A lighter was held out to him, and he turned to see Paul Harris standing close by, his face lit by the quivering flame, a face of angles and hard lines, gaunt, severe. Edmund thought how like one of his own paintings he looked in this flare of dramatic light; he was, Edmund realised, *picturesque* – Raphael might have used him as a model for the tortured Christ.

Edmund looked away quickly, realising he had been staring; drawing on the lit cigarette he stared ahead, hoping that if he said nothing, if he didn't even look at him, Harris would leave him alone. He very much wanted him to; Harris was unnervingly intense, making him feel as though they were both waiting for some momentous event, a dawn execution perhaps. Then he thought that perhaps he should say something – speaking would break this ridiculous tension – but whatever he thought of seemed crass; all he could do was to wait for him to go back into the restaurant. But the man went on standing beside him; from the corner of his eye Edmund could see the glowing tip of his cigarette as it moved to and from his mouth.

He thought of walking away but in truth he didn't know if he really could leave without saying something to him, without leaving some impression of himself other than that of a boy who spoke so pompously and stormed out of restaurants. Besides, if he left, Ann would move on. She would go home with Lawrence Hawker. He knew that would be the end of his relationship with her, such as it was. He couldn't decide if this mattered.

Clearing his throat, Harris said, 'I'm staying at the Queen's Hotel, quite close to the gallery. Do you know it?'

Edmund supposed he had half expected this, somewhere in the pit of his heart. Why else was he still standing here? The evening had been leading up to such a moment; perhaps his whole life had been leading up to this. Now Harris was about to give him the shove he needed. Harris seemed impatient to do this, to not waste any more time. But he needed more time; he needed to lean against the wall and steady himself, to think clearly and carefully; there was much to consider. How would he feel tomorrow, for instance, after it was done with? How would he face his father, even if he could bring himself to go home after such an act? Absurdly, he thought of his honeymoon night and the dirty secret he would have to keep from his innocent bride. He wondered if it would even be possible to live with a woman happily whilst keeping such a secret. He wondered if it would be possible to live at all, afterwards, tomorrow when he would still be able to feel Harris's touch on him, smell him, taste him still.

He glanced at Harris, wanting to make sure that he was as extraordinary as he surely had to be. The man was unsmiling, deadly serious, handsome in a way that seemed complicated to him, as though he could go on looking and looking and still not understand what it was about his face that sent such a charge through him. And so he looked and looked and realised that no one else mattered, *nothing* else mattered; he had reached an

25

understanding: this was what he wanted, this man.

Briskly Harris said, 'Have I made a mistake?' His impatience made him unlikeable, dangerous even; not that it mattered: he was extraordinary, not real at all, but a man he'd invented. Edmund had to look away, aware that he had been staring. Harris repeated, '*Have* I made a mistake? I don't often.'

Often. He did this often. Of course he did – he supposed there could be no restraints to his kind of promiscuity. This encounter would mean little to him and that was good; there really was no substance here.

Edmund cleared his throat. He forced himself to meet his gaze. 'No. No mistake.'

Harris looked relieved but all at once vulnerable too – and younger than he had thought back beneath the bright lights of the gallery, only a handful of years older than he was. He really was beautiful, if a man could be described so, and he wondered how he hadn't noticed as soon as he had seen him – he usually had an eye for beauty. Perhaps his lust had blinded him, that hot filthy feeling, running him through with want.

This beautiful man placed his hand briefly on his arm and Edmund jumped so that Harris grinned at him and became boyishly ordinary. 'Steady. I don't bite. Not enough to break skin, anyway.'

'No, no. I'm sure. Sorry.'

'*Sorry*.' Harris laughed as though he found him as sweetly charming as a shy child. He was standing too close so that Edmund recoiled, afraid he would touch him again; he wasn't quite ready to be touched, to have his skin bristle so, as though he had been stripped of a protective layer; he wasn't ready to lose so much control; he could be mistaken after all. But Harris seemed not to notice that he had stepped away from him and was saying, 'Listen, Edmund, I've made my excuses already, said my goodbyes. Say an hour? The Queen's Hotel, room 212. Yes?'

Edmund nodded; he knew that if he spoke his voice would be a broken, feeble travesty of itself. It was shaming enough that he was nodding, acquiescent, that he wasn't punching Harris's face in, because surely this wasn't what he really wanted, he *had* to be mistaken. But he had an erection, he couldn't be so mistaken, and even if he wasn't he didn't have to be governed by lust. No, he didn't have to do anything he didn't want to do. He drew breath, was about to speak, when Harris turned and walked away.

Chapter Four

PAUL HAD SAID, 'DAD, I wish you hadn't come.' He had taken George's arm, guiding him to a less crowded part of the gallery. 'I'm sorry … It's just –'

'Just what, Paul? Am I embarrassing you?'

In his hotel room, Paul remembered glancing past his father's shoulder, to the portrait of Patrick on their bed. He had felt sixteen again, as though George had discovered him masturbating. He had even felt himself colour – something he hadn't done for years. But even through this embarrassment, he had noted that Patrick's portrait had gathered a seemingly appreciative group.

'I'm really pleased to see you, of course,' Paul had said.

'Of course.'

'Really. But it's a shock – how did you know I was here?'

George hesitated. 'He wrote to me. Patrick wrote to me.' Paul heard the effort it took for his father to say Pat's name, but he seemed to recover himself quickly enough because his voice had an edge of impatience as he went on, 'I wonder why he didn't tell you. Did he want my turning up like this to be a shock, do you imagine, or was it just some kind of practical joke he played on us both?'

'A joke? No, he wouldn't make fools of us, you should know better.'

'Should I?'

'Yes.' Trying to keep the anger from his voice, Paul said, 'He shouldn't have troubled you.'

'*Trouble*? You're my son, Paul. For God's sake, boy – I *wanted* to see you, to see your work –'

Paul had laughed, wanting only to dismiss his *work*,

fumbling in his pocket for the fresh packet of cigarettes. As he was about to take one from the pack, George stopped him. 'Don't, not now. I won't have you fiddling about with those things while I'm talking to you.' He sighed. 'You're very thin. Are you well?'

He'd shoved the cigarettes back into his pocket although he'd craved one, needing to take a great, calming lungful of smoke; he was shaking. From the moment he had seen his father he had been shaking because all he could think about were the questions he had to ask, how he might phrase them and still sound like a normal human being and not a wreck of grief and guilt. He cleared his throat, looking past his father as he managed to ask, 'How's Bobby?'

'He's well.'

Paul heard the note of softness in George's voice and forced himself to meet his gaze. 'He's all right?'

'Yes! He's a fine little boy.'

'They let you see him?'

George smiled bitterly. 'From time to time.'

'Often?'

'As I said, Paul, from time to time. He understands who I am, if that's what you mean.' After a moment he added, 'I show him your photograph. I say, *That's Daddy.* I say, *Your Daddy loved you very much.* Is that all right, Paul? Am I saying the right thing to him?'

'Yes.' He had heard how sullen he sounded and tried to sound less so as he said, 'Yes. Thank you.'

'Don't thank me! I have to lie! I have to lie to your son that you died! He asks me if I'm sad! How do you imagine that feels? And for God's sake, don't cry. I won't have you crying over this. If you'd behaved with more backbone, if you'd stood up to them and hadn't run away with that man –' George broke off. 'I'm sorry. Please don't cry.' Stepping closer to him he had put his hand on his back, saying intently, 'Paul, pull yourself together, don't make a show of yourself, not here.'

His father had taken a handkerchief from his pocket and pressed it into his hand. 'Come now. There's nothing to cry about. Bobby's such a good boy, and so like you. Oh, Lord. I'm making things worse, aren't I?'

Yes, he had made things worse, so bad in fact that Paul had to go outside. Even there, on the dark street, he couldn't cry openly. His throat had burned with the suppression of tears. George had followed him, but at least he was silent, awkward and angry still – Paul was certain of his anger – but silent. Until, at last, George had said, 'I shouldn't have said what I did. I know you didn't run away … I'm truly sorry.'

On the hotel bed, Paul pushed the heels of his hands hard into his eyes: *no backbone; run away;* his father's words kept coming back to him, repeating in his head like a playground taunt.

From his pocket he took out a photograph George had given him and traced his finger around Bobby's face. 'I took him to Evans's,' his father had told him, 'that studio on the High Street. Evans gave him that funny little toy dog to hold.' Sitting on a child-sized wicker chair, Bobby clasped the dog to his chest and looked solemnly at the camera. Paul stared at him, trying to make out the resemblance George said was there; he couldn't see it, try as he might.

He got up and placed Bobby's photograph in an envelope, sealed it and put it in a pocket in his suitcase. He went into the bathroom and washed his face in cold water, avoiding his reflection in the mirror above the sink. Going to the bedroom window he lifted the curtain aside and looked out on to the street; the pavements were shiny from the London drizzle, reflecting the hazy lamplight. He wondered, without much caring, if that boy Edmund would come.

He let the curtain fall back and lay down on the bed again, the springs creaking a little. The boy's weight would make them complain even more, quite a body he had, and tall; he had always preferred tall men: big, strong, handsome men – dark or blond but muscular, hairy, well hung. He liked it best if they hadn't shaved for a little while so that their bristles scoured his skin. He liked it when they grasped his hair and forced his face down to their thick, impatient, greedy cocks; he liked it when they called him *fucking little queer, dirty, cock-sucking little bastard*. To be humiliated, to have his guts soft with lust and fear, his own cock so hard and crushed in a fist – that was what he wanted more than anything else. There was nothing he wanted more; nothing was more important, nothing. Nothing. Unbuttoning his flies, his hand grasped his flaccid cock. He closed his eyes and tears ran down his face.

Margot, his wife, had cried and shouted, 'Why did you marry me? Why, when you knew, you knew ...' She was sobbing, hardly able to get the words out. All at once she was flailing at him with her fists. 'You're filthy! You've made me filthy! Everyone knows! They all know how filthy dirty we are!' He had tried to hold her, but she pulled away from him furiously. 'I hate you. You'll never, *never* see Bobby again.'

On the hotel bed, he buttoned his flies and wiped his face impatiently with his fingers. *No backbone*. And no self-respect, his father might have added. He had got on his knees to his wife, as though that would have made any difference, and he had begged for his son. She had only been even more disgusted. Could that have been possible – could her disgust have been greater still? Her disgust had been palpable; she had quaked with it, she'd pressed the back of her hand to her lips as though her mouth had filled with spittle. He thought how if she had been anyone but Margot she would have spat in his face.

The room was becoming cold. When he'd first come in he had switched on the light, a single bulb hanging from a fraying cord in the centre of a ceiling yellow from all the thousands of cigarettes that must have been smoked on this bed. After a few minutes of this unforgiving glare he had switched it off again – the thin curtains let in enough of the streetlight. The only furniture apart from the creaking, too narrow bed was a wardrobe and a bedside table where he'd placed his glasses in their case, his cigarettes and lighter and a pile of pennies and half pennies that had seemed so shockingly foreign and heavy when he'd first arrived back in England. Only his suitcase by the door looked smart and new, a present from Patrick. 'Leather,' Pat told him, 'no cardboard rubbish. And there – see – I had them emboss your initials on the side. *F.L.*'

F.L. He was Francis Law now, not Paul Harris any more, although sometimes he used his real name. He felt more like

Paul in England. Francis belonged to Patrick, to their house in Tangiers. If he ever left Patrick, left Morocco, he would revert to being Paul and wouldn't care if the past came back to kick him in the teeth.

Footsteps sounded in the corridor outside, and he sat up, listening, but the footsteps carried on past his door. If the boy didn't come he would go out; there was a likely-looking place near by, an underground public lavatory, its wide flight of steps divided by an ornate iron balustrade and lit only dimly by a streetlight a few yards away. Risky business, though. You never knew if a policeman might be watching, or even waiting inside, a smooth-faced boy used as bait, but easy enough to spot, if you weren't too stupefied by nerves and desperation. He would go to a pub first, a shot of Dutch courage, and he might even be lucky – have no need to scuttle down those slippery-looking steps into the piss-stinking darkness because there might be the right kind of man standing at the bar. This man might catch his eye, nod, comment on the weather perhaps. Such an encounter would be unlikely but not hopelessly so.

More unlikely would be the chance of this stranger being as handsome as the boy he'd met tonight; not a boy – this Edmund wasn't that much younger than he was; young enough, though; young enough not to have seen service, he was certain of that, relieved there was no possibility that he had ever been a fellow officer.

Very occasionally during his encounters, a man would take a guess at his likely past and ask him which regiment he'd served in. Not that there was ever that much conversation, although a few liked to talk, if the conditions allowed. One had even asked, 'Where did you lose your eye?'

'It popped out one morning over breakfast. Gave the wife a start, I can tell you.'

Silly bastard for asking. He supposed that if he had told him how he'd lost his eye the man would've had an excuse to talk about his own war wound, the ragged scar he'd glimpsed as he was tugging at his underwear. And of course a response would be expected: '*Ypres, you say? That's a coincidence – I got shrapnel in the thigh at Ypres. Gassed too? I know, I know.*

Ghastly, wasn't it? I thought my lungs were being burnt right out of my chest!'

The only other man's war he knew about was Patrick's, and only the part – those last few months of 1918 – that they had survived together. He didn't want to know about the rest of Pat's war, couldn't bear to think of it. Often he wondered how Patrick had survived so long, such a big man, such a difficult target to miss. 'Christ, it's Goliath,' Corporal Cooper had exclaimed on seeing Sergeant Patrick Morgan for the first time. Paul remembered smiling to himself, enjoying the look of astonishment on the corporal's face. That Patrick had joined their platoon cheered everyone; he supposed they had all forgotten Goliath's fatal flaw.

Again, he heard footsteps in the corridor outside. These steps were more hesitant than the last; he should have recognised that those others were too brisk, too sure of their direction. These footsteps were quieter, cautious. Paul got up from the bed, catching sight of himself in the mirror set in the wardrobe door; he had been thinking about Pat and he should have looked guilty; instead he noticed how eager he looked. He paused, making an effort to appear less predatory, and tried to push Patrick from his mind as he turned from the mirror and went to open the door.

Chapter Five

THE NEXT MORNING IN the bookshop Edmund hung back in the storeroom, unwilling to show his face to the few customers who ventured in out of the rain. Occasionally, if there was more than one customer waiting, Barnes would call him in his brisk shop voice, only to make no comment when he slunk back into the storeroom after the shop had emptied again.

Pretending to catalogue books, most of the time he stared out of the storeroom window overlooking the back yard. He watched a cat stalk a fat pigeon and when his breath misted the glass he rubbed it away only for it to mist again, so he drew a smiling face in the condensation and then watched as the smile slowly trickled out of shape. He listened to Barnes moving about the shop, jumped a little each time the bell on the shop door rang, dreading Barnes' call. Barnes was behaving with great discretion, and he was grateful for this. But it was also as if he knew what had happened last night, as though he could smell it on him; if this was so, all Barnes had been was sympathetic. But it was this sympathy he couldn't stand: men like Barnes weren't supposed to pity men like him.

Late morning, Barnes appeared in the storeroom doorway. 'I'm having a cup of tea, if you'd like one?'

'No, thank you.'

Barnes gazed at him. 'Would you like to go home?'

'No.'

'Are you sure?'

'Yes, I'm fine.'

The older man nodded. Touching his own eye, he said, 'It looks painful.' He sighed. 'If it was down to me you could stay in here all day if you wished, and I'm sure even the customers you've served hardly noticed – they barely see us at the best of times – but Mr Graham is coming in this afternoon to do the banking and if he saw you with that black eye …'

'I should go then, shouldn't I?'

'Yes, I think so. I'll tell him you were taken ill.'

Edmund fetched his coat. Following him to the door, Barnes said, 'Stay out of trouble, eh? I'd like to see you back here, when you feel you can face it.'

He went to a Lyon's Corner House and, although the waitress looked at him sideways, no one else took any notice of him. He was a young man with a black eye, a common enough sight he supposed on a Saturday morning. He touched his eye gingerly; the swelling had gone down a little. When the waitress brought his tea he caught sight of his contorted reflection in the metal teapot and touched his face again. He had a feeling that he had become someone else; this face was not the one he was used to. This feeling had nothing to do with the black and blue bruising: his body felt changed too, as though a defter, more imaginative god had remade him.

When Paul turned to him from closing the hotel room door, even in the dim light Edmund had the impression he'd been crying. But he had been his old self then and had said nothing; besides, of course Harris hadn't been crying and even if he had it was none of his business. He didn't even feel concerned, only went to the bed and sat down on its edge without acknowledging Paul, without looking at him, embarrassed in every way, by everything, not least by the shabbiness of the room and of Paul himself. Without his jacket, collar and tie, without his shoes, with his braces hanging at his sides and his sleeves rolled up, Paul looked too ordinary, dishevelled, like nothing, nobody. He wasn't beautiful – that ridiculous, over-blown word – just a skinny nonentity. Even his voice seemed to have changed, as though he didn't have to disguise his northern accent now other pretences were done with. Here he was, in the rough, and Edmund could only feel appalled.

He had imagined standing up, walking to the door, leaving, all without looking at him, without a word. But Paul was standing over him; if he were to leave it would mean an awkward, clumsy business of stepping around him because he was standing so close, so close; he sensed Paul looking at him. He should say something, just some ordinary remark to break this silence. He suspected that Paul was smiling at him, his smile becoming strained as his silence went on, a shame because when he arrived his smile had been so welcoming, flattering because he seemed so pleased that he had come. This man had been unsure of him after all and now he seemed unsure even of himself, gauche, even; and that voice of his – not officer class, not any class at all that he could rank him by. This voice was softer, with none of its earlier, edgy irony that had made Edmund feel so ready to despise him.

Paul had walked around the bed then and lain down, taking his cigarettes from his pocket and lighting one. It was as though Paul had decided that he could stay or go and it would be just the same to him. Edmund had turned to look at him; outside the clouds had cleared the bright face of a full moon, and this uncommon light made the sculptured quality of his face even starker, like that of a statue on the new war memorials that were being erected everywhere; he thought of his paintings of soldiers and how he had made them look like wistful boys. He thought how he could go on looking at him, mesmerized by his extraordinary beauty.

Edmund lay down beside him, as close as he dared, shy as he hadn't been since he'd left school. Paul passed him his cigarette and it went between them until all that remained could be pinched out between his finger and thumb, until there was only the taste left and the thought that in a moment he would light another … in a little while, there was no hurry. Edmund closed his eyes, and felt the bed shift beneath him as Paul began on the buttons of his shirt.

He thought about stopping him, grasping his wrist and holding it tightly, twisting his flesh, saying that he wasn't like him, wasn't sick and perverted like him; yet he was lying on a bed beside him, eyes closed against responsibility because he was like him, really, and he wanted him, all of him; he had never felt so greedy in his life.

*   *   *

Afterwards Edmund had dozed, only to be disturbed by the sound of a tap running. Naked, he had got up. Standing in the bathroom doorway, he had seen Paul holding his false eye beneath the stream of water before returning it to the socket. Catching sight of Edmund's reflection in the mirror above the sink Paul looked down quickly and turned off the tap.

Embarrassed, Edmund had said lightly, 'I didn't notice your eye when we met, even in the restaurant –'

'You're not meant to notice.' He had glanced at Edmund's reflection in the mirror and it seemed as though he didn't want him there, that he had angered him in some way. He had certainly sounded angry as he'd said, 'But now you can't take your eyes off it.' Brushing past him into the bedroom, naked too and seeming to take care not to touch him at all, Paul snapped, 'Are you staying or going?'

'Staying, if that's all right.'

'Then for God's sake get back into bed.'

In the café, Edmund remembered that it was then that Paul had seemed ordinary again, and not only ordinary but awkward and angry, his too-thin body repellent. As though he had sensed his repulsion, Paul got into bed quickly, covering himself with the sheet before reaching for his cigarettes and lighting two at once, wordlessly holding one out to him. Edmund got into bed too, taking the cigarette although he hadn't wanted another. He allowed it to waste away between his fingers, all the time wondering what he might say to a man who seemed to him to be at turns ugly and breathtaking, as though Paul was two men and he could only see one of them at a time. Perhaps the duality was his own, a sudden schizophrenia triggered by too sudden feeling.

In the café Edmund poured his tea and wished he had ordered toast as his stomach growled hungrily, surprisingly – shouldn't he be robbed of his appetite? Stirring sugar into his cup he remembered how Paul had turned to him, seeming to make an effort to suppress the anger that had come over him so abruptly and finally breaking the silence Edmund hadn't known

37

how to end.

'Have you always lived in London, Edmund?'

Edmund had laughed; it seemed such a facile question, given the circumstances, as though they were strangers meeting at a dull party. Smiling, he turned to look at him, intending to ask if he would like a potted biography, but found that he could only look at him, and that nothing he might say could matter less. He supposed he was dumbstruck, ridiculous, because Paul laughed self-consciously as he said, 'Don't look at me like that.'

He had looked away at once. 'Sorry.'

'It's disturbing.'

'Sorry.'

Another silence expanded between them, one that this time grew until it seemed possible he would never be able to bring himself to speak to this man again, knowing what an idiot he had been with that look of his. He could imagine just *how* he had looked: his eyes all wide with amazement that he could want another person so badly. Desperately trying to think of something to say that would be light-hearted and not at all disturbing, he failed and so he repeated, 'Sorry,' and then, out of masochistic politeness, asked, 'Would you like me to go?'

'No. I'd like you to stay. And you didn't answer my question. Have you always lived in London?'

'Yes.'

Paul lit another cigarette. Exhaling smoke, he said, 'And how old are you? Twenty-one? Twenty-two?'

Edmund laughed uncomfortably. 'Why?'

'Just wondering.'

Too quickly Edmund said, 'Twenty-two next month.'

'And what do you do? To earn a living, I mean.'

'I work in a bookshop.'

'Do you like it?'

'Yes. Yes, actually I do.'

'And you walk out with Ann.'

'Walk out?'

'I don't want to presume anything.'

'Yes, we *walk out*.'

'And what about your work, your painting – was she right

about that? Have you given up?'

'That's enough.' Agitated, Edmund had got up and begun to dress, hunting around the bed for his clothes. He sensed Paul watching him and wondered which Paul he would see if he dared to meet his gaze: a skinny, disfigured *queer,* he supposed, an impertinent queer who asked too many questions, one who must be some kind of magician to have made him imagine he was anything but ordinarily vile. This nasty little trickster had made him vile, too; he wondered how he would ever be able to hold his head up again.

He hadn't been able to find his socks. In the café, as he drank his tea, he wondered what would have happened if he had found them; no doubt he would have put them on quickly, shoved his feet into his shoes, run out the door. Odd that it hadn't occurred to him to put on his shoes *without* his socks. But looking for the socks had given him an excuse not to look at him, an excuse, he supposed, to be watched; it gave Paul an excuse to say something, perhaps even to ask him to stay.

But Paul had said nothing and finally Edmund had said, 'Can you see my blasted socks?'

'Were they thrown out the window in the heat of lust?'

'Don't talk rot.'

'Wear mine if you can find them.'

'I don't want to wear your bloody socks!'

'Then come back to bed.' After a moment he said less impatiently, 'If you'd like me to help you look for your socks, I will, if you feel you really need to go.'

He had found himself standing at the end of the bed, half dressed, the cracked lino cold beneath his bare feet, his shirt hanging open to reveal his vest. The room stank of cigarettes and sex; he could still taste Paul. Remembering the feel of him in his mouth he closed his eyes, groaning with lust. 'Oh, Christ.'

'Come back to bed.'

'I'm not like you.'

'No, all right.'

'I don't know if I can stand the sight of you.'

'I could take out your eyes, if you like.'

Edmund had finally met his gaze. 'I don't know what to do.'
'Then perhaps it's best you go.'
'No. I'll stay.'

His tea had grown cold. He caught the waitress's eye and asked for a jug of hot water and a round of toast. He watched her walk away, neat in her black dress and frilled white apron, although the cap she wore had slipped a little, one of her hair pins hanging redundantly beside her ear. She seemed a common little thing, really, the way she had made eyes at him, pert, easy to fuck and forget. He thought of Ann, who often took waitressing jobs, and was ashamed of himself.

He had climbed back into the bed and Paul had fucked him and he had realised how strong he was, hard and aggressive, not as gentle as he had been with Paul. He had been gentle because Paul had seemed so slight and easy to damage. No, that hadn't been gentleness; he had just been inept and shy, distracted by the inhibiting, amazed voice in his head asking what he thought he was doing.

There was no commentating voice when Paul broke into him. There was no thought of anything at all. He was nothing but flesh and breath and pain; he had not expected such exquisite pain, as though Paul would annihilate him, as though he would tear him apart if only he could be ruthless enough. Not so ruthless, though; he slowed, he murmured to him, *there, there, all right, all right, relax, relax*; there had been laughter in his voice; he stroked the back of his neck, his hair, whispered in his ear *there, there* as he became ruthless again, the bed banging against the wall so hard and fast that flakes of plaster fell down on their heads.

Edmund had tried to hold back, and it seemed that Paul had sensed this, slowing again, but he had already reached the edge, there was no control, no trick Edmund could play to keep from falling, no matter how much he wanted to stay teetering on the brink. Paul came too, allowing his weight to pin him down only for a moment before rolling on to his back, panting; Edmund could hear his triumph even in his breathlessness; he waited to hear him laugh, sure that he would.

Paul only reached for his hand and squeezed it. 'All right?'

Too breathless to speak, Edmund shook his head. Eventually he managed, 'Yes.'

Paul had laughed then, as though he had been afraid to before. Leaning over him, he brushed the plaster from Edmund's hair. 'We've damaged the wall.'

'*You've* damaged the wall.'

'Weren't we in it together?'

'Yes. Of course. I'm sorry.'

Paul had laughed again, picking another piece of plaster from his hair. 'Don't be sorry. Don't be ...' He had gazed at him and Edmund realised it was the first time Paul had looked at him properly, carefully, tenderly, he supposed, so that a feeling he'd had earlier came back to him with this one look: Paul was the only person in the world he would ever care about again.

In the café, Edmund remembered how he had reached up to touch Paul's face, tracing the outline of his mouth, and how he had almost said, 'I love you.' But how could he love him? He was never so reckless, never so cavalier with the truth; and, astonishingly, this did feel like the truth, a truth best left untested by words that anyway seemed too trite; words he had said before easily, without thinking.

Paul had gone on smiling. He'd said, 'You were about to say something?'

'No.'

'You're a very good-looking boy. You know that, don't you?'

He'd referred to him as a *boy* too easily; there had been that touch of loathsome feyness in his voice and it had made him angry that Paul could switch like that; it was terrible that this man was suddenly everything, then just as suddenly nothing. Worse than nothing: a man he could easily despise. Edmund had known that he could have turned away from him then, climbed out of bed, taken his time to dress, and when it came to say goodbye he wouldn't have looked at him. He shifted away a little.

Immediately he'd wanted Paul to pull him back, to say

41

something in the ordinary, classless voice he used in the restaurant: he wanted him to be *ordinary*. Christ: he wanted him to be *manly*. Perhaps he should just say, 'Make love to me but don't speak. If we never speak to each other that would be for the best. And perhaps if you only wear the clothes I choose for you, and if you never become tired or ill or ridiculous or older than you are now ...' He'd covered his face with his hands, dismayed, but this seemed too unlike him, too theatrical, and he dropped them again. Paul smiled at him, tender again, and Edmund had looked away at once, afraid of pitying him. 'I should go.'

'Should you? Why not stay the night?'

'No, I should just go, that's all. Just go ...' He'd made himself look at him. At once, overwhelmed by him, he said, 'I love you.'

The hammering on the door began then, at that moment, as if to save them both.

In the café, as he buttered his toast, Edmund realised that Paul seemed not even to understand what he had said, but had looked towards the door fearfully. The hammering went on. Paul had turned to him, making a sign that he should be silent, and got up; going to the door, his voice was calm and measured as he said, 'Who is it?'

'Open this fucking door before I break it down! I know you're in there, Coulson. Get out here now, you fucking little pervert.'

Paul turned to him. Angrily he'd said, 'Do you know who it is?'

'Joseph Day – he was at the gallery, the restaurant – he must have followed me –'

'Weren't you careful? For Christ's sake! Get dressed and get out before the porter calls the police.'

'I'm sorry – I don't know what he's doing here –'

'And I don't care! Just be quick –'

The door burst open and Day staggered in, almost falling, obviously drunk. Recovering himself, he shook his head, staring at Edmund's nakedness before barking out a laugh. 'Fucking hell.' He turned to Paul. 'Been having a smashing time, the pair of you?'

Paul turned away and began to gather his clothes. Coldly he said, 'Would you like to sit down? A glass of water, perhaps? You're obviously rather over-excited.'

'Listen to him. The wee shite thinks I'm *over-excited*. You think this will excite the police, do you?'

Paul took his wallet from his jacket. Taking out a few folded notes, he said, 'How much do you want?'

He snorted. 'I don't want your money. I just want to see that this one gets what he deserves.'

'Get dressed, Edmund,' Paul said. 'Take your friend home, get some coffee inside him and sort out whatever the problem is between you.'

'The problem? The problem is he's messing about the best girl that ever lived! A girl he doesn't deserve. The problem is he's buggering a nasty little pervert like you.'

It had seemed to Edmund then that Paul changed again. No longer contained, no longer caustic, no longer anything other than a mass of furious energy, he almost leapt on Day, pushing him hard so that he staggered back. 'You foul-mouthed bastard! Why did you come here? What does he deserve? A good hiding from you? Is that it? You want to start with me?' He pushed him again. 'Come on – you're not scared of me, are you? A *pervert* like me?'

Edmund had pulled on his trousers. He stepped forward. 'Day, just leave, please. Please, Joseph –'

He hadn't seen the punch coming. In the café Edmund touched his black eye, the humiliation still fresh enough to make him wince at the memory: Day had knocked him out.

He had come round on the floor, Paul kneeling beside him. He had helped him to his feet and sat him down on the bed. Through his befuddlement, he sensed that Day had gone; the bedroom door was shut as though he had never been there at all. He might have imagined him except that his brain felt as though it was too tightly encased within his skull and his eye had swollen closed. Paul handed him a flannel wrung out in cold water.

'Press this to it.'

'I'm sorry.'

'Be quiet.'

'Really. I'm really sorry.'

Harshly Paul said, 'I told you to be quiet.'

He had hung his head; his mouth had filled with saliva and he concentrated on swallowing back the bile rising in his throat, but there was too much and he spewed at Paul's feet. 'Sorry,' he wiped his mouth with the back of his hand. 'Don't shout at me.'

'Shout at you? For Christ's sake don't talk like a child! Lie down. You should lie down.'

'I'm all right. I'll go.' He made to get up but Paul pushed him back.

'Lie down. I don't want to be blamed if you fall dead in the street.'

He did as he was told. After a moment, Paul lit a cigarette and Edmund turned painfully to see him lie down next to him, leaving a hand's breadth of space between them, as much as the narrow bed would allow. 'I'm sorry,' he repeated.

Paul was silent. Edmund wondered if he should repeat his apology again, but his silence was too discouraging, too stonily tight-lipped; he could see that Paul's hands were trembling. When his cigarette was finished, Paul got up. He fetched towels from the bathroom and began to clean up the vomit.

'Let me do that.'

'Rest. The sooner you're rested the sooner you can go.'

'I don't want to go.'

Paul straightened up and took the towels back to the bathroom. Edmund heard the taps running, the slap of the cloths as Paul threw them into the bath. He got up unsteadily and stood in the bathroom door.

'Forgive me?'

'I'll walk you home.'

'Would you?'

Paul had gazed at him for a moment, and in the café Edmund wondered if he only imagined his hesitation as Paul said, 'Yes, I'll walk back with you, of course.'

* * *

44

As they walked in silence, Edmund had wondered if this escorting meant that Paul felt some responsibility and that he didn't blame him entirely for Day. It wouldn't be fair if he blamed him; he couldn't have known that Day would follow him.

In the café he cringed over this childish petulance. His brother Neville would sometimes tease him over such behaviour and call him a monstrously spoilt brat. He had thought of Neville last night, too, as he walked beside Paul, because the two of them were much the same height and build, very much the same age, he would guess. And Neville could be silent like this too, judgemental and superior. Neville had often disapproved of him; in his brother's eyes he lacked moral fibre. But he was so much younger – Neville might have made allowances, just as Paul might.

He remembered that he had looked at Paul resentfully. He couldn't help saying, 'It wasn't my fault.'

Paul had glanced at him. 'Please be quiet.'

'Stop telling me to be quiet! Why are you so angry with me?'

He ignored him.

'Paul, I can't bear this –'

Paul stopped. 'I'll leave you here, I'm sure you'll be fine.'

'No. Please, wait … Don't go.'

Paul laughed shortly, glancing away. Meeting his gaze he said, 'Edmund, I'm sorry. You're a nice boy –'

'I'm not a boy, stop calling me a boy!'

'All right. You're right. You're not a *boy*. Now, get yourself home, go to bed. Thank you for tonight.'

'Don't thank me. Christ, you'll want to pay me next. Who do you think you are?'

'Goodnight, Edmund.'

He'd made to turn away but Edmund had caught his arm. 'You can't just walk away from me.'

'Why not?' Paul had sighed. 'What do you want?'

'I don't know. You. Don't look like that.'

Paul had smiled as though he had made a bad joke, shaking his head at the poorness of it. 'You want me? What would you do with me? Where would you keep me? How would you expect me to behave?' He lit a cigarette, exhaling smoke on a long breath as he said, 'Because I've a feeling you don't like homosexual men, Edmund. And I know I can be that arch little shirt-lifter I noticed you wincing at. Although you do wince quite discreetly, I do notice and it does make me feel like dirt, if I'm honest, because I would much rather be respected than have false feelings flung at me.'

'Not false.'

'No?'

'No.'

'So, you love me? Edmund, I'm flattered. What shall we do now?'

'Don't patronise me.'

'I mean it. What shall we do? I'm in London for a few more days at least. I'm quite up for a bit of love – I take what I can get. Could I ask if I'm expected to love you back?'

Edmund had looked away, unable to bear his scrutiny. 'I didn't wince.'

'It's all right. Most men make me wince, too – I'm sure I let my own horror slip from time to time.'

'Most of the time you're like any other man.'

Paul laughed bleakly. 'Thanks, I do my best.'

'I didn't mean it like that! All I meant was … All I meant was … I don't know. Maybe I can only look at you sideways.'

'I don't know what you mean by that, Edmund. But I would think it's probably a little insulting, if I wanted to think about it.'

'I don't mean to be insulting. I just want, with all my heart, to see you again.'

'I don't know.' Vehemently Paul said, 'Don't *you* want to be *like any other man*? When I was your age –'

'You talk like an old man – like my bloody father! You're not that much older than me – the war didn't make you a sage.'

Paul laughed, a genuine, surprised laugh, just as he had laughed in that hotel bed, so that Edmund had groaned with the despair of wanting him so badly. Touching his swollen face, Paul said, 'So, you want with all your heart to see me again?

That may be the nicest thing anyone has ever said to me.'

'It's true.'

'Then all right, I would like to see you again, too. But with not so much of my heart … I'm sorry, but I feel I have to be honest, since you've been so honest with me.'

'As long as I can see you.'

In the café, Edmund paid his bill; he left a tip for the waitress, more than he normally would, and he thought guiltily of Ann as he walked out on to the street, turning up his collar against the relentless rain. But the guilt was fleeting; nothing mattered except Paul.

Chapter Six

PAUL ASKED, 'WAS YOUR hotel comfortable?'

George placed his menu down, took off his spectacles and folded them into his pocket. 'You know, whenever I'm in London I have the bitter feeling that I haven't done enough with my life.' Pleased to see Paul looked surprised, he said, 'I slept well, so yes, the room was comfortable. Yours?'

'Yes.'

'Good.'

The hotel Paul had chosen to meet him in for lunch reminded George of the hotels his own father would take him to when he had been a medical student at St Thomas's in Westminster. These hotels were the kind of places where he supposed men took their mistresses: tucked away from the main drags, impressive but not overtly so, discreet and well ordered. He couldn't imagine an irate husband able to make a scene in such tasteful surroundings; the fine china, the sparkling glass and silver, the deep carpets and dark panelling would all conspire against the cuckold, making his jealousy seem petty and ill mannered. But then, George thought, perhaps men didn't take their mistresses anywhere, but kept them in dreary little flats close to convenient tube stations. What did he know? He had slept with one woman in the whole of his life, Paul's mother. Living his day-to-day life in Thorp, the belief that he hadn't had enough sex was a small regret; here in London, reminded of other lives he might have lived, that same regret grew to near overwhelming proportions. He had to marshal all his sensible arguments and excuses to convince himself that he had made the right choices, bolstering himself with the idea that his care for his two sons had to matter more than anything else.

Sitting across the table from Paul he wondered if he had taken the best care, but for the life of him he didn't know what he could have done differently.

Paul had placed his menu down too and was signalling to the waiter. He ordered wine, asking the kind of questions that always seemed to please wine waiters, making them flower from poker-faced boredom into articulate life. This waiter was no exception, and Paul charmed him, which was also unexceptional; his son could be charming when he had a mind to be. The waiter called Paul *sir* often, once leaning quite close to him to point out a wine on the long list. They smiled at one another and George watched all this with uneasy interest, because although he knew Paul was capable of anything, he'd never seen him in action.

When the waiter had gone, Paul unleashed his being-gracious-to-waiters smile on him. 'Well, here we are.'

He must have slept well, George thought, because he seemed so much happier than he was last night, the kind of boyish happiness that he hadn't seen in him for many years, since before the war. But his evening had been successful, all his paintings sold, all those people telling him how wonderful he was, no wonder his good eye was so bright. George looked down at his starched white napkin, still folded on the table in front of him. If he could watch his son closely unobserved there were times he couldn't quite meet his eyes; times when he wasn't strong enough to hide his concerns.

'Dad?'

He looked up at him. Paul had always resembled his mother when he was a child. Even now, when he was so changed, her ghost was still there in his face, in his good eye. He wondered how he might have talked to Grace about Paul, because an explanation would have been necessary. He wondered how she might have reacted; he hadn't known her long enough or well enough to guess.

George unfolded the napkin and spread it over his knee. 'Last night went well. You must be very pleased.'

'I'm sorry I didn't invite you. But I thought … Well, actually I thought no one would come. If it had been a wash-out—'

Another waiter came and took their order. The wine waiter uncorked the wine at their table, pouring a small measure for Paul to taste. When this rigmarole was finished with and they were alone again, Paul said, 'I'm very glad you're here.' He raised his glass. 'It's good to see you.'

George raised his own glass. He sipped the wine and it was delicious, just as he expected their lunch to be delicious, just as there wasn't a stain on the starched cloth or a smudge on the cutlery, just as the rain stopped and a sudden shaft of sunlight dazzled the silver cruet and made the white flowers in their tasteful arrangement appear cleaner and more beautiful. Paul had chosen well. As his son unfolded his own napkin, George noticed his manicured fingernails and his cuff-links that were milky green opals, lustrous, translucent against his immaculate cuffs. The fine tailoring of the dark suit he wore made him appear older, a little broader, a little less like the slight boy he had appeared to be last night. George wondered why he hadn't worn this suit to the opening; perhaps he hadn't wanted to stand out too much from a Bohemian crowd, perhaps he had wanted to pretend to be more like such men and women who didn't care for appearances but only for their Art. Touched by this thought, George said, 'You look very dashing.'

'Do I?' Paul smiled. 'Dashing? It wasn't the look I was aiming for.'

'Which was?'

'Oh, I don't know. Seriousness, I think.' He picked up his glass only to put it down again. 'I suppose I wanted to look as though you don't have to worry about me.'

'I'm not worried. You look happy. Successful.' He raised his glass again, smiling. 'I'm very proud of you.'

Their meal arrived, rare steak and sautéed potatoes and thin green beans, and they ate and talked about Thorp and George's medical practice so that George realised that he had memorised an entertainment of anecdotes for Paul and that he must have been hoping that they would be as easy as this together, as easy as they had been before the war, in that too-brief period between Paul leaving boarding school and joining the army.

There were times even during the war, on his rare leaves home from the front, when they were friends like this; he had always *liked* his son as much as he loved him, and at this moment he loved him terribly, a love that made him fear for his own life – what would he have left if Paul was gone?

But Paul had gone of course; although not dead, but so far away, to a place he would never visit, *could* never visit. He thought of that man: Patrick, who had come to his home, stood in his kitchen, the great, intimidating height and breadth of him blocking out the light from the window as he said, 'I'll take care of him. I know how to protect him, keep him safe. I promise you, Dr Harris, on my life. I would rather die than see him hurt again.'

Such histrionic words, but said with such calm and conviction – Patrick Morgan truly was a paradox of a man. What could he have done except agree that Paul would be safer in a country that wasn't England? He could have said no, and this man, with his love for Paul like a carefully contained but agitating force inside him, would have done what he had to do anyway. George guessed that Morgan had come only out of a calculating courtesy, no doubt reasoning that it was best to have an ally who would help convince Paul that leaving everything he loved was for the best.

The waiter cleared their plates. Paul lit a cigarette, having first asked him if he minded. He did, but he said nothing. Paul ordered coffee and pulled a face as he tasted it. 'I'd forgotten how bad coffee is in England.' For a moment, he seemed far away, preoccupied by a memory that George guessed must be pleasant from the look in his eye, a memory of Morgan, perhaps, and the foreign coffee they drank together in a house he imagined resembled the houses pictured in a child's bible. '*There is a courtyard with a fountain,*' Paul had written to him, shortly after he arrived in that alien country. '*The sun bleaches everything clean. I am well.*' The letters they exchanged were stilted, at least in those early days of his exile. Paul never wrote of Morgan, of course, or only obliquely.

Pushing away his coffee cup, Paul said, 'What time's your train?'

'Half past three. Plenty of time.' George acted on the urge, perhaps prompted by the wine, to reach across the table and cover Paul's hand with his own. Paul smiled at him.

'I'm all right, Dad. Honestly.'

And perhaps it was the wine that caused him to say, 'You could come home –'

Paul withdrew his hand. 'No.'

'No? Why not? It's all forgotten – that business. And now Margot is remarried, settled, she might be happy for you to see Bobby –'

'No, Dad. Please. Let's not spoil this afternoon.'

But he couldn't see the point in stopping, and besides, the words were coming too quickly, as though he had rehearsed them as he had rehearsed the amusing stories. 'Margot is happy, I'm sure. And happiness helps people to forgive. You don't have to live in Thorp, but close – at the seaside, perhaps, where we used to go when you were a child.' He must have been drunker than he thought because he laughed with the excitement of such an idea. 'You could paint the sea!'

Paul was gazing at him, allowing him to babble on until George realised how still his son had become, as though he was keeping some fierce emotion in check. Dismayed, he trailed off. 'I'm sorry. I don't know what came over me.'

'I understand that you had to ask. I would have, if I were you.' Paul laughed slightly. 'Paint the sea, eh? That cold, grey sea.' Suddenly he said, 'I dream of home – at night, I mean. You're in this dream and Bobby is still a baby and Margot has given him to us for good, she doesn't want him any more. And you'd think that this would be a marvellous dream, wouldn't you? But I only want to run away and I wake up and all I feel is relief ...' He stubbed out his cigarette and looked up at him. 'Patrick thinks I'll stay in England now. He thinks I'm brave enough not to run away again.'

'He's right!'

'No. Usually, almost always in fact, but not about this.'

Paul summoned the waiter and asked for the bill. Turning to George, he said, 'Let me get this – it will be the first time I've bought you a meal. It will make me feel like a grown-up.' He smiled, handsome, ironic, more *grown up* than anyone ever deserved to be so that George felt soft with pity and love for him.

'Paul, my home is always your home.'

'Thank you. That means a lot to me.' Glancing away towards the tall windows looking out over the sunny street, he said on a rush of breath, 'It's just that I couldn't survive without Patrick.'

George tried to keep the scorn out of his voice and failed. 'Paul – of course you could –'

It seemed that Paul forced himself to look at him. 'I couldn't. I know it must sound terribly melodramatic to you. Terribly *wrong*. But I don't want you to have any hopes for me, Dad.'

'You were *married*, Paul – and I know you were happy with Margot. You could be happy like that again –'

'I shouldn't have married her.' He had never said this before, and it was as though he realised that there was too much truth in this statement, a truth that was too painful to be aired, too full of renunciation, because he stood up quickly. Too brightly he said, 'I'll walk with you to the station. It will make a change, me seeing you off on to a train.'

On the train going home George thought about them standing on the platform at King's Cross, with a few minutes to spare before his train arrived. The station was crowded, and full of all the smell and noise and grittiness that never failed to take him back to the war, when Paul would stand beside him in uniform, anxiously looking down the track as if only afraid of being late.

As though Paul had been remembering the same scene, he had said, 'I used to imagine I'd come back – *if* I came back – to girls with flowers, to brass bands and bunting ... Can you imagine Thorp Station decked out like that?'

George had laughed. 'No.'

'I'd imagine the station and the bunting, but I couldn't imagine myself beyond that, at home, being *me*.' He'd smiled at him. 'I'll write to you.'

Those were always the last words they'd say to each other,

even from the earliest days of Paul going off to boarding school, another uniform swamping him. George would let him go, standing on a platform until the train was out of sight, reluctant to go back to his empty house. Perhaps this is what he should have done differently: he should have kept him by his side, taught him at home, made him his own and no one else's; and later he should have maimed him in some small way, just enough that the army wouldn't want him.

Resting his head back on the train seat's antimacassar, George closed his eyes. The wine had gone to his head, thickening his brain; he hoped he would sleep away the long journey home, only to be woken by a kindly guard at Darlington. There, he would make his connection home to Thorp, a short fifteen minutes away, hardly time for him to pull himself together enough to be Dr George Harris, smart, straight-backed, dignified, and if not a pillar of the community, then respected by his remaining patients, despite his son's disgrace.

George opened his eyes. Disgrace was the word Paul had used; Paul had stood in his study, still white with the shock of spending a night in a police cell, and with odd, stilted formality had said, 'I'm sorry to have brought this disgrace home. If you want me to leave –'

George had only stared at him, slack-jawed with fear for his son, only managing to say, 'Where on earth would you go? Leave where?'

Paul had bowed his head, trembling; he had never seen anyone tremble so delicately, so thoroughly from his head to his feet, grasping the back of the chair he should have been sitting on, his knuckles white. George knew he should have gone to him, but at the time he felt he didn't have the strength to stand up, and so the strength of the anger in his voice surprised him as he said, 'You have a wife! A son! What were you thinking of?'

Paul had only shaken his head.

'Have you told Margot? My God, Paul – how can you tell that little girl something like this?'

Little girl. On the train, George remembered how a spark of anger had shown in Paul's face, so quick that he might have been mistaken, although he was sure he was not because Paul's voice was hard as he said, 'My wife isn't a child.'

But she was, George thought; Margot had never been more than an eighteen-year-old child to him, immature, too quick to worship Paul, seeing only the boy in uniform, the wounded young officer who was kind and attentive and took such great care of her and their baby. In every respect, he had been a good husband. Every respect but one.

He sometimes wondered what Paul had told Margot that terrible morning, when, still wearing the clothes he had gone out in the previous night, still stinking of the police cell, he'd taken her upstairs to their bedroom and closed the door behind them. What did a man say to his young, *young* wife when he had been caught buggering a man in a public lavatory? That he would go to prison; that the details of the trial would be printed in the local newspaper and that her neighbours would from now on cross the road to avoid her and put excrement through her letterbox along with their hate-filled letters? From his study George had heard Margot cry out, a thud as though something had been dropped; he had been holding Bobby, who had looked up towards this noise, his face crumpling as his mother began to howl.

His son had been disgraced, then, and sent to prison; his daughter-in-law and grandson moved to her parents' house across the road from his; and his neighbours and many of his patients had shunned him, affecting his living. He smiled to himself bitterly; Paul had owed him lunch, especially such a lunch he could no longer afford for himself.

He thought of his home, Parkwood, the ugly house full of unused, freezing rooms his father had designed and built as a very young man. In those days the Harris fortune was still intact under his grandfather's good management. His grandfather and father had both been architects; his father could draw anything, swiftly, with an uncanny, joyful perception; as a child George had thought him a magician for the way he could create a running, jumping dog from just a few strokes of a pencil. His father had adored Paul; the two of them shared the same skills. Perhaps Paul's artistry shouldn't have surprised him quite so much.

Parkwood was on the outskirts of town, close to the park and cemetery. From Thorp Station he would walk the mile or so home through the evening's empty streets. He would unlock his door, turn on the hall light, place his case down and hang up his coat and hat. In the hallstand mirror, he would see that his face was smutty from the journey and he would go into the kitchen to boil enough water to wash. He would make tea and drink it black because there would be no milk. He would light a fire in his study, one he had laid before he left for London, all ready to put a match to. Empty for two days, Parkwood would seem sullen in its cold dampness, showing only how shabby it could be; but everything would be all right once the fire was burning, the tea brewed, some toast made; everything would be just as if he had never gone away.

George stared out of the window as the train sped through the Essex countryside. He had told Iris that he would put a lamp in his study window when he arrived safely home, bright enough so that she could see it from her bedroom. Perhaps her husband Daniel would be out administering at a deathbed and she would be free to slip from the vicarage, across the graveyard and over the road to his house, escaping quick and quiet as a ghost from a tomb. And she would be a little breathless when he opened the back door, shivering in the sympathetic moonlight, smiling. 'I've killed him,' she'd say. 'I stove in his head with an axe.' It was something she sometimes said, her blackest joke. Standing aside he would hold the door wide open. 'Come in. I'll wash the blood from your hands.'

She had said, 'You won't tell Paul, will you?'

He had thought she knew him well enough not to ask such a question. Iris: Margot's mother who knew all about Paul and the disgrace he'd brought home.

George had wondered what she took him for if she thought he could tell Paul anything about his relationship with Paul's ex-mother-in-law; besides, what was there to tell? That they held hands across his kitchen table; that once she had looked so unhappy he had stepped around the table to hold her in the way he would hold a distraught patient. She was another man's wife, and he wasn't absolutely sure she wanted him, although she

56

seemed to. The only certainty was how much he wanted her.

Perhaps he wouldn't put the lamp in the window, and perhaps tomorrow he would go to her and explain that her neighbourly visits were more than his heart could take, but that he could be an adulterer, if she could – it was just that he couldn't go on hiding his desire.

The guard came and checked his ticket and told him that the buffet car was open, if he cared to go along. But the meal he had eaten with Paul lay heavily and he turned back to the window and the darkening fields; he would be home soon enough.

Chapter Seven

PAUL WALKED FROM KING'S Cross, through Holborn to St Paul's Cathedral, where he had told Edmund he would meet him outside on the main steps.

Edmund had grinned. 'Are we to be tourists?'

'I am a tourist.'

It was true he didn't know London very well: not nearly as well as his father, who had lived and worked here before he married. He thought about his father as he walked; his confession that he felt he hadn't done enough with his life had hurt him because it seemed he had wished away his marriage, his children: him. And now, unbearably, he could only think of his father as a disappointed man.

He was early for his meeting with Edmund, had planned it so that he would be: he wanted to see the boy coming and to take pleasure in watching him; he wanted to attempt to read his expression, whether he appeared happy, anxious or only calmly indifferent. Not the last, he thought. 'You will come, won't you?' Edmund had said. There had been a note of pleading in his voice, even though he was smiling, and his eyes had searched his face as though the boy suspected he was the kind of man who would make an arrangement only to renege on it. Paul had wanted only to reassure him at the time, when Edmund was still there in front of him looking at him with such intense, puzzling *want*. Now, on the steps of St Paul's, he couldn't help feeling that perhaps he should have told him that it would be best if they didn't see each other again.

Yet here he was, of course; he couldn't help himself. Besides, he'd thought that he wouldn't be able to be alone this afternoon, prey to an ambush of memories that last night he'd believed would be the only outcome of lunch with his father. As it was, the memories weren't so difficult to cope with; he had the strength for the solitary pleasure of an art gallery and he could almost regret this afternoon's complication, almost, if he wasn't being truthful, if he really wanted to pretend to be the kind of man who would give up on the certainty of sex, no matter its *complications*.

He paced, climbing a few steps only to walk down again. He looked out towards the statue of Queen Anne and the London traffic beyond, an empty open-topped tourist bus making its redundant journey on this changeable, umbrella day. He had bought his umbrella that morning – an oversight in the packing because Patrick had forgotten about rain, it seemed – and now he unfurled it as the rain began again. People dashed past him up the steps and into the cathedral, making his waiting more conspicuous. He looked at his watch: five more minutes, if the boy was on time. He felt sure that he would be.

Patrick had said, 'I went to London once.'

Paul remembered smiling because Pat had sounded so unlike himself, more like a young boy who didn't want the adults to think he hadn't had such an experience. He remembered he had used the tone he would use on a child when he'd asked him, 'Did you have a nice time?'

'It was during the war. I didn't have enough leave to get home.'

Of course: it was impossible to imagine Patrick going to London at any time in his life other than during the war; holidays, sight-seeing, going anywhere just for the sake of it, none of this was in his nature unless he was there to share the experience. He had imagined Patrick trailing around the city streets purposelessly, or perhaps spending his whole, too-short leave in a hotel room, sleeping the exhausted, restless sleep of someone who knows how quickly time passes but who still can't resist the need for oblivion. He wouldn't have gone to a show, as he himself had on a similarly short leave; nor – also as he had – would he have made himself available. Patrick wouldn't have gone down a back alley behind some grand hotel to be buggered by a Royal Marine between overflowing bins, the stink of rotting food mixing with that of expensive dinners wafting from the clattering kitchen. Patrick wouldn't, because he wasn't such a bloody idiot to take such a risk, but also because he had more dignity and pride, and because Patrick wasn't so sure of himself in those days. 'Until I met you,' Pat had told him, 'I didn't know what I was.'

Paul remembered doubting him, thinking that this was only a sentimental lie, with all his lusts and frustrations, all his anguish and self-disgust edited out. He sensed that Patrick needed to tell himself that he was his first and only love, needing that purity because how could he feel like this about another man, *any* man? Wholly discriminating, that was how Patrick liked to think of himself: a man who would have lived and died a virgin were it not for meeting him.

Later though, he came to understand that Patrick truly had been, if not unsure, then fighting hard against his own desires; during that leave he would have kept to himself, Paul was quite certain. And the girls would have turned their heads as he walked by, smiling at the sergeant who was so handsome, so very right and proper in his graveness. Behind his back, the girls would have exchanged looks, laughed a little perhaps, because there was something unaware about this man: he didn't play the game. Perhaps he was a fool, or a god, perhaps.

Paul walked down a few steps, then back again. He should count all the steps, anything to keep from thinking about Patrick and his own unfaithfulness. The rain eased off and he shook out the umbrella; he saw that a rainbow had formed and thought of the colours he would mix to paint it: Cadmium Red, Cobalt Violet, Indian Yellow; the mixing would absorb him, leaving no room for any other thought, such a fine escape. He drew breath, exhaled, steadying himself. The boy was coming, walking quickly, a smile beginning on that sensuous mouth of his. Paul straightened his back and walked down the steps to meet him.

Edmund saw the rainbow too and thought that it was a good omen. He had been worried that the rain would help Paul to change his mind about meeting him: why venture out in such weather, why bother at all with getting wet and cold on the way to meet a stranger? Because, another more sensible voice told him, he likes to fuck you, a sound enough motivation for risking a chill. He listened to this voice and told himself that now he was entirely sober, in the unforgiving light of day, he was under no illusion about Paul-Francis-Law-Harris. Harris was a dog, a filthy, dirty, panting dog, and that was fine by him; that was good, in fact; this was nothing after all, just fucking.

He touched his black eye. Examining it in the mirror in the café's lavatory, he'd thought it didn't look as bad as he'd feared, not nearly as noticeable. Now, as Paul walked towards him, he was less sure. Paul frowned with concern at the bruise, and Edmund found himself laughing self-consciously.

'Do I look a sight?'

'No, not at all.' Paul glanced over his shoulder as though afraid they were watched and that his concern had been noted, before turning to him again. Lightly he said, 'I thought we might walk back to my hotel. You can point out any sights of interest on the way.'

Paul slept and Edmund got up from the hotel bed and went to the window, opening it a little to let in some air. On the street below a couple strolled arm in arm; a man hurried past them, glancing at his watch like the white rabbit. Two porters in the hotel's livery loaded suitcases into a taxi as a woman in a mink coat and an ink-black feathered hat chided her companion. 'And you bring me here,' she said. '*Here,* of all places!' The man looked up and seemed to stare directly at him. There was a vacant look on his face, as though the woman's words were in a language that was just foreign enough to be of no interest. Edmund stepped back out of sight; he was naked, shrivelled by the cold, his body ached and a throb was beginning behind his eyes, lack of sleep catching up with him.

Lack of sleep also caused this mood, he knew, this feeling that the world was bleak and hostile, that everyone spoke in a language that wasn't interesting enough. Behind him, on crumpled, stained sheets, a man was sleeping, a stranger who had thoroughly, systematically fucked him.

He was much practised, this man, in his consideration, in the time he took, in the noises he made and attempted to suppress. There was gentleness and strength, stamina and patience – he had needed all his patience – and there was a kind of understanding, albeit of a superficial kind. Paul had held his gaze only once, only for a moment – perhaps he understood more than Edmund gave him credit for, because surely he would have held his gaze far longer otherwise. He would have smiled that knowing smile of his, perhaps cupped his face in his hand with his well-rehearsed tenderness. As it was, Paul had looked away and his expression became that of a stranger who had inadvertently caught one's eye. A moment later and Paul had brought himself to climax as though he had decided that there was no point in wasting any more time, rolling away and fumbling on the bedside table for his cigarettes, tossing the packet to Edmund when he had finished with lighting one for himself. When the cigarette was smoked – in remarkably little time, he inhaled deeply as though he wished he could draw the whole thing into his lungs at once – Paul slept. Not a single word was said through all of this.

Edmund went into the bathroom. Last night's soiled towels had been replaced, the towel Paul had used that morning hung carefully over the rail to dry. The bath had been rinsed clean, although there was a subtle scent of bath oil, a very expensive, very masculine smell that had him inhaling deeply to catch more of it. There was a bottle of this oil on the shelf above the sink, along with Paul's toothbrush, toothpaste, razor and shaving brush and soap. He shaved very cleanly, and Edmund imagined the care he would take, the time spent looking in the mirror, not seeing his reflection but only the drag of the blade over stretched skin.

Avoiding his own eye in this same mirror, Edmund unscrewed the top from the bath oil and lifted the bottle to his nose. He closed his eyes, concentrating on this essence of foreign queerness. Impossible to buy scent like this in England, he was sure; impossible to smell like this in England. He smiled, despite himself. What *would* his father say?

He replaced the bottle's cap, making sure he screwed it down tightly, and placed it back on the shelf in just the same position. He met his gaze in the mirror and saw how haggard he looked with his black eye, so well and truly done over, and thought how he should run a bath for himself, pouring in too much of the oil so that globules would form on the surface of the water, making him slick and slippery, considerately lubricated. Perhaps he would use Paul's razor so that his cheeks would be soft and boyish, rub some of his toothpaste around his gums so that his breath would not offend. And then he would lie down beside the sleeping stranger on the crumpled bed and wait for him to wake so that he might guide his hand down to his erection.

He wanted Paul constantly; that was the trouble: wanting him and not liking him and knowing that he had never loved anyone like this before. Even though he tried to persuade himself out of this knowledge – because how could one trust a feeling that had come so suddenly – he knew it was hopeless to imagine this was only artful, selfish fucking. In the end it came down to this one, dazzlingly simple feeling: he loved him. 'So there,' he said softly to his reflection. 'I love him, so there.'

He went back into the bedroom and climbed into bed. Paul slept on and Edmund took this opportunity to look at him properly. He saw someone of around thirty, although it was possible he was a little younger, but no older. This thirty-year-old man had dark, neatly cut, very short hair and well-defined eyebrows, and although his eyes were closed, he recalled that they were green, although the eye made of glass was a slightly different shade. He had a straight, narrow nose, and his cheekbones were sharply outlined because he was too thin, really, and fragile-looking in this grey afternoon light. There was a scar beneath the false eye, white and raised against his tanned skin. His ears were small and neat, like a child's. His neck, like his face, forearms and hands, was tanned, but the rest of his body was quite pale, the mass of dark hair on his chest made to appear even darker in contrast to this paleness. He was surprisingly hairy for such a delicate-looking man, but that was all right, he could get an erection just thinking of this contrast.

The sheet covered the rest of his body; Edmund imagined his cock soft against his thigh, against that jagged scar that had earlier stayed his hand and mouth.

Discovering that scar, Edmund had wanted to spring from him – finally reunited with his sense of propriety. He was fucking a man who had worn the same uniform his brother had worn, who had fought in the same battles, a man Neville might have known, might have brought home on leave. And he would have been in awe of his brother's comrade, shy of him, just as his uniform made him shy of Neville, made him a child with no experience of anything at all. Touching Paul's scar, he was thirteen again, and the disconnection between mind and body that protected him from the ridiculousness of sex almost reconnected. Only his overwhelming desire for Paul saved him from shrivelling, his lust too savage to be held back by thought, even thought that involved his brother. The idea that it was heretical to fuck him was forgotten almost as soon as it entered his head.

Edmund wondered how he might bridge the gap between them, how he might not appear as so hopelessly lacking in gravitas as to be no more than a child in Paul's eyes, a *boy*. Though he had told Paul that the war hadn't made him a sage, of course in his heart he believed it had. He couldn't convince himself that such experience wouldn't teach a man everything he would ever need to know.

Paul stirred beside him, keeping his eyes closed and reaching out, as if to check that he was still there. As his fingers brushed his, Paul opened his eyes; he appeared confused for a moment until it seemed he realised where he was. Still he went on frowning at him, as though he couldn't remember his name. His voice broke a little as he said, 'Did I sleep long?'

'No. Half an hour, perhaps.'

Paul took his watch from the bedside table. 'Six o'clock.'

'Have you an appointment to keep?'

'No.' After a moment Paul asked, 'Have you?'

'No.'

'So,' Paul drew breath and exhaled heavily. 'So …'

He was being dismissed. The realisation came to him with a jolt, his stomach lurching as though he had tripped on stairs. He got up at once, too ashamed at his own foolish lack of

64

sensitivity to be still. Making a great effort to be calm he said, 'I should go.' He began to dress, remembering how idiotically he had behaved last night, cringing as he recalled how uncontrolled he must have seemed to him.

Paul reached for his cigarettes, a careless action that all at once incensed him. Shoving his arms into his shirt with such force he almost ripped the cloth, Edmund said, 'Is there ever a moment when you don't smoke?'

Paul shook out the match, squinting against the smoke. 'It's childish, isn't it?'

Edmund stared at him. 'What is?'

'Smoking like I do. I do so enjoy it, though.'

'It makes you stink.'

'I daresay.'

'It's probably all you care about.'

Paul laughed. 'Probably.'

'Because it shows in your work, you know – your lack of care.'

'You're right.' Flicking ash, he said, 'Absolutely right.'

'Why do you paint?'

'Money.'

'Liar.'

Paul gazed at him and Edmund allowed himself to meet his gaze brazenly, as if he didn't care that he might have hurt him. He was still standing at the end of the bed, the same place he had stood last night, the same crack in the lino sharp against his sole, the same perspective on Paul, in bed, the sheets hiding him from his waist to his feet. He would paint him like this, sex soiled, weary, his cigarette burning to a long quiver of ash between his fingers. He would have to keep putting down his brush to fuck him, but this would be serious work, he had no doubt about that.

Edmund turned his back on him and pulled on his trousers. He had hung his jacket on the hook on the door, and he remembered how nervous he had felt when he'd taken it off; he should have left then; he should have behaved decently and not given in to his lust. He swung round to face Paul.

'You were right, last night. I do despise men like you.'

'Do you? You make a bloody good show of disguising it.'
Paul stubbed out his cigarette. Evenly he said, 'Why don't you just fuck off?' He looked up at him. 'Fuck off back to that girl, you spoilt little bastard. I'm sure she'll make you feel better about it all.'

'All what? What the hell would a second-rate, jumped-up little nobody like you know about anything?'

'I'd really like you to go now.'

'I bet you bloody would.'

'Keep your voice down.'

'No – everyone should know what a fake you are.' He glared at him, breathless and knowing how shamingly red his face would be, he could feel it burning. He also knew that if he blinked, the tears would fall down his cheeks and he would be gasping, as blind, deaf, and breathless as a child in a tantrum. All at once Neville was standing in front of him, telling him what a brat he was and why didn't he just bugger off somewhere far away from him. Swiping at his eyes impatiently he said, 'Why did you paint those bloody pictures?' Paul was silent and he repeated, 'Why? You must have known, you must have –'

'Known what? What was I supposed to have known?'

Edmund wiped his eyes again, making an effort to control his voice as he said, 'We have to look. Is that what you think? We have to look at the corpses –'

'No. You don't have to look.'

'And if I don't look, what then? You can call me a spoilt little bastard, is that it – as though I don't know anything? Every painting in that exhibition was facile, sentimental –'

Paul got up and began to dress; his face had drained of colour and Edmund could see that his hands were trembling over the buttons of his shirt. The cuff-links he had placed down so carefully earlier, when Edmund had wanted only to tear off his clothes, glinted in a sudden shaft of sunlight as he struggled to thread them into his cuffs. Paul had transformed again, this time into a frail, humiliated boy. Remembering the scar on his thigh and how often his fingers would go to his false eye, Edmund felt all his anger breached by pity. He crossed the room quickly, making to take the cuff-links from him. 'Let me do it.'

Paul jerked away. 'I'd much rather you left.'

'No – listen, I'm sorry –'

'Please go.'

'No. Paul, listen, please. Please, I'm sorry – that was wrong of me, to criticise your work like that, and maybe I'm jealous ...' He laughed tearfully. 'I don't know ... It's just that you make me weak ... Weak in the knees, heart ... *head*. And now I just sound like some bloody silly song –'

'You sound like a fool. Crying over a man you don't know – it makes me wish I hadn't picked you up.'

'*Picked me up*?' Edmund wiped his eyes, horrified at his tears. 'Is that all I am? Someone you picked up? You do this all the time, don't you? Well I don't –'

'No, I know you don't.' Angrily Paul said, 'Stop crying. For Christ's sake I can't stand it! I don't know what this is about but it's nothing to do with me.'

'It's *everything* to do with you! You must know how much I want you.'

'Well, you can't have me.'

'Why not? I know you're attracted to me. And the sex –'

'Let's not talk about that.'

'Why?'

'Because it's just sex – nothing. Sex is nothing at all –'

'*Nothing*? What – am I terrible at it or something? Christ. Maybe you could teach me all you know!'

'Just go. Go back to your girl.'

'She's not my girl – I'm not interested in her.'

'And I'm not interested in you! Do I really have to spell it out?'

'Yes. Yes you do. Because I see the way you look at me – and you can pretend to be a swine but I know you're not like that, I know that you ... you *like* me and I didn't mean to say those rotten things about your work –'

'But you did say those things.'

'And I'm sorry I hurt you.'

Paul laughed emptily. He sat down on the bed and lit another

67

cigarette; his hands still trembled and Edmund had to suppress the urge to kneel at his feet and beg for forgiveness. He took a step towards him and Paul looked up to meet his gaze. After a little while he said, 'I didn't think the paintings would sell. I was prepared to make all kinds of excuses for them if they hadn't sold, but mainly I thought I would imagine that they hadn't been *understood*.' He laughed again, looking down at the tip of his cigarette. 'But of course they were understood – you understood them. Even the men who bought them knew exactly what they were buying: titillation.'

Unable to help himself, Edmund knelt on the floor and took his hand. 'Paul, you're a fine artist –'

He drew his hand away. 'Edmund …' Searching his face he went on, 'I saw you at the window earlier –'

'I thought you were asleep.'

'You looked so unhappy I was afraid to say anything.'

'I wasn't unhappy. I'm unhappy now, thinking how much I've hurt you.'

'You haven't *hurt* me. Not really.'

'Not really?'

Paul smiled crookedly. 'I'm happy. I sold out – I can afford to buy you supper.'

'Do you want to?'

Paul looked away as though he couldn't bear to meet his gaze any longer. He cleared his throat. 'I don't know, if I'm honest.' He looked at him. 'Do you want me to be honest?'

'Yes –' Edmund attempted to laugh. 'Put me out of my misery.'

'I can't stand it when you say you love me. This isn't *love*, Edmund.'

'I won't say it again.'

Paul nodded, glancing away again. He was collarless, his shirt unbuttoned; there seemed so much intimacy in this almost-dressed state, as though they had lived together for many years. Edmund had the urge to take his hand again, to press it to his lips, at the same time knowing that the better thing to do would be to pretend that they *had* lived together so long. The cuff-links were on the bedside table, he could pick them up and say, *here, it's easier if I do it – you fumble about so.* He could keep up the pretence by asking casually, *where shall we go for supper? You choose, but not that place we went to last time.* He could pretend easily; he could even imagine keeping up this coolness as though they'd had any sort of ordinary conversation and would spend the evening simply being easy with each other, forgetting any carelessness because they knew what deserved forgiveness and what could be overlooked. Edmund knew he could be this actor and there would be no overwrought, overly dramatic scenes; but in his heart he wanted to take Paul's hand and press his palm to his lips and be wild with emotion, begging him to understand that he loved him. But it seemed he could play out neither of these acts. Cautiously he said, 'All right, shall we go out? Find somewhere to eat?'

Paul nodded. 'All right.' There was a note of relief in his voice as he said, 'Yes, all right.'

Chapter Eight

GEORGE WASHED HIS HANDS at the basin in the corner of his surgery. He dried them thoroughly, taking his time. The young woman he had just examined came out from behind the screen, her face flushed. She smoothed her skirt over her hips, picked up her handbag and sat down on the chair angled beside his desk, her feet neatly together, and her back very straight, the handbag held primly on her knee. George thought of the ways women took the news he was about to give her: they would be pleased, anxious, dismayed; some would cry, he had known others to laugh with excitement, to thank him as though he'd had anything to do with it. This girl would be quietly pleased, he thought, satisfied that she had at last lived up to expectations after some years of marriage. This girl's husband waited outside, a young man the same age as Paul. Paul had known him, had said that he was *a good chap – dull as can be, but there you are* ... George frowned to himself – when had Paul said such a thing with such pompousness? During one of his leaves, he remembered, when he and Paul had bumped into this man on the street, both officers in uniform, both of them awkward as school boys, as though they felt it was bad form to be away from the front.

George sat down at his desk. He smiled at the girl. He said, 'You're right, you are pregnant. Congratulations.'

She nodded, bowing her head to hide her smile.

There was nothing much more to say. A few minutes later and he saw her to the door, and the young man whom he remembered as a plainer, less glamorous version of Paul, sprang up from his seat in the corridor, a look of anxious expectation on his face.

She was his last patient of the evening, and he locked up the surgery and walked the short distance home. Since his return from London the horse-chestnut tree in his garden had begun to scatter its pink-eyed blossom to the ground and the daffodils Paul had planted before he first left for France had withered. 'When the flowers are over,' Paul had said, 'leave the leaves to die back naturally.' George had wanted to tell him that he would be back to take care of them himself, but he'd kept quiet, not wanting to tempt fate. That winter of 1916 he'd believed that the war would go on and on, already his oldest son had been at the front for eighteen months, and those months had seemed like his whole life; he'd hardly been able to credit that he'd had a life before 1914.

He walked up the path to Parkwood's front door, noticing the thickening buds on the lilac that had sown itself in the flowerbed like a weed. Paul would have rooted it out: for Paul there was a place for everything and everything should be in its place. George stopped to look more closely at the clusters of tightly closed, white blossoms that would soon block out a little of the light from his study. Each year he imagined cutting down the lilac, each year he put it off, just as he put off any work in the garden. He couldn't help thinking that the garden belonged to Paul, that it was his project, one he shouldn't interfere with.

In the kitchen, he lit the gas under the kettle and went into the pantry to hunt out something for supper. There was some ham drying out in its wrapping paper, half a loaf of bread, a little butter and jam and the hacked remains of a fruitcake. He picked up a tin of sardines, turning it over and over, deciding between the oily fish and the curling ham. He put the tin down gently, keeping still and quiet as he heard the back door open, her voice calling softly, 'George?'

He stepped out into the kitchen, suppressing the urge to smooth back his hair to make himself appear more presentable – he knew he would only look vain, preposterously so. Instead he smiled the ordinary smile he used on his neighbours. 'Iris. How are you?'

She glanced over her shoulder anxiously. 'I've brought Bobby to see you.'

71

George felt his smile break into a grin. He stepped past Iris and lifted his grandson into his arms, kissing his cheek and breathing in his familiar smell. He sat down and settled Bobby on his knee.

He frowned at him. 'Bobby, you look like a poorly boy to me.' Taking a handkerchief from his pocket George wiped Bobby's runny nose. He looked up at Iris. 'Has he caught a cold?'

'Yes. And not sleeping very well – he's exhausted, poor thing. Margot's left him with me so she can get some rest – she's exhausted too.'

George wiped another bubble of snot from Bobby's nose. 'You should be tucked up in bed, Bobby.' To her he said, 'You shouldn't have brought him out. Margot should have kept him at home. She should know better –'

'We wrapped him up warm, and it's such a lovely day –'

'He's not strong, Iris.'

She laughed slightly. 'Yes he is! Of course he is –'

'No. He's like his father – he nearly died of pneumonia when he was Bobby's age.'

'He's fine, George. He has a slight cold, that's all. And Margot was at the end of her tether …'

He looked up at her again. Trying to keep the contempt from his face and voice he said, 'At the end of her tether? She has one small child to look after, that's all, and you told me that new husband of hers has employed a housekeeper –'

'Margot's pregnant.'

The shock must have shown on his face because she said quickly, 'Sorry, I didn't mean to tell you so bluntly. But I won't have you criticising her. It's not fair, and you know it isn't.'

Bobby gazed at him anxiously. George bowed his head, kissing him. 'It's all right, Bobby, everything's all right. Will you let granddad take a look at you?' He set Bobby down, went to his bag and took out his stethoscope. 'Let's listen to your chest.'

'George – there's no need. He has a cold, that's all …' Awkwardly she said, 'Besides, Margot's doctor has examined him. There's nothing to worry about. Truly.'

George couldn't help himself. 'Walsh has seen him? You know that man's a drunk, don't you?'

'He's not –'

'You think I don't know what kind of a man he is? An excuse for a doctor. Now, if you don't mind, I'd like to examine my grandson myself.'

George unbuttoned Bobby's shirt; he remembered how close he was to this child when Paul and Margot lived with him, when he'd take Bobby upstairs to bed so that his son and daughter-in-law could be on their own for a little while. Undressing Bobby, dressing him again in his nightclothes, tucking him into his cot, he would hear Margot and Paul's voices from downstairs, her sudden laughter at something Paul said; a quiet broken by the sounds of a meal being prepared; Paul's quick tread on the stairs as he came to kiss his son goodnight. They had been happy then, it wasn't just his memory casting a rosy glow over the past. And he had been so close to Bobby; he remembered how sturdy he had been, the firm, baby chubbiness of him. As he put the stethoscope to his chest, having first warmed it between his hands, it was even more obvious that Bobby had long since passed that babyish stage; he was becoming a gangly little boy; George had missed his transformation.

Bobby's heart beat normally; his lungs were clear. George took the stethoscope from his ears and coiled it back into his bag. Too briskly, he said, 'There's some medicine I can give you if he develops a temperature.'

'It's all in hand, George, really.'

The kettle was whistling and he went to the stove and turned off the gas. 'I was about to make some tea. Would you like a cup of tea, do you have time?'

'Of course I have time.' After a moment she said, 'I didn't mean to blurt out the news about Margot like that. I'm sorry.'

'No reason to be sorry. Besides, it's not really a surprise – she's been married a little while now.'

'You looked shocked.'

'Did I?'

'Yes, and I'm sorry – I should have told you more carefully.'

73

He spooned tea from the caddy into the pot, forgetting to warm it first, wanting to pick up the pot and throw it against the wall. What would she make of him then? That he was no better than that evil-tempered fool she was married to, and so he bit down hard on his anger and made the tea, going to fetch milk from the cold shelf in the pantry. 'Do you take sugar?'

She sighed. 'No, George, you know I don't.'

He poured weak tea into a beaker for Bobby, adding a little sugar. Handing it to him he said, 'There's a good boy. And do you know, I'm sorry I have no biscuits, but I could make you some bread and jam, how's that?'

'Let's not spoil his supper, George.'

He glanced at her. 'There's some fruitcake. Would you like some? Shop bought, I'm afraid.'

'No, thank you.' Quickly she said, 'Please don't be upset ...' She bowed her head and George saw that she was crying.

'Iris ... don't. I'm sorry.'

'You have nothing to be sorry about.' Impatiently she said, 'Oh look at me, behaving like this. I never cry.'

It was true he had never seen her cry; he had imagined she was the kind of woman who never would, or only in private. This not crying was one of the things he admired about her.

'Something's happened?'

'No.' She wiped her eyes. 'No, not really. Margot's not very well – morning sickness, you know ...'

'That's all?'

She gazed at him as if trying to decide if she should go on. At last she said, 'She's very unhappy with that so-and-so she married.' Bitterly she said, 'I never liked him. Daniel thinks he's marvellous, of course, all but pushed Margot into his arms ... And poor Margot thought no one would ever look at her after what happened.' She looked away. 'Sorry, but it's true. After what Paul did she thought her life was over.'

George went to a box of toys he had brought down from the attic weeks ago; he took out tin soldiers piled in a wooden truck and gave them to Bobby. As Bobby began to take the soldiers out of the truck George said, 'I'm sorry Margot's unhappy. Sometimes, at the beginning of pregnancy –'

74

Iris was scornful. 'Don't tell me what it's like to be pregnant. It's not the baby making her cry.'

'She didn't have to marry him –'

'No, she didn't, not like she had to marry your son! My only wish is that she'd never ever set eyes on either of your boys.'

'Then we wouldn't have Bobby.'

'But she's my daughter, George. And I know that Paul only wanted to do what he thought was for the best when his brother was killed … We should have stopped him, we should have sent Margot away as soon as we found out she was pregnant.'

On the eve of Paul's wedding George had told him, 'I know the baby isn't yours. I know it's Robbie's and that you feel you have to do this for his sake. You don't.'

And Paul, only weeks out of the asylum, had shaken his head, not saying anything at all, because he hardly spoke in those days, but also because he wouldn't admit that the child wasn't his. However unconvincing the lie he and Margot told, he had always stuck to the lie: his dead brother's child was his. He would marry the girl his brother had courted and seduced and there would be no argument. George couldn't help but admire his loyalty. He couldn't help but be grateful that Robbie's child wouldn't be lost to him.

George sat down opposite Iris; he had the urge to take her hands but only said, 'I'm sure Margot will be fine. She's a sensible girl –'

'Sensible! You know she isn't sensible! Any sensible girl wouldn't have married Paul.' She looked down at her hands. 'I'm sorry. I didn't mean that … You know I liked Paul.' Managing to smile at him, she said, 'I haven't asked you how he is. How was your trip – you saw him? How did you get on?'

'Well.' He thought of Paul in his beautiful clothes, a grown, sophisticated man, so changed from the boy Iris had known.

Iris glanced towards Bobby. 'Might he visit you here?'

'No.' He tried to keep the bitterness from his voice as he said, 'Don't worry, there won't be any scenes.'

'Well, that's good. Good. It's for the best.'

'Quite.'

She sipped her tea. Bobby went to her and she lifted him

onto her knee, taking the toy soldier he offered her and stroking his hair as he rested his head against her breast. He thought that Bobby could be her child, she looked young enough to be his mother, and he wanted to say so, but felt that she would think he was trying to flatter her. She looked up and caught his eye. 'Is Paul happy?'

'I think so.' Remembering the lunch they'd shared, he added, 'He's changed. Well, of course he has. Prison would change anyone.'

'Was he with …?'

'No. He stayed in Tangiers.'

Iris nodded, turning the toy soldier over and over in her hand before standing it up on the table. The little model was of a Dragoon Guard, the paint chipped from the tiny face almost as if the expression had been deliberately destroyed. There were many of these soldiers, all chipped or somehow damaged; they had belonged to his father, and he had played with them himself but only in the most desultory way. Robbie and Paul had played with them all the time; he remembered the elaborate games his sons invented, their armies opposed across the sitting room rug. He had always known that Robbie would join the army; it was all he ever wanted to do. Paul, to his surprise, was almost as keen, even before the war began.

'George?'

He looked up at her from the soldier on the table; it was as though all she had wanted to do was gain his attention because she only smiled a little, picking up the toy again and handing it to Bobby. After a while she said, 'When I see soldiers like these I'm always reminded of that fairy tale – do you know it? I used to read it to Margot – *The Little Tin Soldier*.'

'Yes, I remember it: the soldier burnt in the fire until only his heart was left.'

'Yes. Sorry, that's terribly sad.' More briskly she said, 'Enough of sadness. Quite enough.'

'We can't help worrying about our children, Iris.'

She laughed bitterly. 'Daniel thinks that man she married will be *good for her*. That he will *help her to grow up.*' Meeting his gaze she said, 'She misses Paul.'

'No, Iris, I can't –'

'Can't what? Believe that she loved him? She did. He was *kind* to her, George. Not many men are so kind … I'm sorry. I've no right to burden you with my worries.'

'I don't mind.'

'Daniel –' She bit down on her lip.

'Daniel …?'

'Daniel is going away – to see a sick friend … He wants to see him before he dies … So, he's going … He's going to be away for a night or two at least. I'll be on my own.'

She gazed at him, her words hanging between them, weighted, he thought, with her expectation: she needed him to step in now, to save her from saying any more. Only he couldn't be sure, despite the look in her eyes that seemed so encouraging. He wondered what he might say without compromising her while still making her understand how much he wanted her.

He cleared his throat, which seemed to him to be an absurd thing to do, as though he was about to address a patient. How little practice he'd had with women; it was as though he had closed down a part of his heart. He looked at his hands clasped in front of him on the table, hands that resembled his father's in their aging – they always surprised him, these old man's hands. He thought of her in his bed, his hands cupping her breasts, moving down to her belly, then further, between her legs; he wished he was younger; he wished the last thirty years away so that he might start again with her.

He met her gaze only to look away at once.

'George?'

He cleared his throat again. 'When?'

'Tomorrow.' He felt her hand cover his. 'George … I know it's wrong.'

'No.' Forcing himself to look at her he said more quietly, 'Not wrong. Not at all.'

'No? No … And Daniel never goes away, and now he is –'

'And he'll be away for the night?'

'Two nights at least, I think.'

Carefully he said, 'Iris, you do know how I feel about you,

77

don't you?'

'Yes.' She stood up. 'Bobby, put the soldiers back now, it's time to go. Say goodbye to Granddad.'

As he saw her to the door he said quickly, 'Seven o'clock tomorrow?'

She nodded and there was such relief on her face that he wanted to take her into his arms and never let her out of his sight again.

Later, in bed, he stared into the darkness, unable to sleep for thinking of her. He thought to order his memories, the narrative he had in his head about her from the day they first met to this afternoon; he thought that doing so would help him to understand what had happened between them. More than anything, the ordering was sweetly pleasurable and something he did often, starting with the day, a little time after she had moved into the vicarage, when they met in the graveyard.

He had been tending Grace's grave, changing the chrysanthemums in the urn at the angel's feet, the foul-smelling water dripping from the slimy stems as he carried the dead flowers to the bin. She had been walking towards him along the broad path that led from the vicarage, quickly as though she was late for an appointment. He remembered feeling a little dismayed: he would have to touch his hat, say *Good morning!*, and that morning such a small courtesy had seemed beyond him. That morning in 1913 Robbie had left to join his regiment in India. That morning his thoughts were of the nasty diseases his son might pick up in such a country. He tried to convince himself of a sterilizing sun but couldn't help thoughts of open sewers, of flies and lepers. And the withered, once white chrysanthemums dripped their stinking water as his new neighbour approached him, her head slightly bowed as if saying *Good morning* was something she wanted to avoid, too; there was a closed-tight expression on her face, an anger, he thought. He must have looked at her more closely than he'd realised.

She had slowed her pace as she saw him and there was a hesitation in her step as she came closer still, as though she was deciding whether to stop at all. But there was no choice; a politeness drilled into him had him saying, 'Good morning. It's Mrs Whittaker, isn't it?' He had held out his hand, having tossed the flowers into the bin and wiped his palm on his handkerchief. 'Dr Harris – I'm your neighbour, in a sense – I live across the road, just there.' He gestured towards Parkwood standing grimly blank-faced behind him.

'Dr Harris. Of course. How do you do?'

And they exchanged pleasantries, and he saw that she was younger than he had imagined, having not been so close to her before. Younger than him by about five years, her skin smooth and flawless, her eyes bright and lively and quick to smile, although she did seem a little angry still, an anger it seemed she was used to containing.

During that year before the war he would see her occasionally. Sometimes they nodded as they passed on the High Street where he shopped in his rushed, haphazard, and forgetful way. He was sure that she had once spied him in the butcher's queue, heard him make his meagre, living-alone order because she had stopped him on the street outside and invited him to Sunday lunch. There were many Sunday lunches after that; he had even thought about attending church beforehand as a kind of token thanks: in return for a good meal he would swell her husband's small congregation; but it would only be by one, he told himself, and his one presence alone would not help very much, even if he had any faith. And Daniel, her husband, seemed not to mind his absence; it seemed to George that Daniel would have happily done away with church services all together, devoting even more of his time to good works around the parish.

George tried to lead his thoughts away from Daniel, but the man was there in front of him, always larger than life, always full of damnation, of hatred, since Paul married Margot. But there had been a time during the war when he could talk to Daniel. The vicar had no sons at the front and he could tell him of his desperate worry without feeling that the man had worries enough of his own. Daniel listened without seeming to judge him, without saying very much at all, just as he imagined a priest would say little during a confession. When he'd finished talking – and often he talked about nothing very much at all – Daniel had a way of asking some pertinent question, or making some comment that would, temporarily at least, ease his worry. Daniel had followed the war closely; he'd had greater faith in the generals and their strategies, faith that the war would end soon enough, that it wouldn't go on and on and on until there were no young men left in the world.

After these conversations George would feel better for a few hours. Later he'd feel as though Daniel could have no idea of the terror he was going through. Robbie and Paul could be killed at any time; either – both – of them could be dead at that moment and he would have no way of knowing, not for days before the telegram arrived. Boys were being killed every second of every day, and nothing, *nothing* anyone said would make any difference to that. He would pace his room, unable to be still for all his imagining, coming to believe that the Reverend Daniel Whittaker was an unimaginative fool.

George knew that Whittaker had caused the anger on Iris's face the day they met: some facetious remark he'd made, some petty complaint or stubbornness. Whittaker was the cause of Iris's unhappiness and had been for many years. Whittaker couldn't love her, not as he loved her.

Restlessly, he rolled onto his back, despairing of these ordinary justifications of an ordinary would-be adulterer. He despaired and yet he imagined Iris beside him, naked and warm and yielding, wanting him as much as he wanted her; he had always wanted her, since the moment they first spoke, when he saw how lovely she was, warm and attractive and lonely, he thought; as lonely as he was.

Tomorrow he would somehow make the house appear a little less forbidding and cold, less like the home of a sad, weary man who had lived too long with ghosts. He would change the sheets. He would try to change himself, to appear as strong and vital as he had been before the war, before Grace died; before, when he was young and unmarried and full of optimism for the future.

He turned on to his side so that he might sleep, and tried not to think about tomorrow any more.

Chapter Nine

PAUL HAD BOUGHT A postcard from a street vendor, a view of Westminster Abbey still in its paper bag on the table in front of him. He moved it aside as the waiter brought his meal, the man swaying a little but keeping his balance perfectly as the train rushed through the Kent countryside. He had an idea that men who served meals on trains weren't called waiters, but he couldn't remember their proper title. For all the many train journeys he had taken, he had never eaten in a restaurant carriage before, never travelled first class like this, in a plush seat, at a table set with white linen and silver and a lamp with a wine-red, tasselled shade. He had ordered lamb cutlets; the smell of lamb cooking reminded him of his life in Tangiers.

The waiter lifted the silver cloche from his plate, revealing the cutlets with a flourish they didn't seem to deserve. Dressed in dainty, frilled white cuffs, these were nothing like the fat, well-seared chops Patrick and he ate at home but rather small and thin and grey-looking, over-cooked, he imagined, and dry. There were peas and mashed potato, too, reminding him of his boarding-school food. The waiter said, 'Enjoy your meal, sir,' and Paul smiled at him because he liked the way he moved along the aisle between the fixed tables, the way his hips swayed to the motion of the train, showing off his muscled backside in his tight black trousers.

He ate, and the food was less disappointing than he'd imagined, and the view from the window was of a sunny, bright green land, astonishingly green compared with home, and the lamp's tassels swung as the train picked up speed and the cows in the fields went on grazing, used to trains, as used to their noise and smoke and smell as he was. He couldn't count the times he had travelled through this country, always heading south, it seemed – back to school, back to France, always away from Thorp; his journeys north were less memorable because he slept through them; he didn't have to steel himself for home.

He finished the cutlets, and stopped himself from sucking the little bones as he might at home with Patrick where different rules applied. The waiter cleared his plate, and he stared out of the window, putting off taking the postcard from its bag, his pen from his pocket, beginning in the clean white box on the reverse, *Dear Patrick* …

Dear Patrick, dear heart and mind and body. That body, hard and muscular, that broad, dark-nippled chest tapering to that slim waist, the deep belly-button, that cock, casually limp against his thigh as he got out of their bed, the careless, scratchable hang of his balls as he padded naked to their bathroom. And then there was that face, that smile, every way Patrick had of saying his name: a single syllable he could make longer or very short, no more than a grunt of impatience or desire. That desire Pat had, enough to squash him flat so there was no air left inside his lungs, no blood left to shunt around his veins; no spittle in his mouth; if he was eviscerated it was worth it to know him, every part of him, every stroke of skin. And he did know him; he knew him inside and out, every crevice and fold and flaw; the smell and taste of him and the rasp of his breathing as he slept; he knew the dreams Patrick had – their scripts at least. He knew to keep quiet, holding his breath; he knew not to wake him, he knew not to interrupt so that in the morning Patrick wouldn't remember how frightened he'd been and how he'd called out *no, no, no*.

Paul took the postcard from its bag. The waiter brought tea and Paul lit a cigarette, placing the spent match precisely in the clean glass ashtray with its engraving of the train company's initials bold around its rim. He inhaled deeply; he took out his pen from the inside pocket of his jacket and unscrewed its cap. He scrawled the date, underscored it, and wrote quickly, '*On a train going to see Matthew and I bought this card outside the station in a rush because I was late, and now I wish I'd chosen the picture of the very fine guardsman in his very high bearskin astride his very big horse ... Anyway, I shall write again properly tomorrow. Yours, F.'*

F for Francis, that man he was supposed to be growing into. He would tell Matthew that he was shedding Paul's skin, and that he was in flux, a transitional stage that really wasn't very pretty to look at. *I'm that creature that curls against the light when its stone is over-turned: Paul's weakness for fucking exposed whilst Francis scrambles to cover his balls. I can't help thinking that this is Paul's last fling – but of course, it isn't: I don't think I can be Francis for the rest of my life without holidays from his infuriating fidelity. I only tell myself that this is the last fling so that I don't feel so guilty. I am a hopeless sinner, and even acknowledging my guilt is just another way of not taking it seriously.*

Paul stubbed out his cigarette. He knew that he wouldn't say anything so grandstanding to Matthew; besides, it simply wasn't true: there was no Paul/Francis transition taking place, he was only ever himself, a man who wanted to paint to the exclusion of all else.

He thought about the exhibition, his paintings all sold, never to be seen again. He thought of the man who had bought Patrick's portrait, who had smiled at him so knowingly. What did he know? That this was a very beautiful man to hang on his wall, a man who might not have lived any life at all beyond that bed? He thought about how hard he had worked on that painting. Was it hard work? All that concentration, all that doubt, all that starting again, again, again; all that striving and anxiety, all that excitement and joy at the challenge of stretching out for something that was just beyond reach, but there, his for the taking if he only stretched hard enough. Could all that be called hard work? He was only pretending, playing about, trying to get past himself, to be good at something.

Yet he would sabotage himself; he was too full of excesses, of histrionic heat: Edmund had seen this and had known the extent of his failure. He had wanted to explain to the boy how hard he had tried to get at the cold truth. He had wanted to go through each painting step by step: here is the dead lieutenant in the shell hole – obviously dead, not dead-tired-dead-to-the-world sleeping. He is dead and already he looks as if he might have been dead for some time even though it's only a moment since I shot him dead; I know he will dissolve into the mud as if he had never been, as if he had never provoked me so badly I took out my pistol and shot him deliberately dead. Here is the truth of Lieutenant Jenkins then, dead in a shell hole with my bullet in his head. Except the painting isn't of Jenkins; it's of another man I didn't kill, but don't they all look the same dead like that? Edmund would have stepped away from him, horrified.

'Jenkins would have died anyway.' Patrick tells him this, holding him firmly by the shoulders, ducking his head to look into his face, saying, 'Look at me, Paul. Look at me and listen. He would have died anyway – what you did was a mercy.'

Patrick thinks he's a saint.

'He wouldn't stop crying!'

This is his confession. Jenkins wouldn't stop crying so he killed him. Not much of a confession, not the whole truth after all.

Anyway. He should drink his tea, perhaps look out for that waiter and ask if there might be a dessert, something very sweet, the sweeter the better. Anyway, he has begun to manage memories of Jenkins; he has even begun to believe Patrick, because Patrick is so certain: Jenkins would not have survived, so don't think of him. *For Christ's sake, Paul, you'll drive me insane with this!* This is what Patrick says, his anger undermining his certainty, so that he has to bite down on his whining need for reassurance; he has to be quiet and not speak of Jenkins at all. Paint pictures instead; you can do that, can't you? Not say anything to Pat, just show him the pictures you've painted, see if he thinks they are true.

Only Matthew knows the whole truth. Isn't that why he was on this train, leaving Edmund if only for a few hours? He was going to see Matthew, his good friend, his best friend – his only friend because he had never been good at friendship. Matthew knew the truth and it was a relief to be around him, being himself. He might even tell him about Edmund, although he is almost certain he won't; Matthew is a straight man; he doesn't understand everything.

Edmund. There was something about him that moved him viscerally. To look at Edmund was the kindest and most uncomplicated pleasure; he found himself smiling when he thought about him, as though for the first time in his life he was completely carefree.

The train slowed and another sped past in the opposite direction, its wagons full of coal. For a moment the train's window was darkened and became a mirror; he saw how anxious he looked, the very opposite of carefree. His fingers went to his false eye, something he knew they did frequently, but even more frequently when he was around new people. And what was Edmund if not a new person?

He and Edmund had hardly been out of his hotel bed these past few days. Yesterday, during the drowsy afternoon, Edmund had confessed that he had never been with another man before, 'Not truly, not like this.' His head had been resting on Paul's chest and Paul had stroked his hair, thinking that he had not been with another man like this before either, not truly. He had never taken so much time, so much care with anyone in his life because there had never seemed to be enough time. And perhaps he had never cared enough, not even for Patrick. Patrick had always loved him so completely it seemed he wanted nothing from him, only his willingness to be loved and defended from the world. But it seemed to him that there could be equality between him and Edmund.

He tried not to think about this – it was too painful to consider – besides, he shouldn't compare his relationship with Patrick to what he might have with this boy. *This boy*! Weren't he and Edmund almost of an age? He knew that he felt very young when he was around him, like someone he might have been but for everything that had happened since he left school. But for Jenkins, he thought, and, as he did many times each day, he wished himself back in that trench, beside Jenkins who was still alive and who would stop crying, if only he was patient.

Paul lit another cigarette. The train stopped at a station and he watched a group of soldiers alight from a third-class carriage. He watched dispassionately, but it seemed he was always on the lookout, always wanting more, no matter what.

This morning, just before he'd left, Edmund had asked suspiciously, 'Why do you have to go?'

'Matthew's an old friend. I promised I'd visit.'

'You will come back, won't you?'

'Why wouldn't I?'

'I've a feeling you don't really exist.'

Going to the bed, Paul had kissed him. 'Are you usually so whimsical?'

'Only since I met you.'

He'd gazed at him, thinking how beautiful he was; he had wanted to undress and climb back into bed again; he was addicted to his body. He had trailed his fingers over his face, his dry skin snagging on the roughness of Edmund's unshaven cheek; he had kissed his mouth, tasting his own body, and Edmund had grasped his head, kissing him more passionately. Reluctantly Paul had pulled away.

'I'll be back this evening.'

'I love you.'

'Don't say that.'

'I can't help saying it. It's true.'

On the train Paul drew on his cigarette, his hand going to his eye. Edmund loved him, or believed he did. He was afraid of this love, it seemed too ardent, too fierce to be true, and he was flattered by it; only the foolishly vain ever allowed themselves to be swayed by flattery.

Last night Edmund had stopped his hand as his fingers had gone to the glass eye, saying, 'Take it out.' They had been lying face to face on the bed, about to get up and dress, to go and find a place to eat because they were both ravenous after so much sex. Edmund had laughed, repeating, 'Take it out! Take out your eye – I want to see what it looks like – what *you* look like.'

Paul had wondered why the suggestion didn't seem as outrageous as he felt it should have, why he only wanted to laugh, too, to pluck out his eye and offer it to Edmund, saying *There, look – it's nothing very much*, except he couldn't quite bring himself to; he knew how ugly he appeared without it;

Edmund might not mind but then again he might be appalled. He didn't want to wipe that smile from his face, from his own face, because he knew he was mirroring him.

Softly Edmund had said, 'All right, don't let me see. It doesn't matter, it won't make any difference to the way I feel about you whether I see it now or in fifty years.'

'Edmund –'

He'd pressed his finger to his lips. 'Be quiet,' he grinned, 'just listen. In 1975 you'll scoop it out and hand it over, saying, *All right – here! Look if you really must!*'

'And you'll run away in horror.'

'And you'll be better off without me.'

'Imagine living so long.'

'I've made you wistful now.' Edmund had kissed him, brushing his thumb along the scar beneath his eye, only to become brisk. 'Come on, I'm hungry. You need to buy me dinner.'

Edmund *was* very young – he should be honest with himself about this, at least – and looked younger than he claimed to be. Edmund laughed a good deal and talked a lot – more than men of his own age, those who still lived and breathed and hardly knew how to behave around young men like Edmund, younger by those few, crucial years.

Edmund had asked, 'This friend, Matthew –'

'A friend, that's all.'

The train sped on; he would be with Matthew soon enough. Matthew's sister had written to him with the address of the asylum Matthew had been committed to. 'He's well cared for in this new place,' Mary wrote. 'It's a fine old building and the nurses are very kind.'

Paul stared out of the train window, imagining this fine old building, the squeak of the kind nurses' shoes on the lino floors; the wards with their rows of low, metal beds; the freezing bathrooms without locks on the doors; never any privacy, never any peace, no escape from the smell of other men's bodies or the noises they made. Even the dumbstruck ones still open-mouthed in horror were never truly quiet, were the worst, in fact, with their moans and groans, their too-loud breathing.

They should have their hanging jaws tied shut with bandages like a man with toothache, Matthew said. He and Matthew had been sitting together on the lawn of another asylum, both of them in the blue uniform of wounded officers, both of them recovering from his own particular horror. He remembered he had glanced at Matthew, smiled at this cartoon image of dentists' waiting rooms, and that it was the first time he had smiled in months. Matthew had caught his eye, grinning back at him so that he'd believed he was more recovered than he was.

Paul left a tip for the waiter and went back to his carriage, his first-class carriage because he had money to spend and he was, he supposed, on a kind of holiday. His seat was comfortable, there was enough leg room without worrying about nudging the toes of a fellow passenger; he could sleep like the old man in the corner of the carriage, although he knew he wouldn't, despite not having slept much since he'd arrived in England; he was too full of excitement, too full of Edmund, of himself.

The old man stirred, and Paul watched him, hoping he would sleep on; he did, twitching a little, his hand going to his nose as though batting away a fly. But then the carriage door opened and a young couple came in.

He had forgotten about them, boarding the train as they had just as he left for the restaurant car. The girl was wearing a lilac dress, in the new, low-waist, flat-chest, rather sexless style, the skirt drooping around her shins, showing off too-pale stockings and shoes dyed to match her dress. A fox stole hung incongruously around her shoulders, its glass eyes glinting as she sat down. She was too young and slight for such a thing; he imagined her mother throwing it around her protesting daughter as she left, worried that she might catch a chill without it. The fox's paw fell against her boyish, fashionable breast possessively, its eyes staring him out as the girl's companion – husband, he caught a glimpse of her ring as she took off her lilac gloves – sat down beside her.

This young man smiled at him awkwardly. 'Would you mind awfully if I opened the window?'

'Not at all.'

'That's terribly decent of you.' He sprang up – a boy in a dark, formal suit, a white carnation stark in his buttonhole. *Newlyweds*, of course. The lilac ensemble was a going-away outfit. Perhaps the fox was the bride's talisman. A smell of cow dung streamed through the open window on a warm rush. Sitting beside the window, the girl closed her eyes, a look of resigned disgust on her face. He noticed her complexion was white tinged with green; there was a spot of something on her dress.

'I'm afraid my wife is feeling rather unwell.'

'Michael!' The girl's cheeks coloured a little, although she didn't open her eyes.

Opposite her, the boy looked out of the window miserably. Paul took out the bag of barley sugar he had bought for the journey and held it out to him.

He took one, smiling his thanks, and said, 'Enid, would you like a sweet?'

Enid shook her head, a tiny, almost imperceptible movement before covering her mouth with her hand. Her husband watched her anxiously, the barley sugar moving about his mouth as though he wished it would hurry up and dissolve. His anxiety was disturbing; Paul thought how he might as well be rattling along to France, fellow officers jammed up beside him with those same fretful expressions animating their faces; he wanted to tell the boy to buck up, just as he used to tell his subalterns. '*For Christ's sake, pull your bloody socks up!*' A schoolmaster expression used on boys just out of school, the only concession to their pretend adulthood that furious *Christ*.

The girl slept, snoring a little from time to time, so that the boy glanced across at him apologetically. 'It's been rather a hectic day, I'm afraid.'

Paul nodded, unable quite to let go of the sudden, idiotic anger he felt.

The boy got up and closed the window, the fox's fur fluttering into partings in the draught he made. When he sat down again he stared out at the passing countryside, still miserable. He looked about the same age as Edmund and already married and no doubt with a child on the way given the look of his wife, just as he'd been married and a father at his age. He should have felt kinder towards him but didn't. Instead, he felt a mixture of jealousy and contempt and a kind of rage, he supposed, but the rage was always there, lying low like gas in a shell hole.

He had married Margot on Christmas Eve 1919, her pregnancy obvious although she tried valiantly to hide it with her bouquet of red roses and trailing ivy. Red roses against a white dress, reminding him of blood and bandages – but what didn't remind him of such ugliness in those days? He remembered that Margot's father had taken him to one side after the ceremony saying, *If you don't take care of her you'll have me to answer to*. You and whose army, eh? Paul smiled to himself – although at the time Daniel Whittaker had made him feel like something stinking on the sole of his shoe. At the time, he had felt so insubstantial that an idiot like Whittaker could scare him to death.

He glanced at his watch. In five minutes the train would arrive and he would make his connection to the village that was a short walk from the asylum. He imagined Matthew sitting with a blanket over his knees in the conservatory he had told him about in his letters: the palm trees and the black and white tiled floor, the shifting filtered shadows: perhaps this asylum was a fine building. Matthew would look up at him and smile and get to his feet, the blanket slipping to the floor – he didn't really need a blanket, he was stronger, almost well. Paul hoped so; thinking about this scene he became anxious; it could so easily be different; Matthew locked in a cell, a straitjacket contorting his arms; he wouldn't be allowed to see him, not even to peep through the cell's eye hole, to murmur some reassurance Matthew wouldn't understand even if he could hear him.

He had been visiting Matthew in asylums for years now, on and off, as circumstances allowed. *Circumstances*: when he wasn't in prison, in exile, he would visit Matthew as often as he could, and when he couldn't visit he would write to him and Matthew would write back, his letters giving away the greater or lesser extent of his madness. There were even times when he was completely sane, when for a few unsettling settled months he lived quietly with his sister until the delusions came back and he'd insist most adamantly that he was well.

The train began to slow and he got up, gathering his coat. The bag of sweets was on the seat beside him and he handed it to the young man. 'They're supposed to help with sickness.'

'You're very kind.'

'Good luck.'

The boy attempted to smile. 'Do you think I'll need luck?'

On the station platform Paul put on his coat; the sun had gone in. Five minutes to wait for the next train. He looked down the track, hoping the train wouldn't be late; Matthew liked him to be punctual and would be anxious if he wasn't.

Chapter Ten

PAUL CAME EXACTLY ON time, exactly as I expected him – although perhaps a little better dressed. Much better dressed, actually. His suits are obviously tailor-made for him and he has a very good eye for colour and detail, of course. Even his shoes are hand made, on-parade shiny, everything just so, down to his pressed handkerchief and engraved cigarette case. He smelt subtly of sandalwood and when he embraced me I wanted to hold on to him, breathe in that elusive scent, even hoping that it might rub off on me, a reminder of his visit.

Not an embrace, more like a bear hug, and then he held me at arms' length and looked me up and down, grinning. Although he tried to hide it I could see that my ordinary appearance was a relief. I felt very shabby beside him; I always have, even when we both wore the same hospital uniform. He is still very thin, the excellent cut of his clothes only goes some way to disguise this. I told him he smokes too much, one after the other in a chain like the longest cigarette in the world.

I met Paul in 1919. I remember the exact date, July 1st, my birthday. My parents had visited me, and they had brought a cake and small gifts from my sisters – socks, I recall, some writing paper and a pen, and chocolates. Dad gave me cigarettes, slipping them to me discreetly when Mum's back was turned. He winked at me and touched his nose so that we were conspirators, the very best of friends just as we used to be. We sat outside on the lawn, the three of us, and some of the nurses came by, and some of the patients too, and we shared the cake, although a few of my fellows were shy of my father, who couldn't help but talk too loudly, laugh too boisterously, always ready to slap a man on the back, to call him a *grand lad, a credit to his country.* My mother would say, 'Oh hush, Pip,' and smile at some blushing, cringing lunatic. I remember she held out my box of chocolates to those who appeared most shy. 'Here, have a sweetie, dear. Matthew won't mind sharing.'

I remember she said, 'Oh, look at that poor boy, all on his own. Matthew, do go and ask him if he would like some cake.'

I followed her gaze and saw the young lieutenant who had arrived that morning. I had watched from the day room as he'd stepped from the ambulance on the arm of a male nurse, as the nurse led him towards the hospital's entrance, noticing how the lieutenant didn't take his eyes from the ground, walking so slowly that the nurse had a resigned look, as though he knew that he couldn't coax this man into moving any quicker. They stopped, and the nurse ducked his head to look into the officer's face; he spoke to him and must have convinced him of something because they moved on. The lieutenant's fingers went to the eye patch he wore. As they came closer I heard the nurse say, 'Mind the step, sir, that's it, that's the ticket.'

That afternoon, on my mother's prompting – I remember that she did have to ask me more than once – I walked across the lawn to where that same lieutenant was sitting alone, bowed over his cigarette so that it crossed my mind that he had been injured in some way that meant he couldn't lift his head, a little hunchback with his eyes always on the tricky ground. As I came closer to him he seemed to flinch, and so I stood at a little distance because I can't bear flinching, and said, 'It's my birthday today, would you like a slice of my cake?'

For a moment I thought he hadn't heard, and then he looked up at me and I saw that he had been crying. All the same he said, 'Happy birthday.'

Cautiously I took a step closer. 'My name's Matthew Purcell. It's quite a good cake, if you'd care to join us.' I glanced back to see that my parents were watching me as though I'd been sent on a mission I might fail, and at once I wished that they hadn't come, that the fewer times they saw fit to test me the better.

Paul must have seen the change in my expression because he looked back too, his gaze resting on my mother for a moment before he said, 'Is it all right here?'

'All right, you know. All right.'

He nodded and wiped his good eye. I remember that I felt I'd been wrong in not saying more to reassure him, and tried to think of something else that might, but he'd hunched into himself again and I would have left him alone but all at once my father was beside me, his voice full of goodwill as he said, 'There's no moping going on, is there?' He grinned at Paul. 'Come on, lad. We're having a party for Matt. Don't cast gloom over his birthday, eh?'

So Paul joined us for tea and cake and his hands shook terribly so that his cup rattled in its saucer, his fingers constantly searching out the eye patch, not speaking at all except out of the most necessary politeness. In short, he behaved exactly like any other new arrival at St Stephen's Asylum for the Shattered.

The next evening at supper, one of the other men pointed him out to me. 'How did you get on with our new arrival yesterday?'

I glanced at Paul, who sat alone, smoking a cigarette, his half-finished meal pushed away from him. As though he sensed our curiosity he lifted his head to look at us, only to look away again. The other patient – I think that it was Grayson – laughed shortly. 'He's got a *reputation*, that one. Lucky not to be court-martialled, rumour goes.' *Sotto voce* he added, '*Nancy*. Got a little too soft-hearted over one of his subalterns.'

It's tempting to say that I didn't listen to rumours and that I gave Grayson a telling-off for talking such rubbish. But of course I was as curious as the next man; in a place like St Stephen's it's hard not to speculate about fellow inmates once you yourself are on the mend. I found myself looking out for Paul and noticed that he kept his distance from the other men so that I began to believe he'd heard the rumours and was ashamed. He certainly began to appear to me to be ashamed, but that was because I had created my own story around him: the sweet-natured young officer who had taken an even younger man under his wing; I imagined how one thing might have led to another until it all rather got out of hand, appalling them

94

both. This story became quite thrilling; it would keep me awake at night; during the day I found I could hardly keep my eyes off Paul, looking for something more to fuel my imagination.

One morning, as I was reading a letter from home in the day room, Paul came and sat down next to me. He asked, 'Is that from your mother?'

'Yes.'

'I would like to write to her, if I may, to thank her for being so kind to me the day I arrived.'

'Of course. I'm writing to her today, if you would like to put in a note with my letter.'

'I will. Thank you.'

He got up to go but by then, a week or so after his arrival, my curiosity about him had grown beyond measure; I needed not just to look, but to hear him speak, and so I said in a horribly cheerful voice, 'Perhaps when your mother visits she might bring cake for you to share with me.'

'She's dead.'

I think I must have blushed to the roots of my hair; to my horror my eyes filled with tears.

Paul sat down again and touched my hand. Handing me a handkerchief he said, 'Don't let them see I've made you cry. I'll be lynched.'

I wiped my eyes quickly. On the other side of the room, some of the others were playing dominoes and I was aware that there was a good deal of glancing going on. Quietly Paul said, 'Should we get some air?'

I remember that we walked some distance that day, and that the sun was shining and the countryside was very still and quiet as though an arrangement had been made that we might have it to ourselves as recompense. Because the sun was so warm we took off our tunics and rolled up our shirtsleeves and lay down in the long grass of a meadow, the tunics folded beneath our heads. A single cloud moved across our allocation of sky and Paul said, 'The rumour isn't true.'

I followed the cloud's progress, unable to think of the right response after the stories I'd made up about him. I was terribly disappointed, so I kept quiet, watching the cloud become more ragged as the sun reached its zenith. I began to feel large and dirty beside him, my dirty thoughts writhing about inside my head, reluctant to be stilled even by the evidence: he was just a boy, younger than me, sicker than me and even more frightened. I kept my eyes on the cloud, unable to look at him; I thought I wouldn't be able to look at him ever again.

He was quiet beside me, didn't seem to mind me at all, and gradually my thoughts became less hectic and I thought again of the relationship I had invented for him, because actually it was sweet and tender; in my invented world Paul was very well loved. I managed to look at him. 'Might the rumour have been true?'

He frowned, turning to search my face. 'I was told you were once a priest.'

I turned away. He had a look on his face I have very often seen: very needy and hopeful, bound to be disappointed. I really didn't want to disappoint him but there was nothing I could do.

After a while he said, 'It's very quiet, isn't it? I have the feeling we're lost.'

'No, I know my way back.'

'Our way back – or will you leave me here?'

'No, of course not.'

'Were you a priest?'

I thought about lying, telling him no, that he wasn't the only victim of rumour. I sat up, plucking at the long grass, shredding the blades with my thumb nail, aware that he was watching me so that I expected to feel his hand on my back; my skin crawled with anticipation until I couldn't bear it any more and I turned to him.

'If you feel you need to tell me something in confidence –'

'I murdered a man.'

He had come to kneel beside me, very close, and the words were said on a rush of breath with a quick clarity that was not like his voice at all, what little I had heard of it, but more like that of a young boy, one whose voice had only just broken, one who could still sound like a child. I seem to remember that we both stayed quite still, fixed on each other; I seem to remember that I could see myself reflected in the shiny, theatrical black of his eye patch, and that I was pale and ugly and my hair was all sticking up, my lips still parted, still intent on the speech he'd interrupted.

At last he said, 'Please say it's all right.'

'It's all right.'

He bowed his head so low that his forehead touched the ground. 'Please help me. Dear Christ, please help me.'

My hand hovered over his back; I felt that to touch him would release some energy that I wouldn't have the strength to deal with. He was rocking back and forth, a soft moaning sound coming from him. I bent my head low next to his. If someone had seen us I suppose we might have looked as though we were searching for something in the grass, amongst all the bright buttercups, and that whatever we were looking for could only be found in a tiny section of ground because neither of us moved for some time. Despite the warmth of the day my knees became cold; there was something sharp beneath my palm that would leave its imprint, but I stayed still, afraid to touch him, only whispering over and over that it was all right, everything would be all right. I wanted to tell him about the world I had invented for him where everything *was* all right. But he was making that dreadful noise and I couldn't think straight enough to be sufficiently coherent.

I had the feeling that we might kneel in that meadow for the rest of time, that the grass would grow still taller around us then whither and still we would be there, as the cold came, the snow and wind and rain and the sun again, weathering us away. I felt how easy it would be to give in to this process, to return to a fundamental element, unthinking, unfeeling, only time having its slow, slow effect on us. The sun was warm on my back, but moving away from me as surely as the earth was solid beneath my knees and hands. I thought how he had said he had murdered a man and knew that this murder would be excusable because there had been so many deaths, so many that one more would hardly count at all, and I knew that this was a wicked thought, profoundly true and wicked and that I should care about wickedness, although I didn't. He'd confessed that he had murdered a man and I thought *so what?* and said over and over, 'It's all right.' And, eventually, because of the sharp stone against my hand, because of the cold creeping into my knees, I said, 'Paul ... Perhaps that's enough.'

He sat back on his heels. I still had his handkerchief, and I handed it to him. 'Shall we go back?'

He nodded, clambering to his feet and brushing dry grass from his legs. Looking along the trail of flattened grass we had made across the meadow he said, 'I'll write to your mother, to thank her.'

He wrote to my mother often over the following years until her death. He sent her drawings. After my father's death in 1921 he was the only one left in the world who called her by her Christian name. He even wrote to her from prison; I remember that she asked me why anyone should be sent to prison for such a foolish, silly thing. Foolish and silly to follow a man into a public toilet, to bugger him in a cubicle, not having noticed the burly man hanging around outside, waiting to kick down the cubicle door. Nothing could be sillier, or more foolish, unless one felt a need for punishment.

He wrote to me, too, of course, never abandoning me as some have. And this afternoon he came to visit me. Now his visit is over and I'm sniffing the air like a foxhound for a lingering scent of him. Odd, the effect he has on me, but also on the other patients and staff. His mannered courtesy and immaculate turnout offend some of them, of course; some look at him with open hatred. But it seemed that others, like me, only wished that he would stay and not behave with such brittle edginess as he did at first, but like the man that I know him to be, as he came to behave just before he left when he was used to us all at last.

During his visit we walked to the village, but I couldn't face the busy teashop so we sat on a bench in the churchyard beneath a white lilac that had just come into flower. The church is very old, and some of the gravestones slant and lean as though one good push would topple them. The names of their dead are illegible, but not all the graves are decrepit. Some are so new, the lettering on their memorials so bold and clear that they stand out with a kind of vulgar vainglory. The war memorial close to the church has the same unweathered newness, especially the names engraved on its plinth: gold capital letters and precise punctuation, the names ordered alphabetically in their ranks. Atop the plinth there is a statue of a soldier crouching on one knee, head bowed as if in supplication.

Paul and I walked around the memorial; we read the names; he told me that the memorial in Thorp is outside the parish church, a great white obelisk with steps leading up to it, all surrounded by a low, wrought-iron railing with a little gate, kept locked except on Sundays, when wreaths can be laid. He said, 'I counted the names I knew; there are three. I suppose if I'd gone to school in Thorp I would have known ten or more. In Thorp Grammar there is a plaque with the names of old boys and teachers.' He laughed, looking up at the stone soldier. 'For the few months I taught there I seem to remember I used to run past it, looking the other way. *You there, boy! No running in the corridors!*' He smiled at me. 'I was hopeless.'

He had taught in a boys' school just after the war – not for long; he *was* hopeless, his nerves still all shot to bits. I had forgotten he was a teacher. I felt I should have remembered this.

In the graveyard, beneath the heady lilac, he took out a photograph and handed it to me without comment. There was Patrick smiling in front of a wall covered by some profusely flowering climbing plant. He wore an open-necked shirt and pale, loose trousers, bare feet in sandals, hands thrust into his pockets. I turned the photograph over; Paul had written a date, nothing more. Handing it back to him, I said, 'He should have come with you.'

'He won't come back to England.' He put on Patrick's deeper voice: '*Not after what they did to you, Paul.*'

Paul is a good mimic; even his face changed a little to resemble Patrick's, that frowning concern that would darken Pat's eyes. Paul returned the photo to its envelope, hesitating before he took out another. This time he said, 'Bobby.'

I gazed at Paul's son; he is Paul in miniature.

99

'Dad wants me to visit him. I said I wouldn't, but I'm not sure … The very idea makes my knees give.' He took the photo from me and frowned at it. 'He doesn't look very happy, does he? And the way they've cut his hair so short … Anyway …' He put the photo in with that of Patrick and shoved the envelope back in his inside pocket. 'Anyway, I'm not thinking of going to Thorp.' He smiled at me, 'If I did I'd have to buy a wig, I think, and a false beard – dark glasses, what do you think?'

I thought of him in dark glasses as though he was blind, as though they'd scooped out both his eyes in the confusion of the first aid station. I thought that he would never have seen me, only heard me, and I thought how that might be better, that he might like me more than he does. We looked out over the graves and the birds sang and halting music came from inside the church, an organist practising a Protestant hymn. A young woman walked by pushing a pram, a bunch of flowers placed across her sleeping baby.

She stopped at one of the new graves and, taking a milk bottle from the pram, went to fill it with water at the standpipe. She returned and poured the water into the grave's urn before thrusting the flowers into its covering mesh. Daffodils. She had wrapped them in a page of the *News of the World*, which flapped in the breeze, taking off only to flatten against the pram wheel. Her baby began to cry, a newborn's mewling, and she straightened from the flowers and began to push the pram away without a backward glance. The newspaper tumbled after her and I stooped to pick it up, noticing her slim ankles as I did so. Her hips swung as she walked; she had a brassy style about her that had me watching her swinging hips and backside until she turned the corner of the church out of sight.

I balled the paper and tossed it away, realising I must have looked like some deranged tramp to pick up rubbish like that, smudging my hands with ink. But Paul pretended not to notice. He handed me a cigarette and we smoked in a silence that would have been companionable if the girl hadn't provoked such frustration in me.

At last I said, 'I'll be discharged soon, I think.'

Paul glanced at me. 'Do you feel ready?'

'I'm not pretending to be well, if that's what you think.'

'No, I don't think that. Where will you go?'

'To Mary's.' I thought of my sister and her house full of children; she didn't want me but couldn't refuse. The idea of going to live with her made me want to lash out at someone. I thought of Paul, his home with Patrick, his *life* with Patrick, and I was struck with how unfair it all was. I stood up. 'Let's go back. No good sitting here, cold and miserable. Why aren't you being better company? You shouldn't have come if you were going to be like this.'

'Like what, Matthew?'

'Don't sound reasonable. I can't stand it.'

We began to walk back. Half way along the lane he stopped. 'Matthew, you could come home with me – to Tangiers.'

I was a few steps ahead of him, and I turned. 'What would Patrick say?'

'Welcome? You know Patrick. Come for a holiday at least. The sun works wonders.'

'So I need to be worked on?'

He stepped towards me and grasped my shoulders. 'You need what I have – peace and room to think –'

I pulled away from him. 'You have Patrick. *That's* what you have. Would you share him with me too, as well as your peace and *thinking room*? That's if I wanted such a savage, ungodly relationship.'

I shocked him. We stood facing each other in the middle of a country lane, and there was no one in sight, no human sound except that of our breathing. He looked past me, and his voice was quiet even as he said, 'We'd better get moving. I don't want to miss my train.'

'Then walk the other way, back to the village.'

'I've enough time to walk back with you.'

'I don't want you to.'

'I've left my coat at the hospital. My ticket is in the pocket.'

'So you would walk away now if you could?'

He met my gaze. 'I don't know.'

'I've hurt your feelings by speaking the truth.'

He stepped around me, walking so quickly I had to run to catch up with him.

Falling into step beside him I said, 'It *is* ungodly what you and he do. You know it. In fact, I don't know how you can bear to do such dirty, degrading things. Are you listening? Can you hear me?' I ran ahead of him, walking backwards in front of him, my voice rising. 'You have a child! A fine little boy! How could you leave him? Why aren't you home with him now? You care nothing for anyone – nothing! You care only for yourself – your disgusting perversion. Those boys you taught at the grammar school – were you fiddling with them? That's what men like you do, isn't it? Rob boys of their innocence?'

He stopped. 'Matthew, you're ill, that's why I won't listen to this.'

'Your perversion is condemned in the bible! Corinthians chapter six, verse nine!'

He began walking again. He can walk very quickly, and it took a lot to keep up. I taunted him all the way to the hospital, along its drive, up the steps, through the hallway. I couldn't stop. My fist kept going to my mouth, and I bit down hard on my knuckles, but I couldn't stop. He was very pale when we reached the room where he had left his coat, a beautiful, dark wool coat. I tugged it from him, pressing it to my face, inhaling his scent. I could sense his despair, heard it in his voice as he said, 'I have to go now, Matthew. Give me my coat, see me out, let's say goodbye properly.'

'Properly?'

'Yes.'

'You're angry now and you won't come back.'

'I will, if you want me to.'

'You won't have time what with all that fucking you do. Don't think I don't know that you've sodomised every man in England.'

He reached out, taking his coat from me, putting it on, fastening it; his hands were shaking, there was something vulnerable about them that moved me.

'I'll give you my gloves if you want,' I said.

'Thank you, but I think you should keep them.'

'Wait, I'll fetch them from my room.'

'No, Matt.' He stepped towards me and I flinched. 'Shall we say goodbye here?'

I nodded, my fist pressed against my teeth so that I broke the skin and tasted blood. 'Goodbye.'

He touched my arm; I wanted him to hug me as he had when he arrived, but perhaps he was afraid to; I only felt the memory of that hug in my bones, making my longing for his embrace even stronger.

He left and I went to the window to watch him go. I thought he might look back and wave at me, but he didn't. I watched him until a nurse came and led me away; my knuckles were dripping blood, just as though we'd had a fight.

Chapter Eleven

EDMUND SAID, 'I DON'T have to explain myself to you.'

Ann thought that she might cry, which only made her angrier. 'You do have to explain. You do.'

'No. Besides, I can't.' He looked towards the bookshop's door; he had turned the sign to 'Closed' as soon as she'd walked in, drawing the bolt across and leading her through into the shadowy interior. She could hardly see him in the dim light and she wanted to take his hand and drag him to the window, to make him face her so that she would see his shiftiness, so that he would know she saw it and be ashamed. But he wouldn't allow her to lead him anywhere; she couldn't imagine that they would so much as touch each other ever again. She imagined him in bed with that man; it was all she could imagine.

'Why?'

'Ann, I'm sorry. I wish Day hadn't told you, but since he has, well … It's done, and I'm sorry.' Heatedly he said, 'And anyway, it was just a bit of fun, you said so yourself.' Pushing his hand through his hair he said, 'Look, I need to open the shop – if Barnes gets back and finds it locked up he'll give me a row.'

He went to the door, unbolted it and turned the sign around. Now that he was in the light she saw that he didn't look at all shifty, only exhausted and anxious. The bruise around his eye showed yellow against the grey pallor of his skin – Joseph had told her all about how he had punched him, how he had deserved worse, the filthy bastard. 'Standing there bollock naked! Both of them! Jesus! Queer English bastards!'

She had wanted to tell him to be quiet – that she wanted for once to be the kind of woman men protected from knowing about such things. She wished he hadn't told her, hadn't followed Edmund to that hotel, hadn't blacked his eye because now Edmund didn't care about her, only about his own pride.

He held the door open for her. 'I'm sorry, Ann.'

She walked to the Python Gallery, past the second-hand bookshops, the junk shops with their miscellaneous displays: an elephant's foot, a watercolour of Highland cows; past the closed pubs where the publicans would just be waking, going downstairs to the dark bar where the night-time smells of alcohol and cigarettes still hung thickly, a miasma, a fruity old ghost of a drunk, stale and obdurate. She walked past the restaurant where they had eaten after Law's exhibition; the Italian waiters had flung open the door and windows and were sweeping and swilling; a fast, foaming stream of bleach-stinking water ran into the gutter – she had to skip around it – and one of the waiters called after her, laughing his apology. '*Bella*!' he called, and of course she turned, couldn't help herself, saw him pinching his fingers to his mouth, splaying them out wide to set the kiss free. *Bella*. She shouldn't have looked back.

Edmund had said, 'I think you are possibly the most exquisite creature I have ever seen.' The first words he had ever said to her, smiling, drunk, swaying. *Possibly. Exquisite*. She should have known that these words were all wrong. And *creature*. An organism, an animal: something that should be pinned to a board, pared down to its bones, mounted under glass; a thing to be studied, sketched, intensely looked at, intimately explored.

She walked on more quickly, her anger an accelerant. A dray passed so that she had to walk closer to the buildings; there was the sudden country smell of dung, of sweating, powerful beasts, the heavy turn of cart-wheels sending the shuddering dread of crushed bones through her. A policeman smiled and doffed his helmet, an out-of-place man who made her feel that he might think of something to detain her with and so she should walk even faster. And so she did, glancing over her shoulder at the uniformed back, the sausage-meat-like hands clutched behind him. She became breathless, her chest tightening.

She stopped by a Wren church. She was wearing the wrong shoes to walk at such a lick. She thought that if she listened hard enough she would hear her father call out, 'Catch up, Mary-Ann, don't dawdle now!' and he would be grinning, hands on his hips; if she ran to him he would swing her up on to his shoulders. 'There now,' he would say, 'a grand view from up there, don't you think?'

But there was just the noise of the traffic, a bus advertising *Five Boy Chocolate.* Name five boys you've slept with – quick now: Stephen (first, back home, a fumble, a blur), Joseph, Edmund, Lawrence (last). Not five. Only four. *Only!* Only almost five, if you could count Matthew.

You couldn't count Matthew. What had happened with Matthew was nothing, nothing at all, less than that fumble with that first one – what's-his-name – Stephen. Matthew didn't count, not at all, and she shouldn't be reminded, wouldn't be reminded, by such silly things as advertisements on a bus. *Five Boys!* No, only four and not all boys. Lawrence was not a boy.

Lawrence was a man, an angry man but angry only when he'd had a drink and then he'd say, '*Fuck it. Fuck the fucking lot of them! Bloody fools!*' Only to frown at her, '*Sorry. Stop your ears, sweet girl.*' She didn't mind, only words, after all. And when he was sober he was sweet as a lamb and sang and told jokes, happy, mostly happy. '*Finish it with that boy – you know the one I mean – Edmund? He's a waster, I think.*' Turning to her from boiling a kettle for tea in his tiny, ordered kitchen, saying, '*I say – you do look well in my dressing gown.*'

'*I say. Fuck the fucking lot of them.*' Lawrence Hawker, youngest son of a baron. '*No money in it, only for Charles, and then not much – not worth it if you're a gold digger.*'

The London streets were paved with gold: gold plated like that dog's backside, her father said. Her Daddy didn't try to stop her leaving but walked with her the mile or so to the Port of Belfast, saw her off on the ferry. '*Be good, say your prayers – write to us.*' An afterthought, this writing, an untried strangeness.

She hung on to the church railings, her shoe dangling from

her fingers as she rubbed the ball of her foot. Her heels were too high: she had wanted to seem taller to Edmund, more his match, and she had been striding along in these heels, so angry because of Edmund; outraged, amazed because who would have thought it of Edmund? Lawrence had thought it. Lawrence had known all along, and even Joseph had guessed as he'd watched him with that man in that restaurant: *'The way they eyed each other up! As if they couldn't fucking wait!'* Couldn't wait to fuck.

Pure sex, then; no how d'you do; no 'I think you are possibly the most exquisite creature I have ever seen.' Just that eyeing up, that speculation. How did they recognise each other? By scent, by a look, a movement, a handshake, a cryptic note passed under the table, stuffed into a pocket. By their chins, their ears, the length of their tongues ... Just Edmund being Edmund, perhaps that was enough, the vulnerability of Edmund, blond and bonny and bright as the sun, a May sun, elusive, a now-you-see-me-now-you-don't sun. Edmund, who didn't care at all, wasn't responsible at all, only attentive when he could be bothered. And when he bothered, oh then you would bask in his heat; you would burn, not caring; later you would regret such reckless behaviour: you should have known better.

She put on her shoe, wincing. A woman walked past her into the church carrying funeral-white lilies, laughing as the vicar came out of the church door, *'There you are, Reverend! I'd called at the house –'* her words becoming lost inside, the closing door wafting out the churchy smells. No incense, not here, only back home. Only parched dust smells here, cold stone and soft hymn-book smells and brass-rubbing tourists. *'Brass rubbings!'* Matthew's scornful laugh: *'God as arts and crafts!'*

Matthew. She winced again as she let go of the railings, began to walk on, to try not to think about Matthew, who had written to her this morning, had written in big bold letters: *You are a whore.* Only that. The fire in the grate had leapt around the single page, taking a little more time over the fine, thick, well-gummed envelope, as much time as it took for her heartbeat to return to normal. Tomorrow he would write again, a normal letter, no mention of her whoredom. No apology. Matthew had never apologised but he had warned her: *I have to warn you I'm not right in the head.* When he was well, he could say, *I'm not right in the head.* He could warn her. And when he was most ill he would believe that he was most well: he could call her a whore because wasn't that the sane truth and not at all a madman's judgement?

Lawrence had warned her, too. He had said, 'And you're thinking of visiting this Major Purcell at this place he's in?' He had frowned at her over a teapot in the café on Percy Street. Lawrence, a veteran like Matthew, although Lawrence had '*got off scot-free*'. Almost scot-free – he had his moments. She had thought he'd be supportive: wasn't Matthew a fellow officer? But he had only poured the tea, frowning and frowning as he'd said, 'How well do you know this man?'

She had lied, of course. 'Not well.'

'Then for goodness sake don't go visiting him in a mad house! Men like that aren't sick puppies to be petted. I know you mean well, but honestly, you make me fearful.' She had laughed, not wanting him to be fearful, but he had shaken his head, frowning still. 'Seriously, my girl. Be careful.'

Be careful, he had said, and: *there are more things in heaven and earth*: he thought she had no imagination.

You are a whore. The deeply scored, single sheet of writing paper had almost flown up the chimney; she'd had to rush to hold it down with the poker.

She could see the gallery across the road now: smart in the daylight with its new sign and professional paint job; she had washed the plate glass smear-free, squeaky clean, placed one painting just-so in the window as Lawrence directed her from the pavement. Not one of Law's paintings. They'd all sold. Lawrence was delighted. '*I told you so – didn't I? Genius!*' But who was the genius? Lawrence. Not that man. Not that talentless, repellent, one-eyed *creature*.

She waited at the kerb for a taxi to pass, crossed the road and stood in front of the gallery's window. She checked her reflection, smoothing down her hair, pressing her lips together to even out her lipstick, tilting her little hat a fraction more:

jaunty whore. The gallery was empty; there was no one on the other side of the plate glass to see her. Lawrence would be in the back office, on the telephone, always on the telephone; he would wave at her as she opened the office door, perhaps cover the mouthpiece with his hand, '*Won't be a tick.*' It wasn't just in her imagination that his face lit up when he saw her.

She would tell him she had finished it with Edmund. He would nod. '*Good,*' he would say, '*best shot of the bugger.*' No, he would be magnanimous. He wouldn't say anything. Perhaps a smile; perhaps he would allow himself a glanced-away smile. She tried the gallery's door; it was locked. No matter, she would see him later. She would go on to the pub, surprise Susie by starting her shift early. She began to slow her walk, her thoughts, her anger slipping away a little.

'I don't know what you see in that Edmund – posh bugger.' Ann remembered how Susie had flicked her cigarette ash contemptuously as she went on, 'Looks down his nose, talks like an arse. Maybe if he brushed himself up a bit he would look all right. But nah – wouldn't trust him, all that butter-wouldn't-melt act.'

They had been standing together behind the bar of the King's Head, waiting as Fred opened the doors to the small knot of drinkers on the pavement outside, Susie with her arms folded, scowling, belligerent – she wouldn't smile until Fred had locked the doors again, the very opposite of the barmaid Ann had imagined her to be when she'd first seen her. Not that the customers seemed to mind Susie's surliness; it was almost as though they felt they deserved her scathing looks and remarks. The King's Head was not a pub to be comfortable in, but a place of dimness and stuffy warmth, of hard, varnished-shiny surfaces and mirrors so old and mottled they could almost be flattering if any of the customers had thought to look up to catch sight of themselves. Most of the customers were old men, or young men whom the war had made prematurely old, with all the paraphernalia of age: walking sticks, mufflers and heavy coats even in summer, clothes that barely disguised wrecked bodies.

Paul Harris was wrecked with that dead glass eye of his; in

the gallery Harris had caught her studying him and his hand had gone to it. At the time she had felt sorry for him. Now she only felt sorry for his father, having a son like that.

Matthew had told her about Paul Harris, how they had befriended each other and kept in touch no matter the distance between them. 'I owe him so many favours,' Matthew had told her. 'I would like to feel I'd helped him in some way.' And so he had written to Harris to tell him about Lawrence and his new gallery and how he should send him samples of his work.

She had met Matthew on one of her first shifts behind the bar, when she had still been afraid of Susie and her scornful tongue, afraid that she would be too inappropriately friendly with the customers or not friendly enough; ironic, now she came to remember. But Fred, Susie's husband, the man whose name was above the door, had been straight with her: 'You'll soon get the hang of it. Nothing to it, anyway.' From the other end of the bar, she had heard Susie's bark of laughter. Fred had winked at her. 'Don't mind my wife.' He smiled and his voice was quieter as he said, 'Just mind me, all right?'

Soon she did have the hang of pulling pints and taking money and giving change, doing the small additions and subtractions in her head. She had begun to think that there was actually nothing to it when there was a sudden commotion, drinkers moving back in surprise as one of their number fell to the floor, the glass he'd been holding smashing beside him, beer spreading and foaming around the shards. At once, moving from behind the bar with practised agility, Fred was crouching beside the man's body and feeling for a pulse.

Everyone gathered around. Susie had snorted. 'Typical. Why do they have to come in here to drop dead?'

'For God's sake woman, show some charity.' Looking around, Fred's gaze came to rest on a man Ann hadn't noticed before that moment, and an expression that was something like relief mixed with apprehension crossed his face. 'Father,' he said, 'would you come over here?'

'Father!' Matthew had said much later. 'I shall always be Father to Fred, no matter that he's twenty years on me. I shall start calling him *son,* see how he likes that.'

But that evening Matthew had only edged his way through from the back of the little crowd and knelt beside the man's body, careless of the broken glass, not seeming to mind the spilled beer, closing the startled eyes and saying words so softly and intently that no one could hear.

Later, after the body had been taken away, the drinkers shooed out and the doors closed and bolted, Susie said to her, 'Come through. I think we deserve a shot of brandy in our tea tonight.'

In the living room at the back of the pub, Fred and the Father had turned to them. The quiet argument they seemed to be having stopped abruptly.

To Matthew, Fred had said, 'This is Ann. She's come to work for us.' To her he said, 'This is my cousin, Ann. He's called Matthew and whatever you do don't call him anything else but Matthew. Isn't that right, Matthew – or how about just Matt? Nice and informal, Matt.'

Matthew had stepped towards her, holding out his hand. 'Ann. How do you do?'

Almost at the pub, dawdling now, she remembered the feel of Matthew's hard, calloused hand in hers, and how she had thought that a priest's hands should be softer and that their expressions should be softer, too, not angry and impatient, as though he could hardly wait to leave. But he had stayed when Fred offered him a drink and the four of them had sat round the coal fire that Susie, with surprising meekness, had set about lighting.

Matthew drank the whisky Fred gave him and then stood up to go. Fred stood up, too, saying, 'Would you walk the girl home, Matthew? It's late – you don't know who could be out so late.'

Immediately she had protested but Matthew had said impatiently, 'Don't argue with the man. It's pointless.'

Outside the pub he'd said, 'Which way?'

'You don't have to walk me home.'

'And what would Fred say if they found you in the morning with your throat cut?'

She'd had to run to keep up with him. Breathlessly she said, 'Slow down. I've been on my feet all night.'

He had slowed his pace. After a while he'd said, 'I'd say from your accent that you're from Belfast?'

'Yes.'

'Why did you leave?'

'Same reason everyone leaves.'

'Which is?'

'The lure of London's bright lights.'

He glanced at her, smiling for the first time. Looking around him at the dark, grimy street he said, 'They are quite dazzling, aren't they? Especially tonight.'

'Who would have thought life could be so exciting.'

'Who indeed?'

They had walked on, and after a little while she'd said, 'They won't find me with my throat cut – really, you don't have to see me to my door.'

'It happens that this is the right direction for me.' Quickly he added, 'And I shouldn't have said that – it's a nasty image, especially after what happened tonight.'

'Did you know the man who died?'

'Yes.' After a moment he'd said, 'He was one of my congregation. His name was Peter O'Connor. He had ten living children. Ten. He would boast to me about his ten children. I had to be very impressed, of course.' He had stopped at the corner of the street. 'Which way now?'

Matthew would come in the pub often after that night last winter, taking time to talk to her, often walking her home. It was always so cold, their breath hanging on the air, merging. She would pull her scarf high around her face in preparation for stepping out of the pub's warmth so that he would grin when he saw her. *All set?* he'd ask; he always asked this, waiting at the bar as Fred counted out the night's takings from the till. He always said goodnight to Fred, Fred always held up his hand in a half salute – lips too busy mouthing his sums to answer. Matt always smiled at her then, and then always offered her his arm. All set. Weren't there murders on the street? Men who would cut your throat for fun? But she was on the arm of Major Matthew Purcell who had won a medal for bravery: Fred had told her this. He had told her this as though he was justifying something to himself and to Susie, who had only said *Watch your step, madam*, as she would have expected Susie to say.

He'd walk her home and she would hold on to his arm tightly because the pavements sparkled with ice; close to him, in step with him, he wasn't so much taller, but stocky, compact, she could feel the strength in the tenseness of his arm as she leaned on him too heavily, afraid of falling in her wrong shoes. Walking home and he talked; he always talked, telling her about his life before the war, his father Pip who was a gamekeeper, who took him out to shoot grouse on the Yorkshire moors, that beautiful land, rugged and desolate, then soft and beautiful, a tapestry in a certain light. Pip the gamekeeper, short for Phillip, odd to have a father called Pip, he said, a child's name, after all. Things became confusing when Pip called his son Father; he'd smiled at her then – a mild smile, a mild joke.

She wondered why he had left the church, why he had given up on the respect, all those men and women and children calling him Father, bowing heads to him, deferring to him, believing him wise. She thought of the priests who came to call at home, her father saying Father too often, her father wanting the priest gone, wanting to be father himself again in his own home.

But Matthew had left the church during the war. From the church to the army – one institution to the other, he'd said. He didn't speak of the war, or his medal that Fred had boasted about. He only told her of the explosion that sent him flying off his feet – *I could feel myself lifted – lifted, extraordinary, like flying* – to land on his head, his helmet gone and his skull cracked. *Never the same since*. That look again, that smile. Perhaps you end up in love without much noticing that you were heading in that direction, as you might suddenly come across the glittering sea after a walk down a green, shaded lane. Unexpected, exciting, such a thrill when you suddenly realise it, when it's there in front of you suddenly, suddenly when he stops and takes your hand and pulls you into his arms so that your bodies collide, powerful and urgent, hard and strong, fast as the sea to drown you.

Outside the pub now, she hesitated before going in because it seemed to her that her face would give too much away – she knew how thinking of Matthew changed her, made her soft-looking and vulnerable. Susie would eye her speculatively, and Fred would look guilty, as he often did around her now, as though he knew, as though he realised he should have warned her, properly warned her; as though he should have told Matthew to keep away. So she made herself think of Edmund, and that creature he had left her for, drawing on her anger to make her hard again; this would work, for a time, although her anger had abated a little – Edmund was becoming nothing more than a boy she once knew; her thoughts would return to Matthew soon enough. She drew breath and pushed open the pub door.

Chapter Twelve

LAWRENCE HAWKER HAD MADE him coffee – decent, proper coffee. It cooled in a blue and gold bone china cup on Hawker's desk, beside it a matching plate on to which Hawker had spilled arrowroot biscuits from a tin. Snapping one of these biscuits in half Hawker dunked it in his own coffee to which he'd added a slug of the Scotch that Paul had refused. Frowning at the bitten-off biscuit, Hawker said, 'I acquired a taste for these during the war – odd because they're fairly dull. We were sent a whole bloody crate of them once. I seem to remember one of the chap's uncles had a biscuit factory ...' His frown deepened. 'Christ – sounds like I made that up, doesn't it? An old war story with which to entertain ...' He grinned at him. 'Drink your coffee. Have a biscuit. For God's sake, relax. You're my star turn, can't have you flaking out.'

Paul realised he was sitting on the edge of his seat; reaching for his coffee, he sat back and the cup rattled in its fine saucer. Lawrence caught his eye and looked away again. Rather too cheerily, he said, 'Do you miss foreign climes?'

'No. Yes, sometimes ...' He sipped his coffee, aware of the other man watching him as though he wondered how likely he was to *flake out*. He supposed he looked nervous: jumpy, fey probably, through lack of sleep, through an excess of guilt and worry. He took another sip of the coffee, hoping it would buck him up, hoping that this man was not just remorselessly business-like but someone he could like. He felt that they would have got on all right during the war, as he had got on with other men like Lawrence Hawker: straight and easy going, jolly-good-show men. But that was unfair; it was obvious Hawker wasn't that kind of fool.

Lawrence lit a cigarette and pushed the box over to him. He took one gratefully. Blowing smoke down his nose, Lawrence leaned back even further in his chair, tilting on its back legs. 'So. What are you working on at the moment?'

Paul thought of his studio at home, the canvases turned to the wall, all his paintbrushes cleaned, all neat and tidy for his return. He had closed the shutters and the trapped air would become staler because Patrick wouldn't even open the door on this tidiness; he never intruded, never asked the impertinent question that Hawker had just asked. And if Patrick did ask – he never would, thank God, but *if* he did, he would answer, 'Nothing! For Christ's sake, why don't you just leave it? It's all *nothing*, all right?' No. He wouldn't say that, not even to Pat.

Hawker frowned at him. 'Are you quite all right?'

'Sorry.' He exhaled. 'I'm thinking about a series of portraits.'

'Oh?' Hawker looked encouraged.

'Some of the traders in the market close to where we live.'

'Oh.' He looked less encouraged. He tapped his fingers against his mouth thoughtfully. 'Perhaps not very decorative … Still, neither is a bombed landscape...' He frowned at him. 'Would they sit for you, those people? It's against their religion, isn't it? Or rather you are – *you're* against their religion.'

Paul thought of Matthew, shouting biblical verses at him on that terrible walk back to the hospital. His rant filled his head still, skewering his thoughts, his actions, until it seemed that everything he touched, everything he laid eyes on was made wrong by him, even Edmund. Since he'd returned from visiting Matthew he couldn't look at Edmund without knowing he had debauched him. He had begun to feel as though he had ruined the boy's life. But hadn't his own life been ruined? Why shouldn't he do some ruining? He flicked cigarette ash into the ashtray on Hawker's desk. The man smiled at him as though he hadn't been insolent at all.

Lawrence got up and went to the barred window. 'You know, I've rather been thinking that perhaps I could do something out here – make more of it in some way. It's very sheltered, gets all the sun – obviously not as much as you get back in Tangiers. I feel obsessed with the sun at the moment, too much winter. If I whitewashed the walls … Perhaps if I put a glass roof on it … In the summer it could be an extension of the gallery – it's such a small space, I need more space …' He turned to grin at him. 'More of your work, if you'll let me have it. Paint what you must, of course, you will anyway.'

Paul got up and stood beside him. The window looked out on to a yard. An elder bush grew in a corner, soon to blossom into the lacy white flowers that would turn into clots of black berries, weighing the branches down. Dandelions grew from the cracks in the paving stones; along the top of the walls someone had concreted shards of broken glass – green, brown, clear – a random, striking effect, like the upright quills of an exotic bird. He could see the yard would trap the sun; the imprisoned sun would make the glass glint and the window's metal bars would send their shadows across the walls of this little room as the day wore on. At once he was back in his prison cell, a space that captured the noon sun like this. Sundays at noon he would lie on his bunk and watch the sun make shadows of the bars; Sunday afternoons and he would have time to crouch in the shell hole beside Jenkins, cradling his body in his arms, ineffectually wiping the blood from his face; he should have closed Jenkins' eyes, *that's* what he should have done. Lying in his cell he'd imagine slapping his palm to his forehead in exasperation at the obviousness of this revelation because exasperation made him feel as though he could lose himself in a harmless, meandering derangement. But there was too much comfort in such behaviour, he needed to be harder on himself and be truthful; he needed to remember his spite and lack of patience and pity, his childish, wanton rage at Jenkins, who was a coward, a cry baby, but still he shouldn't have killed him. And truly he shouldn't think of Jenkins as anything other than a fellow officer, scared as he was scared, because this was the truth and it wasn't enough to be able to watch the shadows like this, safe in a sunny cell; there should be some harsher retribution.

Paul sat down. His legs were trembling; he clasped his hands together to disguise their shaking, proper shaking now, not just the ordinary tremor Lawrence had noticed earlier, but the proper shaking memories of Jenkins. Aware that Lawrence was watching him intently, he made himself look up.

'All right?' Lawrence's voice was sharp with impatience.

'Yes. Sorry.'

'Do you need to put your head between your knees or something?'

'I'm fine.'

'Perhaps you should try harder to get a decent night's sleep.' Lawrence sat down and his tone was even more abrupt as he said, 'May I give you a piece of advice? That boy, Edmund. If you've dipped your wick that's fine, I really don't care what you do. But he's a leech – and Christ –' he laughed shortly ' – you do look as though he's bled you.'

Paul stood up to go. 'Thank you for the advice.'

'Oh sit down. Bugger for Britain, I don't care, but he's indiscreet and foolish.' He snorted. 'You people really are led by your dicks, aren't you?'

Paul sat down. 'I'm sorry – I thought you were pretending not to care. But now I'm not sure of the ground. Do you still want my work or is who I fuck too much of an obstacle?'

'I don't care. I thought I should warn you, that's all. The police throw out their nets occasionally.' Becoming more animated he went on, 'All right, listen – just so you're *sure of your ground* – I'm not good at coping around men like you, and by *men like you* I mean the shaking, the sudden … I don't know – starts? And if you are going to throw yourself under the desk and cover your head with your arms I can't help feeling that I might dive under there with you from sheer funk. You make me nervous. There you are. This honestly has nothing to do with the other thing. *Who you fuck.*' He glanced away as though the profanity embarrassed him. Clearing his throat he said, 'Not much, anyway, if we're being frank. And I'm sorry but I've really made an effort to put the war in a box, if you understand me, and I can't help thinking that you could too, if you tried … Sorry.' He attempted to laugh. 'Stiff upper lip, and all that. It's not all bollocks, you know, what they taught us.'

Paul felt his fingers go to his eye and he stopped himself. He had an idea that he should sit on his hands. His face began to twitch. He cleared his throat. 'You're right, of course. I do understand you.'

'Do you? Because sometimes I think I'm being an arsehole. That I'm being too harsh, you know? And I know you lost your eye – that must have been bloody hell ...' He groaned. 'Jesus. From biscuits to this. What a pair we are.' Lawrence stood up. 'Come on, I'll buy you a drink.'

Lawrence was laughing, hardly able to get the words out, saying, '... and this corporal, little face all serious as sin, says *I'm very sorry, sir, I just cannot bring myself to eat it.*' Lawrence wiped the tears from his eyes, laughing so much that he fell against him. '*Just cannot bring myself*! He was vegetarian or something ...' He frowned at him with a drunk's exaggerated concern. 'Do you hate my guts?'

'No.'

'I don't hate queers, you know.'

'No. I understand.'

'You're very understanding.' He seemed to become aware of how he was slumped against his shoulder because he made an effort to sit up straight. 'I do hate *some* queers, but not because they're queer. Well, I don't know ... Maybe that is the reason ... Some of you buggers ... Not you ... I suppose there are types ... Types who wouldn't get past the recruiting sergeant ... Am I making sense?'

'Yes.'

'Have you stopped shaking?'

'Yes.'

'Good man! Keep buggering on, eh?' He began to laugh again. 'Well, no perhaps not in your case, what?'

'*What*?' Paul laughed at this affectation.

'I know. Horrible, isn't it? But then, you're a prim little lower-middle-class boy with a grammar-school accent, so don't let's start on all that.' He downed his Scotch and wiped his mouth with the back of his hand. 'Another?'

Paul got up and went to the bar. He was more or less sober – one drink to Lawrence's two, pacing himself, wanting to be in control. Lawrence barely noticed that he wasn't matching him drink for drink. He drank a lot and often, Paul guessed, his way of buggering on, his war not held in *a box* but drowned in a bottle.

The barmaid came out from the snug, wiping her hands on her apron, calling over her shoulder, 'Oh, yes? That'll be the day!' not looking at him as she said, 'Yes, sir, what can I get you?'

Paul had the cowardly idea that he might simply turn and walk out. Ann still hadn't seen him, she was looking past him to Lawrence, he saw how her expression softened; and then she turned to him and at once she was the hard-faced barmaid again.

'Yes?'

'A Scotch, please.'

'Single or double?'

'Single, thank you.'

'Anything else? To *drink*, I mean.'

The landlord came over. 'Everything all right, sir?'

'Yes, thank you.'

'Could I have a word, when you've finished serving the gentleman, Ann?'

When he'd gone she said, 'You've got me into trouble now.'

'I don't think so, do you?'

Lawrence came over; he slapped Paul on the back and then draped his arm over his shoulder, leaning on him. 'Hello, Ann, darling girl. This is Paul whom you've met. You're being very slow with the drinks, old man. Or is it you, Ann? Are you the slow one?'

She turned to Paul. 'You shouldn't have let him get so drunk.'

'Did you let me, Paul?' He frowned. 'Christ. Were you meant to stop me?'

Ann said, 'Go home, Lawrence, you've had enough.'

'No.'

'Yes. We don't serve drunks.'

'Yes you do. Anyway, you're not serving me, you're serving him, and he is mysteriously sober.'

The landlord came back. 'Hello, Lawrence. Maybe you

should think about getting on your way now.' To Paul he said, 'Maybe you could see him home, sir.'

'No! I think it's appalling that you're all ganging up on me. Fred – am I not your best customer?'

Paul took his arm. 'We should go.'

The fresh air seemed to sober him a little. Outside the pub, Lawrence lit a cigarette, passing the open packet to him. Cupping a match to Paul's cigarette, he said, 'I don't need a chaperone. Go back in there. Tell Ann you are very sorry that you took off with her sweetheart. Her *lover*. She's quite a girl – she might even say not to worry – *not to worry because he's a bloody bleeder and you're very, very welcome to him.*' He met his eye. 'I am actually very grateful to you. I know I warned you off but it would be a relief if you took him away somewhere. Back to Tangiers, perhaps? He'd make a charming pet.'

'Lawrence –'

Passionately Lawrence blurted, 'I can't stand that she's with him as well as me.' He frowned at him. 'My God. Now you look shocked. Are you shocked? I thought queers were unshockable, but look at you – you're shocked.' He laughed. 'Oh, you *are* a little provincial, for all your airs. Or is it just the thought of cunt? Never mind. Won't get into that again … I'm going home. I think you should go and apologise to Ann. It was very ungallant, what you did to her.'

Ungallant; Paul thought so himself, of course. He had felt guilty about the girl, even when he was sitting next to her in that restaurant; he had known even then he would have Edmund.

Have him. To have and to hold. He thought of the fifty years Edmund had talked of. From this day forward. In fifty years, he would be seventy-eight; he would be dead. 'Til death do us part. He thought of Edmund dressing, knotting his tie in front of the mirror in the hotel room, smoothing back his hair with both hands, catching his reflected eye, smiling. No one smiled at him like that. 'You're always smiling,' he'd said.

Edmund had brushed passed him, squeezing his hand

briefly. 'Ready?'

Ready to go out into the damp spring air, to walk side by side to a *little place* Edmund knew. Greek. *'They do a very weird thing with leaves.'*

Yes. He knew of stuffed vine leaves: *koubebia*. These were nothing like the ones he had eaten in Athens. And the lamb – he had such a hankering for lamb – was nothing like the lamb he ate at home. Nothing was as it should be and everything was as he remembered: the soft rain and washed-out sun; the belting rain and cold and skies the colour of iron bars, and the blossom everywhere, making a Japanese painting of almost every window, even the barred windows that looked out on to yards.

He shouldn't have remembered that window and the shadow bars but it was very easy to be back in his cell where he had concentrated all his memories by working on them so diligently. He could tune out the clatter and clangs of the prison, all its stinks, the stifling Augusts and the cold despair of Christmas, and revisit taking his pistol from its holder and pressing its barrel to Jenkins' left temple. In his cell he could begin to see those things he hadn't properly noticed at the time: how small Jenkins' hands were, and soft like a child's when he'd tried to rub some warmth into them, how clean Jenkins' fingernails were compared with his own – his own hands were filthy compared with his, and too quick and furtive. He could see how shrouded the moon was and that there were no stars and no sound but the ringing in his ears from the single shot. One shot, not two – he began to doubt himself, perhaps he had shot him twice? No, he should think more carefully, remember exactly in careful detail the specifics: the clean, small hands and the missing button on Jenkins' tunic and how, when he licked his parched lips, he tasted blood and thought he might have hurt himself, not thinking about this blood as clearly as he might.

In his cell he would watch the sun move the bars across the wall and remember the smell of churned earth and muddy, stagnant water: hadn't he sunk a little into this oozing quagmire, hadn't he believed that it might claim him, although perhaps the mud had been too slow for that. And when the ringing inside his head stopped wasn't the sound of his own breathing indecently loud, like that of a monster? A monster he couldn't see, of course he couldn't see himself, only his hands moving about Jenkins' body, feeling for a heart beat … No, no need, only going through his pockets. Yes, he did that: he searched him for letters, for photographs, for cigarettes and matches, for something he could use or keep or throw away, he hardly knew what might be important, after all. He had an idea he would write to his mother; he also thought he might hand himself in and so evidence would be needed. He didn't think he would get away with it.

Outside the King's Head, Paul pressed the heels of his hands hard into his eyes. He felt that his legs were about to buckle and he leaned against the pub wall. He imagined turning to face the wall, rolling his forehead against the brick, whimpering for Patrick; it took all his strength not to do this. But if he did Pat would hear him and run from the house and crouch beside him as he lay curled up beside the fountain in the courtyard. Patrick would stroke his back, his hair, murmuring, 'I'm here now. I'm here.' *Where were you?* A step away, that's all, always close by. A letter hidden in his shoe or under his mattress; he could read his letters even in the dark of his cell, like Braille. Patrick was always close by, and there waiting for him outside the prison gates like a vision, one he couldn't trust, too astonishing to be true.

He took a deep breath and stood up straight. He had survived, hadn't he? All those memories of Jenkins, all that concentrating on the details of Jenkins – he had survived this self-inflicted punishment – not much to survive after all, but still, he was here. Wasn't he strong now, even away from Patrick? He took a long drag on his cigarette. There now. Stiff upper lip, what? Not everything they had been taught was bollocks. He smiled. In fact he could laugh his head off at that one.

He tossed his cigarette down; he wouldn't light another from its stub; he was fine. He was fine. He wouldn't think of Jenkins or Patrick; he wouldn't think of Matthew and his ravings that had seemed like the true words of a prophet. He wouldn't think of crouching in that trench, not caring at all that Jenkins was crying as he pressed his pistol to his head. He wouldn't remember murdering Jenkins. He didn't have to remember it any more, not ever again. In fact he would make a great effort not to think of the past at all.

He thought of the barmaid, Ann, Edmund's girl. Hawker was right, he should apologise: apologising would be a kind of penance, perhaps the kind of penance Matthew would give: abase yourself, pay for your sins in humiliation, be free of the guilt, at least the small amount of guilt he felt for what he had done to this girl. He thought of Edmund in her bed and his jealousy was quick and painful, an epiphany; he had never been jealous in his life before; he must love Edmund if he wanted him so wholly, so entirely for himself. He must love him, despite the filthy feeling Matthew's words had left him with.

Lighting another cigarette, he inhaled deeply and went back into the pub.

Chapter Thirteen

SHE WASN'T FAT, NOT really, not very; she was plump, perhaps. Iris frowned at her reflection; she knew that when she took off her corset there would be red weals on her skin, flesh that resembled pastry with that orange-peel effect above her private hair. Her *pubic* hair – she shouldn't mince words, not even in her head, bad habit. She was not to be prissy. Besides, he was a doctor and had seen it all before.

Standing in front of her bedroom mirror Iris turned sideways, splaying her hands over her stomach. Perhaps she could go to George corset-less so there would be no red marks; knickerless, without stockings or garter; perhaps run across the road only in her dressing gown, like wee Willie Winkie... Barefoot? With a candle, its flame cupped by her hand, but if she saw someone she would have to blow the candle out, hide behind a tree, shivering amongst the graves, all those angels and crosses and obelisks, all the dearly departed, George's own wife amongst them; *Grace Harris, beloved wife and mother*. Grace who had pushed out Paul and fell back dead before he even cried, Grace's doctor being so busy saving the baby he barely noticed the mother. 'He was frantic,' George said, 'and so was I. But she just gave up. Gave up. Nothing I could do.'

She'd thought how unfeeling he was to say that Grace had given up; he had surprised her because he seemed caring. But his wife's death had been a long time ago, and he was a doctor, men she often thought to be impatient in the face of frailty. She forgave him, but didn't forgive herself for the ridiculous rush of pride she had felt at her own perseverance in childbirth.

He had told her about Grace's death years ago, before she met Paul or Robbie, before she had seen those two boys in their officer uniforms and greatcoats, impersonating men. Two brothers of the same height, same build, with the same dark, too-short hair beneath their eye-shading caps. No wonder Margot fell for them both, one after the other, quick as spit-spot. If she had been seventeen she would have fallen for them herself, although she would have guessed how dull Robbie was.

And, even at seventeen, she would have guessed that Paul was not quite right. All the same she would have fallen for him, hoping for some change, just as Margot had. She would have bought a pretty dress and some silk and lacy nonsense, a lipstick even: she would have *made* him see her; but it would all have been for nothing, a waste of time and money and tears. 'I love him,' Margot had said, and the tears fell down her face just as they had when she was a little girl, unchecked, her nose all snotty. 'He says he loves me! He says he does!' Perhaps he did. He loved Bobby. That was love. All that terrible, raw affection, as if he'd never loved anyone in his life.

She turned away from the mirror. Of course she would dress. She had bought new underwear – silk and lace that would be just as wasted on George: these garments would be off in no time, she knew this. It wasn't vanity to know how much he wanted her; she wanted him as much. Their courtship – she couldn't think of the last few years as anything else – had been too long, too agonised.

That morning Daniel had said, 'I'm not sure about going to see Reverend Carter. What if he doesn't remember me – he's quite senile now...'

Too loudly she had said, 'You can't let him down!'

'Let him down? But if he doesn't remember me ... I don't know ...'

'He'll remember you – you say yourself even the senile have moments of awareness.'

'I do say that. You're right, of course. Of course I must go. It's only that I don't like leaving you here alone.'

'It'll be fine. I'll be fine.'

He didn't notice the rush of smiles her relief brought, only nodded absently and turned away, searching his desk for something. She left the room before he could ask her if she had seen whatever it was he had lost, running up the stairs to look across the cemetery to George's house. He wasn't home, he was hardly ever home, but seeing Parkwood helped her to feel she might see him at any minute. Any minute he could walk up the path, up the short, shallow flight of steps with the loose slab that rocked when it was stepped on. She would watch him take his key from his pocket and unlock the door, perhaps stoop to pick up the post from the mat as he walked inside. He might turn and look towards the vicarage – he had once, she remembered, once he caught her out; he had turned and raised his hand as if to shield his eyes from the sun so that he might see more clearly. But she could have only been a shadow – the distance between their two houses that little bit too great. She could only hope that he had sensed her watching.

That afternoon she had waved Daniel off at Thorp Station. The station master had tipped his cap at her as she walked out, smiled at her as though he understood that now she was a free woman, one with a spring in her step, she could do as she wished: not go home, perhaps, but to Robinson's Department Store, browse around the dress floor before taking the lift to the top floor café, where the tables looked out over the High Street and waitresses in lacy white aprons would call her madam. She could order tea and chocolate éclairs because there was no supper to cook or spoil. Or she could go straight home and read a book in the bath, turning the hot water tap on and off with her toes until there was no more hot water to be had, no one banging on the door to ask what on earth she was doing in there so long. No one to ask anything at all; no one glowering in their study, or worse coming out of their study, wanting cocoa, wanting something, they didn't know what, couldn't pin it down, neither could she, a different life, perhaps, one that hadn't run into the buffers.

At least she knew what she wanted even if she also knew the fulfilment of that want wouldn't change anything. She would still be the vicar's wife when she left George's house, still dutiful to Daniel and the parish, still Margot's mother and Bobby's grandmother. Nothing would truly change, she would only know a little more about George. She would know if he was shy or bold without his clothes, or padded around naked quite unselfconsciously. She paused, struck by this thought; she would know another man's body, and this was astonishing to her after so many years of Daniel.

George was not like Daniel, but shorter, slimmer, more elegant and not at all untidy; his voice was lighter; he had more hair on his head and less in his nose; his eyebrows were tamed; his ears were smaller, as were his feet. He was younger than Daniel, only by a year or two, but it showed. And he had a different smell, of course; George's smell was soapy, near clinical, a smell that wasn't his own, unlike Daniel, who smelt only of himself, of nothing very much, a faint whiff of sweat perhaps, pipe tobacco sometimes. George wore rather good suits: she suspected that clothes were his one indulgence; Daniel wore his cassock, sometimes stained with soup, always faded, his dog-collar cutting him off at the neck so that she wondered how he bore it day after day. In the same way she bore her corset, she supposed. One became used to life's discomfort.

Leaving the station that afternoon, she had smiled back at the station master, happy because that was the first moment in a long list of moments that she had looked forward to: the moment Daniel was gone and she could allow herself to show her excitement. The next moment would be standing in front of her mirror, bathed, dressed, powdered, finished. The next – perhaps the best – would be the moment George saw her, the moment she saw him, his lovely face. After that she couldn't think further, couldn't really imagine following him upstairs to his bedroom and closing the door behind them. She had never been upstairs in Parkwood. She thought of Grace falling back dead on the bed. She closed her eyes and bowed her head because the guilt she felt was like a slap across the face, snatching her breath away.

She pressed her hands to her body and breathed in. She wouldn't feel guilty; she wasn't doing any harm, not even to Daniel who would never know and never suspect. She loved George, and had loved him for a very long time, and she knew him so well, almost as well as she knew Daniel. Tonight she felt she would know him better than she knew her husband.

At five to seven she let herself out of the house. She walked quickly, as she always did – no one would think anything of her hurry. But there was no one about, and even Oxhill Avenue was quiet. She closed Parkwood's gate softly, but didn't go up the wobbly steps to the front door but around to the back. The light was on in his kitchen and she put her hand to her chest in relief, smiling and smiling as she opened the door.

He didn't walk around naked at all. He wore a beautiful silk dressing gown, tied loosely with its tasselled cord, although his feet were bare and she worried he might catch a chill because Parkwood was a cold house as well as a gloomy one and only his bed was warm. He had given her another dressing gown to wear, an older, warmer garment, the one he used when he couldn't sleep and got up in the night to make tea, he said, and to stare across the road to see if there was a light on in the vicarage. He had smiled, drawing her into his arms, and she had felt the spring of the hairs on his back beneath the smooth silk; his hairiness had been a surprise, his toughness, his strength and stamina, all a surprise as though she had expected him to be somehow insubstantial; before that evening he had only ever been his face, his voice, his hands; she hadn't known him at all.

In his kitchen, wearing the silk robe, he said, 'I've made soup, and there's that good bread from Marshall's. Is that all right? Is that enough? I wasn't sure.'

'I wasn't expecting you to feed me … You made soup?'

'Now you look terrified.'

'No! I'm sure it will be delicious.'

'Well, the boys always liked it.'

She had heard him refer to his sons in this way occasionally. But now the informality of it touched her; more than that, he had made her feel as though they were her sons, theirs. She sat down at the kitchen table, drawing his red tartan dressing gown closer around her, watching as he lit the gas beneath a pan and moved from the pantry to the stove, setting out the loaf of brown bread, butter, plates and spoons and knives in front of her. He smiled at her from time to time; once he had to walk

129

around her to fetch a breadboard from the dresser and he placed his hand lightly on her shoulder, brushing his lips against her hair.

He placed a bowl of soup in front of her and she breathed in its steam: leek and potato. She smiled up at him and without thinking said, 'Daniel's never cooked a thing in his whole life.'

'He's always had you to do it for him.' He smiled and she realised it was all right that she had mentioned her husband; they had always talked about him, often alone in this kitchen, at this table.

Relieved, she said, 'Yes, I suppose he's never even needed to learn to boil an egg.'

He sat down opposite her and cut some bread. 'I can't stand boiled eggs. I do make a good omelette, though. That's what we'll have tomorrow night.'

'What else do you do?'

He glanced at her from buttering bread. 'I can't cook much else, really. I live on bacon and cheese and bread ... I eat too much cake, which is very bad. During the war Paul would say he should be sending me food parcels, not the other way round. Have some bread.' He frowned, 'Are you as hungry as I am?' He laughed. 'You look very beautiful. You're here, and I can hardly believe it. When I was making the soup ... I thought; *this is an awful lot of soup for one.*'

'You thought I wouldn't come.'

He hesitated. 'Yes, I thought you might not come ... But you're here ... Anyway, we'll eat the soup – and I have cake, I always have cake.' He reached out and squeezed her hand. 'And then we'll go back to bed, yes?'

His eyes were so bright that she laughed. 'Yes, we'll go back to bed.'

Chapter Fourteen

ANN CLIMBED INTO LAWRENCE'S bed and he rolled on his side, opening one eye to look at her. 'Are you angry with me?'

'Yes.' She sighed. 'No. Except you promised you wouldn't drink during the day.'

'I know. Bad, bad boy, eh?'

'I worry.'

'Do you?' He sat up, groping on the bedside table for his cigarettes. Lighting one he asked, 'Will you stay here tonight?'

'Yes.'

'Good.' He got up. 'I'm going to bathe and then I'm taking you out for supper. Share the bath with me?'

'Yes, all right.'

He ran the bath, singing *All the Nice Girls Love a Sailor*, happy because he was usually happy; 'I never lose my temper,' he'd once told her. He did lose it, especially when he was drunk. She didn't believe that he had never lost his temper when he was sober: how could anyone not get angry, not want to scream and shout and jump with rage and frustration? Even if you suppressed that rage, how could you not feel it getting big inside you so that you couldn't keep still but had to pace or throw a vase at the wall or say something vicious so that another person had to step back, away from you and your nasty, vicious tongue, as though you'd spat in their face?

Paul Harris had stepped back. He'd said, 'What a foul mouth you have.' He'd sounded astonished.

'Not as foul as yours,' she'd said.

Earlier that day, in the pub's back room, Harris had shaken his head as if trying to clear it of the names she'd called him, as if his ears were ringing, although she hadn't shouted, aware of Fred's thin walls, of the drinkers just beyond them in the bar who had watched her lead Paul into Fred's private living room, who were listening now, she could sense their straining to listen. Paul glanced over his shoulder as though he sensed them, too. He turned to her and she saw how white he looked, as though she'd shocked all the blood out of him. 'Would you mind if I sat down?'

Too angry to speak, she gestured towards one of the two easy chairs in front of the banked-down fire. He sat on its edge, fumbling through his pockets for his cigarette case. His hands shook. Finally, with his cigarette lit and the case and lighter returned to his pocket, he said, 'Sorry. I just need to catch my breath and then I'll go.'

They were mirroring each other, each on the edge of their seat, their bodies angled towards the door.

He drew on the cigarette and looked around for an ashtray. There was one on the mantelpiece and he got up, taking it back to the chair, sitting down on its edge again, his awkwardness showing in every movement. Unable to look at him, she looked around the room instead. She had only been properly inside this room once before, on the night she met Matthew: there were the two white pug dogs facing out on the mantelpiece, the thin line of gold paint around their necks that couldn't be seen from the door. There on the sideboard was a bowl of wax fruit with Fred's *Racing Post* folded beside it, on the wall a picture of the Virgin, blue and white, the same shades of virgin on her daddy's wall. Beside Paul's chair was Susie's sewing box, a darning mushroom rolling on top of it; he had kicked the box as he'd got up, surprising her because she hadn't imagined such a man would be clumsy. Then she remembered the glass eye, that lack of peripheral vision. The wooden mushroom made a peculiar noise on the sewing box's tin lid and he reached down blindly and stilled it.

Unable to tolerate him any more she stood up. 'I have to get back to work. The pub's busy.'

She had held the door open for him and he had got to his feet. Quickly he said, 'I've been a fool – it's only just occurred to me – you're Ann McNamara, aren't you? Matthew Purcell's friend? He wrote to me about you. He wrote that you worked in a pub called –'

'What of it?'

'I went to see him yesterday ...' He paused; more hesitantly he went on, 'You are his friend, aren't you? Ann McNamara? You do know about that place he's in?'

She nodded.

'He's very poorly, isn't he?' Harris's voice was pained. 'I don't know what you think but he seems so ill ... more ill than I've known him to be for a while, and I've been wondering if anything happened before he was committed this time ... I know there isn't always a cause, only sometimes ...' Despairingly he said, 'It's just I've never seen him quite like that before ... Ann?'

She had looked away, wanting him to be quiet because the pain in his voice was too much, as though he loved Matthew, properly loved and cared for him, making her ashamed and frightened. She saw Matthew crouched like a troll in the corner of her room and her hand tightened around the door handle.

'I have to get back to work. The pub's busy.'

'Please –'

'I don't know anything.' She felt her face colour, the heat spreading to her chest; she needed to get away from him looking at her like that, like a nice, kind man; she didn't want him to be any of those things, she only wanted him to go away and not care about any of this.

'All right,' he said, 'you need to get back to the bar.' Quickly he added, 'Matthew did write a lot about you, for a time – I was so pleased he'd found such a good friend.'

She had held the door open for him and he had stepped past her into the corridor that led to the public bar. He turned back. 'I hope you can forgive me.'

She couldn't help herself, the words were too easy to say, and she said them harshly. 'You *hope* so, do you?'

He held out his hand. 'Goodbye, Ann. Thank you for seeing me.'

* * *

In Lawrence's bed she remembered how hard and cool his hand was, but still she had wiped her own hand down her skirt when he let her go, not caring if he saw her do this and immediately ashamed that he had. She watched him walk through the pub – all eyes were on him, everyone curious, speculating. She'd had an urge to run after him and say that she was sorry, but sorry often led to the truth and at that moment she had felt as if she would rather die than tell Paul Harris the truth.

Lawrence's bed was warm and soft and she wished she could sleep; she wanted oblivion from herself, from her anger and guilt.

A smell of roses seeped in hot water came from the bathroom along the passage. Lawrence stood in the doorway, a towel wrapped around his waist. He had stopped singing and was gazing at her, such a look on his face. All at once he was beside her, pulling her into his arms, rocking and hushing her as she wept.

Chapter Fifteen

'I WANT TO TAKE you somewhere,' Edmund had said. 'I want to be seen with you.'

Paul had taken some persuading, but he had persuaded him, cajoled and teased him into coming to this club – he supposed he could call it that: a room above a warehouse with a bar and a dance floor, a discreet, half-guarded staircase leading up, barely lit, barely noticeable. Edmund knew about this place because he *knew*; knowing came from looking and listening, from walking the streets at night alone; he didn't have to go that far, a few streets, that was all, and he would be hanging about outside the door, watching the men come and go, afraid to go in because what would he do once he was inside? Now he was inside, all he wanted to do was leave, to take Paul home with him.

To take Paul home with him, to have him follow him up the stairs to his room, to stand back to allow him in first when he opened the door, to say, this is where I live – these are my pictures, my books, this is where I sleep alone – no one else has ever been here with me. He would make him tea on the gas ring. Perhaps the baby upstairs would not, for once, be crying and his downstairs neighbours would not be having one of their alarming fights. His room was neat and clean, he always kept it so, and perhaps Paul would take him seriously if he saw that he lived in this self-contained way.

He imagined showing him some of his drawings, how Paul would stand beside him, some careful expression on his face; how Paul might say this is not quite right or this could be improved if you did this, changed that. He might say nothing at all and there would be an awkwardness between them unlike any other, because Paul would know that there was some pretence going on, that he was seeking the opinion of a man whose work he didn't respect, and what was the point in that, other than a desperate kind of showing off?

Edmund glanced at Paul, who was watching the dancers on the tightly packed floor, his face wreathed in smoke so that he could barely be seen. The lights were very dim – although there were many: lamps on the table in front of them, on every table, all darkly shaded in purple and trimmed with silky bobbles that frayed and unravelled to show dull brown cork. Cigarette smoke seemed to rise from these lamps as though they were chimneys, a trick of the light because the smoke was everywhere; every man in the place seemed to be smoking except him. Behind the bar a row of Tiffany lamps, their purple dragonflies spreading their glass wings wide, was reflected in a wall of mirrors. He could watch the two young barmen both front and back as they moved deftly, gracefully, stepping around each other like dancers, the only dancers not touching, not so close that they seemed to be melding into each other's bodies, their hands down and down one another's backs so that they moved still closer, grinding close, crushing close in the heat of pressed tight bodies. Not dancers, then, not truly, nothing so decorous. He watched Paul watching them behind his smoke screen.

Paul had said, 'I've been to those types of clubs, Edmund. They're places you go to *find* sex. We've no need –'

He repeated, 'I want to be seen with you.'

'Why? Besides, in those places no one looks at anyone except themselves and their victim.'

'*Victim?*'

'Target, then. You know what I mean.' Exasperated he'd said, 'I'm surprised at you.'

But Edmund had persuaded him, and here they were, and Paul had been right when he'd talked of victims and targets; there were men sitting at the bar who stared at him or smiled at him or pursed their mouths and blew kisses at him; men who wore lipstick and eye liner, who made Paul smile and whisper, *'I'd have that one on a charge: gross misuse of the powder compact,'* Paul's lips so close to his ear sending a shock through him so that he'd actually jerked away – this was too much intimacy in such a public place, even a place like this, even especially in a place like this that was so serious with intent. He'd realised that Paul was very comfortable here, despite his earlier protestations. Paul would grope and be groped on the dance floor; Paul would grasp another man's head and shove his tongue down his throat, backing him against the wall, just like the pair they had passed on the stairs; they'd had to edge past them sideways; Paul had grinned at him over his shoulder. He had wanted to go home from that moment.

Paul turned to him. 'Don't you like your cocktail?'

'What is it?'

'Vodka, mainly.' Paul smiled slowly, and again his lips were close to Edmund's ear as he said, 'Thought I'd get you drunk.' The smile in his voice, the warmth of his breath, sent that same shock through Edmund, and this time he didn't jerk away, the dancers had had their effect on him, and Paul could be as intimate as he liked, press his hand to his erection and unbutton his flies if he wished. But Paul only took his hand and squeezed it tightly. 'Would you like to go back to my hotel?'

'Soon.'

'Not seen enough?'

'We could dance.'

Paul gazed at him, such a long, long look, his expression softening his features so that he almost seemed like someone else; no, not someone else, only Paul without Paul's experience, as though a kinder hand had written his fate. Edmund felt himself unable to look away, he wanted to touch his face and feel this transformation, but he thought how that might disrupt the process and bring the other Paul back, the man who should go away for a while.

He was about to speak, to explain more convincingly than he had before how much he loved him, when Paul stood up and led him on to the floor.

And the little band plays, and the singer sings some forlorn chanson, and he is held in the boy's awkward embrace because he is too tall for him, just as Patrick is too tall, and he shouldn't think of Patrick, not here, not as he rests his head on the boy's shoulder and feels his arms tighten around him, feels the smooth, fine wool of his jacket against his cheek and thinks of the body beneath it, beneath the evening shirt and vest, the pale, smooth firm skin of him, the soft belly and gold-blond hair tapering from his navel to become luxurious again. He had taken the boy in his mouth and he didn't believe that anyone else had ever done this for him because he had bucked and groaned so extravagantly, his big hand too heavy on his head as if he might not ever let him go: he would suffocate him in that lush gold hair. Such a memory this one's becoming, one that will stay with him until death, the smell of him too, the taste and the silkiness of him, and the way he'd cried *Oh Christ, my God, sweet Christ*, like a martyr in the flames. He'd had to swallow and swallow, held down, all of his mouth, his throat, his sinuses, all his soft tissues, all full of the scent and taste and feel of him, his ears full of blasphemy.

He hadn't realised he was such an accomplished cock sucker.

Now, why have such a thought? Why not concentrate, keep the memory sweet: no irony, no bitterness or distrust – no thinking that the boy is someone other than he is: guileless and innocent, like a child really. No, not a child, an adolescent. Old enough, just. Older than he was when he'd first … Concentrate now, on the shuffling steps, on his warmth, the tenderness of his embrace. The singer is singing about love; the singer is a man dressed as a woman, convincingly: he is fine boned and slim as a girl in his lovely satin dress, but singing about love in an experienced woman's voice; how strange this is, complicated, he needs to concentrate to make sense of it; the vodka has gone to his head. The boy is stroking his hair. *Edmund*. Use his name; he hates it when he is *boy*.

Bodies nudge them, deliberately he thinks; there may be hands other than Edmund's on him, quick, speculative, nothing-ventured-nothing-gained hands. He keeps his eyes closed and pictures Edmund's face, tries to, but it's elusive; there is only this warmth and tenderness and that's enough. His smile is extraordinarily warm, strong in his memory, a light he can turn on when other memories crowd him; those memories scuttle back into the dark when he thinks of Edmund's smile. Sunny boy, sunny and untroubled and fine. Edmund has told him he loves him; he should be troubled by this, but not now. Not as Edmund is stroking his hair, not when he is being soothed. He needs to be soothed, smoothed out, straightened and put right by this boy. *Edmund*. Edmund. He has an old, old name, the name of a Dark Age king, one that brought light to the nation, peace and goodwill; a king that lived to a great, great age. *In fifty years' time,* Edmund said; if they aren't dead; they may not be. They may not be. Edmund is an optimist; the sun rises day after day, and he won't think of Matthew, who is not a prophet, only a deranged man, a sick man; he won't think of Jenkins weeping; most of all he won't think of Patrick, who deserves more from him, that faithfulness he hasn't until now been able to find in his heart; he imagines being faithful to Edmund; yes, he must think only of Edmund, who is nowhere in his past, only in his future.

The song ends and segues into another; the man/girl/woman hardly pauses for breath. Edmund steps away from him a little and says softly, 'Come back with me. Not to the hotel …'

He nods; this is the right thing to do; he is brittle in that hotel room, a man he loathes but can't help being. In Edmund's room he will be someone else; he will keep his temper, his impatience and brittleness to himself. Edmund kisses him, long and deep and slow, grasping his head with both his hands. When he breaks from this kiss, Edmund touches his mouth so that he can't answer back when he says, 'I love you.'

Edmund fumbled with his key in the lock; the lock had always been awkward and there was a knack to it – lifting the key a little and turning it sharply; sometimes he can do this easily and the spring of the yielding lock is satisfying, but not now. Paul was too quiet beside him, like a child woken from a deep sleep and made to walk to another room. Perhaps he had drunk too much, although he didn't think so. He was tired, perhaps. They both were. He imagined Paul falling asleep on his feet, heavy against his shoulder as he struggled with the lock. But the key turned at last; he opened the door and his voice was much too bright and loud as he said, 'Here we are, then,' like the sleepy child's older, braver brother.

He lit a lamp and his enormous shadow played on the wall. He turned to Paul. 'Would you like some tea? Or cocoa? I've nothing stronger, I'm afraid.'

Paul sat down on his bed; he seemed not to have heard him. A print of Canaletto's *Return of the Bucintoro to the Molo on Ascension Day* was on the wall in Paul's eye line, a picture Edmund had bought on the Portobello Road, one of his first buys after leaving home, a picture that he had thought serious, full of detailed life. Now he hardly saw it at all, its busyness lost amongst all his other pictures.

Looking at this print, Paul said absently, 'I've been to Venice. We stayed for a day and a night, in winter … January, I think, cold and damp – we didn't think Italy could be so cold.'

He didn't want to ask whom he was with in Venice; that *we*: said twice, so painfully, as though a confession was being tortured from him. Perhaps he was referring to his father, the nice, courteous man who had looked at Paul with such a mixture of concern and exasperation, the same expression he saw too often on Paul's face. In his heart, though, he knew that he was talking about a lover; he suspected the man Paul had painted naked on a bed, the painting many of the men at the exhibition had gathered around as though under some compulsion; there was something in the man's face they recognised, something he himself had recognised; he remembered how he had avoided that portrait, and how he had looked with such contempt at the man who had bought it. Now his contempt seemed extraordinary in its arrogance, an adolescent ignorance.

Edmund turned back to the lamp, the kettle beside it on the gas ring; he had filled the kettle earlier in anticipation, not wanting to have to leave Paul alone even for the little time this took, hoping that such foresight wasn't tempting fate. He shouldn't be superstitious, although it was hard not to be since he'd met Paul; he needed to touch wood, to cross his fingers, to not walk under ladders or on cracks in the pavement because

140

Paul-who-was-sometimes-called-Francis was unreliable, he knew this in his heart, too. Paul would go away to be Francis, never to be seen again. He tried to ignore this knowledge; it wasn't certain, after all, and he was doing away with certainties.

He made tea, sweetening Paul's without asking because he had noticed how Paul spooned sugar into his tea, how he always seemed to have sweets in his pocket, humbugs and mint imperials, so that the taste of mint had become erotic for him over the last few days. He handed Paul his cup and sat down beside him, keeping a little distance, not wanting to proceed too quickly as they always seemed to. They should drink their tea, talk about nothing very much, like normal people. He thought that perhaps he should have sat on the chair – his only chair – but couldn't bring himself to; it was always difficult not to touch him, not to keep touching him, and that was not how a normal person behaved.

Paul sipped his tea then placed the cup and saucer on the floor and took out his cigarettes. Edmund had the idea that he should ask him not to smoke – he didn't smoke in his room, didn't like the smell that lingered and stained the walls and ceiling. But he hardly ever saw Paul without a cigarette; his fingers were yellow from tobacco, the only thing about him that he found disgusting – an admission that seemed to him should have the correlation he would inevitably find him disgusting because of what they did together, acts he had never, ever done before. His life could be said to be divided in two, now: BP and AP. He smiled to himself and Paul caught his eye as he lit his cigarette.

'What are you smiling at?'

'You, I think.'

Paul winced against the smoke as he inhaled. 'Always smiling isn't natural. They might put you away.'

'If they caught me.'

Paul looked down; he seemed to be making a decision about whether he could be bothered to pick up his cup or not. He did, saying, 'Do you have an ashtray?'

'No. Use your saucer.'

'I don't like to.'

'I don't smoke, Paul. Not really. I don't have all the *accoutrements.*'

Paul snorted, an odd, dismissive sound he wouldn't have thought him capable of, giving him the uncomfortable insight that he really, truly didn't know him very well at all. Afraid that this mood Paul seemed to be slipping into would make him even more of a stranger, he got up and fetched one of his most crazed and chipped plates. 'Use this.'

'I'm sorry I smoke so much.'

'I don't mind.'

'Then you're the only one who hasn't minded so far.'

'In that case you don't have to go any further – you can stop with me and no one will have to mind ever again.'

He was still standing in front of him, holding out the plate, and Paul looked up at him, frowning. 'It's tempting.'

'Be tempted.'

'Why do you like me?'

Edmund laughed, dismayed at the self-pity in his voice: this wasn't Paul; perhaps it was Francis. He was sure the man in the portrait had called him Francis. 'What kind of question is that?'

'A bad one.' He looked down at his cup. 'You're right to look at me in that way. Edmund ...' He looked up at him again. 'Sit down, don't tower over me.'

They sat in silence, a little space between them that caused Edmund's whole side to ache with the strain of not touching Paul. The Canaletto was directly in his line of vision now, too, and he stared at it, thinking of Paul in a wintery Venice with someone else.

His room was taking on the alien smell of cigarette smoke, and although the cigarettes Paul smoked were particularly expensive and not as disgusting as they might be, he got up and opened the window a crack. As he sat down again Paul said, 'I got lost in Venice. I walked out of the hotel and couldn't find my way back. There was a mist from the sea, you could hardly see a thing, and I couldn't remember the name of the hotel to ask directions ... I panicked, I was so frightened. He found me. I hadn't gone so far. I was crying my eyes out, like a baby ...' He laughed brokenly and looked down at his cup.

Edmund waited. He waited and swore to himself he wouldn't speak until Paul spoke, Paul or Francis or whoever this person was who seemed to want to confess so much. He waited, he even sipped his tea, he even thought about the Canaletto, how he had knocked down the seller's price a little. He wouldn't think about Paul crying so pathetically.

At last, flicking cigarette ash on to the plate, Paul glanced at him. He said, 'His name is Patrick, Edmund. We have been together for a long time. We met during the last few months of the war; he was my sergeant ...' he laughed, the same broken, self-conscious noise he had made a moment ago. '*My sergeant. My rock.* He did everything, ran everything, but he had to call me sir. He used to make *sir* sound like an endearment. *Sir, are you all right?*' He laughed again. 'I was, until I met him, but then there was Patrick, asking if I was all right and I realised I wasn't all right any more and I couldn't cope any more, not without him. So I gave up. Caved in. And I know I was weak and cowardly but I just couldn't seem to help myself.'

Paul had returned his gaze to the *Return of the Bucintoro*. For once his cigarette was ignored between his fingers, his lips parted as if he was about to say something else, something he couldn't quite find the right words for; he blinked and his hand went to his eye, and it seemed that the right words still eluded him because he turned to Edmund and frowned, as if they were schoolboys asked some tricky question. Edmund felt that he should say something. But the only words that occurred to him were, 'Buck up, old man.' He would sound like an idiot. Floundering he said, 'You don't have to tell me any of this – none of my business, after all,' and his voice sounded false to him, a bad imitation of his father's.

Searching his face, Paul said, 'I should have kept quiet, shouldn't I?'

'No!' He was blustering now, and he laughed, a harsh, desperate noise that had him getting to his feet in a rush of cringing embarrassment. 'No, of course not – you can tell me anything –'

'I've said enough, I think.' On a rush he added, 'I've been thinking about staying in London. How would that be, do you think?'

'I don't know –'

'I could start again. I could find a place to live, a studio to work in … And if we were discreet and careful … And now you look horrified.'

'No –'

'I've said too much. It was just … I don't know … I wanted you to know, and now you look like you want to run away, as though you have finally come to your senses.'

'No, no I don't think so.'

Taking his hand, Paul said, 'Don't think so, eh?' He smiled unhappily and looked down at their hands clasped together. 'We should just go to bed, shouldn't we? Not talk.' Looking up at him he said, 'Is that all right?'

'Yes, of course.'

Edmund went to the window to draw the curtains; catching sight of himself in the dark glass he thought how pale he looked. He turned to speak to Paul, only to close his mouth hard on the words. Paul was undressing. Tugging the curtains closed, Edmund sat down on the chair and began to untie his shoelaces.

Chapter Sixteen

DANIEL SAID, 'I NEED to speak to you.'

In his shirtsleeves in his garden, wondering where to begin on the weeds that had grown up under the close protection of the viciously thorny roses, George turned to see Iris's husband standing over him. At once he turned back to the roses, concentrating on the grey thorns that grew thickly all along their stems. He felt as though his heart might break out of his chest, a cowardly feeling, one, he supposed, that adulterers must endure from time to time. Only he hadn't expected this feeling so soon; he had hoped that a fair god might have given him a little more time with Iris. He should have known that there was only Daniel's god, vengeful and pedantic.

He took off his spectacles, folded them and placed them in his shirt pocket; he didn't want them broken; nor did he want to appear older and weaker than he was. Turning to face him he said, 'Shall we go inside?'

'Yes. That would be for the best, I think. More private. I think you will want this to be kept private.'

George looked up at those few windows that overlooked his garden. He wasn't on speaking terms with any of his neighbours, not since Paul's conviction; it didn't matter to him at all if they witnessed his further humiliation. But he supposed it mattered to Daniel, and he owed him privacy, at least.

He led him across the lawn that needed mowing, past the summer house that needed repainting, up the steps to the terrace that needed the sludge of last year's leaves removing, this year's horse-chestnut blossom, twigs and moss swept from its corners. He led him through the French doors to the dining room he never used, where the dust had settled thick enough for the mice to leave prints, where the sun had worn holes in the curtains. Grace had chosen those curtains, he realised, as he led Daniel Whittaker along the passage and into his study. Grace had asked him if he thought they were ugly. He wondered why he thought of this now; it wasn't one of those few memories of her that came most often to him. He remembered Grace because of Iris, of course. She had made all kinds of memories resurface, as though he was reconnecting with his life – coming back to life. And now his resurrection was to end. He imagined telling Whittaker that he couldn't stop him from seeing Iris – and that they were running away together; how defiant he would sound, how idiotic.

In his study, where the grate was still grey with last night's ashes, a newspaper, tea cup and crumb-strewn plate still on his desk, the curtains still closed, George motioned that Daniel should sit down and went to draw back the curtains. The sun would shine into Daniel's face, disadvantaging him. He opened the window because the room was warm and stuffy and he was ashamed of this stuffiness as much as he was ashamed of anything. He felt horribly resigned, and also that he might cry, once left alone.

Sitting at his desk, he cleared the cup and plate to one side and his voice was quite calm as he said, 'How may I help, Daniel?'

He saw Whittaker's face become a little more set, a little grimmer: Daniel didn't like him to use his Christian name. He should call him Reverend; as the father of a criminal he had no right to be on such familiar terms; George knew Daniel thought he used his name to irk him; Daniel was right.

He was about to repeat his name, when Whittaker said sharply, 'I hear you went to see your son in London?'

George wondered what this had to do with Iris and him; perhaps he was playing for time, unable to bring himself to the point. He realised he was holding his breath and exhaled. 'Yes. I went to see Paul. There was an exhibition of his paintings.'

'I'm not interested.'

'Then why mention him, Daniel?'

'Because he's the reason I'm here. How long will he stay in

146

London?'

'I don't know –'

'Has he any intention of coming here?' When George didn't reply he said, 'You must see that he doesn't.'

'Must I?'

'Yes. Because if he comes anywhere near my family again I will kill him.'

George laughed. 'You'll kill him?'

'Yes, I will. I will not have him shaming my daughter again – making her cry with shame *again*. If I ever set eyes on him –'

'Daniel, go home. I think enough has been said, don't you?'

'Give me your word he won't come here.'

'No, Daniel. This is his home.' More gently, because his relief allowed him to be kind, he said, 'He won't try to see Margot. He understands what he did to her.'

Whittaker looked astonished. 'Understands? He *understands*? No, he doesn't! I almost lost her! For months she didn't eat, didn't sleep – I thought she'd cry herself to death … Her mother and I …' His hands became fists. 'Her mother and I had to see to her as if she was a baby again …' He brought his fist down hard on the desk, making the cup jump in its saucer. 'He doesn't understand anything! And I would like to know where he is … I would like to know so that I can *make* him understand.'

George had an idea that he should stand up, walk around his desk and put a steadying hand on Whittaker's shoulder, just as if he was a patient. He would say, 'I'm sorry,' knowing how little he could do to help when a man was as angry as this. He would say, 'I understand,' as sometimes he did, but the word would only make the man more furious.

All the same, he did understand Whittaker's anger, sometimes he even shared it; his anger at Paul could flare up like a boil because he had come to love his daughter-in-law – she was tender and patient, the wife he would have chosen for poor, shattered Robbie; more than that, he had loved her because she loved Paul and seemed to want him and because Paul seemed to love her. Sometimes he had wondered if Paul wasn't simply a very good actor. Most of the time he was just enormously relieved: he had been wrong about Paul, or at least only partly right. The day he had found out he had been mostly right he had wanted to give him the kind of good hiding another father might have meted out.

Getting up, George went to the window and drew the curtain so that the sun wasn't in Daniel's face. He sat down and almost used his name again, only to stop himself and say, 'Reverend, I've talked to Paul and I believe he won't come to Thorp again.'

'You see that he doesn't.' Whittaker stood up. He was a big man in a black cassock, stooped a little now, his grey hair a little too long, his hands knobbly and arthritic; he had aged since the war as they all had, sagging into their grief. Robbie had liked this man: *'He doesn't talk any guff, Dad.'* Robbie had gone to Whittaker's church every Sunday during those few fine months after the war. George bowed his head, the familiar panicky grief making him want to rock back and forth in his chair. Instead he clasped the chair's arms; his grief had a peculiar comfort he shouldn't take refuge in, not in front of this man. He should be robust, responsible; he should face his guilt decently; he remembered Iris naked in his bed and said as evenly as he could, 'I'll see you out, Reverend.'

George turned the lawn mower on its side and stared down at the helix curve of its blades. They were blunt, encrusted with last year's grass. Paul would have cleaned and sharpened and oiled the mower before putting it away last autumn. But Paul hadn't been here to do any of those things. He hadn't been home for years, he would never come home; he had to face this stark truth: *Don't have any hopes for me, Dad.* Such modest hopes he'd had: that his sons would live and be happy.

He pushed the mower back inside the shed, where plant pots and watering cans, trowels and trugs were arranged neatly on the cobwebbed shelves. Hanging from nails on the walls were the spades and forks and hoes, the shears and lawn edger. There was some kind of feed for roses in bottles on the floor, there were canes and pieces of netting and a hessian sack folded neatly beside a bucket. There was the oilcan, its long, fine spout connected by a grey cobweb to a can of linseed beside it. The spider was dead between these two cans, had been for some time, like the butterfly caught up in another web in the corner above the spade, its blue wings still remarkably vivid after so many months. But inside the shed was always dark, there was no chink for the sun to penetrate to wash out the colour, and no one ever went inside any more except him, and then only to fetch the lawn mower once in a while. He must have left the shed door open one late summer evening for the butterfly to become trapped.

He had found Paul in this shed the morning of his trial. He had been rubbing a rag along the blade of the shears and there was the engine-like smell of the lubricating oil he'd used. Paul had been wearing his gardening clothes, a soft, collarless shirt and trousers that were so old he believed they must have belonged to his grandfather. His head was bowed over his task, his face pale in the dim light from the open door, wearing the same expression he'd had since his arrest a few weeks earlier: a kind of surprise that seemed to George to be the seeping out of a deep shock that was otherwise strictly contained. It seemed to him that everything was contained behind this disconcerting expression, all Paul's fear and grief for the life he had just lost, everything he had ever experienced since 1916. Paul had become silent again, just as he had in the months after the war's end. He worked in the garden and in the shed and everywhere was tidy, swept, weeded, pruned, sharpened, and oiled. Even these shears, even their wooden handles, wiped with the oily rag before he hung them on their nail. Paul had turned to him, alerted by the blocking of the light from the doorway. 'I'm just coming.'

'It's all right, Paul. Plenty of time.'

'Yes, but I need to bathe, to shave. I should press my suit. My good shoes need polishing.'

'I've done it.' He'd attempted to smile. 'Suit and shoes done, shirt too, and tie. All present and correct.'

'Thank you.' Paul placed the rag down on the bench he worked at when filling pots with compost and sowing seeds; there was always something he was tending to in here. The bench was clear now, scrubbed down. Paul picked up the rag

149

again and looked around as if wondering where it might best be placed. He stared at it. Absently he repeated, 'Thank you.'

'That's all right. Come in now, eh? I'll make you a sandwich.'

'No. No, I'm not hungry.'

'You should eat, Paul.' He had stepped inside cautiously, afraid of approaching him, of touching him, of showing any sign of his own anxiety that flapped uselessly around his head, his heart, his guts, keeping him from sleep, from the food he would try to make Paul eat. He was afraid that Paul would collapse, that the police would have to come to carry him to court because they wouldn't allow him to get away with it; they wouldn't let him off just because he was frail and badly damaged and might not survive prison. No, they believed that what he had done was much too bad for any show of leniency. Touching another man's private parts was much too heinous a crime for compassion. They would be on the doorstep to take Paul away because the law's the law, no good coming up with your sob story about your sick son – you-mean-your-sick-in-the-head-son – no good at all.

George remembered how he had taken another step towards Paul, then another, as though he was playing Grandmother's footsteps, and that he had said, 'Let me take that from you,' and had reached out and taken the rag from his hand, felt its greasy pliability, as though the oil had made something else of it. He saw Paul place both hands flat on the bench, bowing his head, his shoulders, his breathing coming too quickly and too shallowly, and for a moment he'd thought that he couldn't do anything at all but watch him.

He wondered now, these few years later, if his own son had repelled him. But no, that feeling of repulsion couldn't have been true, it couldn't; it had only been his fear that made him pause, even though that fear was so agitating it had never given him a moment to pause before. He *had* only watched Paul, however; he knew he hadn't tried to comfort him immediately; he knew his watching seemed to go on and on, the rag twisted tight in his hands so that he had left oily marks on Paul's back when finally he had pulled him into his arms.

George picked up a cane and swiped at the dead butterfly, knocking it down onto the bench. He stared down at it; one wing had detached from the desiccated body. He'd thought butterflies were meant to turn to dust at such a blow, to become indistinguishable from the ordinary dirt. But that couldn't be, of course; there was substance, still, and the cornflower colour. He found a dustpan and brush under the bench and swept the insect up, the wings fluttering as if such things could never truly give up on flight.

He thought about Iris and her shyness when she undressed for him; she hadn't wanted him to look at her. Not until afterwards, when he held her in his arms and they talked a little, did her body relax against his; and later she put on his dressing gown as though she wore it every day, as though he had seen her wrap it around her naked body every day. He thought of her in his kitchen eating bread and soup and laughing because it occurred to her that he looked like a character from the *Mikado* in the red silk robe he wore. 'Paul sent it to me one Christmas,' he'd told her, 'Paul's idea of a joke.' He thought how everything came back to Paul.

He carried the dustpan outside and flung the butterfly onto the lawn, the least he could do; he locked the shed, went into the kitchen and returned the key to its hook beside the back door. At three o'clock Whittaker would be leading mourners up the aisle of his church, climbing the steps of his pulpit to make his funeral address – Iris had told him last night, their last night together before Daniel's return this morning. 'I'll meet you in the park,' she'd said. 'We'll have an hour, at least. I'll bring Bobby, if I can.'

He glanced at the clock; quarter to three. He would have to hurry if he wasn't to keep her waiting.

Chapter Seventeen

IRIS CROUCHED AT THE edge of Thorp Park duck pond, holding Bobby's hand. The geese crowded them, the two beady-eyed swans circling and aloof from the mallards that mobbed each other over the crusts of bread Bobby threw with ineffective force. She hugged him to her as a swan came nearer. She had heard that one of these swans had attacked a small dog that had come too close to its young, and drowned the dog, although she could hardly credit it; she mustn't think of it; she had decided long ago not to dwell on the gruesome and cruel. Yet these thoughts came, she couldn't stop them, couldn't not picture the little dog. She kissed Bobby's cheek; he smelt of Margot and she kissed him again and again.

They sat down on the park bench that looked out over the lake towards the backs of the houses on Oxhill Avenue, where Parkwood, the oldest, most austere house amongst all the gothic mansions, could be glimpsed looming over a mass of pink cherry blossom. She looked at her watch. He would be here soon.

Taking *The Tale of Tom Kitten* from her handbag, she began to read to Bobby. She turned the pages and read the story, and he didn't seem to mind that she was distracted, that she constantly glanced along the path for George. She saw him, walking quickly as though he were late, and the excitement she felt made her feel like a very young girl. If only some way could be invented of distilling such a feeling so that it could be bottled and stored for a day when there was no George, kept for a day when there was only Daniel, or no one, only her, alone to drink in this memory of this man walking, smiling, hurrying to be with her. She stood up to meet him.

But it seemed his smile was only for Bobby; he hardly looked at her as he kissed him and said, 'How's my best boy?' He only glanced at her and she saw that his smile was only in his voice and on his lips and only for Bobby, and all her excitement left her; she no longer felt young; the disappointment aged her a hundred years.

'What's happened?'

George sat down, Bobby held close on his knee. 'Sit down, Iris.'

'Tell me what's wrong.' Her voice rose in panic and he frowned.

'Sit down.' It seemed that they had gone back to a beginning; she thought of snakes and ladders, that silly game she would always lose. As she sat beside him, he said, 'Daniel came to see me.'

She felt as though he had put his hand around her heart and stopped it. 'Why?'

George kissed the top of Bobby's head. He gazed out over the pond, the ducks and swans and geese dispersed now. She was about to repeat her question when he suddenly lifted Bobby from his knee and stood up. Curtly he said, 'I can't sit still. We'll walk to the swings.'

'George –'

'Come on. I need just to walk.'

She pushed Bobby on the swing, back and forth, back and forth, her palm light on the centre of his back, pushing him away and away again as George stood beside her. She felt as if she might cry with rage. George's anger with Daniel, with her – because why should his wife be spared? – was infectious. She stopped pushing the swing, it seemed too innocent a thing to be doing; she wished Bobby wasn't with them, a little witness to all this sordidness.

Bobby climbed down from the swing and ran off towards the roundabout. She called after him to be careful but George said sharply, 'Let him go. You don't want him growing up a sissy, do you?'

She rounded on him. 'How dare you!'

153

He had the grace to look ashamed. At last he said, 'I'm sorry.'

'Don't take your guilt out on me. Don't you think I feel guilty? All of a sudden you feel sorry for Daniel? Fine. Good. You know how it feels – you know how I feel every time I look at him. So, what shall we do, George? Confess and break his heart – and don't think that's some romantic figure of speech because I actually think it would kill him.'

'Of course I don't want to confess –'

'Then be quiet. Don't mention him to me ever again.'

'Iris …' He caught her hand. When she pulled away from him he said, 'I've spoilt everything, haven't I?'

'Yes!' She closed her eyes, shaking her head. 'No. No … It's just …' She laughed brokenly. 'You talk as if the pain of what Paul did to us came as a shock to you, that seeing Daniel still so angry was a *shock*! Had our hurt really not occurred to you, George? Did you really think it was only you and your child who truly suffered? Daniel and I thought Margot would never recover. At one time … at one time …' She stopped and thought of Margot curled up so tightly on the floor of her childhood bedroom, silent, Bobby's teddy bear clutched to her chest, her eyes staring and big in her gaunt face. She had knelt beside her and tried to hold her but her daughter's body had been limp in her arms, and she had smelt different, as sour as her breath, and felt different too because she was skin and bone and not soft and plump as she had always been. Daniel had come and carried Margot to bed, murmuring to her, brushing back her rat-tails hair from her face, tucking her in, murmuring her name, murmuring, *Daddy's here.* She'd had to go to Bobby, who was crying from his crib beside Margot's bed; she'd had to hold her grandson, *Paul*'s son, and watch Daniel comfort their child.

She watched Bobby now as he stood gazing at a group of older children on the roundabout. He was such a timid child. Perhaps this was Paul's fault, too. She remembered Paul holding Margot's hand, fearfully shy as he was then, as he told her and Daniel that he was going to marry their daughter. She remembered how astonished she'd been because although

Margot looked frightened, she also looked at Paul as though she was besotted by this odd boy. She'd had the idea that she would take Margot aside and explain Paul to her, only of course she couldn't – Paul was Margot's way out of disgrace.

She turned to George. 'I should take Bobby home.'

'Iris, I've decided to go back to London to see Paul again, spend time with him while I still can. He can't come back here – I know that now … I might just as well go to him …'

As coldly as she could she said, 'Yes. I think that's a good idea.'

She could see how her coldness surprised him; he glanced away, shifting from one foot to another like a child who had been caught out in a lie. After a moment, plaintively, he said, 'I did try to talk to Paul before he married Margot, Iris. I tried to make him understand that if he married her … Well, he would have to *change* … Perhaps I wasn't firm enough – clear enough, I remember that it was excruciating –'

She laughed harshly. 'Excruciating. An agony of pussy-footing.'

'Yes! It was – agonising for us both! Paul didn't have to do what he did – he did only what he thought would be best for all of us. Would it really have been better if he hadn't married Margot, if we'd had to give Bobby up? And I thought at the time that he could change. I *wanted* him to change, and the last thing I wanted to do was discourage him by telling him how hard it would be. So blame me – blame me for being an ineffectual father.'

'All right, I will.'

'And I'll blame you for not watching Margot every minute of every day.'

She turned away from him, too angry to meet his gaze, and watched Bobby watching the other children. He was so like his father, so like the Harris family, hardly theirs at all, a little cuckoo in her nest. She loved him; she felt like his mother, had been his mother for all Margot had been able to look after him; but sometimes she wished he had never been born, never conceived; she couldn't, no matter how hard she tried, feel the same enormous love George felt for him, as though he was all he had left in the world.

She turned to George. 'When will you leave for London?'

'Tomorrow, the first train that leaves in the morning.'

She nodded and began to walk towards Bobby. She thought George might follow her, but when she reached her grandson and glanced back he was already walking away. *Coward,* she thought, like his son, that pitiful boy who had seemed to quake whenever he saw Daniel, as though he knew that he would never be able to keep his vows to Margot. 'Coward,' she murmured aloud, her bitterness so potent she might have shouted the word at him, her anger making her cry out like a mad woman – 'Don't you dare walk away from me!'

She took Bobby's hand, snapping at him that they had to go home, but he pulled away from her and ran after his grandfather. George stopped and swept the little boy up into his arms, holding him close as she walked towards them, their faces level, both watching her as though afraid of what she might do next. They were so alike, the two of them; she wondered if Bobby would grow up as flawed as all the Harris men seemed to be, one way or the other. But they were also kind, she thought, and patient in the face of the worst troubles, accepting that trouble was as much their due as anyone's. Daniel said they brought their troubles on themselves.

She was in front of George, Daniel's condemning voice in her head, full of self-righteous hurt. How could she think of Daniel's hurt now, how could she think of her husband when she stood so close to this man who last night had undressed her, kissed her over and over, repeating how much he loved her, adored her, who had been so gentle with her when she wept that this would be their last time, there would be no more nights like this. And it seemed to her that George's heart had been breaking just as hers was, even as he'd laughed, as though ashamed of his tears, saying, *'I'm sorry, I'm ridiculous. Listen, listen – no one knows the future –'*

She thought of her future without him and said, 'What time does your train leave?'

'Seven thirty.'

'From Thorp Station?'

He frowned. 'Yes – Iris –'

She touched his mouth. 'Be quiet. Let's go home.'

Lying in bed beside her husband, as Daniel rolled over, tugging at the bedcovers, she kept still on her back, hoping he was asleep. He had to be asleep before she could remember properly, remember her first night in George's bed, how he had kissed her deeply and passionately, drawing back only to murmur, 'Iris, Iris ...' No one had ever said her name like that, with such tenderness, and his hands were tender and his mouth and the way he looked at her the whole time, holding her gaze, only closing his eyes for a few moments at the end, his face transformed as she knew hers was. She had closed her eyes too, alone in that moment, there was only her own body becoming fluid, mindless. He stopped, and still she went on as he buried his face in her neck, his breath coming hard and warm against her skin.

Why hadn't she married him? Why hadn't she met him when she was nineteen and thought she needed someone to marry? Where had he been, anyway? She could have searched for him, found him, stood before him: *here I am.* She shouldn't have settled so young, but gone on her quest, found him, stood her ground: *here I am. I love you and you'll love me.* And we won't have sons to be maimed in wars, or daughters to marry men who break them; we shall have children who are perfect and no one will ever hurt them if we are their parents, you and I together. She should have known when she was young that he was out there, somewhere, she could have found him. But she wouldn't have had Margot.

Only this thought saved her: her darling girl who wouldn't be Margot if George was her father, but another girl, quicker, brighter perhaps and not steadfast and modest, not compassionate, with such a soft heart as to fall in love with frail young men because she felt such a mix of pity and admiration and desire, a toxic love potion of feelings. 'He's asked me to marry him!' *Who, darling?* Who? Because there had only been Robbie, dull, ponderous Robbie, as though he'd had all his senses knocked out of him in France, all his wit so that he

seemed middle-aged, staid: *Pleased to meet you, Mrs Whittaker.
How do you do, Mrs Whittaker? Thank you for having me.
You're very kind, Mrs Whittaker. Very kind.*

Robbie didn't shake like Paul, twitch like Paul; he didn't
raise his eyebrows behind Daniel's back like Paul, didn't catch
her eye and smile like Paul, as though she was in on his joke.
Robbie didn't do any of these things. Robbie just went to visit
his brother in the asylum one day and was knocked off his
motorbike and killed. And she had held George as he had wept
and tried to steady him when he raged and she had thought that
Robbie had always been his favourite, secretly, in his heart, but
she had been wrong. There was no one to compare with Paul for
being a favourite; even Daniel had admired Paul more than his
brother, at first.

Iris stared at the ceiling as Daniel snored beside her. The
curtains didn't quite meet and outside the moon was full and
bright, lighting up the familiar shapes of their room, the
wardrobe and the chest of drawers, the chair where Daniel sat to
tie his shoes, the picture her mother had left her of Jesus
holding up a lamp beside a half-open door, *The Light of the
World*.

Her mother had said, 'He's every inch the vicar, isn't he?
Vicar in the making.' Daniel had been a curate then. She could
tell her mother didn't quite take to him, even before she said
this. But she had thought Daniel honest and steadfast and
handsome in a way she tried so hard to make more of. And
Daniel *was* honest and steadfast, and she knew that if he wasn't
easy then at least he wasn't glib or silly: he wasn't a fool to
make her squirm with embarrassment or shame. They would
have a serious, useful life together; there was a lot to be said for
respect and trust. So, she married him and Daniel had slept
beside her every night since, every night but two, so that they
knew each other so well and could say anything to each other,
although mostly they said hardly anything at all. She could
almost blame Daniel for going away – he must have known it
would be dangerous to leave her; he knew everything about her
– he must know how much she loved another man.

She turned onto her side, away from him, and saw her

suitcase there on the floor, packed and ready. She gazed at it, unpacked and repacked it in her head, making sure that everything was there. She knew she wouldn't sleep, or she would sleep restlessly and wake up each hour until it was time to get up, to dress, to wake Bobby from his bed in the room next to theirs, to meet the taxi on the road outside; she wouldn't wake Daniel, wouldn't disturb him. She would dress in the half-light leaking through the curtains and close the bedroom door quietly behind her.

Chapter Eighteen

PAUL HAS BEEN A lot on my mind lately, since he visited me. I've been thinking how changed he was, how much happier; his suntan suited him, he looked fitter and healthier than I think I have ever seen him; more *virile*. Virile is from the Latin *virilis* meaning *man*. So Paul is at last manly, in an elegant, off-the-cuff way, although I overheard one of the nurses make some sniggering remark about him after he had gone; but that particular nurse is an uncouth fellow and I didn't pay any attention. Although this place is very much more civilized than some of the other hospitals that have detained me, the nurses and orderlies are all cut from the same rough cloth as nurses and orderlies everywhere. I don't trust them and they don't trust me. One of them asked me rather slyly how I knew Paul, saying how it seemed that I thought very highly of him. I ignored the man, of course; he won't get a rise out of me.

I wonder if I do think highly of Paul. That nurse made it sound as if I've put him on a pedestal, so high that I can't see his faults, and also that I am naïve to admire such a man, that only someone as uniquely inexperienced as me *could* admire him. I think the staff believes that I haven't truly escaped my adolescence, despite the war, despite everything – despite even my friendship with Paul – a brush with whom would surely initiate anyone into the ways of adulthood.

I am thirty-five. Not old, not young, a nowhere age. During the war, at my lowest and most afraid, I'd hoped to achieve these milestones by now: marriage, children, a career – perhaps in a bank, safe behind a counter as a big clock kept me rigidly in check. When I was a little boy my father wanted me to be a priest because it was what my mother wanted more than anything in this world. Her only son, her youngest child, a priest: *Father Matthew Purcell.* I was not a devout child, but rather ordinary and grubby as any boy, always out with my father, stalking across the moors for miles and miles, the two of us quiet together, the very best of companions. If I'd told him I would rather be like him, follow only in his footsteps, he would've been disappointed only for my mother's sake.

I would have been a gamekeeper, like him, had it not been that Christ came to me when I was fifteen, an experience of such astonishing clarity that I couldn't speak for days. Nothing else mattered, only Christ and our mutual love. Christ could make me weep with joy or pity; he made me quicker, sharper, brighter than I would ever have been without him. I was his, heart, body and mind. I was spilling over with love for Christ, and the energy I had then seems miraculous to me now, such energy as though I could shoot all the birds from the sky and bring each one back to life again by blowing on its feathers.

Occasionally I would wonder if perhaps I loved Christ too much, that I should be more tied to the earth than this energetic love would allow me to be. In the seminary I tried to keep much of this energy to myself but still the others looked at me as though I intended to show them up, like a miner who digs too deeply, too quickly as his workmates chip away slowly, taking care not to give so much away.

Paul asked me once if I missed the priesthood. I should have told him that I miss Christ, but I was afraid that I would seem odd to him – *odder*. I do so want him to think of me as any other man.

After his visit I was taken to my room and left there to contemplate my foolish behaviour. My room is a space just big enough for a bed and a chest of drawers. There is a high, arched window with a deep stone sill, the glass divided into leaded diamond-shaped panes that make a tiring pattern on the wooden floor when the sun shines. The walls are painted white and although we are allowed to put up pictures, I haven't. When I described this room to Paul in a letter, he sent me a painting of the sparrows that visit his courtyard in Tangiers; I wrapped it in newspaper and stored it under my bed.

Today I was thinking about Paul so much I took the painting out. I can't think why I hid it away for so long. The little birds around the fountain are so lively one almost expects them to fly off the canvas; he has captured the way the sunlight sparkles on the fountain's spray very well, I think, although of course I am no judge of art. In the bottom right-hand corner he has signed the painting *Francis Law*. I know Paul Harris as Paul Harris, and I do wish he wouldn't change about so as if he is trying to lose his past and all his old friends. Paul Harris and I have been friends for a long time now, since July 1st, 1919, my birthday. Perhaps Paul didn't paint this picture of the sparrows hopping around the fountain; really I don't think he's capable of such fineness. Perhaps he is a liar, pretending that this Law's work is his own.

July 1st, 1919, was the third anniversary of the 1st Battle of the Somme. 'Were you there, Paul?' I once asked him, and he said no, that he had been gassed and was recovering by the sea in England. 'Piece of luck,' he said, and his smile was ironic. 'And you, Matthew, were you there?' and his voice was ironic too, and I said yes, I was. Piece of bad luck. We talked that little bit about that little bit of the war only because it happened to coincide with my birthday and the day we met. We never discussed the war otherwise. What was there to say?

We used to talk about his wife sometimes, when he'd visit me at a place I was in near York, a place not as nice as this one: I remember I slept in a ward with nine other men. Five beds down each side, high-up windows with belt-and-braces bars. I wasn't as well then as I am now, so when Paul visited he did the talking – he used to talk about his wife, and I listened.

She sounded like a silly little piece to me, from what he said. Her name was Whittaker, before Paul married her. I remember because that was the name of one of the priests who taught me at the seminary. Paul has a son called Bobby. Paul showed me his picture. He showed me a picture of a little boy who'd had all his lovely curly hair shorn off; at least I imagine he once had lovely curls. I imagine the locks of dark hair falling to the floor around him as he cries. I imagine how he cannot be comforted, not for a little while. Not for a little while at least.

Paul would say that his wife was very sweet. *Very sweet*! I remember in York I could hardly bear to listen to him talking about her, hardly asked two words about her the whole time he was going on. I did ask something – and it's excusable because I was very poorly then – I asked if he liked to fuck her. He only looked down at his cigarette and didn't answer. Maybe he didn't hear me. Sometimes I think I've said things aloud when actually the words are only in my head – and the other way round: vice versa, which is Latin for the position being reversed and nothing to do with vice.

Another time, another visit, I asked him if he had finished with buggering men now that he was married. I think I did ask. I certainly wondered to myself about it, even if I might not have actually got the question out because it's a bit of a mouthful. Mind your own business, Matthew, after all. He was teaching at a school in Thorp then, and I was in that institution near York, and he used to take the train to see me on a Sunday and he didn't look virile as he looked the other day; he looked ill and unhappy and I didn't believe him when he said his wife was very sweet. And when he told me that his baby was born and he was a boy I thought that it was very, very wrong of him to have a baby like that because it didn't seem fair to me. And it's no good him being nice to me, being ironic and funny and bringing me toffees because he likes them. He's not really a good person, he's a *wrong* person, I think, but all the same he gets everything he wants and always has.

He got Patrick. He showed me a picture of Patrick, too, the other day. Before the little boy's photo, Patrick's, Patrick in front of a wall. The wall was covered in some climber: it didn't look as though he was going to be shot or anything – the wall was too pretty for that and he was smiling, anyway, that smile he has for Paul which makes me think he doesn't know Paul as I do because the smile is straightforward love and no doubt about it.

Paul started on Patrick when he was still married; I know because Paul used to mention him sometimes in passing, when I was in that place near York, when he wasn't talking about his wife and his baby boy. He said he had met up with a man he had served with during the war and that he was a good friend. Wasn't I his good friend? I did ask him this, I know I did, and he said yes, of course, none better, none *gooder*, he said, and smiled. There is no such word as gooder, of course. It was just his joke; he thinks I need jokes and games with words and to hear about men he meets up with because they served together in the same platoon and are *good friends*. He wears his heart on his sleeve. I see right through him, past his bones, right through him.

I wish I'd told him about Ann when we were sitting in that graveyard during his recent visit. I thought to when I saw that girl with her pram and her daffodils and hip-swaying walk. Telling him about Ann would have made him realise that he's not the only one in the whole world.

I first saw Ann behind Fred's bar, and she was so lively and happy I thought she wouldn't mind me. The evening Peter O'Connor dropped dead I had thought of approaching her, of saying something careless such as, 'It's nice to see a pretty face,' risking Susie's sarcasm. More likely I would have risked only her surprise because of course I would never say such a thing: it's the kind of remark men who have had experience with women make; men who leer and flirt quite openly; the kind of remark that might lead somewhere once everyone has got over its boorishness. But then O'Connor fell dead to the floor and the atmosphere changed so completely.

He was dead before I reached him but I said a few words anyway, for Fred's sake. Fred's a suspicious man; I think he believes O'Connor would be haunting his pub now if I hadn't been there to placate his departing soul. Placate. Is that the right word? Direct, perhaps, is more accurate. In Latin I said, *go in peace.* Fred knew those weren't the official words, there weren't enough of them – I'd left out God and he knows the Latin for God, but he didn't complain. I was very angry with Fred, I remember, although I understand now that really I was angry with O'Connor, allowing myself to believe that were it not for his inconsiderate dying I would have approached Ann that evening in a way that would have got our relationship off on the right foot. This is nonsense, of course. More likely, I wouldn't have spoken to her for weeks; weeks spent trying to pluck up my courage.

Sometimes I imagine her coming to visit me, and how we would go walking arm in arm along the lane; the rain would have just stopped and there'd be the smell of the damp woods hemming us in on either side, the muddy ground a little slippery underfoot so that she'd hold on to me tightly as she used to. There'd be many rabbits, as ever, hopping quite unperturbed amongst the cow parsley in the verge. Perhaps a pheasant would come clattering out across our path causing me to imagine the hunters with their guns broken over their arms, the soft-mouthed dogs trotting ahead of them, home with the day's kill. This image is so vivid that I half expect my father to come striding towards us, a brace of grouse dangling from his fingers. He would be pleased to see me with a girl like Ann.

I shouldn't think about Ann because I know I can get upset about her, all my thoughts coming like a speeded-up Keystone Kop film with pratfalls and chases.

The weather is sunny and warm and if I look out of my window, I see that there is blossom on the trees like the blossom that was on that climbing plant in the photo of Patrick.

I wrote to Patrick and told him that I have seen Paul, and how well he looks, very well with all the attention he is receiving in London. *He glows*, I wrote, *as he used to when he met you*. He'll take my meaning, I think. I do like Patrick very much. He doesn't *shift* so much as Paul; he is not so much of a chameleon. I have written to him, he'll take my meaning, he will come, and Paul will have to be good, for once.

Chapter Nineteen

'I CAN'T DO MY bottom belly button up,' Lawrence sang. He straightened the picture, stood back, frowned, stepped forward again and straightened it again. He cocked his head to one side. 'There. I think that will do.' He began to sing again, knowing the words more often than not. She caught songs off him as if they were germs; his songs became stuck in her head until she had to sing them out. His/her songs had annoyed Edmund to death.

Lawrence had a light tenor voice. Ann suspected that he had a longing to perform on stage. He would call himself *Larry*, a more likely name for one of those comics who sang, who carried a walking cane and wore spats and a top hat to tilt to the back of his head when he was pretending to be perplexed. *I say, I say, I say,* he would say. *Why did the Irish girl cry herself stupid?* There's no answer to that.

He'd held her as she'd cried, the towel he had wrapped around his waist in preparation for his bath coming loose, displaying his flaccid penis so that even through her tears she felt embarrassed for his nakedness. She smelt the Scotch on his breath as he whispered, 'Don't cry, sweet girl,' tasted the alcohol when he kissed her, and she could hear the distress in his voice, feel the tension in him. Beneath her ear his heart beat too quickly and she felt sorry for what she was doing to him, that she was shortening his life by a few minutes by setting off his heart like this; couldn't hearts beat only so fast for so long only so often before they stopped dead? She sat up, wiping her eyes with her fingers. 'Sorry.' She had sounded as though he had made her angry the way she spat out sorry like that. He'd reached out and stroked her back and she glanced at him,

166

wanting to ask what he thought of her for crying, for making his heart work so hard.

He'd said carefully, 'You're crying over him, aren't you?'

He meant Edmund and so she said no scornfully, as though he was a fool for thinking so even though her tears were partly over Edmund, only partly, and actually it was the gallant thing to think. Lawrence liked *gallant*, it was one of his words. He was gallant not to have guessed about the other men; he didn't know her history was so colourful. If she told him about Joseph Day, about that first boy back in Ireland, he would be shocked. He would be even more shocked if she told him that her tears were mostly over Matthew. She imagined how he would draw away from her; he would look at her as he had sometimes looked at Edmund, as though she was contemptible, not worth his shock, arranging his face into its cold, *not-one-of-us* mask.

Now he turned to her from straightening the picture on the gallery wall and said, 'What do you think?'

'It's straight now.'

'I mean about you – up there on the wall. What do you think about you?'

She thought that Joseph Day had made her look like someone else, a good thing to do but not the truthful thing. Joseph had seen her through the eyes of a man who was jealous and angry and hurt and he couldn't bring himself to talk to her when she went to his room each day so that he could finish this picture, the last one he had painted of her, the last one he would ever paint of her. But finish it he did, despite his anger – because really he wasn't angry when he was painting, he was just a concentration of energy; and when he was painting she was just a thing, better than a vase of flowers or a bowl of fruit because she had blood under her skin, bones to get right, eyes to light properly, an expression to capture. Yet he had still managed to paint an expression she didn't recognise.

She stood beside Lawrence; he put her arm around her waist and pulled her close, his eyes on the painting as he asked, 'Well?'

'I'm not as nice as she is.'

He laughed, holding her even more tightly as he kissed her

cheek. 'Oh, yes you are. You are very, very nice.'

'Really, I'm not.'

'Really?' He turned back to her portrait. 'I think he was being very *real*. He's very good, isn't he? Dreadful man, bloody good artist. Don't tell him, though – well, you can tell him he's dreadful, just not that he's good. He'll be insufferable.'

'As insufferable as Paul Harris?'

He frowned at her. 'Harris is a good chap.' His frown deepened. 'Is he a good chap? I don't know. Probably, underneath all that … fraught. Not insufferable though. But I understand why you think he is.'

He didn't understand, couldn't see past Edmund, as though Edmund still stood between them. Although Lawrence was not as jealous as Joseph had been, he still couldn't get over his small amount of jealousy. Again, she imagined how he would react if she told him what a slut she was.

Lawrence squeezed her to him. 'All right, you can stop staring at yourself now, vain creature. We should get on, hang the others. I do hope it goes as well as Harris's exhibition. All those queers do like his work, don't they?'

'Were they *all* …?'

Picking up another of Joseph's pictures from those leaning against the wall, his voice was distracted as he said, 'Were they all …? Oh. Yes, of course.' He laughed shortly, his eyes serious, searching Joseph's painting of her head and naked shoulders before glancing at her. 'My dear girl – you didn't think normal men would buy those pictures, did you? Now, help me with this.'

Afterwards, when they had hung all the paintings to his exacting standard, when she had helped him to stick a card with its title and catalogue number typed neatly by her beside each one, when he had walked around the gallery again just to make sure *that it was right, my darling. Things must be right!* they went back to his rooms and he made her scrambled eggs and sang as he buttered toast: '*I can't do my bottom belly button up* …' She had told him that it was a silly song, one he shouldn't sing because people would think he was insane. He'd frowned, pretending to be perplexed so she'd imagined that tilting top hat again. 'Silly? It's about a young girl about to give birth to a bastard.' He sliced the toast in two with the buttery knife. 'Unless I've got that wrong and she's eaten too much cake. What do you think?' He looked at her. 'Cake or bastard, silly or sad?'

She thought how happy he was, even for him, and that this extra happiness made him look younger and more handsome than he was; actually he was a plain man, most of the time quite ordinary-looking in the way that most men were: average height and build, mousey hair receding a little, his lips a little too thin so that he sometimes tried living with a moustache until she made him shave it off. He was plain compared with Edmund with his lovely body he was so easy in, that smiling face like an angel that had just thought of a risqué joke. Lawrence was plain compared with Matthew who has so handsome. Matthew; thinking of him was as shockingly painful as biting down on your tongue, pain caused by your own greediness, your lack of attention to anything but your own greedy want.

She looked down at the plate of scrambled eggs Lawrence had set down with a flourish in front of her. Paul Harris had made her feel guilty over Matthew and it wasn't fair – Harris was the guilty one. *Matthew* was the guilty one. Wasn't he just as much to blame for what happened? He had hardly pushed her away. Probably he had expected her to behave so badly – still a priest at heart, imagining that all women were harlots.

Perhaps she was a harlot. Wasn't she here, in the worst part of London, taking off her clothes for a living; serving beer for a living; hanging dirty pictures for a living, for Lawrence who said *fuck, fuckity fuckity fuck* just because he dropped a spoon on his kitchen floor? And she had slept with Joseph only because he had actually got on his knees and begged her to, and she had laughed, and been thrilled and touched because he had paint on his face, because he had painted her and made her look so beautiful. And it was all right; she liked Joseph.

And then she met Edmund and when she brought Edmund to the gallery, after he had gone Lawrence had laughed and said, 'Honestly?' Just that: *honestly?* seeing something she didn't.

And Lawrence had said, 'This Matthew fellow. I really do think you should keep away from him.' But sometimes she couldn't take Lawrence seriously because of all the songs and top-hat tipping – even though that was only in her head, even though Lawrence had been in the war and had checked men's feet for rot and been lucky to get off scot-free, although not really scot-free because his dreams were bad and he drank and drank because of the dreams that he said were only that: dreams; *roll me out of bed when I shout. Roll me over in the clover ... Roll me over. Lay me down. Do it again.*

How could you take a man seriously who sang such songs and said such things as, 'I know you're with that boy Edmund, but I really don't think I can go on in this world without you. You'll see sense, eventually.'?

She had been made to see sense. She thought of Joseph, his face alight with the filthy thing he had to tell her about Edmund. She thought of Harris in the pub's back room, how he had apologised without saying what he was apologising for, because how could he? He was an arrogant man in expensive clothes, wearing an expression that must have cost only a little time in front of a mirror, apologising to a barmaid in the back room of a back-street pub. He had apologised but actually he was telling her that he was entitled to Edmund, that he had a more valid claim on him. She had hated Paul Harris more than anyone else in the world then; she hated him still, even if he was Matthew's friend; *because* he was Matthew's friend, making all that guilt rise inside her when what happened hadn't been her fault. She couldn't accept that it was her fault.

She realised she had finished the scrambled eggs Lawrence had made for her, had hardly tasted them, and that he was watching her, a look of concern on his face. He smiled sadly as if he knew she didn't love him. 'Will you stay the night?'

She nodded.

'Will you marry me?'

She laughed in dismay. 'I should, shouldn't I?'

'Yes.' He reached across the table and took her hand. 'In the meantime, shall we go to bed?'

Chapter Twenty

PATRICK IS HERE, IN England. He has been to see me, looking marvellous because he always does. Tall, dark, handsome Patrick, like the prince from a fairy tale – don't ask me which. One where the prince has his heart torn out – although I don't think that happens to princes in stories.

My letter and he crossed, probably somewhere at sea. He was coming here anyway, couldn't keep away, couldn't bear to be apart. Almost as soon as Paul left he was following him. He had fully intended not to. But jealousy is a demanding child, taking your hand, dragging you along, always looking over its shoulder at you, chivvying constantly. Poor Patrick, at his wits' end with worry; *Wits' End*, this could be the name of the prince's home, the palace he sets out from on his quest.

We sat on the lawn in wicker chairs that Patrick carried from the Orangery where no oranges grow. He has oranges in his garden, figs and lemons too. He told me that Paul tends them, that Paul is the gardener. He said, 'Paul misses England, the seasons, the weather, far more than I do.' He laughed, and glanced at me from gazing at the china blue of the English sky. 'I think we've all had enough of cold and wet.'

Oh, I would so agree with that.

I asked him what he was going to do about Paul, *to* Paul. Perhaps I looked too eager to know, sitting on the edge of my seat like that. I had grasped the arms of the chair so hard the basketwork pattern imprinted on my palms. He only said, 'Perhaps they could bring us some tea? Do they do that here?' He has visited me in hospitals where tea is served, others where it is not. He has seen the best and the worst. I told him that here tea was brought out at four o'clock, but that was too late, he had to catch his train to London. He was only on his way; I was only a stopping-off point.

I have to think myself very lucky he came to see me at all, the state he was in over that man he is so obsessed with: Paul. I told him that Paul had visited me and about how he'd behaved. Patrick only nodded and glanced at his watch, no doubt worried about his train. I didn't like this impatience, it's unlike him, so I told him how promiscuous Paul is; he only nodded again, frowning this time as though I had told him I had a headache, and asked if they were treating me well here, if there was anything he could send me to make me more comfortable. I told him that I wouldn't be here much longer and yes, of course, he nodded again and smiled. 'That's good,' he said, 'good.' He was being insufferable, a great big insufferable *butcher* – how could Paul live with a butcher, anyway? It's unseemly, preposterous. His butcher's hands looked as though they were ingrained with blood.

I wasn't in hospital when I first met Patrick. I was living with my sister and Patrick alarmed her, walking up her garden path with his great big butcher's stride. She said, 'Matt – what have you done now?' She thought he was some kind of plain-clothed policeman like those in the detective novels she reads – and he did certainly look like such a man with his inscrutability and quiet clothes, except he doesn't have a policeman's face; he has Gabriel's face, I might add.

I remember we sat alone in my sister's parlour, such a cold, unnecessary room, facing each other across the empty grate. He wrung his hands, I remember that, I couldn't take my eyes off his wringing hands as he said, 'I know you write to Paul. I know you know about him and me. I need you to help me, Matthew – may I call you Matthew? – I need you to help me find a way of getting him out of that prison.'

I thought about jailbreaks: dynamite and rope ladders flung over walls. I had a vision of the jails in western novels, a barred room behind the sheriff's office in some raw, American frontier town. Or perhaps that is only the vision I have now. Of course, I knew about real, English prisons, I had visited men in prison often, and they stank of English bodies too crowded together, of too many men using too few buckets. And the prisoners inside these prisons were not sturdy, sunburnt cowboys fresh from the prairies but grey, weasel-faced men who were stooped and wary, shifty, fidgeting as they said, 'Father, I'm an innocent man, Father.' Those men were very much older than me – or looked it, at least – men who would pray fervently with me, as though they really were afraid of God. They made me think of all the other priests who had prayed with them so ineffectually over the years so that my faith became a little less buoyant and a little more connected to the earth. I knew about prisons, then, and about prisoners. I knew that Paul might die in such a place; I pondered this: he would be a martyr, of sorts.

In my sister's parlour, Patrick wrung his hands and I put my own hands over his, wanting them to still. Still thinking of rope ladders, I asked him how I might help and he only looked lost and desperate and I said, 'There are people we could write to, perhaps. We could campaign for clemency, a reprieve …' He began to cry; I think he had thought of this and didn't think it would work, didn't know why he was sitting there in my sister's little room with the garish picture of the Sacred Heart looking down on us from the chimney piece. He had looked up at Christ and his bloody organ and laughed shortly, drawing his hands from mine and wiping his eyes. 'I'm Catholic. I keep wanting to call you Father …'

I remember I sat back from him.

Fumbling in his pocket for a handkerchief, he said, 'I have written to everyone I can think of, but I was just a sergeant, Matthew, and you were a major, and perhaps you know more people, from the church, the army … And even if you just go to visit him … I'm sorry … I know it's hopeless, but that judge was so biased … That may be something we can work on – and Paul's war record, how he was commended, mentioned in dispatches … You know him as well as I do, I think. He wasn't innocent, I'm not saying that. He did what they said he did …' He blew his nose and shoved the hanky back in his pocket. 'I'm angry with him, Matthew. I don't know how to stop the anger I feel, except by doing something. Christ knows what. Sorry, excuse me. Excuse my language.'

'You love him,' I said, and he looked away from me, his jaw set, his eyes fierce with some fiery feeling he must have struggled with often. He swallowed and his big Adam's apple bobbed in this throat.

'I feel I should go to confession more often.' He looked at me, another man wanting to spew his shame all over me. I should have said *confess then, and give up the sin*.

I remember he stayed for supper. Cottage pie and cabbage. My sister looked at him the whole time as though he had fallen out of the sky.

I wrote letters, I'm not saying I didn't; I went to visit Paul more than once, meeting Patrick afterwards when he would look at me as though I could somehow save them both. But then my sister's doctor decided I wasn't well enough to be at large after some trifling incident in a shop, and I was sent back to hospital. Anyway, everyone wrote to everyone, as far as I can remember – both before, during and after Paul's trial. The judge had been a disgraceful old fool, everyone knew that, but the law is the law, ass or not. Don't go buggering other men in the park's lavatories, that's the moral of the tale, even if you have a distinguished war record as long as your arm, even if they did dig out your eye and gave you a piece of glass instead.

Sitting on the lawn today in the Orangery's chairs, I think Patrick and I must have looked very companionable. He told me I had been a good friend to them both and that I must say if ever I needed anything, anything at all. Such as, I wanted to ask him, such as? What could he and Paul possibly have for me? I only said, 'Paul is fucking someone else. I smelt it on him when he came to see me. You know how he behaves when he's fucking other men – so *full* of it.'

He winced. He looked away and pretended he hadn't heard me, but he had winced so I knew he'd heard. I said, 'You knew, of course – guessed, at least, that he would revert to his old ways. That's why you're here.'

He made such an effort to look at me, his body stiff, as though he had lost all of his lovely grace and fluidity. He's a fine man and he makes me feel grubby. I only said those words to him today because he had angered me and I regretted them once they were out. I know I did speak aloud because he winced. I hated how he winced, showing himself up for what he is. So I said more. I said, 'Will you leave him?'

He laughed so painfully I wanted to weep for him. 'Matthew … No, I won't leave him.'

'You should. He's wicked. You should go home and never have anything to do with him again.'

'You're right, of course.' And then he said something quite surprising. 'He loves you, Matthew. We both do.'

He didn't stay very long. Before he went he carried the chairs back inside. He said, 'Matthew …' and hugged me, his way of telling me he would never ever see me again. I know this; I sensed it in my bones when he crushed me to him, when he patted my back as I pressed my face against his shoulder. 'Matthew,' he said, 'Matthew.' He has a way of making my name sound like *Father*.

Alone, I went to my room. I should have told him about Ann; he wouldn't have felt so sorry for me then. I would have told Paul about her, but he would only think I was making up stories; he doesn't think me capable of fucking a girl.

I have written to Ann. I have asked her to visit me, suggesting that she could bring me records for the gramophone. We could dance together, then. I would have to roll up the carpet in the day room first, move the chairs out of the way, and chase the others out. I could hold her close and lead her in a waltz; we could pretend to be somewhere else, a grand ballroom full of the whirl of dancers, full of the light of a thousand candles. And all the men smart in black tails or dashing in dress uniform, all the women in sweeping skirts, all beautiful, none more so than Ann. I have medals I could wear. I forget this – that I have medals – ribbons and metal all glinting on my chest, a strange kind of ornament for a ball, perhaps, for what they represent: pulling men from a shell hole under fire. Ha! What else was I supposed to do if I wanted to go on living? Was I to say *never mind them*? Even Paul has medals. No, I shall not write any more about Paul. We were at the ball, Ann and I, amongst the dancers.

She used to put her arm through mine.

She used to search out my hand and entwine her fingers with mine; she used to smile as she held on to my hand, as she looked up at me, smiling and happy. She used to look at me and only smile, only see me and smile.

She used not to be afraid.

She used to be a girl I knew.

I mustn't think about her.

I have propped Paul's picture of birds against the wall where I can see it from my bed. I imagine I am standing by the fountain with the birds all around me, that some of them fly on to my outstretched hands to feed from my palm. The fountain splashes my face, the bright drops of water darkening my shirt. I wonder what orange blossom smells of, and what a fresh fig might taste of, and I try very hard to imagine these things and find I can only truly see the birds, their sharp, frail claws, and Paul, who is there, painting his picture, not seeing me, not imagining me at all.

Chapter Twenty-one

EDMUND SAID, 'I HAVE to go to work.' He groaned. 'I don't want to go to work.'

Paul lifted his head from the pillow to look at him. Edmund's head rested on his chest, he was circling his nipple with his thumbnail, never still; this boy was never still. Paul had woken to find Edmund gazing at him, he'd had to tell him to stop, stop looking, honestly, Edmund, and the boy had only laughed and kissed him and told him that looking was allowed and quite natural, and then he had kissed him again more sensually as though he could never have enough of him.

Now Paul said, 'Tell me where you work again?'

'Graham's, *dealers in rare books and first editions*. And terrible books, second-hand books, books that no one will ever, ever read again. And it's very quiet and peaceful and it has the advantage of being only around the corner.' Edmund reached up and touched his mouth. 'And I don't want to go.'

'Then don't.'

'But these are hard times. I need the money.'

'Then go.'

'You're not being very helpful.' He exhaled. Decisively, he said, 'I'll go.' Less decisively, he said, 'Is that all right?'

'Yes, Edmund, of course you must go to work.'

'What will you do?'

Sleep, he thought, *because you have done for me, very near killed me. Even the thought of leaving your bed, of going out of your room, of walking and talking* ... He reached for his cigarettes on the floor, lit one and exhaled smoke at the ceiling. 'I have to go back to the hotel.'

Getting out of bed, Edmund asked, 'Why?'

'I need a change of clothes, a bath –'

Edmund laughed at his pronunciation. 'A *bath*! Where are you from? It's bath.' He looked at him from buttoning his flies. 'Oh. You look hurt. I like your accent. Really. Don't look like that.' He frowned. 'Where are you from, anyway?'

'Have you heard of Newcastle?'

'Coal.'

'Just a bit further south.'

'Where?'

'Edmund … I shall say bath as you do in future, all right? I shall mind my ps and qs.' He got up and dressed in the clothes he had taken off on Saturday night when they returned from that club; he hadn't dressed since, and now it was Tuesday morning and Edmund had to go to work in a bookshop and he had to go back to the hotel and see if there was any letter from Patrick; he thought of sending him a telegram: *I may stay longer. Stop. I may need more time. Stop. I may be able to live without you after all. Stop.*

He stepped around Edmund to put on his tie in front of the mirror above the chest of drawers. Laid out on top of the drawers were Edmund's brush and comb, a saucer where he kept loose change, his soap and shaving brush, his razor, these last beside a folded towel, all ready to be taken down the hall to the shared bathroom.

The orderliness of the little room, even the bookcase where the books were lined up level and alphabetically, had surprised him; when Edmund had gone out briefly yesterday to buy bread and milk and tea, he had got up from the bed and looked through his books, every one about art or an artist's life. He'd opened a book at random, saw a glossy reproduction of Van Gogh's *Starry Night*; he closed the book, put it back carefully, and looked at the pictures on Edmund's walls.

Some of these pictures had been cut from the books, he'd guessed, and framed like photographs: Turner's views of the Thames, a horse by Reynolds. Edmund seemed taken by Renoir, Monet and Manet. French beaches, French men in boats in boaters and moustaches, French women in striped muslin dresses and parasols; blues and golds and whites, sea and sky merging and punctuated by sails. And then there was the Canaletto, and he had stood for a while, staring at this picture that he liked less than the others, that seemed out of place, in the wrong room, and he had thought that perhaps fate had made Edmund place it there, so that he could come along and be prompted to say things he otherwise wouldn't have said.

In front of Edmund's mirror he began to knot his tie and Edmund put his arms around his waist, drawing him close. 'Shall you meet me for lunch?'

'Where?' He met his eye in the mirror and smiled because Edmund looked so relieved. It seemed that even after all they had said to each other Edmund still thought he was about to say thank you and goodbye. 'Where shall I meet you?'

'There's a café on Percy Street near the gallery. It's nothing much –'

'Not the Ritz?'

'Nor the Savoy. But I'll buy you a bun, or bacon and eggs?'

'Good enough for a man who says *bath*?'

'I'm sorry. I'm an idiot.' He gazed at him in the mirror. 'Your voice is lovely. And you make me sound like a chinless wonder … Which I am, I suppose. I'm from Kensington, lived there all my life. My people still live there.' He smiled shyly. 'I don't go far, haven't *been* far.' He brushed his lips against his shoulder and stepped back. 'I have to go. The café is called *Bright's*. Say half past twelve?'

Before he'd left for England, Patrick had asked, 'Will you go to Thorp?'

'I don't know. No.'

'Maybe you should try to see Bobby.'

Paul felt that this was a challenge: go and see your son, be brave, and if you can't be brave then face up to losing him, come home and start to live without making both our lives a misery. At their table in the courtyard, eating the supper Patrick had prepared, Paul had put down his fork. 'They've told Bobby I'm dead. You think I should rise from my grave?'

'He's still a baby –'

'He's four, Patrick. You know he's four.'

Patrick had only held his gaze, the tension between them worse at this time of day when he had been working for hours and hours without stopping and only wanted to go back to work; but Patrick insisted he stop, sit down, eat, *eat with him*. Patrick didn't even necessarily want him to talk to him, just sit at this table in the relative cool of the late evening beneath the fig tree and later go to bed. Go to bed, and lie beneath the thin sheet watching Patrick undress; Patrick would climb into bed beside him and pull him close, murmuring, 'Why are you so tense? You never relax,' rolling him on to his front, kneeling astride his back, massaging the tension out of his shoulders and arms. Then they would talk, but only about the day-to-day things, of the customers who haggled with Patrick at the market where he butchered the lambs, of the men he worked with, and drank mint tea with in the cafés after work. And if they made love, Paul would sometimes think that he could smell the blood on him. Even though Patrick was always clean sometimes all he could smell was blood and he thought that it must be his mind playing tricks, that this stink of blood was something to do with the fear he still felt, because Tangiers scared him, the heat and the noise and the smells and the crowds, and being so far away scared him, because he had lost his grip on the life he'd imagined for himself before the war: the life of an Englishman in England in a house with a garden, with his wife and child.

Walking back to his hotel, Paul thought about Margot, as he often did when he was alone; he missed her, and sometimes he believed that missing his wife showed on his face and that Patrick would be hurt; he felt he hurt Pat enough without allowing him to glimpse this particular sense of loss. And it was quite particular – he missed the certain way she looked at him when he came home from work, smiling, worried, questioning, *was it all right?* She had known he couldn't teach a classroom of boys, couldn't even keep them under control, and this smile she had for him when he came through the door made him feel that his uselessness didn't matter so much, he would find something else to do and she would support him. But more than that, more than just particulars, he missed her voice, her softness, the smell of her, and he missed the pride he felt when he walked down the street beside her. Odd, this pride, more like hubris, thinking about it now – he should have been more circumspect, he shouldn't have allowed himself to become the kind of man who believed he could be anyone.

At first he had been that careful man; at first he had hardly believed that she'd consented to marry him. Couldn't she see what he was? Not only a one-eyed wreck; not only a feeble stand-in for his brother but worse than that – couldn't she see? Her innocence shouldn't have surprised him as much as it did, but he couldn't help being astonished by her, astonished again when his body responded to hers.

He stopped walking, fumbling in his pockets for cigarettes as he remembered the charged quality of his happiness with his wife; he'd been given Robbie's life to lead, granted his dearest childhood wish. But all the time it was as though he was waiting for his brother to come back, to take over as he always had, saying, 'What the devil are you doing now, Paul? Out of the way, for God's sake.' Where was Robbie when he needed him?

He lit a cigarette, inhaling deeply as he walked on. He was beginning to know his way without worrying that he would become lost. It seemed to him that he had never travelled more than a mile or two in London since he got off the train at Waterloo. And Kensington wasn't far, he knew. A cock stride and Edmund would be with his family, his *people*. Bath not *bath*. Edmund thought he had hurt his feelings by remarking on his accent, but he had only been surprised, brought up short he supposed. Edmund out-classed him; he wasn't used to that.

He stopped at a tobacconist's and bought cigarettes, a quarter of mint imperials and a newspaper. He had time to kill; after going back to the hotel, if the weather remained fine, he would find one of those squares to sit in; if not he would go to a museum or gallery; or he would simply walk around, wander to Buckingham Palace, see the guards on parade, on horse back, riding down the Mall if he was lucky. There would be the clatter of hooves, the gleam of breastplates and swords, of polished boots; the controlled, straight-backed rise and fall of the riders. He would have stayed in the army, if he could have, he liked the discipline, and the knowing where one stood, the rightness of it. 'I think you're mad,' Patrick would say if he ever mentioned this. 'Insane. Jesus. Fucking army.' He hardly ever used foul language, but it was always the *fucking* army, he was always glad to be fucking out of it.

He walked on, a mint dissolving on his tongue. A policeman was walking towards him and he felt the urge to stop and stare into a shop window until he'd gone by. Still, his knees had weakened, fear dancing its fandango in his guts. He wouldn't think of his arrest, of prison, of one particular warder saying softly: 'Get up you little bugger, get up, get up, I know you can get up.' This man, Barker, spoke as though he was singing sometimes – singing a chorus with all the repeats. He could get up if he made a great effort; to his knees first, holding on to his bed, pushing himself up. But his legs would be jelly and it would be hard to stand to attention, shoulders back, head up, hands by your sides: the governor's coming, the governor's coming, stand up straight you little bugger, stand up straight or I'll kick your fucking arse into next week. But hadn't he already done that? Tripped him so he fell back into his cell, kicked him when he was down. No, that's not kicking your arse into next week. Keep up, stand up, head up, eyes front! Sing-song screaming in your face, so close the spittle flecks you and you smell his breath: onions and cheese, and his eyes are big and bulging and wild like those of a frightened horse.

Paul stopped and stared into the window of a music shop. The policeman's reflection moved across the glass and he was gone. There was a violin, lying in its open case; there was a music stand, a score set up. He'd thought that the governor might have noticed his black eye, noticed that he was shaking so, but the man was only doing his occasional rounds. He supposed he didn't see him at all. The governor had walked past his cell door, was framed in it for an instant, and then he was gone and Barker was whispering in his ear, I'm coming back, don't you worry, don't you worry, I'm coming back.

Paul rested his forehead against the shop's window and the glass was cold and soothing; the mint was a sharp sliver now, almost nothing but sweetness that would make his tongue sore if he ate too many. He realised he stank, as unwashed as he had been in prison; he thought of their bath at home and how Patrick would wash his back, and how he would wash his in return, his beautiful tanned skin slippery smooth beneath his soapy hands.

'Do you think God is watching us?' Patrick had turned to him, hair and face wet because he had just surfaced, drops of water on his eyelashes; he was smiling, showing such white teeth in his darkly tanned face. 'Do you think he's watching?'

'I hope so. Taking a good look.'

'Owes us.'

'Yes.'

'The bells of hell go ting a ling a ling.'

'We know because we've heard.'

Patrick grasped his face; he laughed and there was joy in voice and his eyes shone with an overwhelming passion. 'Christ Almighty I love you!'

And prison warder Barker whispered, what are you so afraid of, Harris? What what what? Because I can only kill you once so what you fucking shaking for? What what what? And he wanted to tell him that he was afraid of everything, everything, to confess to this man who had power of death over him that he was afraid of everything, but he didn't have a voice, there were no words for how afraid he was.

And Patrick said, 'You're all right. I'm here, I'm here,' sing-song too, but a lullaby: 'Go to sleep, I'm here, go to sleep, I'm here.' And *Christ Almighty I love you!* – the force in his voice startling Paul so that Patrick had frowned, his wet hands holding his face more gently, saying more softly, 'I love you, God help me.'

Paul stepped away from the music shop window. His forehead had left a mark on the glass and he wiped it off with his handkerchief; can't go around leaving marks, some kind of evidence. He walked on, lighting another cigarette as he crossed the road, dodging the buses and the taxis, moving as if he had purpose, somewhere to go like the men and women walking around him and past him, quicker, more purposeful; he should keep up and not think; perhaps think about Edmund, be kind to himself and think about Edmund.

Edmund. What was there to think of except he should confess everything to him, as he'd tried to the night they'd returned from the nightclub. But that night Edmund had worried him – there had been something distant about the boy so that he'd had to keep a tight rein on himself so as not to say too much, although he'd said enough, almost too much.

He was always ready to tell him about Patrick; to speak his name in Edmund's presence had become a compulsion he had to keep in check. But sitting on Edmund's bed he had seen the Canaletto and been transported back to Venice, and the fear he'd felt by the side of that freezing canal he'd felt again: he had lost Patrick and would never find him again and he would die. And so he'd had to talk of Patrick just to remind himself of the life they had together. Yet this talking now seemed a kind of boasting, a nasty little betrayal of both men, even if he didn't believe in the love that both professed so easily.

'I love you,' Edmund had told him again, after the sex was done with, and he had said all right so that he would be quiet, so that they wouldn't have to talk any more, already ashamed of everything he'd said. And they had sex again, but this time slowly and tenderly, or at least Edmund had been slow and tender, as though he felt he should minister to him as a nurse might, tending wounds that were too painful to be touched without the utmost care. He had only accepted the boy's ministrations passively, his guilt making him useless, until at last Edmund had whispered, *tell me what to do,* and there had been despair in his voice and desperation, as though he was ministering to the dying, and so he had forced himself to respond, to make less of his guilt for Edmund's sake. He stopped him and took over their love making and Edmund had been relieved so that he felt his heart would break for this boy because he was so young, so flawless; more than that, there was something in his eyes he hadn't seen before and he realised that it was fear: perhaps Edmund didn't want to be this man. Yet, this morning, in the bright sunlight, he had seemed happy; he had seemed to want him all the more.

Paul walked on, almost at his hotel now, almost breathless

so that he slowed. He thought how he would bathe and put on cologne and dress in clean clothes and polish his shoes so that they shone; and he would look at himself carefully in the full-length mirror set in the wardrobe door and he would part and comb his hair which was too short, which he would allow to grow a little, for Edmund. For Edmund he would look less like a convict; he would put on a show – hadn't this kind of showmanship worked during the war, before he met Patrick? He quickened his pace again, eager to begin this transformation.

Chapter Twenty-two

BARNES ASKED, 'DID YOU have a nice lunch?'

Edmund grinned. 'Splendid, thank you.'

'Splendid? How splendid. Where did you go? I shall go if it's so good.'

'Only to Bright's.'

Barnes snorted. 'I'm very pleased you're so easily pleased. Very pleased you're at all pleased, in fact. It seems lately that the gloom of the past months has lifted. Hoorah.'

Glancing at him from shelving a pile of books, Edmund said, 'Do you know places around Newcastle, south of Newcastle?'

'*Everywhere* is south of Newcastle.'

'No, seriously … I suppose I mean towns around there … You're from the north, aren't you?'

'I'm from Leeds. A place which is, undoubtedly, south of Newcastle. Why the interest?'

'No reason.'

'He could be talking about Durham, of course.'

Edmund kept his eyes on the books. 'He?'

'The man you're trying not to talk about. The very gorgeous man I saw you with the other night. Come to think of him, he did have a very *northern* air. Rather dangerous-looking, I think. A northern Barbarian.'

Edmund felt his face colour. He had put all the books on the shelves, straightened them, there was nothing left to do; unable to go on just staring at the spines, he brushed past Barnes and went to the shop counter. A customer came in and he almost leapt on the man, serving him with an enthusiasm he had never found for his work before. All the time he sensed Barnes watching him. When the customer had gone he made himself say, 'He's just a friend.'

Barnes laughed as though this was genuinely funny.

'Listen –'

'Edmund, it's all right. No one thinks any less of you, actually the reverse. So, tell me, what did you think of the singer in the club? He's overrated in my opinion. Good dress sense, though, beautiful bias-cut frocks.' Barnes came to stand a little closer to him. Gently he said, 'Tell me to be quiet if you will, but I do have to say be careful. I've known men like that, all charm one minute and the next … well … Maybe next he'll do more than black your eye.'

Edmund laughed in astonishment. 'He didn't, that wasn't him –'

'Gosh, we are living a busy life.'

'It's not like that.'

Barnes patted his arm. 'I'm only saying. If it wasn't him who blacked your eye then it had something to do with him.' He sighed. 'I know the way of it, Edmund. I've been around too long. No doubt he's married. Men like him – good-looking, hard-faced – are as faithless as can be.'

'He's not married.'

Barnes snorted. 'Sure about that, are you?' He sighed. 'All right, that's enough out of us both. Fetch the books in from the front. Let's make a head start on closing up.'

That lunchtime Paul had been waiting for him in Bright's, sitting at a table near the door. As he'd sat down opposite him, Paul said, 'I've ordered egg and chips twice. Be quick to tell the man if you want something else.'

'No, that's fine.' He'd glanced at Bright behind the counter, all twenty stone of him, his apron greasy as ever, his sleeves rolled up to reveal the smudgy anchors tattooed on his forearms. What had he made of Paul? Nothing, he supposed; he had to keep reminding himself that not everyone looked at him as he did, or as Barnes did. He imagined Paul actually blacking his eye, finally turning all that pent-up anger on him. He couldn't imagine defending himself.

Paul had said, 'How was your morning?'

'Fine.' He'd smiled at him and because Bright's back was turned he risked touching his hand. 'Yours?'

'I went to the National Gallery.'

'You didn't have much time – you could spend a week in there –'

'Then maybe we'll go back together. Take a tent and a camping stove.'

Paul had shaved; he had bathed, just as he said he would; Edmund could just about smell the delicious scent of him above that of frying chips. He looked as polished and immaculate as he had looked on the steps of St Paul's, when he'd had to stop himself grinning with pleasure at the sight of him. This was the dressed-up, detached Paul, although this incarnation had a slight variation, like an extra pin tuck on an evening shirt: this one made jokes and smiled back at him and touched his foot with his under the table. Quietly, smiling, Paul had said, 'What time do you finish work?' and Edmund had at once had the beginning of an erection.

Lifting up a box of books outside the shop, Edmund thought how Paul had finished his meal, all but a few of the chips. 'How can you leave chips, for God's sake?'

'You eat them.' Paul had lit a cigarette and grinned at him. 'You're a growing boy.'

Don't look at me like that, he had wanted to say, or speak with that inflection; don't be funny in that queer's way.

Carrying a box of books inside, he stopped short, the box heavy in his arms; he concentrated on its weight, the bulk of it hard against him. Barnes was queer. His friend Andrew was queer. The men in that club were queer. And Paul. The box of books might have been empty, weightless, he could only think of this, the idea that he didn't think of himself as anything like them, like Barnes, like Andrew; like Paul. He could almost laugh with the absurdity of it. He thought of his father telling him about French letters and scrupulous girls; he thought of Ann, but the fact that he had made love to her seemed absurd too; his relationship with her belonged to a life he was walking away from, as though it was a room he'd stopped renting.

He put the box of books down and stared at it. He thought of Paul who was ordinary, really, a man he would have passed on the street and not seen because he was so undistinguished, a slight, insubstantial man. Paul didn't even behave in ways that would cause him to despise him; the way certain types of effeminate boys had behaved at school. And if Paul did behave like those boys, it was only sometimes. He thought about those sometimes: how could he love a *sometimes* man? How could he love a man? He must be mistaken. How could he have made such a mistake, as though he didn't know himself, his own body, his own heart and mind?

Barnes had come outside and was watching him.

'Edmund?'

'I'm sorry. I have to go.'

'Wait.' Barnes caught his arm. 'Edmund … Listen, think about what you're doing.'

He shrugged him off. 'It's none of your business.'

'He's a user, Edmund.'

'I don't know what you're talking about.'

'No. All right.' Suddenly he said, 'It's just that I like you, Edmund. I do. And when I saw you with such an obviously self-centred –'

'As I say, I don't know what you're talking about.'

Barnes sighed. 'Then I'll just say this – we're not all like him. Some of us – *most* of us – are faithful and honest.'

Despite himself, Edmund said, 'You don't know anything about him.'

'I know what's written all over his face. I know …' More vehemently, he went on, 'I just know, that's all. Don't let him eat your heart out.'

Edmund laughed; he had never felt so much scorn for another man. '*Eat my heart out*? For Christ's sake –'

Barnes picked up a box of books. 'Go, if you want. Throw yourself at him. With a bit of luck he'll be so appalled at your enthusiasm he'll fuck off before he's completely wasted you.'

Walking towards Paul's hotel, Edmund suppressed the urge to go back to the shop and have it out with Barnes. He imagined grabbing the man by his lapels, pushing him up against a wall of bookcases, lifting him off his feet in his outrage. He thought he knew him! Barnes thought he knew everything about him and Paul just from seeing them together in that nightclub. Edmund slowed his pace; he was breathless with anger. He glanced back toward the shop and saw a customer go in. He couldn't cause such a scene. No one he respected ever caused scenes – such bad form. He thought of his father, always so calm, never losing his temper. As far as he could guess his father had never felt like this, so full of rage it was all he could do not to punch a wall.

His father had said, 'I'll give you a year, Edmund. A year to do just as you like – to paint, if you must, but to be out from under the wing.' He'd smiled. 'Make mistakes – tilt at those windmills, eh? And then we'll see. If after this year you would still prefer to go to art school instead of Oxford, well, so be it.'

He hadn't painted for weeks. Since he'd met Paul he hadn't even thought about painting, or about anything but him. He had thought one time after they'd made love, when Paul was relaxed and not so waspishly edgy, that he and Paul might discuss art together. *Art*! He almost laughed. What kind of discussion would that be? A painful discussion, awkward and faltering and exposing them both as frauds: Paul because he tried too hard and him because he didn't try hard enough.

Edmund drew breath in an effort to steady himself. He thought about Paul's paintings, seen so briefly at that exhibition. Perhaps they were better than he remembered; he didn't like to think about it because perhaps they were worse. And perhaps Paul really was worthless; he knew he was faithless. He thought of Patrick – he knew this man, the noble, long-suffering lover, so much an archetype that he could believe Paul had invented him.

He should go back to his room, be alone to think: he hadn't been alone for days – Paul had taken over his life, taken over his thoughts, invaded him like a virus, leaving him weak. He should go home, would if he was sensible. Instead, he walked on, towards Paul's hotel.

Chapter Twenty-three

THE RECEPTIONIST SAID, 'NO, sir, we have no Mr Harris staying with us.'

'Yes, yes you have. He told me he was staying here, at the Queen's Hotel. Please, please check again. Paul Harris.'

The man glanced down at his ledger, a brief glance, he had already checked after all. 'No sir. Not even a Mr *Paul* Harris.'

George looked at Iris. She was holding Bobby in her arms because he was tired, his head against her shoulder, she was smiling and murmuring in his ear, not panicked as George was, not frantically wondering what to do. Desperately he said, 'I know he said this is his hotel, it's so near to the gallery ... The Queen's ... This is the Queen's?'

'Yes sir.'

'Listen, he's a young man, slight ...' How could he describe his son; he looked to Iris, but she was setting Bobby down, steadying him, taken up with him. On one breath he said, 'He has a false eye ...'

'Oh. We have a gentleman ... with ... yes, but his name is Mr Law. Francis Law.'

George felt as though he might collapse with relief. 'Yes. Mr Law. It's a name he uses ...' The receptionist raised his eyebrows. Beside him, Iris touched his hand.

'Perhaps we could book a room, George. Bobby's so tired.'

He looked down at his grandson who had been so good on the train, a child who hardly ever said a word, still less asked a question, trusting these two adults who had whisked him away from his mother. George had a sense that the world had stopped behaving as it should; he had stepped outside his life and he was lost and if Bobby started to cry for Margot he would cry

191

too; Iris would have to contend with both of them, man and boy.

He crouched down in front of Bobby. 'Well, we're here …' He couldn't think what else to say, only lifted him into his arms. Turning to the receptionist, he said, 'Do you have a room for the three of us?'

'Yes, I think so, sir.' The man looked down at his book again and George thought of St Peter at the gates of heaven and wanted to laugh, a feeling of hysteria rising inside him. 'A double room, we can put up a bed for your son. What name is it?'

'Harris,' Iris said. 'Mr and Mrs Harris.'

She had been there, on the station platform, holding Bobby's hand. He'd thought only that she had come to see him off, not seeing her suitcase at first. When she'd told him of her plans he had only stared at her.

She had told Daniel she was going to her aunt's in Carlisle, taking Bobby because Margot was tired and ill with morning sickness, and Margot was grateful. There, all arranged: tell the same lie to everyone and you won't be caught out. 'And I think Paul should see Bobby one last time, perhaps we owe him that.' She'd taken his hand. 'Besides, I can't let you go yet.'

'What if he finds out?'

She had shrugged.

As they travelled on the train, he had thought about that shrug and wondered at it. She had caught him watching her and smiled and didn't seem to be surprised at all at her own audacity. He thought how marvellous she was and had laughed, turning away to look out of the train window because she was too marvellous for words. He had seen his reflection in the glass and hardly recognised himself.

George sat Bobby on the reception desk and signed the hotel's registration card. The receptionist smiled and said, 'Here's Mr Law now, sir.'

Iris said, 'I'll take Bobby up to our room, George. You talk to Paul.'

George took a step towards his son, afraid that Paul might

faint with the shock of seeing them. There was a couch opposite the reception desk, and he took Paul's arm to lead him to it, but Paul shrugged him off, staring at the stairs that Iris and Bobby had just ascended out of sight. He made to follow them but George said quickly, 'Wait. We'll give Iris time to settle him.'

He looked at him. 'I need to see him now.'

'Paul, think a little about what you might say to him first.'

'*Say*?' He seemed to panic. 'What shall I say? Will he recognise me, do you think?'

George hesitated. 'No. No, I don't think so.'

'Because they told him I was dead ...' He shook his head as if to clear it. His fingers went to his eye and he glanced back towards the doors on to the street. 'I don't want to frighten him –'

'You won't!' George laughed as though the idea of Bobby being afraid of Paul was preposterous, even as he knew that the child would be afraid of this man. He felt as though he was seeing Paul for the first time as a stranger might see him, perhaps even as Daniel had seen him: a highly strung, unpredictable boy. Gently he said, 'Paul, try to be calm –'

'Calm? You do this to me and say I should be calm? Is Margot here too?'

'No, she doesn't know –'

Paul's voice rose in alarm. 'She'll be worried!'

'No, she knows he's safe with his grandmother. Paul ... Iris and I thought you should see him.'

Paul slumped down onto the couch. He glanced towards the stairs and then back to him. 'I wouldn't have recognised him. He's grown up.'

'Still a baby –'

'No. A little boy. He'll wonder who I am. What will I say to him?'

George sat down beside him, lost for words. He hadn't expected to feel so deflated, so utterly foolish. He'd been thinking only of himself, himself and Iris, not even Iris alone but how she was with him, away from her ordinary, responsible life. He hadn't thought of Paul, still less of Bobby. Ashamed, he said, 'I'm sorry.'

'I want to run away.' Paul laughed painfully. 'And I want to go to him now and crush him to me –' He looked again to the door out on to the street. 'I should go – if you're staying here I'll find another hotel – best if I go. Do you think so? Do you think I should leave?'

George gazed at him; he saw the child he once was, given to these agonising indecisions, always afraid of doing the wrong thing, the bad thing; he had never known a child to be so wracked by his conscience, made so timid by the fear of self-reproach. He'd always wanted to tell him not to be afraid in this way, but instead to make sure to do only what was right and honest, but he could never bring himself to be so forthright with Paul; even as a child Paul had known his life would never be so straightforward.

Paul stood up suddenly, so agitated it seemed that he might run up the stairs. 'I'll go to him now,' he said. 'Now before I change my mind.'

Iris buttoned Bobby's coat. She looked at Paul. 'You'll take good care of him?'

'Of course.'

George saw how impatient Paul was to go; he didn't look at Iris, it seemed he could hardly see either of them, just Bobby, his impatience animating him so that he almost looked like a child again, a nervous twelve-year-old boy. This boy held out his hand to Bobby, who was shy and hung on to Iris's hand. Gently she said, 'Go on, Bobby. You'll have a lovely time.'

When they had gone, Iris said, 'He looks terrible.'

'Yes.'

'What did they do to him in that prison?'

'Iris …' He sat down on the bed; if she said any more he would cry and that would be shaming. She had looked so shocked when she saw Paul, and he had forgotten that the last time she had seen him he was just her daughter's husband – not ordinary, exactly, but beginning to be less … *odd*, he supposed. When Iris had last seen Paul he was Bobby's father and more than anything else being Bobby's father made Paul *right*: a twenty-three-year-old man struggling like any other with the responsibilities of a family.

Iris sat beside him. 'George … I'm sorry … He's fine. I'm sure he's fine.'

George stood up. He went to the window and there was Paul, holding Bobby's hand, walking away. He imagined running after them because suddenly he didn't trust Paul not to keep walking, to never come back because why would he? Why would he lose his son again? *Go,* he thought. *Take him. He's yours. He was always yours more than he was anyone's.* He put a hand against the wall to steady himself. Another man's wife was watching him from a hotel bed, outside the afternoon sun was shining as if it would never give up on the day and he had run away from home.

He felt Iris's hand on his arm. 'Come and lie down. You're tired, such a long day …'

She led him to the bed; she took off his shoes and lay down beside him, taking his hand in hers.

George slept and Iris lay still, not wanting to move in case she woke him. She felt she should get up, wash and change because she smelt of the train; her hands felt sticky, her feet sore from walking from the station to this place, this shabby little hotel hidden away down a back street.

She shouldn't have brought Bobby here; *she* shouldn't be here: Daniel was bound to find out; Bobby would say something to his mother. She breathed in, held her breath, exhaled. Margot wouldn't give her away; she had to count on that, on her daughter's need to keep the peace. And perhaps Bobby wouldn't say anything at all; he was such a quiet little boy. All the same, she had told him that this was a game and that the fun of the game was not to tell anyone, not even Mummy, that Granddad had come on this trip too. Wasn't that fun? Wasn't that wicked to ask a child to lie? Not lying, not really, just a game, a not telling. And perhaps Margot suspected, anyway. She knew Paul was in England. She'd asked her, 'Do you think he'll come to Thorp and try to see Bobby?' Her face had such a look on it, hopeful and horrified at once.

George mumbled something from his sleep, frowning,

anxious. She turned her head to look at him because he was a fine-looking man and there would be few chances to look at him soon enough. It was masochistic to come here with him, knowing that she had to give him up, and yet she wouldn't regret it, even if Daniel found out and never spoke to her again.

She gazed at George; the women of Thorp would quite envy her this gazing, even though it made her feel rather silly and self-indulgent. The women on the parish council, on the church-cleaning rota, those who had volunteered with her during the war to serve tea to soldiers on Darlington Station, all of them had a good word for Dr Harris; some had a fancy for him, too, always a smile in their voices when they mentioned his name. At least, they had behaved like this before Paul shamed them all so badly. Before this George was always *poor Dr Harris* and none of them understood why he had never remarried.

She had said to him once, laughing, 'Mrs Simms wonders why you remain single.' He had only shaken his head, exasperated; she'd been told by others that more than one mother had thrown a daughter at him in the early years after Grace's death. But men grow older and set in their ways, and their children grow older too, from adorable little boys into awkward adolescents, although perhaps there had been a brief time, when both George's sons were in uniform, that the little family became glamorous again. A brief time, when Thorp could overlook Paul's *manner* because he was fighting, one of the brave boys; and in that uniform he almost looked like anyone, like his brother. But the fighting ended and Paul came home.

When she saw Paul walk into the hotel, before he noticed her or his father and son, she had wanted to hide away; she wouldn't be able to speak to him, or behave in any normal way around him at all: he was utterly changed. The boy she'd been expecting, the ironic, kind boy she had grown to like, was nowhere to be seen in this man. This man would make her want to look away if he passed her on the street; she would be afraid of him, he was so obviously possessed with anger; and his hair was so short, his face reduced to sharply defined cheekbones as though he had been planed from wood. Always slim, now he was thin, angular, hard-looking, full of an energy that made him seem as though he was about to launch himself into a fight. Despite his beautiful clothes, the fine cut and expense of his coat and suit and shoes, he was a thug.

She had thought of lifting Bobby down from the desk and running away with him, back to King's Cross, home, away from this man she didn't recognise as Bobby's gentle father. And then he had seen her; before he saw his father and son he'd seen her and looked as if he would kill her.

Perhaps she shouldn't have allowed him to take Bobby out of her sight. But she had never seen a man change so quickly from hardness to soft, smiling joy. Bobby transformed him; she could see the old Paul again, although his voice was rougher, as though he had to live down to his appearance, but soft again when he spoke to Bobby. He had knelt in front of him, *'Hello Bob,'* and cupped his face in his hand. She had always known how much he had loved him – of course he had loved him. But this was love like no other she had ever seen before. Bobby had turned to her, unsure of this man whose face shone with such intense feeling.

So as not to disturb George, Iris got up as quietly as she could and went to the window. There was the narrow street they had walked down, unsure that this dingy place could really be their destination. The building opposite was an unbroken mass of red brick punctuated with haphazard windows and doorways that might open on to anything – a warehouse, a factory, a workhouse, perhaps. The city sprawled beyond these buildings, all its shops and restaurants and hotels, parks and palaces, all its bridges, all the places made famous by nursery rhymes and songs. Paul was out there with Bobby; she might never see them again, and then Margot would be lost to her too, and Daniel.

Softly she said, 'Don't come back,' to test the words out, the feeling behind them, but there was only hollowness; Margot was her whole life; Paul knew this. Paul would bring Bobby back because he *was* Paul, and not that man she'd glimpsed in the hotel's lobby.

* * *

Bobby whispered, 'That man is very fat.'

'Yes. He is. Perhaps he ate too much ice cream.' Paul took out his handkerchief and wiped a chocolate ice cream smudge from Bobby's mouth. Quietly he said, 'Perhaps you shouldn't stare at him, Bob.'

'He has drawings on his arms.'

Paul smiled at him, and then glanced towards Bright, who was smearing tables with a grubby cloth. 'Those drawings are called tattoos.'

Bobby looked at his empty ice cream sundae glass, its long spoon resting on the glacé cherry at the bottom. 'What will he have in it?' Bright had asked. 'Everything,' Paul had answered. And now he worried that it had been too much. He reached out but stopped himself from stroking his son's hair. 'Are you all right, Bob?'

He didn't look up, only touched the spoon, making it clink against the white, pink and chocolate brown smeared glass. 'Thank you for my ice cream.'

'My pleasure.'

He wanted to hold him, to sit him on his knee and hold him very close and breathe in the smell of his hair and skin; kiss him over and over and say I love you, I'm sorry. Instead, he was sitting beside him in Bright's Café where there could be no such carrying on. He could only look at him and stop himself from stroking his hair because Bobby didn't like him to, he flinched away a little, but such a little. It seemed as though Bobby felt that he had to endure whatever grown-ups did and to duck away from them was impolite.

'He's very shy,' his father had said to him in the hotel room. Shy because he held on to Iris's hand and didn't seem to want to let go. But Iris had fetched his coat and buttoned Bobby up in it, saying, 'This is Francis, Bobby. He knew your Daddy very well and he would like to take you out.' And then she had looked at him pointedly, as if he might challenge this explanation, and asked if he would take good care of him. He had pretended hardly to hear her, only said *of course* and only because he was so desperate to take Bobby away and not show how much he hated her, in case she stopped him.

Bright began to wipe their table. 'How was that, Sunny Jim? Want another? Go on – ask your dad if you can have another.'

Bobby stared down at the table and Bright laughed and ruffled his hair roughly. 'Maybe Dad would like a cup of tea?'

'No, thank you.' Paul stood up and held out his hand to Bobby. Turning to Bright he asked, 'Is there a park around here, somewhere he'd enjoy?'

'Enjoy?' Bright laughed. 'He's getting spoilt, is he?'

'Yes.'

He continued to wipe the table. 'There's nothing round here for kids. You'd best get on a bus, see where the fancy takes you.'

On the street outside the café, Paul crouched in front of Bobby. 'I'm a bit lost, Bob. I don't live here, you see...' He gazed at him, searching his face. He looked exhausted; he wanted to take him back to his room, tuck him up in bed, lie beside him and read the stories George had read to him. He would watch over him as he slept and when he woke up … When he woke up, then what? He would take him away, home.

Paul touched Bobby's cheek, imagining this; they would be together and Bobby wouldn't have to wear the stiff wool coat and schoolboy flannel shorts they'd dressed him in even though he was just a little boy. He wouldn't have to wear those shoes like a grown man's shoes in miniature, those thick, itchy-looking socks showing off his white knees. In Tangiers Bobby could run around barefoot and his skin would become brown, his hair becoming as blond as it had been when he was born. They would be together and he would take care of him … He would cry for his mother, he would miss her, but he'd get over that – he'd never had a mother himself after all, just a father, just George. He hadn't needed a mother. He and Patrick would look after him; Patrick wouldn't mind, he never minded anything he did. He imagined opening the door to their house, calling Pat's name as he held Bobby's hand, and Pat would appear. He tried to imagine the expression on his face. Impossible.

He searched Bobby's face, as though this child might all at once tell him what to do. But he only hung his head, a confused little boy.

'You're tired, aren't you? Do you want to go back to Granddad?'

He nodded.

'All right.' He straightened up from his crouch. 'It's not far, is it? We'll be back in no time.'

No time. He held Bobby's hand, small and soft and ice-cream sticky and thought of things he might say to him. He should say something, make the most of this time; he wanted Bobby to remember him, didn't he? But he couldn't think of a single thing, the street was too grey, too bleak, there was nothing to point at, to remark on, there was just the two of them and no fat men or ice cream in funny glasses with awkward spoons and wasted cherries. He wouldn't have eaten that cherry, either; he'd always hated glacé fruit. Eventually he asked, 'What do you like to eat best in the whole world, Bob?'

'Ice cream.'

'Ah. I suppose that was a silly question?' He smiled at him. 'Is ice cream better than cake?'

Bobby shrugged. At last he said, 'I like chocolate.'

'Me too. When I was your age, Granddad –' he hesitated and corrected himself, 'my daddy used to keep chocolate and sweeties in a tin on a very high shelf and one day my brother Rob …' Again he hesitated, wondering how he hadn't realised how difficult this would be, or how Rob's name would make his voice catch. Bobby glanced up at him. Quickly he went on, 'My brother and I would take a chair and piles of books and use them to climb up … And Rob could just about, *just about* reach, if he stretched really hard … I'd worry he would fall …' He smiled at him again, remembering Rob and his horrifying bravery. 'I'd be scared he'd fall but I never tried to stop him from trying to get those sweets.'

'Were you naughty?'

'Oh very.' He squeezed his hand lightly. 'I bet you're not naughty?'

He shook his head.

'Do you play in Granddad's garden?'

Again he shook his head.

200

'Oh you should! It's a lovely garden.' He forgot himself, saying, 'I built a tree house – right at the end behind the vegetable patch, in a sycamore tree – the tree with the seeds that float down like little propellers? I wouldn't let Rob up – no room for the both of us, anyway. I had candles up there, and this and that I took from the house.' He laughed. 'Robbie must have helped me, now I come to think. I think Rob probably helped quite a lot …'

He smiled at Bobby, bringing himself back from the garden, from Robbie climbing on the rope lassoed around a thick branch of the sycamore. He could see Robbie in Bobby's rare smile, in his shy seriousness.

'*I want to call him Robert*,' Margot had said, and he had wanted to say, no, no, he's mine and I'd like to call him Guy. But he hadn't had the nerve or the strength, and Margot looked so hopeful, wanting this one thing. He had glanced at her, hardly able to take his eyes from his baby son, but he had, at last, and saw how exhausted she was, pale and sweaty from her labour, that thick, fecund smell coming off her, blood and something else, milk leaking from her breasts perhaps, a fundamental female scent. Holding their baby, he had lain down beside her and stroked back her damp hair. 'Yes,' he'd said, 'we'll call him Robert, of course. I love you, anything you want. I love you so.'

He brought himself into the present again; these memories were relentless, taking him back and back as if he couldn't concentrate on the here and now, on his son's hand in his. He made himself smile again, to say, 'Ask Granddad if you can play in his garden. Perhaps he's not so busy nowadays that he won't help you build another tree house. It is a lovely, garden, Bob … I'm sure you can go and play there.'

'Daddy says I can't.'

A feeling that someone had collided violently into him, sending him spinning, made him stop, and this was ridiculous and melodramatic' stopping so suddenly like this as if he had forgotten something and was about to run back for it. Bobby was looking up at him, small, impassive, tired; he shouldn't have to bother with this strange man who didn't talk and then talked too much and asked him silly questions and stopped dead as though someone had brained him. Paul was still holding Bobby's hand. He looked down at him. He wouldn't have recognised him; he had always imagined a one-year-old baby, as he was on the evening he walked out ... He walked out ... On the evening he walked out to Thorp Park ... to Thorp Park where there was a place ...

'Paul!'

He spun round, automatically lifting Bobby into his arms. He was no weight, slight and small just as he himself had been as a child. He held him tightly.

'Paul?' Edmund frowned at him. 'What's going on?'

'This is not right! None of this is right –'

Edmund said, 'No, I know, I understand, I understand, Paul ...'

As Paul paced his hotel room, Edmund watched helplessly from the door he had closed behind him; he'd taken no more than a step inside; he still held the door's handle, as though this might reassure Paul that he would leave at any moment if he wanted him to. Paul stopped and turned to face him; he looked as if he was about to spring on him and tear him to pieces.

'He's my son! Mine! And I'm to pretend, pretend –' He looked up to the ceiling. A few minutes earlier Paul had taken the child up to the next floor where Paul's father waited for him. Paul had told Edmund to stay there, outside his room, his voice like that of an extremely angry teacher who was just about controlling his temper. And he had stayed there, like a schoolboy, with the same sick fear he used to have waiting outside the headmaster's study for the cane.

In Paul's room, Edmund dared to step a little closer to where Paul stood staring at the ceiling. 'Paul ... Go up to him now. I'll leave – or I'll stay if you want me to, whatever you want.'

'I pretended to be someone else! A stranger – I am a stranger, a stranger keeping a secret, hardly able to speak for giving it away. He must think I'm wrong in the head –'

'He's just a little boy, Paul, he doesn't think anything.'

He looked at him. Quietly, as if afraid to be overheard, he

said, 'They told him I was dead. I am dead. *I'm dead.* What can I say to him? What? What do dead men say?'

Paul sat down on the bed. Sullenly he said, 'Do you have any cigarettes?'

'No, I'm sorry –'

He sprang up again. 'Christ Almighty! Why don't you smoke properly – messing about, taking or leaving it! Why smoke at all? Useless –' He pushed past him, out of the room and down the stairs.

Edmund followed, catching up with him on the street outside. 'Paul,' he caught his arm. 'Wait, you'll need this.' He handed him his wallet.

Paul took it, shoving it in his pocket without looking at him. 'Did you bring my key as well?'

'No, sorry.'

'Then I'm locked out.'

'They'll let you back in.'

'Will they? Sure about that?' He met his gaze. 'I need cigarettes. Where's closest?'

'I'll take you.'

There had been a shop close by; Paul thought how he could have walked there alone, without a guide, and he would have tried to buy cigarettes, searching his pockets for his wallet, having to go back to the hotel, back through the lobby with the receptionist watching him avidly, back up the stairs, afraid of bumping into his father, or her, his ex-mother-in-law, a woman who looked at him as if he was something not right. But Edmund had saved him from all that, bringing his wallet, even though he had shouted at him as though he was some bloody snivelling kid of a second lieutenant, fresh off the boat. Edmund had saved him and in the tobacconist's shop Edmund had even asked the man for the right brand, even asked for matches because he couldn't speak for himself he was so angry and Edmund seemed to understand this, and on the street he opened the pack and took one out and lit it and handed it to him. 'There,' he said. *There.*

'I can't go back to the hotel.'

Edmund had nodded, 'All right. Come back with me.'

Paul lay on Edmund's bed, fully clothed apart from his jacket and shoes. Edmund sat on the chair, talking about a cricket match he had once played at school, quite a grand school where he was a better bowler than a batsman, and anyway, he had bowled five of them out … And this story went on, and he found it easy to drop in and out of it, listening to the musical sound of Edmund's voice, light and easy and confident. He had a sister, Caroline; another sister, Diana; a brother Rupert – in the Household Guards, who thought he was the bee's knees in his uniform, apparently. Edmund talked about how Rupert was the eldest and he only the baby of the family … The baby, the youngest, he might have guessed.

He listened to him and smoked and smoked and Edmund got up and opened the window and he could hear the traffic on the street outside, feel the breeze that smelt of exhaust, of people going about their lives, and the breeze made his cigarette taste different, worse. Upstairs a baby cried; a woman called out; a door slammed. Edmund talked on; he made school sound as though it was only last week, that cricket-match tea with its egg-and-cress sandwiches and sultana cake, all its who said what to whom, that sunny cloudless day only last week so that he knew how young Edmund was, the youngest, the baby, whose father was a doctor, like his, but so much more grand, Harley Street, treating dukes but still as useless as any doctor, although he didn't tell Edmund what he thought of bloody doctors. He only smoked, and Edmund seemed so proud of his family, and of his father; he loved them as he should.

He thought Edmund wouldn't run out of words: he was so confident, light and breezy, he would go on and on, but he trailed off, stopped. Paul noticed that the plate-cum-ashtray beside him was full, the pack of cigarettes Edmund had bought half empty. He noticed that Edmund was gazing at him, that look he had. It was a look he must surely only use on him because it was so strange, no one else would be able to bear it; they would think Edmund was mad and no one seemed to think this, not his family who loved him, or the boys at his school, in his cricket team. It seemed everyone adored him and always had.

At last Edmund said, 'I had another brother. Neville. He was killed. First of July, 1916.'

Paul closed his eyes. Robbie had been there that day, and Patrick, and Patrick's brother, and Matthew, and it had been Matthew's birthday: happy birthday. He wouldn't tell Edmund this; he didn't want to take the focus away from this Neville by mentioning so many others, all of his platoon in fact, most of his regiment. He didn't want to mention that he should have been there but wasn't. He was on a beach in Dorset, fucking a sweet-faced second lieutenant; a second lieutenant just like him, gassed like him, recovering like him; recovering in the sand dunes, hidden by the sharp sea grass, grass that could cut paper-thin cuts, salt-stinging wounds, nothing, worth it for the chance to be obliterated by sex for a little while. But it seemed they could hear the guns like distant thunder rumbling relentlessly, doggedly, across the sea, and George was frightened, as he was, and they'd clung together. George Atkins – that was the second lieutenant's name. George. *Christ*, he'd almost said, *I wish you hadn't told me your name, George. I do wish you'd kept your mouth shut on the introductions.*

'Paul?'

He opened his eyes; he had forgotten Edmund, and that was inexcusable. 'I'm sorry, Edmund. I'm sorry for your loss.'

Edmund had stood up; he took the cigarette from his fingers and stubbed it out, putting the plate-cum-ashtray on the floor. Paul thought he would go on talking, lie down beside him perhaps, but go on talking about his brother, telling him everything. But his face had become like that of all the officers he had ever known; men who had snubbed him, men he couldn't be brave enough for, no matter what he did, because they saw what he was and nothing mattered compared with that.

Paul found himself gazing at him. Edmund's transformation was horrible but it was only what he expected, he shouldn't be stunned, he shouldn't feel as stunned as this by an expression of such commonplace disgust; besides, he deserved it: hadn't he been remembering George Atkins? Edmund must have seen into his thoughts; he must think him worse than disgusting to think of such a thing as he was sharing his grief so diffidently.

Ashamed, he made to get up; he would go, of course, he had to go now. Only Bobby mattered anyway; and yet he couldn't face his son, which was why he was here, on a near-stranger's bed that smelled of sex, the sheets stained with him, with them both; how could he see Bobby again when he was such a man, how could he face anyone ever again? He gasped for breath and covered his face with his hands. He thought it might be possible to die of shame as Edmund lay down and with wordless resignation pulled him into his arms.

Chapter Twenty-four

ON THE TRAIN TO Victoria, Patrick stared out of the window and thought that he would never return to England again; this was the end of it. He thought of the station guard at Canterbury, where he had changed trains, who had stared at him with such hostility, muttering *wog* as he walked past him. Pasty-faced little bastard.

Patrick stared at his reflection in the train window. Who would have thought he could look like anyone other than an Englishman? Who would have thought he could pass for a *wog* as he stood on the platform of a provincial station? Catholic, queer and now this; what a good joke. If Matthew had been well he would have shared the joke; Matt would have laughed. If Matthew had been well he wouldn't have been on that station; he would have been in Soho, where no doubt *wogs* like him were so common as to be unremarkable.

The train stopped and more passengers boarded carriages that were already full, so that they stood in the corridors, trying to keep a little distance from each other, bags strategically placed. Patrick had given up his seat two stops ago to a bone-thin girl and her baby. She had smiled at him gratefully, wearily, as her child grizzled and worried at the buttons on her cheap coat. They all looked so *ill*, Patrick thought, pale and exhausted; their hair greasy rat-tails that the women valiantly tried to style, a losing battle in the damp air. The sun had shone for them today, though; some were burnt red, sore-looking, some even a gentle shade of brown, not so dark as him, more like honey, sweet like honey, too: he had forgotten how unwashed his countrymen were.

How could Paul miss this country? He knew he did miss it,

although he never told him so. And it wasn't just his family he missed – his father and his son. He actually missed England. He supposed exiles did miss home more than those who had made a choice to leave.

He was tired, he would like to sit down, lie down, close his eyes; he should have travelled first class, as Paul would have: officer class – Paul had always had a certain sense of *class*. 'I'll call you sir if you like, you arrogant little get,' he had shouted at Paul once: a kind of truth that would surface during an argument. *Sir*. Sir, would you care to stop being a wanker and come home? Because I've come to fetch you, sir. Surprise.

Patrick leaned more heavily against the train window and closed his eyes; perhaps he could sleep on his feet, as he used to; he used to be able to sleep anywhere, in a shallow dip in the side of a trench, curled up in his greatcoat, ignoring the grunt and whisper of other men's voices, their snores and farts, ignoring the cold and discomfort, trying to at least, trying to think of something else: hot sausages and mashed potato, a clean, warm bed; trying not to think too much about the young lieutenant Paul Harris who could never look him in the eye but looked to his side, past him, away from him: *Thank you, sergeant, that will be all*.

Little Nancy, the men called Paul: tough little Nancy though, like he would kick your teeth down your throat if you looked at him sideways, raise his pistol and shoot you in the head if you didn't carry out his order at once: jump to, man, jump to. Jump to. Paul used to say that a lot, shout that a lot. *Get your bloody heads down! Keep your bloody heads down,* holding his watch, eyes fixed on its face, his other hand raised, waiting to fall when the time came, the signal to scramble up the ladders, Paul first, or sometimes last, making sure there were no stragglers. No one would dare to straggle when Paul was around. Lieutenant Harris aiming his pistol at you meant business. *Jump to, man, jump to*. The men respected him – they knew where they were with him, there was respect for his fairness, his willingness to lead, despite the dirty-queer jokes they made behind his back.

Curled up in a hollow in a trench, Patrick would try not to

think about those jokes. It was difficult enough loving Paul as he did without all that filthy rubbish. Difficult! Easy, really, because Paul never looked at him, never spoke to him unless he had to, quick and to the point, looking to one side, away, as though he couldn't stand the sight of him; easy to love someone so secretly without the loved one's acknowledgement.

'I actually wanted to throw myself on your body,' Paul had told him years later. He didn't believe him; it couldn't be true, they were both too exhausted, too bowed by responsibility, too scared too often, too cold and hungry and miserable to care about sex. At least he was. He only loved Paul, and it was a soft and sentimental feeling; he only wanted to protect him, to comfort him, keep him alive. Paul was the most beautiful man he had ever seen, and kind and tender when a man was sick to death: St Paul then, touchy little sod, beautiful and mad and foul-mouthed and up for it, always, always. Always up for a fight, for a fuck, always, always. *I actually wanted to throw myself on your body*. Perhaps it was true.

The train's motion was rocking him to sleep – he hadn't lost his old knack of sleeping anywhere, after all. He remembered sleeping on ferries in storms, too sick even to care about staying awake for fear of drowning. He had slept on trains that sped across Belgium and France, fast and straight as the French poplar-lined roads he had marched down on blistered feet. Marching, marching, either scorched by the sun or soaked by the rain, men to his side, men behind, men to the front; men staggering, out of step, look lively, keep up! *It's a long, long way* – fuck that, fuck the singing, just keep on, not thinking, not thinking, make the pain in your feet all that matters, the whole world, no past, no future, just a pair of feet bleeding into your boots.

Pat opened his eyes; he wouldn't think of this. He would think of the train in Italy, the wine, bread and tomatoes they had bought when the train stopped, passed to them through the windows from the vendors with their baskets, their quick smiling hands and faces coming at them through the windows. *Signori! Signori!* The smell of that bread, flat as a pebble, warm and delicious; the tomatoes that were so sweet, bursting pips on to his shirt, the wine so rough it made Paul splutter. And the train that was nothing like this one but rickety, more *wooden,* like a toy, rattling through the olive groves, slow as you liked. And Paul slept against him, his head on his shoulder, hardly able to talk to him.

Months passed before Paul could talk to him. Months of travelling from Durham gaol through Europe because it had seemed to him that they had to have this time as travellers, homeless, country-less; time for Paul to become used to him again away from any idea of being settled, pinned down to a life Patrick was so afraid he may not want.

From the prison gates they travelled through England, boarding a ferry to cross the sea to France, a country they couldn't escape fast enough. Then down more slowly through Switzerland, slower through Italy. And at the end of Italy, at the very toe of the Italian boot, they took another ferry to Sicily and it had seemed to Paul like the end of the world: he'd told him so on a Sicilian beach: *I have nothing left to live for.* You have me. Paul had nodded, pressing the heels of his hands hard into his eyes as if he could squeeze out the few tears he had left. *All right,* Paul said eventually, dropping his hands from his eyes to look at him, pitifully brave. *All right.*

Finally he took Paul to the life he'd made in Tangiers, the life he'd first escaped to when Paul had decided he must at least try to be honourable towards his wife, try to be faithful, to be *ordinary* as he put it. Ordinary. Patrick had even imagined he'd understood. He had imagined Paul could live this ordinary life.

He had imagined this for a few weeks, long enough for him to leave England and travel to the place he had an idea of, a tolerant and cosmopolitan place where he could be ordinary in his way. Only then, after those few weeks, did he realise that Paul had merely been testing him and he should have stayed until Paul realised this, too. Paul would have realised that he could live with his wife and still have him, it would be fine, fine … He would have stopped Paul walking out one dark evening. He would have stopped him following that stranger; he would have pulled him back. He imagined his anger as he dragged Paul away from that place; but his anger would have been tempered by the knowledge that Paul had to go there: there could never be enough sex for Paul, there never had been enough, and there never would be enough.

A man edged past him in the train's corridor saying, 'Sorry, mate, sorry.'

Patrick pressed himself against the window, trying to take up as little space as possible. He was a big man; there were times when other men looked at him fearfully, looked at him slyly, sizing him up: *big bastard – looking for trouble.* Well, he was in the right place for trouble: England with all its pettiness and snobbery and its *You have committed an offence that is debauched in the extreme and must be dealt with accordingly, properly and severely. Two years hard labour. Take him down.*

He remembered standing up in the public gallery, shouting, 'No! No – that's not right!' Not right, not just. 'Do you call that justice?' Paul's father had shouted. Paul's father, George, who had wept, who wouldn't allow him to speak even when he tried to tell him that Paul would survive, that he was tough, the toughest little Nancy in the world.

And soon he would be with him again in the Queen's Hotel. There'd be two queens staying at the Queen's. He tried to smile at this joke.

The train slowed into Victoria Station. Patrick rubbed his hands across his face, he needed to shave; he was beginning to smell like them, the men pushing past him now to be the first off, his compatriots. Perhaps Paul and he would share a bath.

The train stopped and doors were flung open; the platform was crowded because this was Victoria, London, not some backwater. No one would see him here; no one would take any notice of him. All the same he hesitated before he stepped down.

Chapter Twenty-five

PAUL HAD FALLEN ASLEEP on his bed and Edmund covered him with a quilt as carefully as he could; he couldn't wake him, he was afraid that Paul might begin to cry again. He didn't want to think less of him for this crying; he truly didn't. He had asked him not to cry, but only as one might ask a child, knowing that it was just a way of saying something, a reassurance: *Don't cry, I'm here.* In all truth he had wanted to say don't cry because he was embarrassed; at least he was at first. But eventually he became used to this crying, he had stroked his head and kept silent, waiting for him to stop. He had no idea how long this would take because he had never seen a man cry before, not even his father when they received the telegram advising that Neville was missing in action.

'They presume dead,' his father had said, and his voice was as calm as it ever was, except for the inflection on that *presume*, as though the word was one he had never come across before, as though he didn't know what *they* were talking about, sending out their incomprehensible nonsense. Edmund had been home from school for the weekend and he had wished desperately that he hadn't come home, that he hadn't witnessed the boy resting his bike against the railings outside their house, walking up the steps, adjusting his cap, his hesitation before pulling on the doorbell. All this was seen from his father's study, over his father's shoulder as his father had reprimanded him for his poor school report. He couldn't take his eyes off this boy in his cap and uniform, this harbinger of bad news, only bad news, how could he do such a job? And his father had sighed, 'Edmund. What are you staring at now?' A moment later and the doorbell rang and Edmund had run out into the hall, racing the maid to the door.

His sisters had cried for Neville; his mother went to her room and didn't come out very much until the memorial service. He, his father and Rupert had not cried, at least not in front of anyone. For all he knew his father cried every night and as for Rupert, he only looked dazed when he came home on leave. 'It should have been me, old son,' he'd told him. 'Neville was the good one.'

So, no tears; dry your eyes, be strong, a man. Hold your head up, face the world, proudly, straight and direct. This is what he was taught at school; this is what his father taught him, when he wasn't telling him not to go tilting at windmills. Who would have thought his father had read Don Quixote? Who would have imagined he would allow him to go after the giants who were not giants? Perhaps he wouldn't have allowed it if Neville had lived; if Neville had lived his father might still have believed that everything was as it purported to be and that propriety truly mattered.

He sat down on the chair; he couldn't go on standing over Paul, couldn't lie down next to him, couldn't leave him, although he would like to go outside, to draw himself up straight, stretch and fill his lungs with air tainted only by traffic fumes and not the stink of cigarettes, of Paul's hot, salty, snotty grief.

When Paul had eventually stopped crying he hadn't known what to do, how to hold him, what to say; Paul had frightened him, but what was there to be frightened of? Paul. A stranger; more strange than ever, now, with his little child and, therefore, presumably, a wife he had loved. He presumed he'd loved her, perhaps he still did, or perhaps he never had; perhaps he had never married, just fucked a girl, fucked off when things became messy. He didn't know. He felt he could almost believe anything of a man who cried as Paul had cried this afternoon.

It occurred to him to wish he had never met him, to wish that he had stayed in bed with Ann the other evening. The *other evening*! He closed his eyes, remembering that restaurant, the taste of garlic and spaghetti, the sound of Day and Andrew laughing at the other end of the table, the sight of Paul looking up at him, so handsome, wry, the question in his eyes, the smile in his voice as he asked, *What conclusion have you reached?* He remembered how Paul had made something in him rise to the surface, an urgent, needy feeling he hadn't recognised until later.

Before Paul had begun to cry he had talked until he was almost hoarse and Paul had listened, or seemed to listen, smoking, smoking, one pristine cigarette lit from the disgusting remnants of the last. When he told him about Neville he seemed hardly to have heard him at all and this was excruciating, because it had taken a lot to tell him, a lot of working himself up. He had wanted him to ask about Neville, even the kind of inane questions he imagined Paul, a veteran, would ask: regiment, rank, length of service, comparing these details with his own record, contrasting their fortunes, being secretly relieved that Neville was the dead one and not him: he had been in a luckier place further up or down the line. But Paul had kept silent, behaving as if Neville didn't matter enough even for those questions in the scheme of things, and in the scheme of things he didn't, he understood that, he understood that Paul had seen it all, everything; he understood.

But understanding didn't stop him thinking that Barnes was right: Paul was a self-centred bastard, and pathetic in his self-pitying silence. Edmund had gazed at him, hardly able to believe such a person was there on his bed. And then Paul had started to cry. He didn't know if he'd felt repelled or not; still didn't, there was just a worm of a feeling he couldn't bear to examine too closely.

He stood up, unable to sit still. Paul's jacket had slipped from the end of the bed to the floor, and he picked it up. At once he was lifting it to his face, inhaling Paul's scent, feeling the weight of his wallet in the pocket bump against his body. He remembered snatching the wallet up from the table in his hotel room, going after Paul, afraid for him, needing to take care of him. He remembered the intimacy of another man's wallet in his hand as he ran down the hotel's stairs, and yet at the time he had thought nothing of this intimacy: it was just Paul's wallet and Paul was everything; nothing was too much a part of Paul that was not also a part of him.

He hung up the jacket, smoothing out a sleeve; he closed the window, the evening had become windy, the curtains were billowing into the room; Paul would be cold. Sitting back down, he watched over him as he slept.

Chapter Twenty-six

GEORGE WENT TO PAUL'S room and knocked gently on the door. Room 212, the receptionist had said, that mannered, painstakingly polite man who nevertheless had raised his eyebrows so expressively when he'd told him that *Francis Law* was Paul's alias. At that moment George had understood why Paul had chosen this hotel; even walking through its anonymous-looking door into its dim, neat lobby was like walking into an exclusive club; for Paul it must have felt like an oasis; the calm of acceptance, of no questions asked, must have been an enormous relief. He had felt the same kind of relief himself.

George knocked again, a little more urgently this time, although he knew instinctively that Paul wasn't in his room, that he wouldn't have been able to settle after he brought Bobby back. He had looked as though he would run right out of the hotel and keep running, such was the energy that seemed to charge through him. Only Bobby's presence helped a little to keep that energy in check. Paul had knelt down in front of his son so that their faces were level. Taking both his hands, he said, 'I have to go now, Bob. Perhaps tomorrow –' He had looked up at him, 'You'll be here tomorrow?'

George had stepped towards him. He had an idea that he would catch hold of him when he got to his feet again; he would hold him and make him be still, keep on holding him until he was calm and still, as he used to hold him when he was a child and had woken from bad dreams. But Iris had stepped forward; she had said, 'We'll be here.'

Paul had turned to her. He had clambered to his feet with none of his usual grace, as though some inept puppeteer was

216

controlling him; his face was ugly with hatred as he said, 'Do I look like a dead man to you?'

'Paul, please –' George had taken another step towards him, but couldn't bring himself even to touch his arm. This man was too unlike his son, too much like a man he would make an effort to avoid.

Without looking at him, only stretching out his hand as if to stop him coming any closer, Paul said, 'I'll come back. I'll come back to Thorp and take him when you least expect it and you'll never see him again. Do you understand? I will take him. I *will* do this. Tell Margot, tell your husband. Don't think any of you will have any peace from now on.'

Iris had put her hand to her throat, her face so pale that George went to her; but he couldn't touch her, either. He only stood uselessly, emasculated by the hate-filled power of this man.

When Paul had gone, George had slumped onto the bed, unable to look at Iris, who had gone to Bobby, who was taking off his coat, speaking to him too quickly, with too much bright reassurance.

George stepped back from the door to Paul's room. About to turn away, to go back upstairs to Iris and Bobby, he reached for the handle. The door was unlocked, and he stepped inside, closing the door behind him.

'Paul?' He went to the bathroom, cautiously pushing the door that stood ajar. On the threshold of these two rooms, he turned to face Paul's bed.

The bed was made, neat and tidy like the room itself. Nervously, George went to the wardrobe and opened its doors; there were Paul's shirts, the suit he had worn when they'd had lunch together, his silk ties coiled carefully on the wardrobe's shelf, beautiful ties in jewel colours. There was a leather box and he opened it: cuff links, tie pins, a gold signet ring. He picked up the ring and saw the two Ps engraved, entwined. George gazed at it, turning it around and around; he slipped it on his own finger, the third finger of his left hand; it fitted, slipping easily over his knuckle. He wondered why Paul didn't wear it, why he left it in a box. He thought of Patrick, who had told him how much he loved his son, of Paul saying, *I can't live without him, Dad,* as though this was not just a romantic figure of speech but the literal truth: he would die without the man who had met him at the prison gates, who had taken him in a taxi to Durham Station, who had turned to him as he followed Paul on to the train and said, 'I'll take care of him. I promise, Dr Harris, I'll take care of him.'

George took off the ring, replacing it in the box, putting the box back on the shelf and closing the wardrobe door softly. The air inside the wardrobe had smelled of Paul – no, of *Francis Law* – Paul had only ever smelled of soap, carbolic or sometimes *Pears* or *Lifebuoy*, whatever soap he'd bought for the bathroom at Parkwood, neither of them caring. But Francis Law, he was quite a man about town, urbane, wearing his experience lightly. And such experience! Such knowledge of the world: a man who had lived in countries George had never even dreamt of visiting, had barely known existed; a man who knew exactly how to dress, how to carry himself, how to behave in whatever hotel he found himself in – how to find the appropriate hotel in the first place. Francis Law, the artist who could sell out an exhibition of his work to other men who behaved with the same urbane air as him, men who were the opposite of George himself. Although he had lived and worked in London he'd only ever wanted to go home to Thorp, to Grace, the girl along the road, whose parents knew his parents, who was so shy and sweet that even his father was careful of her.

His father. Even on his death bed that man had been laughing at him; his father, a man with *experience*, who could have become Francis Law just as easily as Paul could – more easily perhaps, not having Paul's more unique experiences to bring him down to earth.

George sat down on the bed and stared out of the window. Paul would come back to this room, he had to, there was the ring in the box, and he wouldn't leave such a thing behind, not when he had deliberately brought it with him. Paul would come back, to this hotel where eyebrows were only raised ironically, and he would be here, waiting for him, alone, because Iris would not stay now, would not keep Bobby here close by a man who could transform into the very devil, a vengeful, pitiless sprite, cursing those who had crossed him, who had killed him if only in their heads and hearts.

He went to the window and looked down on to the empty, shadowed street. Paul would come back, or Francis; he didn't much care which, he knew both, he was caught between them, could reach out to either of them.

Iris stepped inside Paul's room; she was shaking, a pulse throbbing in her head, a fearful, metallic tingling on her tongue; she had never been as scared as this. But there was only George there, sitting on the bed, his back to her, staring out of the window at the prison-like building across the road.

Cautiously, she said, 'Did you speak to him?'

He stood up, seemed to make an effort to stand up straight, to make a show of not minding that she was still here in this hotel. 'No, Iris. He wasn't here. I hardly expected him to be here.'

'Where might he have gone?'

'I don't know. I've really no idea.'

She turned to go. 'I've left Bobby alone. I should go to him in case Paul comes back.'

'Iris –' He exhaled sharply. 'I'm sorry. What Paul said – you know he wouldn't have meant it – he's just so angry … He loves Bobby.'

'Yes, George, I know he loves him. And now I know just how much he hates us too.'

He stepped towards her. 'Iris … I have never been rash, never in my life, until these last few days. I don't know what I'm doing, what to say –'

He was disclaiming their relationship. She felt as though he had slapped her across the face. Yet she heard herself say stiffly, 'It's all right, George. We've both been rash. Now, I must get back to my grandson.'

'He isn't at any risk, Iris, *wasn't* at any risk. He was with *Paul* – he wouldn't hurt him.'

'No. But he might have taken him. Might still, I think.'

As she turned to go he said, 'I'll stay in this room tonight. If Paul comes back then I'll ask if they have another room.'

She nodded. 'I think that's for the best.'

For the best not to make love to him again, ever again; for the best to be alone as Daniel's wife for the rest of her life, no more intimacy that wasn't the intimacy of her marriage.

Half way up the stairs to her room on the next floor, Iris stopped. She thought of her bed at home in the vicarage, how in the darkness Daniel's hand would go to her breast and how she would turn to him so that they were face to face in the darkness, her nose brushing his as he stroked back her hair. There would be such an intense look in his eyes, so serious, as though desire couldn't be taken lightly, as though it was too deep inside him even for words. At most he would murmur her name, a whispered word lost in a kiss, his hand moving down her body, slowly and patiently so it seemed that he thought she would stop him, never expecting her to want him as much as he wanted her. Afterwards he would roll away and reach across the bed for her hand, squeezing her fingers lightly, *goodnight*, he would say. No darling words, there was never any need for words; in a moment he would be asleep, his hand becoming limp in hers, and she would move away from the heat of his body, sleepy too but thinking of the next day, its busyness whirling away before her. Daniel would begin to snore; she would touch his back lightly and he would stop and the bed would creak beneath his weight as he turned over, *goodnight* repeated as though he was dreaming it, his voice thick with sleep.

On the hotel stairs, she gripped the banister rail. She closed her eyes and saw Daniel's face, and it was as though her infidelity had torn a hole inside her, damaging her beyond repair. She gripped the banister and bowed to the pain of it, gasping with shame so that she didn't hear him, only felt George's arm around her waist, helping her upstairs.

Chapter Twenty-seven

PAUL FELT HIMSELF BEING shaken awake: they had come for him: he would be taken to the showers where the blood could be washed away more easily, Prison Officer Barker's hand clamped against his mouth, frog-marching him along, quick with anticipation – perhaps Barker loved him, wanted him urgently, because he could hear a voice close to him saying, 'Quiet, quiet,' a loving voice, full of alarm. The voice became calmer, softer, 'Quiet now. Everything's all right. Hush … hush, that's it, that's it.' There was a hand on his chest, another on his face; they had come for him: he fought back.

'Paul! Stop now, stop … It's all right. It's me, Edmund …'

Edmund. He stared at him, disorientated; Edmund. He closed his eyes and fell back onto the pillows that were too warm, too creased and sweaty from his dreams. He covered his face with his hands. Edmund; he had witnessed this, too, then: the shouting out, the fighting with apparitions, the bloody idiotic drama of it all. Edmund, who was too young, much too young, his only fault was that he was too young, born too late, lucky boy. Too young to be kneeling over him now, frightened and appalled by his histrionics; too young; what had he been thinking of? Himself, of course.

'Paul?'

He lowered his hands; covering your face was nothing, if not drama. 'I'm sorry.'

'Why?' Edmund laughed a little, making Paul ache for him. 'It's not something you can help, is it?'

Paul made to get up but Edmund pushed him down again. 'Give yourself a moment.'

Edmund's hand was on his chest and Paul lifted it away.

Despite himself, he held on to his wrist, not wanting to relinquish him yet; he could feel his pulse, strong and steady, perhaps a little too fast. He had held other men's wrists like this, counting as a life pulsed away despite his frantic reassurances, his hasty tourniquets. Could he not have been calmer and less scared; not a speeded-up, charged-up version of an officer, but considered, careful, calm? And then he could have saved them. He could have, he could have.

'Paul?'

'I have to go.'

'Then I'll go with you, see you safely back.'

He was still holding Edmund's wrist, his fingers only just meeting around it, his flesh firm beneath his touch, his veins blue: blue blood and no calluses, and if he turned his hand over to see his palm he knew there would be a long, long life line. *In fifty years' time.* How could he live without such optimism, without the warmth that drew him out of the past and into the present? He should live in the present, day by day, and the past could be done away with because Edmund had no part in it; he was only part of the present, and the future perhaps, those fifty years. How could he live a day without him?

'I should go, Edmund.'

'You keep saying that.' Edmund lifted his wrist as if to show him that his fingers were still gripped tight around it. 'You say it.'

What should he say now; that he should go because he was bad for him, because he was weak and had cried? That he had a child he missed and missing him was a pain that never went away? And why would Edmund want to be with someone like him, whose pain made him angry every day? Why would Edmund want to be with a man who couldn't be optimistic, or even know if he truly wanted those fifty years? And he couldn't tell him about his past, all the mess of it, he could only look at Edmund's face, the extraordinary warmth of his smile; only look at him and know that he would be himself with this man, the self he had thought he would be before the *past.*

'Edmund.'

'Say my name like that again. Always say it like that.'

Paul closed his eyes. 'Edmund …'

Edmund kissed him and he could feel the warmth in his kiss, hear it in his voice as he murmured, 'Stay with me. Stay, stay.'

Patrick stood at the hotel's desk and the receptionist nodded towards his bag. 'Do you need any help with your bags, sir, or is that all the luggage you have?'

'This is all I have, thank you.'

'Room 214, then, next to Mr Law's room. I hope you'll be comfortable.'

'Is Mr Law in, do you know?'

'I believe he may be.' The man glanced over his shoulder at the compartments for the room keys. 'His key's not here, so he might well be in his room. Here we are, sir, your key, room 214.'

Patrick took the key and found he couldn't move; he had made a mistake in coming here. Paul would only be astonished, angry. He could imagine how angry he would be, so light on his feet with anger, buoyed by it, unable to be still for it. Always so graceful and quick he would suddenly be beyond grace and quickness, soaring with a kind of mania, running at him, pushing at him, shouting 'Tell me why you're here? Here, with your bloody jealousy and possessiveness! Here, because you don't trust me! And you can't tell me you don't trust me and say you love me in the next breath.'

He could hear this rant, feel Paul's hand pushing at his chest, at his shoulder, but he would stand firm as Paul pushed against him, and eventually he would calm down and he would say, 'Will you let me speak now?'

'Mr Morgan?'

Patrick looked at the receptionist. 'Sorry. Long journey.'

'I quite understand, sir. Second floor, to your left.'

Patrick paused outside Paul's room; he thought that perhaps he should wash away the long journey before seeing him, before he became the wall Paul had to bounce off. Bastard, he thought, angry little bastard who wouldn't let up, wind down, stop. He raised his fist to knock and stopped himself. He would wash first, shave – he wouldn't be the unkempt man Paul liked him to be when he was angry; he would look and smell respectable, calm, less likely to push back. He would give himself time.

In his room Patrick looked around: a double bed, a wardrobe, a chair, little else. Paul would be comfortable in such a stark place; he had always preferred the unadorned; at home they lived so simply he found he hardly had to work at all because there was so little to spend money on; even Paul's tailor came inexpensively at home. Good clothes were Paul's only luxury and cigarettes his only necessity; he hardly ate, preferring to spend the time working; he would live on fresh air – no, on smoke. Patrick felt the familiar feeling of defeat creep over him so that he couldn't resist lying down on the bed; he would close his eyes for five minutes.

But sleep wouldn't come. He got up and paced the spartan room; knowing that Paul was only a step away was torture. He went back to stand outside Paul's door, raised his fist and knocked this time, called his name, softly, then more loudly, knocking again, not caring about the noise he made, about how angry Paul might be. Perhaps he might not be angry, but pleased – why shouldn't he be pleased? Overjoyed, he might say, *Let's pack up and go home now, at once.* He knocked and knocked but there was no answer.

Patrick went back to his room and ran a bath. He thought about unpacking, but only left his small suitcase open on the bed. He wouldn't be staying long, whatever happened.

He bathed, wrapped a towel around his waist and shaved, brushed his teeth and combed back his hair, kept very short because otherwise its curliness made him feel and look like someone he wasn't. Even so, his hair wasn't as short as Paul's was. 'Grow your hair a little,' he'd say, wanting to add, 'you're not in prison now, why look as if you are?'

But he didn't look like that prisoner, not really. Patrick remembered how Paul had looked the day of his release, as broken as he imagined a Catholic martyr would look after a few months with Protestant torturers. He hadn't believed it possible that a man could look so broken and still be able to walk, although he couldn't walk far. He limped and couldn't lift his gaze from the ground, as though terrified to meet anyone's eye.

Patrick remembered how he had raced across the road as they closed the prison gate behind Paul, how Paul had backed away from him, from an embrace which must have seemed to him overwhelming, frightening: just a great big man running at him. With hindsight, Patrick wondered what he'd been thinking of to do such a thing, but he knew he had only needed to hold him, that he didn't know then that Paul had changed beyond any imagining.

For weeks Paul wouldn't allow himself to be embraced; Patrick had had to keep all his relief, all his need inside and not let it spill out all over him because Paul couldn't bear it. Couldn't bear to be touched, talked to, even looked at. Couldn't bear it if he left his side, couldn't bear being by his side; Paul was scared of noise, of crowded places and groups of men, of lone men who looked at him wrongly, who looked at all. He would find Paul trying to make himself invisible, standing very close to a wall, his hands scrabbling at the mortar, his forehead rolling against the bricks; he would keen.

He had never heard such a noise before: keening, like a trapped, wounded animal; Paul would make this noise and within it Patrick would hear the fractured syllables of his name. He would take his hand, gently, gently, and lead him away to somewhere quiet, if he could find such a place on all the noisy stations, all the busy ports, the trains and ferries, the foreign, confusing streets. He would hold his hand as though he was a little child and not care if anyone saw them. Two men holding hands, one so slight, so damaged – everything damaged so there were times when Patrick could hardly bear to be near him. He was ashamed that Paul's keening made him want to block his ears, ashamed that he longed to pull his hand away, run away, far away from so much pain. He thought he might go mad alone with Paul, that he might kill him and then kill himself because there seemed no other escape. He thought how Paul would finally be at peace.

In front of the hotel bathroom mirror, Patrick stared at his reflection. He was thirty, in his prime, he supposed, and fit – he had always been fit; fit for slaughtering pigs and butchering their heavy carcasses; fit for running towards the enemy lines, bayonet fixed. He'd been worked hard since he was fifteen, since his father took him out of the grammar school and put a meat axe in his hand. He was tall and strong with all that hard work and there were men at home in Tangiers who had loved him much more than he had loved them, who loved him still – *wanted him* still, men who asked why he was so faithful to Paul. He could have anyone, *anyone*, they told him, yet he stayed with Paul, who wasn't good enough for him, they said, who was, they said, a selfish little drama queen. I know, he'd say. I know. No accounting for taste.

Those men would be surprised to know that sometimes he couldn't stand the sight of Paul and he would have to get out of their house and walk and walk until he was too exhausted to be angry with him. Sometimes there wasn't even anger, only boredom and impatience. But not often; most often Paul was just Paul, a fragile version of the shockingly beautiful, recklessly brave man he had fallen for so desperately in 1918.

Lately he had even begun to see in Paul that calmer, sweeter man he had become after the war, during those few months of his marriage when every Wednesday and Saturday evening they would be together. During those evenings he fell in love with him properly, confirming to himself what he had known all along: this wasn't just lust – he really did love this man, his voice, his manner, the gentle grace of him. More than that, he loved Paul for the way he made him feel about himself: whole; right. Until then he had only felt that he was wrong and had never believed that there would be a man like Paul who would love him and be loved in return.

Decisive now, Patrick dressed; he put on his coat because outside a wind had started up, throwing rain at the hotel's rattling windows. He took his key and closed the room's door behind him, going swiftly down the stairs and out on to the street to search for him.

Chapter Twenty-eight

A GOOD CROWD HAD turned out for Joseph's show. Lawrence was happy – even happier. He caught her around her waist, kissing her cheek. 'Ann – they adore you!'

He had been drinking champagne. Champagne, he said, didn't count as drink. He held a half-empty champagne flute and raised it in a salute. 'Here's to us.' He grinned at her. 'You and me. The gallery. Success.'

Joseph was with a woman; he had his arm around her; when he saw her noticing them he kissed the woman's neck, his eyes on hers. Beside her, Lawrence laughed. Many people she didn't know milled around her; the gallery was warm and becoming warmer with the press of bodies, noisier as more champagne was drunk. Her face was all around her, her body, draped, posed, unrecognisable and yet her exactly: skin tone, expression, the way she held herself, only unrecognisable in that this wasn't how she saw herself – she wasn't as serene as the woman on the walls.

That morning she'd had a letter from Matthew. It had begun as an ordinary letter with its questions after her health, asking after Fred and Susie and if she had heard from her family. He wrote a little about the weather, touching on the sky in a way that made her know he was only just keeping his madness in check. He'd had a visitor, he wrote, a man who would sometimes drop from the heavens to see him. No doubt she would see him, too, because he followed Paul everywhere.

At the end of the letter, he had written, *I still think of what happened between us often. Often! Every single moment. I think about your pretty little cunt opening up to me, and how you groaned when I slipped my fingers inside you and I think about*

227

the smell of you on my fingers, the taste of you, as though I had pulled you from the sea, a mermaid gasping for breath as my fingers probed inside. You are folded inside, wet, concertinaed, not as I expected but stronger, tighter and not passive at all – as though you had the power to crush me. I may have been rough, forgive me. I think I may have frightened you, and that is a terrible thought in my mind. But how could you not warn me?

She thought of Matt, suddenly changed, suddenly bold and commanding and handsome on the street as he walked her home – why had she not seen how handsome he was before that moment, the moment when he suddenly took her hand and pulled her towards him so that their bodies collided and she realised how solid he was, strong and not odd or strange or *wrong in the head* but a man like any other. And men were all fine by her; she never had any trouble falling for them, wanting them, finding some part of their faces, their bodies, their voices, smiles and gestures desirable.

But this man, this changed Matt, was more desirable than any other, and he looked at her as though he would eat her alive, as though he had never seen anyone he wanted so much in his life. He had walked her home every night for weeks, every night, unfailing every night, and he'd hardly given her any clue at all, a look perhaps, nothing more, a quick widening of his eyes.

There were voices all around her, champagne voices, a hand was light on the small of her back. 'Ann, sweetheart ...' Lawrence, speaking to her softly, his lips at her ear, concerned for her; he cared for her, she knew this.

She knew that she would still have given herself to Matthew that night if he had told her the sky was made of gold paper about to tear, that it was full of holes that only he could fix. All the things he wrote to her about later he could have told her then and still she would have taken him up the stairs to her room, taken off her clothes and helped him off with his. Still she would have held him and kissed him and wanted him so badly that her hands were everywhere on him: how hairy he was, how dense his flesh, firm and muscled; he smelt of driftwood warmed by the sun so that she buried her face into him, straddled him. And then he had rolled her onto her back, their position all at once reversed as if he wanted to keep her still so that she'd look at him and see that he was so full of want for her, as if she didn't know. She'd looked at him and he'd touched her face. '*Ann.*'

'Ann?' Lawrence squeezed her to him, said, 'Come on, darling girl. Buck up, eh? Rodney is speaking to you.'

She saw a man in front of her, leering at her; he'd asked a question of her but she hadn't heard him. Lawrence's arm tightened around her waist. 'Rodney was asking, is it very difficult to hold a pose for so long?'

Now that's a funny question. Lawrence – Larry – should tip his top hat, lean on his cane, cross one ankle over the other. '*How long did the Irish girl hold her pose?*'

She had kept very still, lying on her crumpled sheets, gazing up at Matthew's face that she had somehow managed not to see before, his eyes searching hers as though she was playing a game he couldn't believe in. For a moment she had thought he wanted to stop her because he was once a priest, perhaps still a priest in his heart and – wicked girl – she had wanted him all the more. She had thought of him in his vestments, in the confessional – all the sins he must have heard, all that shame and sorrow, and now he was gazing at her, his lips parted, his tongue wetting them as though nervousness had robbed him of his voice. She had sat up, propping herself up with her hand flat on the mattress, and put a finger to his mouth. He drew it in and bit down gently.

Lawrence said, 'Ann?' He laughed a little. 'Roddie, I think she may be a little tired – would you excuse us?'

In the office at the back of the gallery, Lawrence sat her down. He handed her a large measure of brandy. He sighed; leaning against the desk he folded his arms and said, 'All right, shall I tell you a secret? I'm not the biggest fool in the world. I know there's something wrong and it scares me to death. When you cried the other evening –'

She made to speak to stop him talking, he talked too much, but he held up his hand to stop her.

'When you cried like that it scared me because it makes me think … Well, it makes me think something has happened that you can't tell me about. But I have to know, so I'm going to ask, no more shilly-shallying around. Are you pregnant?' He pushed himself away from the desk in one quick movement and crouched beside her. Taking her hand, he said, 'Because if you are, you know I would help you … take care of it.' More softly he said, 'Are you pregnant?'

She pulled her hand away.

'Ann … I would marry you – you know that. But if the baby's Edmund's –'

'It's yours.' His face was all frowning softness and she took his hand and pressed it against her body. 'Yours. Aren't you glad? Aren't you looking forward to *taking care of it*?'

He bowed his head. 'If it was mine. If I could be sure it was mine.' Looking up at her he said quickly, 'How can I be sure? I'm sorry, but you must have known I couldn't bring up a child if there was any doubt.'

'It's yours.'

He took his hand from hers and straightened to his feet. 'I'm sorry, my darling. I can't be made a fool of. I'll help you find a discreet doctor, no back-street butcher for my best girl. No one need know. You'll be fine. We'll be fine, a fresh start, all that. We'll be as if it never happened.' He gazed at her. 'You understand, don't you?'

She nodded although she wanted to tell him again that the baby was his, that Edmund had always been so careful, too careful. Lawrence had never been careful; she should tell him that he should have taken more care. If he had he wouldn't have to look so pained now, so torn, guessing that the child was his but unable to let go of his doubt. He would kill his baby for the sake of his pride.

Gently he said, 'Will you come home with me tonight?'

'Yes.'

'Good girl.' After a moment he said, 'Everything will be all right. Everything usually is, in the end.'

Alone, she sipped her brandy. She remembered how Matthew

had bit down on her finger, as gently as his hunting dogs would carry the dead birds between their jaws. He straddled her, his back straight, and she was propped up, her arm quivering with the weight of her body, the mattress giving beneath her palm. His face was so close she could see the bristles on his cheek, the tiny place where he hadn't shaved cleanly enough; she could see her reflection in his eyes, two tiny Anns, both startled, both wondrous because he was so beautiful and she hadn't noticed this before.

She drew her finger from his mouth, supporting herself now on both hands, her breasts high on her chest; they had seemed so *presented* to him, she realised, so brazenly offered; she had looked down at herself, her small, pointed breasts with their hardened nipples; she looked down and saw how hard he was, his cock risen against his flat belly. She had expected him to be more boyish, a virgin boy who would be milder and less rankly male; but his cock was thick, and he closed his hand around it, to hide himself from her perhaps, even as his balls brushed against her body. He closed his eyes.

Matthew had closed his eyes, tilting back his head, not virginal at all but ecstatic, so yes, perhaps virginal then – one of those types of flawless martyrs the Romans would have fucked to death. Dirty, violent stories, wasn't her head full of them – wasn't everyone's head full of such profanity? Maybe not, maybe she was the only one, wrong in the head, like him, and he was shutting her out, his eyes closed against her so that she reached up to him, pulling him down on top of her, taking his hand, guiding it although he resisted, guiding it more forcefully between her legs.

And she was soft and wet, too soft, too wet, she should have known, should have realised, but the blood was too soon in showing itself, too soon, too painless; it was the shock of him, she thought, the shock of his unexpected lust. But she shouldn't have been shocked by him – wasn't he a man like any other? The same as any man, until his fingers hooked inside her and were still, his face still, keeping its ecstasy fixed for a moment in his eyes and mouth, not realising at first, perhaps never knowing at all how ordinary blood was.

231

But when he realised, it was as though a spell had been broken and he had scrambled away from her, moving quick as a wild animal to crouch in the corner of her room, his hands clasping his head, his forearms covering his face. He became a squat bundle of hands, of arms and elbows and knees, of shins and feet, hairy, a creature from the pages of a dark fairy tale, weeping. And she was naked too, although she should have covered herself, only didn't think to, there was no time, no time except to jump from her bed, to go to him. Matthew. He was still Matthew even then. Matthew, flailing at her so that she smelt him even more strongly, that smell men have when they want you very badly; and there was her smell too, the blood on her thighs, unexpected but still nothing, only blood after all, her blood on his fingers and smeared on his face.

All this was her fault; hadn't she been warned? Silly girl fucking around with a madman, making him madder, making him cry; daft girl thinking there'd be no consequences, none; thinking she could be free to do as she pleased away from home, away from her daddy and her brothers, from her mother and sisters who had shown her how to wash the bloody rags each month, secretly, furtively, away from the eyes of the men, the shame coming as naturally as the blood itself. But Matthew had made her feel her shame as though it was a living, vicious thing, so how could she go on loving him as she did? She couldn't be right in the head to carry a burden of love like this.

She swallowed the last of the brandy. She would go out into the gallery and put on a show for Lawrence, flirt with this friend of his – this Roddie. Lawrence would see that she didn't care; he would be relieved that she was still his best, flighty girl. Later she would tell him that there was no baby and that they'd both been mistaken. He might guess that she'd been testing him and be ashamed.

Chapter Twenty-nine

PATRICK STOOD ACROSS THE road from the Python Gallery. He thought how smart it was, brightly lit – the rest of the street was in darkness, and the gallery was an oasis of light and noise – it seemed there was a party going on, but it was small for a place that had taken up so much space in his imagination.

The party seemed to be coming to an end; Patrick had to step to one side to allow people out on to the street before he could go in. Inside, small groups were breaking into smaller groups, making their goodbyes and heading for the door. A man stood with his arm around a girl. The girl caught his eye and smiled a little drunkenly at him as the man said, 'Hello. I think you may be very late, we're just about to close – but look around –'

'I'm looking for an artist called Francis Law. I believe he had an exhibition here?' Patrick glanced at the pictures hanging around the walls. None was Paul's.

Another man said, 'Law isn't here.'

The man with his arm around the girl said, 'May I introduce you to Joseph Day – the artist. This is his show tonight, but don't mind him. I'm afraid the talented Mr Law isn't here.'

'Talented!' Day laughed harshly. 'Aye. We all know what he's talented at! Can you tell us why you were looking for him Mr ...?' He frowned at him. He peered more closely and laughed. 'Jesus. You're the one in that picture! Well, you'll know all about his *talents*, eh?'

Patrick made to turn away but Day caught his arm. 'Fucking queer – don't turn your back on me!'

'Let go.'

'Or else?'

The first man stepped forward. 'Or else, Day, I'll throw you out on to the street and all your unsold paintings after you.' He held out his hand to Patrick. 'Lawrence Hawker. Come through to the back – it's a little bit more civilized.'

This was Hawker, then, the man he'd worried about most, who might flatter Paul, who would understand his work far better than he did, perhaps take him out to dinner and listen to him talk about painting – something he never talked to him about. A bond would grow quickly between them; he imagined the two of them walking back from the restaurant together, through London's more knowing, blasé streets, to Hawker's rooms where he lived the kind of life Paul wanted to live: alone. And there would be works of art on the walls and books everywhere and there would be an *Englishness* about the place, the smell of coal fires, a damp dusk settling against the windows, the sound of rain against the glass. Hawker would have been an officer, of course, served in Gallipoli, not France – there had to be some little difference between Paul and him. Or perhaps he had served in Palestine, in Egypt, and they would talk about those countries, the pyramids that had so impressed Paul that for once he didn't care about the heat or the flies or that he was so far from home. *You're home now,* Hawker would say. Paul would nod, realising it at last, such a sweet realisation: home.

Patrick sat down on the chair Hawker pulled out for him. He heard the man laugh nervously. 'You look rather shattered.' He went to a cupboard, brought out two glasses and a bottle of brandy. 'Here,' he handed him a glass. 'Sorry about that lout out there.'

Patrick took a sip of the brandy; it was expensive – the brandy they would serve in the officers' mess. He should look at Hawker properly, not sideways, not snatching quick, reluctant glances. He should know what he was really up against. Meeting his gaze he said, 'Do you know where Francis is?'

'Paul – sorry – I know him as Paul … Does he prefer Francis? He never said –'

'Do you know where he is?'

The man held his gaze; he seemed to be sizing him up;

234

certain officers would do this: look him up and down, up and down, speculating as if he was a bull in a cattle market. *Are you a sound man, sergeant? Able to get the job done, what?* Tossers. He swallowed his drink, put down his glass and stood up. 'I'll go back to the hotel, wait for him there.'

He swayed, lack of sleep, of food, the brandy coursing through him, made him hold on to the back of the chair, flimsy under his weight. He felt Hawker's hand on his arm.

'Whoa. Steady. Don't want you breaking anything … Sit down, sit down, for pity's sake. You look done in to me. Get your breath back, eh? Good man.'

'Don't *good man* me!'

Hawker held up his hands. 'All right – sit down.' He shook his head. 'Figure of speech – perhaps you aren't a good man – who knows?' He smiled at him, a joker; the worst type of officer was the type who made jokes.

Patrick sat, all the exhaustion, all the worry and jealousy bowing him. Another glass of brandy was put into his hands, Hawker's voice more gentle as he said, 'Paul – Francis – is fine. No doubt he'll be delighted to see you.'

Hawker sat down behind his desk. He lit a cigarette and pushed the box and lighter towards him. 'Francis sold out on the night. Great success.'

Patrick thought of his own portrait, how Paul had made him look bolder than he was: idealised, although Paul had argued with him over this. *It's just how I see you, Patrick, just how you are.* But he was wrong; it was as though Paul didn't know him at all because he didn't see how scared he was, how angry and jealous and scared: wasn't an artist supposed to see more, understand more?

He looked down at his drink, swirling it around and around like some connoisseur warming the alcohol between his hands, releasing the brandy's aroma; this is what he'd seen other men do, at home in Tangiers, in houses where Paul was the little star to be remarked on, marvelled at; where he was Paul's guard, watching him, watching him, never more than a few steps away from him. He tasted the brandy, a sip, he could get drunk, falling-down drunk, something he rarely did, drunk with this man, this ex-officer with his mess voice, his lightness and jokes, his straightness. This man would be a welcome change of company: he'd had enough of bent men who looked at Paul, looked and looked and whispered behind their hands to each other, smirking, wondering which of them would get to him first.

Patrick reached for a cigarette and his hands trembled over the lighter. All the time he knew Hawker was watching him, wondering who this man was sitting trembling in his office. But Hawker knew who he was – he'd seen the picture: Paul's lover. He felt ashamed, even though he wasn't ashamed, not of himself: of Paul, perhaps that was it: Paul's bad behaviour shamed him. His only compensation was that he would never have to see that bloody picture again.

Hawker said, 'You didn't tell me your name.'

'Morgan.'

'Is that it? Come on – we're not on parade.'

'Patrick.'

'He told me you have a beautiful home in Tangiers, a haven he called it. I very much liked his pictures of the birds and the fountain, the fig tree … They're not sold, didn't go in the exhibition, I'm saving them for another kind of show … I do hope there will be another show, more of the fountain, more of the flora and fauna, if you will – very decorative, very lovely.' After a moment he said, 'Those other pictures of the soldiers – the ones I did sell – have a market. I can sell those kind of paintings easily. Not sure it's what he should be doing, though. Perhaps it was something he needed to get out of his system, eh?'

Patrick made to stand, but couldn't find the strength. 'I should be back at the hotel.'

'Plenty of time. Perhaps you should eat first. There's quite a decent little place round the corner. If I were you I'd get a good meal inside me, get some rest. In the morning –'

'The morning? I'll see him before then – he'll be back at the hotel.'

'Yes, of course.'

Patrick saw how awkward Hawker was, unable to look at

him now. Flatly he said, 'He's with someone.'

Hawker shook his head as though all at once exasperated by him and everyone else in the world. 'I don't know if he is *with* someone. I don't know – and even if I did know … Listen, he may be back at the hotel, it's really none of my business.'

Hawker saw him out. At the door on to the street he said, 'I'm pleased to have met you.' He shook his hand. 'Tell Paul – Francis – about the bird pictures. Remind him, would you?'

Patrick walked back in the direction of the hotel, buttoning his coat, pulling on his gloves – May, but England was cold, the drizzling rain meeting his expectations. The street was filthy; the wind rolled an empty beer bottle into the gutter where there was a kind of black soil, slimy-looking, stinking. On the side of a pawn shop was an advertisement hoarding for Hovis Bread – golden wheat, blue skies and yellow sun, the colours garish and ugly in the greyness and making everything else uglier. This country! This bloody hole he'd almost got himself killed for, for nothing – nothing! This country was nothing but weather and cold and hatred and spite, nothing but men spitting out *wog, queer, don't-turn-your-back-on-me-fucking-queer.*

He heard footsteps running behind him and turned, instinctively ready to fight; but it was the young woman from the gallery. She put her hand to her chest, gasping for breath. She was blonde and pale, frail-looking, as though she needed the sun, some warmth in her bones. Breathlessly she said, 'Patrick?'

He stepped back from her because the momentum of her running seemed to have brought her to a stop too close to him and because she had that smell English women had: cheap perfume hiding a faint whiff of sweat. Kohl was smudged around her eyes and her wispy hair was escaping from its grips; there was that hint of drunkenness he'd noticed in the gallery. No more than a child, he thought, a waif. He put out his hand to steady her because she looked as though she might collapse.

'Patrick?'

'Yes.'

On a rush she said, 'I know where Paul is.'

Patrick wanted to walk away, to have nothing to do with this girl and her tales. But she was shivering; he couldn't help but think he should take off his coat and put it around her shoulders, but it would swamp her and trail to the filthy pavement. A few doors away a pub cast an oblong of stencilled light on to the street. She glanced towards it, repeating, 'I know where he is.'

'All right,' he said. 'Let's get out of this cold.'

The pub was like those in Thorp, one pub in particular, all dark wood and dimly lit corners, where he would meet Paul from time to time, as though they were two old comrades out sharing reminiscences; and who would suspect them of anything else: Morgan, the big, burly butcher, Mr Harris, schoolmaster, with a wife and a baby on the way. You'd have to be a suspicious bugger to suspect anything, but all the same they'd had to keep to themselves, pretend. The pretending was a waste of their precious time, it got so they didn't bother with the pub any more, got so that their lives became only the flat above his butcher's shop, only its bedroom, the bed, the dip in the mattress where they rolled together, so close, so close, not a breath between them.

At the bar, Patrick glanced back at the girl, Ann, settling herself in a seat in the far corner by the fire, blindly pinning back a strand of her hair, dabbing at her eyes as though she guessed the black had ran. She'd asked for a port and lemon, reminding him of his mother, a sweet drink for a sweet drinking woman. His mother had had the same vulnerable look this girl had, too. He sighed, taking out his wallet and handing the barman his money. He looked along the bar where meat pies were arranged under a glass dome, pale, lardy-looking, a hole in the centre of each one where the gravy had bubbled through burnt and sticky. He wondered if he was hungry enough and decided he was. He bought two and another for the girl because she looked half-starved.

Settled with their drinks, the pies on plates in front of them, Patrick took out his cigarettes and lit one, offering the packet to the girl as an afterthought. She shook her head shyly like one of those little girls who would hold his hand in the school playground when he was a child.

Quickly she said, 'Lawrence told me you were looking for Paul. I know where he is. I know who he's with.'

Patrick picked up his drink only to put it down again; he should eat first. There was no knife to cut the pie, no napkin; this was a pub in England, what did he expect? The girl shifted beside him, so awkward in his presence he could hardly bear to look at her; he wondered what her motivation could be for chasing after him like this, only to make sense of it, only wondering at how slow-witted he was: Paul had snatched away some boy she loved.

He pulled the pie towards him, pushed it away again, thinking he should go to the bar and ask for a knife and fork or would they have him drip gravy down his chin, down his shirt? And then how would he appear to Paul, who was so neat and precise?

The girl said, 'Did you hear me? I know where Paul is.'

He turned to her; she was pretty, more than pretty; even with her eyes smudged and red from crying he could see that she was delicately beautiful, with no breasts to speak of, no soft curves, the kind of girl certain types of men would be attracted to. She dropped her gaze from his. Making trouble obviously didn't come naturally to her because it seemed to him that she was regretting this, afraid of him and what he might do. Perhaps she had expected him to be the mincing nancy-boy of happy imagination, not someone who was capable of smashing her lover's face to a pulp.

His cigarette had burnt down almost to nothing, most of it wasted, forgotten. He stubbed it out, saying, 'Are you hungry? I'll fetch some knives and forks. Do you think they have napkins? Maybe that's too much to ask.'

'I'm not hungry.'

He looked at the pies; it had been a long time since he had eaten English food. 'No,' he said, 'I don't think I'm hungry, either.' He sipped his beer, piss-poor London beer, but all the same he could drain it in one, return to the bar for another. He wondered if it would be better to be drunk when he finally faced Paul, better to rage and throw his fists about and put an end to the tension that had grown between them since Paul had decided to come here. And if he did behave so badly Paul might decide to stay. Best not to be drunk, then, but to behave properly and with dignity; his dignity had always been his best weapon.

He said, 'You're from Belfast, aren't you? My mother came from Belfast. She'd take me to see my grandmother for the summer holidays and I'd come back with the same accent you have.'

She glanced at him, only to look away as though even meeting his eye was inappropriately familiar. Quickly she said, 'What will you do?'

'About what?'

'Paul.'

He laughed shortly. 'Take him home.'

'Do you want me to tell you where he is?'

'Maybe he's back at his hotel, eh?'

She stared down at her drink. 'Yes. Probably.'

She was just like those little girls who would befriend him, who perhaps sensed his otherness as children seemed to. He remembered his first holy communion, how he'd been made to walk down the aisle with a little girl on his arm, a blonde little girl in a white dress and veil. He smiled; he would tell Paul this.

He said, 'I used to go to a church with my mother and grandmother on the Falls Road. St John's. Do you know it?'

She nodded.

'I was a good Catholic boy in Ireland, not so good in England.' He thought of Matthew, the good priest giving the last rites to men at the dressing stations early in the war, his faith ebbing away with each death. He had asked him why he stopped being a priest and Matthew had told him, 'I began to feel like a coward. Dying men were calling me Father – *Father*,' he laughed bitterly, 'I was just a frightened boy, quaking with fear, garbling the sacrament because I was so scared of all the blood. How could I go on like that?'

Matthew. He had told Matthew that he loved him and he wondered if this was true. Paul loved him, such a deep feeling he had never been able to fathom, and perhaps his own love for

Matthew was only a pretence, an attempt to feel what Paul felt, to be more like him. He had been jealous of Matthew at first – who was this man Paul travelled to see so faithfully? The letters they exchanged were long and sometimes Paul would say *Read this* – laughing as he passed him Matt's latest letter, full of jokes and cleverness, nothing to hide, nothing but this easy friendship. And when Paul was in prison Matthew would visit him when he was well enough, and afterwards he would meet him in a pub in the shadow of Durham Cathedral, drinking amongst all the hard drinking men. He had loved Matthew then, he was sure; it was easy to love Matthew when he was well. It was Matthew who had told him how much Paul needed him, Matthew who had said, 'When I see him it's you he asks after. You're in his heart, Patrick.'

He looked at the pies again; perhaps they didn't look so bad, and he was hungry. He smiled at the girl. 'I'll fetch some knives and forks, and then we can eat, and you can tell me about where you grew up.'

Chapter Thirty

IRIS KNELT BESIDE THE folding bed the hotel had put up in the room and covered Bobby more snugly. She kissed his head. 'Sweet dreams, sweetheart.' He was almost asleep, his eyelids heavy, he was no longer sucking his thumb with such concentration. Margot didn't like him to suck his thumb; it annoyed her new husband, who thought that it was a babyish habit. Well, he was a baby still, she told Margot. She would stand up for Bobby because it seemed that his mother wouldn't; perhaps Margot saw too much of the Harris boys in her son.

When she was certain he was fast asleep, Iris stood up and went to the bed. George held his hand out to her and she lay down beside him.

Quietly she said, 'Let's run away with him.'

He rolled onto his side to look at her. 'Where shall we go?'

'Anywhere. Cornwall – Land's End ... John O'Groats. Doesn't matter.'

He gazed at her; almost dusk, the curtains were open still and the light was soft and flattering; she thought how young he looked, young enough to be mistaken for Bobby's father without a second glance, without any question. He frowned, and she put her fingers to his mouth, but he drew back a little.

'He would miss Margot.'

She laughed and felt like crying. 'Of course he would.' Bobby had cried a little for his mother as she'd bathed him. 'Tomorrow,' she told him. 'As soon as you wake up, we'll go back on the train – you loved the train – and after the train Mummy will be there, waiting to give you a big hug.' Perhaps not a big hug, perhaps only a *Were you a good boy? I hope so, Bobby*. But he had been soothed, he had been a good boy; too good, she thought. His step-father had warned him often enough.

George rolled onto his back. 'Cornwall is beautiful. I took the boys there when they were quite small. Hotel by the beach, ice cream everyday … Padstow, that was it …' He closed his eyes. 'Lucky with the weather, Robbie and Paul brown as berries … They always took to the sun.'

He seemed to be remembering, picturing that beach; his two sons tanned by the sun. A nerve twitched almost imperceptibly in his cheek and he put his hand to it. He said, 'Robbie was such a bright boy – I wish you'd known him better, before the war … And brave! I remember he would swim far out to sea … climb the cliffs like a little monkey – little monkey making my heart stop. Half the time I hardly knew where he was and Paul was so watchful of him, in awe of him …' He looked at her. 'Paul not as bright, not as brave, not then … later, when he had to be, not then … I don't want you to have the wrong idea of them, Iris. The war changed them but they would have changed back, I think, become my boys again … No. Perhaps not, not entirely mine …'

He pulled her into his arms and she rested her head on his chest; he stroked her hair. She thought she might sleep but didn't want to; she wanted only to stay up all night with him. His heart beat steadily, and this was soothing. Outside on the street a young man laughed; a girl answered with some remark she didn't catch; there was only the boy's laughter moving off, away. She thought of Robbie in his greatcoat and cap, his puttees and shiny, shiny boots; she had thought him handsome and dull and not brave or bright. Bobby's father, climbing cliffs, brown as a berry, swimming out to sea; one day she would tell Bobby about Robbie Harris; but George would have already told him; somehow he would find a way around the lies they had told.

'Yes, we could run away with Bobby,' he said.

'Where shall we run to?'

He was silent for some time and she thought he was tired of this game, and that he may even have fallen asleep, but his hand became heavy on her head as if to hold her still. 'Tangiers.'

George had described Paul's house to her: how he imagined it, at least, its thick white walls and flat roof, its narrow, shuttered windows, tiled floors and heavy wooden doors, some doors opening out on to a courtyard where a table was set in the shade of a fig tree, where a fountain splashed and cooled the air. The fig tree and the table and the fountain: these were the things about his son's house he knew for certain, the things that Paul had written about and painted for him. The rest he only imagined. She imagined the heat at noon, the blinding sun; the sun was all she could imagine of that country; she had never taken to the sun as Paul had.

'I miss him,' George said. 'Every day I think, *go to him, just pack up and go – what's to stop you*? Every day. Nothing to stop me ... I just think, why stay? Why stay when Paul would welcome me, I'm sure. And if he lived alone out there ... but then he wouldn't be *out there*, would he? He'd be in Thorp, with Margot and Bobby ...' He lifted his hand from her head. 'I don't go to my son because he lives with a man. I am just as bad as everyone else.'

She knelt beside him. 'Come home with us tomorrow.'

'Yes, I'll go home. Paul won't want me to hang around here.' Quickly he said, 'I'm sorry, Iris. Sorry that this is the end of it. How shall we get along, do you think, once we're back in Thorp? Will you avoid me? Shall I cross the street when I see you or behave as I always have?'

'As you always have.'

He laughed painfully. 'God help me. God help me, I don't think I'll be able to do it.'

'We'll be friends again.'

He nodded, mute because of the tears she could see in his eyes. She kissed him, and he pulled her into his arms and held her tightly.

Chapter Thirty-one

EDMUND WATCHED PAUL DRESS. He said, 'Where are you going?'

Paul turned to him, frowning, thin and drawn in the unforgiving light of a sunny morning, unkempt because his hair stuck up a little and he hadn't shaved. A few days ago Edmund would have thought he was nothing, no one; he wouldn't have looked twice at such a man. Now he didn't want to let him out of his sight ever again.

Paul stepped towards the bed. 'Edmund, go back to sleep.'

'Where are you going?'

'To see my son.'

'Will you come back?'

'Yes. Yes, of course.'

'Promise?'

He sat on the bed, reaching out to press his hand against his cheek. 'Yes, I'll come back. Yes, Edmund, yes. Go to sleep, it's early …' He kissed him. 'Go to sleep.'

Edmund sat up. 'I love you. Believe me?'

'Yes.'

He watched Paul put on his jacket, smooth back his hair quickly in the mirror and shove his wallet into his pocket. He watched him hesitate at the door and look over his shoulder; Edmund thought he might get up, one last kiss and the erotic sensation of his nakedness against Paul's clothed body, his arms around him. Perhaps Paul would come back to bed then, stay a few more hours. But he was so tired and Paul was closing the door softly behind him; he heard his quick footsteps on the stairs. Edmund rolled onto his side, his arm stretching out to that warm place where Paul had slept beside him.

The sun was shining, that careful English sun he missed so much, and the London streets were crowded, men and women going to work in the sunshine, and if he caught a girl's eye she would smile at him as girls often did, and he would smile back, speculate a little, not seriously, only if, perhaps, maybe … There was promise everywhere. His life could take any direction, any direction at all, but always forward, with Edmund, no more looking back, no more memories that Edmund couldn't smile away; there would be new memories, a future full of them. He would never leave England again but take some rooms with Edmund – a better place with light and space to work, that looked out over rooftops to the river. He would paint the views Turner painted, the sun slipping into the Thames, briefly dazzling the cool evening sky; there would be softer colours, a different, calmer light; there would be winter and then spring, always changes, new beginnings. And there would be Edmund; smiling, carefree, only-in-the-present Edmund.

Paul stopped; he was smiling and breathless with this smiling. In a dress-shop window he caught sight of himself; he could be Edmund's age with all this smiling. He could be eighteen again and never have blasted Jenkins' brains all over his face. But Jenkins wouldn't have survived, he wouldn't have, his was a mercy killing. Tell yourself this, that you didn't kill him because of his crying, his horrible, infectious fear. You killed a man because you had to – a kindness; you were a good soldier, you were good at something.

But look at yourself in the dress-shop window and you could be eighteen again, fresh from Edmund's arms, his scent still on you, his breath still inside you; you could be his age. His age. With all his smiles, that lack of experience, he could be no more than eighteen. You step closer to the window, dumb with realisation. Eighteen. He is eighteen. So young, too young. Perhaps it doesn't matter how young he is. When you were eighteen the bodies were piling at your feet; perhaps he is older, twenty; when you were twenty you had shot Jenkins; this doesn't matter. Edmund will be immune from your past.

He could not love anyone more than he loves this boy, has never loved anyone more, he knows this. Edmund has taken him back in time and he is eighteen and the sun is shining, and there are new fashions in the dress-shop window, a smiling boy reflecting back at him as the traffic moves past him, around him, handsome men and smiling women at the start of a sunny day.

The window is cool against his forehead, his breath mists the glass; he is smiling still but there is something deeper, harder, colder inside him; he can't smile this coldness away, even Edmund's smile at this distance cannot warm him enough; he is cold and sinking deeper into coldness, and there are voices in his head he can't quiet, voices of the other prisoners so close to his ear, warm on his neck, *easy, easy* grunting, snuffling voices, triumphant, shunting themselves deep and hard so that they will always be inside him – *there there easy easy don't make this hurt more than it has to.* There is a stink, there is iron on his bitten-through tongue and stone cold beneath his face: the flags will press an imprint into his cheek, a graze, a gentle graze because he is giving in to the ground, the cold, the grunting, snuffling voices *easy easy easy.* He calls out for Patrick, but quietly so they won't hear him; Patrick who should only be a step away, was only ever a step away, but has gone from him now because he has been so faithless, so wicked and faithless he deserves this punishment.

'Young man.'

There is another reflection in the window, between his and the mannequin in its pale lilac dress. Lilac is the colour this season, it seems, and he cannot take his eyes off this dress, its lacy shapelessness; the glass is no longer cool, no longer soothing, only warm and hard beneath his forehead; the coldness is all inside him and the dress is so ugly, he must concentrate on it and not this man behind him who is wearing such fine clothes, a tall man, blond and beautiful. He can smell him: he is expensive, upright, twice his age but fuckable, certainly; perhaps he's followed him for a purpose; he looks as if he might have *purpose.* He might be mistaken; he sometimes is, not often. But not everyone fucks about as he does; he should remember this, remember this, think of Edmund, remember him.

The man spoke again, a rising inflection as though he was preparing to be mistaken. 'Young man?'

Paul stepped away from the window. He can't do what this man wants him to do, not now, perhaps not ever again. 'Sorry, excuse me.' He made to step past him but the man caught hold of his arm.

'Wait. A moment, if you will.'

'I'm sorry, I have to go –'

'Yes. In a moment. I won't keep you.'

His voice was soft, that cultured English voice that could make his insides curdle with fear or lust: the colonel's voice, the medic's voice, the judge's voice. Edmund's voice but older, colder, still a trace of him though, a trace. He managed to look at him; he was unmistakable. 'Dr Coulson.'

'Sir Richard, but Dr Coulson once, yes. I'm pleased you understand who I am – it makes this a little easier. Would you mind awfully?'

The man led him into the doorway of the shop, its closed sign turned out amongst the advertisements for silk stockings. There was no sun here, only deep shade, a mosaic of terracotta tiles beneath their feet, scraps of bus tickets and sweet wrappers blown into the corners. Paul kept his eyes on the wrappers swirling in a sudden breeze. Coulson was so tall, he might lean on him. He must not; he must concentrate and not make it worse for himself.

Coulson said, 'I'm so sorry, I don't know your name –' he held up his hand although Paul hadn't thought to speak. 'And I don't want to know your name. I only want to say this: you must keep away from Edmund. You must, because if you don't you will find yourself in a police cell. Now, I'm sure you had no intention of seeing him again, I know how men like you behave, I'm sure you wonder what the fuss is about, a nineteen-year-old innocent couldn't possibly detain you long. So, all well and good, as long as you do keep away from him from now on. You do understand me, don't you? I will go to the police if you don't stay away.'

The sweet wrappers blew around their feet, dry and rustling and raggedly bright like the scraps that would sometimes be caught on the barbed wire; odd, the things that could be snagged on the barbs. He began to shake; he would lean on this man; he would, if he didn't concentrate.

Coulson said, 'You do understand. I've seen men like you, wrecked by prison, and you wouldn't survive, by the look of you. Now, I need to hear you say that you will keep away from my son. All right. So speak up now.'

Paul lifted his head. Perhaps he hadn't heard him correctly. He frowned.

Coulson sighed. 'Listen, my boy, I very much pity you. I think you may have seen service, am I right? No doubt you fought alongside my older sons and that's why I haven't gone to the police already. But I lost one boy and I will not, *will not* lose another for whatever reason. Now, please tell me you will leave my young son alone. I must hear you say it.'

Paul stepped past him, out into the sun again; he wouldn't be made to speak; no one had ever made him speak, not even Jenkins with his crying and pleading, not even the prison warders, or the men who shared his cell, who came to his bed at night. Not even this doctor, a man who wanted his voice along with everything else, everything, all of him. He couldn't be made to speak, there had to be a little pride left.

He could hear Coulson calling after him; his voice was so like Edmund's but older. Edmund was a boy, so young, too young, and he could remember his smile if he tried very hard, but it was slipping away from him. There would be a memory in time, warm as a patch of sunlight to fall back on; enough, more than he had ever had before.

He walked quickly, quickly. His son was waiting; he would say goodbye to him, lift him into his arms and say goodbye.

Edmund heard the voice but it made no sense except in the persistent repeat of his name, the soft command: 'Edmund, wake up now. Wake up, Edmund, please.'

His father stood over him, smelling of outdoors, frowning and pretending to be cross with his *Late again, Edmund* face,

249

only his eyes giving him away. Edmund groaned, pushing his hands across his face, catching Paul's scent on his fingers, making him smile. He smiled at his father, puzzled as to why he should be here, but he was here, one of his occasional appearances, like an actor with a bit part in his life. 'Papa.'

'I've come to see you.'

'So I see.'

'I've come to tell you the man who was here is gone. He will not come back. You will not look for him. He won't be found.'

Edmund sat up. He would get out of bed, but he was naked. He stank; his room was stuffy and cold at the same time, and his father was dressed warmly in his outdoor coat, yet smelt of the cold. He could hardly understand what he had just said, because it seemed so unlikely that his father should look so unchanged and still know that he had changed so much. He stared at him until his father sat down on the bed where Paul had sat and reached for his hand, holding it tightly between his own so that he thought he might be dreaming, an odd, untimely dream.

'Perhaps it's time you came home now, Edmund. Your mother misses you so. Home for the summer and Oxford in October. I wish my own life was ahead of me so wonderfully.'

'No.'

'Yes.' He smiled at him. 'Shall you argue like a child, Edmund? Shall I have to put my foot down? Enough now. Time to come home. I shall send the car for you, for your things.' He looked around, then back to him. 'A year, I promised you a year, it's over now.'

'He'll come back.'

'No, Edmund, he won't. How could I allow it? What kind of father would I be if I didn't watch over you?'

'Watch …?'

His father stood up. 'I must go. Get up now, bathe. The car will be here this afternoon.' He went to his shelves and looked at the books. After a moment he said, 'He was very decent about it. A decent young man. Really, Edmund, you mustn't lie about your age, he was shocked. And you might have got him into very serious trouble. Very serious trouble indeed, I know how indiscreet you are – boys like you are always indiscreet. And I think a man like that doesn't need any more trouble than he has already, don't you?' He turned from the books to look at him. 'You might go to the bookshop and thank Barnes on my behalf. Thank him for his kindnesses. Be back here for the car at two o'clock. Don't leave your lovely books behind.'

He was gone. Edmund fell back onto the bed. He thought he might wind back the last few minutes, say something, do something that would change the present so that he could still believe he would see Paul again. His father had seemed so much larger than life standing over his bed, dressed in his coat … Perhaps he had dreamt him, just as he had been dreaming that Paul had gone; Paul had found him out and he had gone.

In this dream of his he seemed to be confusing Paul with Neville because Paul was in uniform, his eye restored, and he was saying, 'I'm dead. What do dead men say?' And he was gone, his father there instead, insisting, insisting as though nothing had changed at all.

Chapter Thirty-two

GEORGE SAID, 'WELL NOW, Bobby, this has been an adventure, hasn't it? And before Grandmamma takes you home on the train, we shall have breakfast. Eggs and bacon and toast, how does that sound?'

He held Bobby's hand as they walked downstairs, leaving Iris to finish dressing. His own voice rang in his ears, too hearty, full of guilt. He held his grandson's hand too tightly; he had the shameful idea that he might at any moment sweep him into his arms and say, 'You'll keep our secret, won't you, my darling boy?'

He had only intended to hold her, too aware of Bobby's presence to do anything else, and for a long while he had only held her, and the room became darker, Bobby's breathing more settled into sleep so that it became easier to forget about him; there was just the two of them, face to face, the necessary darkness and quiet kind to them both, slowing the time they had left together until it seemed that they had stepped outside time and there was nothing beyond themselves. When she moved against him, she was languid, so much time they had, after all, all night in the dark and quiet; she made him live every fraction of every second, made each breath and heartbeat keep time with hers; this was to last for the rest of their lives.

He paused on the stairs and lifted Bobby into his arms; he needed to hold him, feel his warmth and weight, his too-big-to-be-held awkwardness. George was too full of energy not to. She had sent this charge through him and it had nowhere else to go except to fuel his guilt; he needed to steady himself; this mania wouldn't do at all. He put Bobby down again at the bottom of the stairs. 'Sorry, Bobby. Your granddad is a very silly old man.'

He went to the reception desk. The same man was there, as though he never left his post; he wondered if he could ask him if he had a home, or did he sleep here in the hotel, and what was it like to live and work in such a place? He should tell him that he was glad that the hotel existed, but perhaps it didn't exist; there was that trick it played with time, after all; he should ask this man how he stopped time like that. He said only, 'Have you seen Mr Law this morning?'

'No, sir.'

George nodded. He had already knocked on Paul's door, sensing he wasn't there. 'If you see him, would you tell him I'm still here?'

'Of course, Mr Harris.'

He was still here, waiting. He imagined waiting in this hotel for the rest of his life for Paul to come back, time expanding and contracting like metal bars heated in the sun, keeping him here as the world changed around him, because how could he resist pausing his life in such a way. He thought of Iris and the slow, careful way she held him, and how they would leave this hotel and go back to their old lives. They would be friends, she had said, as though nothing had happened between them at all, nothing they might be ashamed of.

He became aware of Bobby's hand pulling his. 'Granddad. It's that man who bought me ice cream.'

There was a lounge tucked away like a secret place to be revealed only at the receptionist's discretion. The man had led them along a corridor and held open a door. 'Here we are. Would you like me to bring you some coffee, perhaps some milk for the young man?'

'Yes, thank you.'

This was a room of chairs and low tables, of tall windows looking out on to a walled garden. French doors were open on to a small terrace where a wrought-iron table and chairs warmed in a square of sun. Paul turned to him. 'Shall we sit outside?'

The iron table and chairs were wet with dew and Paul wiped the seats with his handkerchief. 'Is this all right? Not too cold?'

'It's warm, Paul. Spring.' George sat down, the chair cold beneath him and rocking a little on the uneven flag stones. Bobby stood at the edge of the terrace, and he said, 'Bobby, why don't you go and explore the garden whilst Francis and I talk? See what you can find.'

Paul watched Bobby run across the small lawn. Without taking his eyes off him he said, 'Thank you for bringing him to see me. Thank you for staying.' At last he managed to look at him. 'I'm so sorry, Dad. I've behaved very badly.'

'You're here now. We won't say any more.'

'Nothing more?' Paul watched his son chase a pigeon that landed a few feet away. The bird flew into the air in a panic of grey-blue feathers; Paul kept his gaze on Bobby, such longing on his face that George turned away. He heard Paul strike a match and smelt his cigarette smoke. He waited for him to speak, knowing that whatever he said himself would be wrong, too desperate or too brusque in an effort not to seem desperate at all. The smell of Paul's cigarette mixed with the damp smells of an English garden in late spring; he turned and there was a lilac tree heavy with white flowers, a little out of the sun, not warm enough yet to perfume the air too densely. He breathed in deeply: Paul's peculiar cigarettes and lilac, something else to remember him by.

Paul turned to him. 'I was wondering how I might pretend to be Francis, for Bobby's sake. But I think that whenever I saw him I wouldn't be able to stop myself saying *I knew your father* and sometimes his father would be Robbie and sometimes he would be Paul, mixed up together, confusing ...' He shook his head. 'Even if I could keep quiet – just be *Francis*, the man who buys him ice cream, who imposes himself on his life, even then he'd only wonder what to make of me.'

'He'd recognise you as he grew older –'

A waiter came with coffee, a basket of sweet rolls and a glass of milk. Paul stood up and walked towards Bobby. He held out his hand to him. 'Bob, come and have some breakfast.'

Bobby hesitated and George willed him to take Paul's hand, willed the child to recognise him. It shouldn't take so much, after all, for Bobby to see that this was his father. George concentrated on pouring the coffee, on adding cream to his own cup, sugar to Paul's. From the corner of his eye he saw Paul swing Bobby into his arms and up onto his shoulders. Bobby was small for his age, as Paul had been small, but his father was strong now – stronger than he looked. He heard Bobby laugh, the first time he had heard him laugh so happily for days.

Patrick bathed; he brushed his teeth and shaved carefully then studied his face in the mirror. Practise an expression, he thought. One of mild, anything's-all-right-by-me acceptance, one that says *Stay in London longer, if you wish; go to Thorp if you can bear to; come home with me. Whatever you want to do*. Practise this nonchalant expression so that it stays on your face without any effort, no ragged emotion to give you away. No anger, no pleading, no fear. He only had to be careful, steady, contained: himself.

He went downstairs. The receptionist called to him, 'Mr Morgan. Mr Law is here, sir.'

Patrick looked at him blankly. Who was this Mr Law? He leaned on the reception desk, afraid of how weak he had become.

'Are you quite all right, Mr Morgan?'

'Has Mr Law gone to his room? I'd knocked …'

'No, sir. He's with another gentleman in the lounge.'

'This other man …?'

'Mr Harris and his son.'

'Where? Where are they?'

'Along the corridor to your right, sir.'

George had left them alone together and Paul held Bobby on his knee, both of them watching the London sparrows hop closer and closer to the table for the crumbs from the breakfast rolls. He had told him that in France bread like this was called croissants because they were shaped like the crescent moon, and where he lived they were called krachel and were flavoured with orange-flower water and anise. And the sparrows were a little tamer, expecting their crumbs each morning, payment for the poses they made.

255

He held him closer and kissed the top of his head. He thought of saying, *I knew your daddy and he loved you very much*. But saying this now would make him someone else. For now he was Bobby's daddy. He shifted Bobby's weight on his knee, no weight at all really; he was small and agile as Rob had been. He kissed his head again and Bobby looked up at him. 'Will you come on the train with us?'

'No, I have to go home.'

'Back to where they eat the funny bread?'

'Yes, back there, Bob.'

'Nobody calls me Bob.'

'No? I used to. Do you mind me calling you Bob?'

He shook his head and scrambled down from his knee to face him. 'Bob's better. Bob's a grown-up's name.'

Paul thought of the grown-up Bob, how he might find him and ask for his forgiveness; he wondered if he would be brave enough. To be forgiven he would have to confess everything – how could he be fully forgiven unless all of his trespass was known? He would have to throw his most intimate self at his grown son's feet and it would be as though he felt some perverse pride in himself: see what he'd been up against? His very nature. Hadn't he tried so hard to be faithful? Forgive me, he would say, I really couldn't help myself.

There could be no confession, then; his pride wouldn't allow it; Bob would never know the truth and perhaps that would be best: best to keep away and not intrude on his son's life with his need to be understood. He would bear the consequences of his own actions, the grown-up thing to do.

They left the garden. Paul watched his son run along the corridor towards a man he didn't recognise for a moment because the sun was in his eye, a tall, powerfully built man who caught Bobby in his arms, holding him close before setting him down and taking his hand. Patrick, here to save him if he needed to be saved. For a moment he imagined walking past him, on, out into the London streets, not stopping until he had made his own life, something he had never done before. But his relief was too great, his need too great. He walked towards him, quickening his step.

Epilogue

Soho, one year later
FRED SAID, 'SHE WANTED the wedding do here. Now I couldn't turn her down, could I, Matt?' He stepped down from the chair he'd been stood on to polish the mirror behind the bar. Susie had hung bunting everywhere; she had made a sign that read *Congratulations Mr & Mrs Hawker!* That exclamation mark surprised me; then I thought that perhaps Susie was being ironic.

Susie caught my eye and raised her eyebrows as if to say, *Well, could Fred have turned her down?* No; Fred was giving her away; I'd glimpsed through his open bedroom door his good suit hanging brushed and ready. Already Susie was wearing her new dress and an odd little hat: feathered and flighty and unlike her, another irony, perhaps. She said, 'You've missed a bit, Fred – there, look, where it's smeary.' As Fred climbed on the chair again, she said lightly, 'You coming to the church, Matt?'

'Yes,' Fred said. He turned to me, duster still raised. 'Come. There's to be a full mass.' He stepped down again, tossing the duster under the bar. 'Bells and smells, Lawrence calls it. I don't think he's being disrespectful.'

'No, I'm sure,' I said.

'He's going along with it to keep her happy.' Fred began polishing glasses. 'I think he'd do anything to keep her happy. Besotted.'

'He loves her,' I said.

Fred laughed. 'Who bloody wouldn't, eh? Gorgeous girl like that.'

Susie was watching me. I thought that her hat should have a

veil, and then she could watch more discreetly. I smiled at her. 'I won't come to the church.'

'But you'll come down after and have a drink with us all?'

'Perhaps.'

'You'll like Lawrence,' Fred said. 'Grand lad he is.'

'Yes, I've met him. Would you both excuse me?'

'Of course, you go and have a lie down. Rest.' Fred grinned at me. 'I always say it's best to get your head down whilst you can.'

I went upstairs and lay down on my bed. My room is above the bar and I can hear Fred and Susie's bickering, their laughter and clattering. There are gaps in the floorboards so that if I have a mind to I can lift back the rug and spy on them. I know that's the kind of thing I am capable of, that I'm keeping a tight rein on. I am being very careful, as though I'm carrying a sleeping baby that might at any time wake and start to scream. Even when I'm alone I can never put the baby down; it's difficult to relax, to *rest*, as Fred says. He must see how tense I am; he must worry that asking me here wasn't the most sensible thing to do; only the kind thing, the charitable thing, although he would swear he doesn't think of me in those terms.

He came to visit me at Easter, when I was almost as well as I am now, and told me I could live with them. 'You could maybe help us out behind the bar. I could often do with a strong lad like you backing me up.' Lad. I suppose I am a child when I'm in the hospitals. Not a man, anyway.

The bedroom Fred has made over to me is quite large; there is space enough for a desk and an armchair, space for my books; I am really quite self-contained and can be alone whenever I want to be, although there is always noise from the bar and from the street. I don't mind this noise; there is life going on around me, and this makes me feel connected. And I do serve behind the bar, and there are fights occasionally and sometimes the drunks weep on my shoulder. Sometimes Lawrence Hawker comes in; he sometimes buys me a drink – *whatever you're having*, he says. He keeps an eye on me rather as Susie does. They are both curious, both of them wondering

258

what my next move will be; Susie knows that I love Ann; Hawker only has his suspicions that I'm not to be trusted.

During the war Hawker would've addressed me as sir. 'Yes, sir, Major, sir.' A snappy little captain, not a bad officer to have under one's command, if a little wearing perhaps. Now he doesn't call me anything, only tosses off his *whatever you're having*, not looking at me as he takes his change from his pocket, only looking when he thinks I'm busy elsewhere. Once I caught his eye in the mirror behind the bar and he didn't look away; I had the chance to study him as he had the chance to study me. He looks as though he has lost something, someone, perhaps, and that he can't quite understand why he can't get over this loss, him with his bright future ahead. I imagine telling Ann not to marry him, but for all I know Hawker might be the best of our generation: who of us hasn't lost something, after all?

I imagine telling Ann that I am sorry. I rehearse my apology in my head. I would go into Hawker's gallery where she works behind a desk he set up for her, displaying her like one of his works of art. I would pretend to be studying one of the pictures or a sculpture perhaps, and she would approach me, not realising for a moment that it was me, just another customer to charm into a sale. When I turn to face her she would step back; I imagine her hand going to her mouth to stop her exclamation escaping. And then my imagination runs out; I can't think of the words I would use. Sorry really doesn't seem good enough. I do imagine how lovely she is, but also that Hawker has polished her so that she is almost unrecognisable from the girl I knew. Susie refers to her as the Queen of Sheba and Fred catches my eye and shakes his head as if I know all about women and their talk. 'She's just a nice lass who's done well for herself,' he says. Not a queen, then, not the beautiful astonishing woman who comes to me night after night after night so that I wake in a fever of desire. A nice lass; it's what my father would have called her, and he would have been as wrong as Fred is wrong.

The walls of this room are papered in a busy pattern of trellised roses and ivy. I could paint over this pattern, plain white, Fred wouldn't mind; he says I should do as I like. Paul's pictures would look better on a bare wall. A few weeks after I came here, a picture arrived from him of a boy lying in a meadow. Buttercups grew around him, gold strokes of paint dashed amongst the greens of the tall grass. A peaceful boy, a self-portrait. The letter he sent with this picture invited me to his home, an open invitation, he wrote. He wrote, *Patrick and I would be so pleased to see you.* He writes this often, although I think he knows it's a journey I'll never make. Hawker has invited him back here, he wrote, there'll be another exhibition of his work. He'll come to me, then, just as he always has.

I must have fallen asleep, because when I woke there was gramophone music playing in the bar and the sound of people laughing and talking a little too loudly, rather as though they were relieved: this is what wedding parties sound like when they are released from church, I'd recognise the sound anywhere; I could even feel the slap on the back, the hearty handshake from a bride's father, *Thank you, Father, lovely service, will you come back and have a drink with us, Father?* Not wanting me there, not really, weren't they to have a party, an unloosening of ties and collars? Some priests would have loosened their own collars too and drunk the good health toasts. I was too young, I think, too fervent.

I got up only to stand, tense and listening; I felt like a chanced-upon thief with no escape open to him. I could hide in my room or I could go downstairs and face them. My help would be needed; there would be plenty of drinkers to serve.

I turned and she was there, standing in my doorway.

'Matthew.' She was hesitant, afraid. She carried a bouquet of white roses, cloud white against her sky-blue dress; their perfume filled the air between us. She glanced back down the stairs, turning to me again as I stepped towards her. 'Matthew.' Very quickly she said, 'Forgive me?'

I wanted to hold her, to toss those flowers aside and crush her to me. I only gazed at her, and I could feel myself shaking my head; I heard myself saying, 'I should get down on my knees to you.'

'No! No …' She laughed as though she might cry. 'No. Matthew …'

I heard him coming up the stairs; I saw him; he stood behind her and put his arms around her waist and pulled her to him gently, all the time holding my gaze. Then he kissed her shoulder; he said, 'Come downstairs, my darling girl.'

'Yes, yes. I will...'

There were shouts from the bar, the bangs of popping champagne corks. I said, 'Go back to your guests.' I smiled, bright as could be. 'The pair of you shouldn't be up here.'

She turned and left the scent of her roses, and a feeling inside me that I could put the sleeping baby down for a little while.

The End

Prologue and First Chapter of
Paper Moon

Soho, January 1939

THE ROBE THE MAN had given her to change into was dark blue silk, printed with storks and Japanese gardens and tiny bridges on which pigtailed men crossed shimmering streams. The silk felt cold and slippery against her bare skin, and she shivered as though snakes slithered over her flesh. She raised her hands and lifted her hair free to fall around her shoulders.

From behind the camera, the man who had introduced himself only as Jason held up a hand as if to silence her. She hadn't thought to speak – the idea that he thought she might surprised her, because she was scared and cold and her teeth were chattering. The camera flashed and Jason lowered his hand. She blushed darkly.

'Well done.' His voice was posh and effeminate, and she remembered what was said about certain types of Englishmen. 'Now,' he said, 'take off the robe.'

There was a café across the road from the studio in Percy Street, off London's Tottenham Court Road. It was the place where Jason had first introduced himself and told her she had good bones for the camera, as though the camera was a beast in need of feeding. The tables were covered in oilcloths in red checks and steam hissed from a tea urn on the counter. Bath buns sweated beneath a glass dome smudged with an intricate pattern of fingerprints. Men sat at the other tables, hunched possessively over fried bread and bacon and eggs that ruptured

263

and spilled yellow yolks over the thick white plates. Nina looked away, remembering she was hungry.

At the counter, her companion pointed at the buns. She heard him laugh and looked up. In the studio he had seemed serious, not given to friendliness; he had barely spoken to her at all, only watched as Jason took photo after photo. Behind the café's counter the woman lifted the glass dome and dropped two buns onto a plate, obviously charmed.

He carried the tray of tea and buns to her table and sat down opposite her. His face was serious again. He took cigarettes from his pocket and offered her the open packet. When she shook her head he frowned.

'You don't smoke?'

'It makes me sick.'

'You get over that.' He went on frowning at her, shaking out the match he used to light his own cigarette. 'If you want to be an actress you should smoke. Smoking gives you something to do with your hands.'

He poured the tea, pushing a cup towards her along with the plate of buns. 'Come on, now, eat up.' He imitated her Irish accent so accurately she blushed, bowing her head to hide it. She heard him laugh and forced herself to meet his eye, intending to give him a fierce gaze. But he was smiling at her and once again she was struck by how beautiful he was, like the colour plate of Gabriel in her Children's Illustrated Bible.

She said, 'He takes your picture, too, doesn't he?'

He nodded. 'And afterwards I come here for sticky buns.'

'To feel normal again.'

He gazed at her. Holding out his hand he said, 'Bobby Harris, pleased to meet you.'

His hand was cold and dry in hers. Letting go, she said, 'Nina Tate.'

'Tell me your real name.'

She looked down, stirred sugar into her tea. At last she said, 'Patricia O'Neil.' She met his gaze, daring him to laugh. He only nodded. Taking one of the buns he bit into it and discreetly licked the sugar crystals from his lips.

'Nina, would you like to go to the pictures after this?'

He was eighteen, only months older than her. He was posh, like Jason, but not like him, because she guessed that the photographer had trained himself to talk as he did, whereas Bobby had been born to it. In the dark warmth of the cinema she studied his profile as the lights from the screen alternately shadowed and illuminated his face. There was a perfect symmetry to his features; his hair was thick and dark, falling over his forehead so that from time to time he pushed it away from his eyes that were green as a cat's. His nose had been broken – there was a small bump on its bridge where it had mended, and she stared at it, wondering how anyone could have hurt him, until he caught her eye and smiled. She looked away. On the screen Fred Astaire danced his impossible steps and sang, *'If you're blue and you don't know where to go to, why don't you go where Harlem flits …'* Bobby leaned towards her, his mouth close to her ear. Softly and in tune he sang, *'Putting on the Ritz,'* and a shiver ran down her spine.

He lived in a room above Jason's studio. They lay on his bed, fully clothed, side by side like effigies on a tomb, his hand closed loosely over hers. An oil lamp cast shadows but left the corners of the room in darkness so that she couldn't see the things he might possess. The bed was big enough to leave a decent space between them – she could sleep without touching him, she could pretend to be innocent, even though he had seen her naked. But that had been an odd kind of nakedness; she hadn't given anything away. Daring herself to look at him, she turned her head on the fat, feather pillows. He'd lit a cigarette, releasing tremulous rings of smoke into the dull yellow light. The silence between them made her feel safe and lazy, as though she need never talk again.

As the smoke rings flattened against the ceiling she imagined he could hear her heart beating. She wondered if he guessed she loved him, although she had only realised it a moment ago, recognising what Jason must've seen – that they were the same, a matching pair like the Dresden shepherd and shepherdess on Father Mitchell's mantelpiece. It seemed immoral to love someone because they looked like you, and she thought of the orphanage nuns who had told her that only the soul was important, although in their pictures Christ was always exquisite, even in agony.

He turned on his side and edged closer so that their noses almost touched. He said, 'I'm learning to fly,' and at once she imagined wings sprouting from his narrow shoulders, heavy, immaculate wings, white as doves. He was Gabriel, after all, grounded for a time. She smiled and he touched her mouth with his fingers. 'It's true.'

He was silent again, staring at the ceiling where it seemed the smoke rings had left indelible marks like halos. She believed she would sleep – her limbs felt weighted to the bed. She would dream of smoke and flying. His hand squeezed hers.

He said, 'I'd like to make love to you, but it won't mean anything. I don't want you to love me, or think I might love you. Loyalty is what matters.'

She felt as she had when she'd allowed the Japanese robe to slip from her shoulders, a catch-your-breath mixture of fear and excitement that came from knowing she was as wicked as the nuns said she was. She wasn't disappointed that he disregarded love – she suspected men did, at first. She wondered about loyalty, deciding it was safe. He looked at her. He seemed very young and all at once she felt powerful. She smiled, hiding it with her hand.

'You're shocked,' he said.

She stopped herself smiling and arranged her face into a suitable expression of seriousness. Lowering her hand from her mouth she said, 'It won't mean anything?'

'Except that I think you're lovely.' He seemed to think the word inadequate because he frowned. 'Beautiful. Is that enough?' He gazed into her face before closing his eyes and pressing his mouth to hers.

She became his girl. He bought her copies of the latest Paris fashions made by refugees in back-street tailor shops. He bought her gloves and high-heeled shoes and sweet, sexy hats with polka-dot veils or flighty feathers. He taught her how to speak as he did and to smoke; he taught her how to hold her head up and sway her hips when she walked so that men smiled after her and whistled. In Jason's photographs around that time she looked as if she was keeping a secret, although Jason guessed she was in love and told her to keep it to herself, that it showed in her eyes and ruined his composition. She guessed that he was jealous, newly sophisticated enough to know that Jason loved Bobby, too.

That summer in Hyde Park they watched workmen dig trenches, cover from the bombs no one could imagine falling. The smell of the cold, disturbed soil reminded her of graveyards and she shuddered, slipping her arm around Bobby's waist and leaning close to him. His blue RAF tunic was rough against her face; she traced her fingers over the wings on his chest and pictured him flying in his comical little plane: Bobby the pilot, her delicate, fine-boned boy. He seemed invented for the air, for light and space and speed; the drudgery of the trench diggers would break him in two.

He said, 'Jason took his last photograph of me today.' He didn't look at her but went on gazing at the men waist deep in the earth. 'He doesn't know yet. He thinks we'll go on as we were.'

His cap shaded his eyes and he bowed his head to light a cigarette, shielding the match with cupped hands. She wondered how anyone could imagine they could go on as they were when Bobby was so changed. After Jason took his photographs he'd discarded the ordinarily beautiful clothes he'd arrived in for the extraordinary transformation of his uniform. He'd adjusted his cap and straightened his tie in front of Jason's wall of mirrors, mirrors they'd used to check other dressing-up costumes. There was no irony in his pose; he didn't smile to include her in this new, elaborate joke. She'd watched his reflection, seeing at last the way he saw himself: serious, intent on the future and a war that couldn't come fast enough. Soon he would look at her and not see the same person but someone he'd known ages ago, a shadow from his childhood.

The workmen climbed from their trench. Clay clung to their boots and smeared their faces where they had wiped sweat from their brows. They looked like creatures of the earth, as weighted to it as she was. Only Bobby could escape.

Chapter One

Soho, April 1946

STANDING BEHIND HIS FATHER'S wheelchair, Hugh Morgan scanned the crowded room, looking for the blonde he'd noticed earlier. A moment ago she'd been flirting with Henry, his father's editor, whose cheeks had flushed the same shade of red as the girl's dress. She had laughed suddenly, flashing her teeth and reminding him of the shark in *Mac the Knife*.

Hugh lit a cigarette and blew smoke into air already thick with tobacco fumes. He'd noticed that the girl used a cigarette holder and that her dress clung to the curve of her backside and plunged between her breasts. He imagined he'd seen the dimple of her belly button through the sheer fabric, realising with dismay that he must have been staring. It seemed as though he had forgotten how to look at women.

Hugh had arrived in London that morning. His ship had docked in Portsmouth the day before and he was now, officially, a civilian. The London train had been full of service men and women, all looking like misplaced persons, grey-faced and anxious, as though the prospect of facing those left behind at the start of the war filled them with dread. What would they say to them? *The bed's too soft.* The line from one of his father's poems had come back to him as the train rattled through the English countryside. Beside him, an RAF sergeant had fallen asleep, his Brylcreemed head almost resting on Hugh's shoulder, his body a heavy, warm weight against his arm. The WREN opposite had smiled in sympathy and he'd realised that women in uniform would never call him sir again. He'd felt liberated, dislodging the still sleeping airman to lean across the carriage and light the girl's cigarette. It had been an uncharacteristic move; all at once he'd found himself too shy to strike up the kind of conversation that might have led to an end to his months of celibacy. He'd spoken to the WREN as though he was still her superior officer. Henry would've had a better chance of getting her knickers off.

Hugh sighed, and gave up looking for the girl in the red dress. She had probably left, bored by his father's middle-aged, bookish friends and the awe-struck fans that turned up to his poetry readings. All Hugh's life his father had been famous, or as famous as poets could be. A crippled veteran of the Somme, turned war poet, Mick Morgan had struck a chord with the British public. A Kipling for the modern age, *The Times* had called him in its latest review, a great populist. Hugh knew that the article would have angered Mick: the last thing his father wanted to be was popular.

The girl in the red dress appeared again. Twisting round in his wheelchair to look at him, Mick said, 'Her name's Nina Tate. She's a model.'

'What's she doing here?'

Without irony his father said, 'She loves my work. She had a dog-eared copy of Dawn Song she wanted me to sign.' Watching the girl he said, 'You should introduce yourself, Hugh. Tell her I wrote *Homecoming* for you – you'll be irresistible.'

'I'd say I'm not her type.'

'How do you know that? For God's sake, boy, if I were your age …'

'Weren't you married when you were my age?' Hugh frowned at him, pretending he didn't know. 'Anyway, why don't you go and talk to her? As the writer of *Homecoming* you've got a head start on me.'

'I've already invited her to dinner. You can come too, if you like.'

They watched the girl together. A blonde ringlet had escaped from her chignon, bobbing against her long, white neck, and she tucked it behind her ear. Her fingernails were painted scarlet. Hugh imagined their scrape across his back, feeling the stirring of desires too long suppressed.

* * *

A week earlier, a few days before Bobby left London, Nina had told him she was going to the book launch. He'd laughed shortly. 'What's he writing about now? Don't tell me – the pity of war, *again*. More books should be burnt – I was with Adolf on that one.'

Bobby was walking her home from her job as sales assistant in Antoinette Modes. She knew he had spent the day alone in her room and that boredom had soured his mood. Only a week since his release from hospital, he still waited for the cover of darkness before braving the streets. She'd sighed, searching out his hand from his pocket and holding it gently, as though the burns that disfigured it were still raw and painful. After only a few steps he stopped and lit a cigarette, an excuse to draw his hand away. The match flared, illuminating the taut, immobile mask skin grafts had made of his face, and he held her gaze, his eyes challenging her to look away. He would often test her like this, always alert for expressions that might betray her.

He shook the match out, tossing it into the overgrown garden of a bombed house. Bitterly he said, 'Do you have to go?'

'Not if you don't want me to.'

He sighed. 'Go, buy a pile of his books – we'll have a bonfire.'

She'd laughed despite herself and he'd smiled, reaching out to touch her face before drawing his hand away quickly. 'Be careful of Michael Morgan, he's a womaniser.'

Sitting opposite Morgan now in an Italian restaurant, Nina began to eat the spaghetti the waiter had set in front of her. The pasta was over-cooked, the sauce too thin, sweet with the taste of English ketchup. The bread grew staler in its raffia basket as the poet, his son and his minder ate their meals without comment. They were all used to worse, and the taste could be washed away with the sour red wine, but suddenly she was tired of terrible food and she pushed her plate away and fished in her bag for her cigarettes. Mick Morgan leaned across the table with his lighter.

'Would you like something else?' he asked.

Henry Vickers said, 'They used to do v...v...very

g…g…good ice cream here, before the w…w…war.'

Sitting beside her, Morgan's son pushed his own, cleared, plate away. 'You brought me here as a child, do you remember, Henry? Chocolate ice cream in a tall glass and two long spoons. I believed you when you said they wouldn't serve grown-ups ice cream.'

'I didn't think I was such a g…g…good liar.' He smiled at him lovingly. 'I thought you were humouring me.'

'No.' Hugh caught Nina's eye and laughed as though embarrassed.

Nina got up. Smiling at Henry to lessen his discomfort she said, 'Would you excuse me? I have to powder my nose.'

In the ladies' toilets, the sole concession to a powder room was the cracked mirror above the sink. Taking a lipstick from her bag she unscrewed it, then paused. There was no need to put on more – it was simply an automatic response to a mirror, but it helped, sometimes, to look harder than she actually was. She applied it quickly, pressing her lips together to even out the stain. Her reflection smiled back at her, glossy and seductive. Turning away, she went back into the dim, red light of the restaurant.

'She's lovely, isn't she?'

Hugh sighed. 'Dad, just stop. I'm tired, I could sleep for a month – I'm not interested in her.'

'Then why come with us tonight? Henry can manage quite well on his own.'

Hugh looked at Henry's empty chair. 'I hurt him, didn't I? I didn't mean to. I suppose I'm out of practice when it comes to dealing with men like him.'

'Oh? I thought the navy was stuffed with queers. I would've thought you'd get plenty of *practice*.' More harshly he added, 'Anyway, Henry loves you like a father. Maybe if he had been your father you wouldn't be so bloody …' He seemed lost for words and Hugh looked at him.

Levelly he said, 'You haven't asked me how Mum is.'

'How is she?'

'Fine.'

Wanting a drink, Hugh turned towards the bar. The same bunches of dusty wax grapes and vine leaves hung from the walls, looking less exotic now than when he was a child and ice cream was on the menu. They sat on the same plush-covered banquettes he remembered itching against his short-trousered legs and the same posters of Pisa and Rome curled their corners from the walls as red candles cascaded wax down the sides of wine bottles. Only one thing had changed – the man who had been proprietor then, who had pinched his cheek and smiled his rapid, incomprehensible endearments, had been interned on the Isle of Man. He'd died there, so Henry told him. Hugh sighed, trying unsuccessfully to feel anything but exhausted.

Failing to catch the waiter's eye he turned to his father. 'Do you want a Scotch?'

'No, I've had enough.'

As Henry came back Hugh said too heartily, 'You'll join me, Henry, won't you?'

'Will I? In what?' Henry and Mick exchanged a wry look. Irritated, Hugh turned away.

Nina Tate sat down beside him. She touched his arm briefly and at once turned her attention on his father. 'Would you mind if your son and I go dancing?'

Hugh laughed, astonished. 'Shouldn't you ask me first?'

He felt her foot brush against his ankle; she had taken her shoe off and her silk-stockinged toes worked their way beneath his trouser leg. To Mick she said, 'Thank you for this evening.'

On the street outside the restaurant Hugh said, 'I'm not a very good dancer.'

The girl linked her arm through his. 'Come on,' she said. 'I'll teach you how to jive.'

On the Empire's dance floor, Nina rested her head against Hugh Morgan's shoulder. The lights had been dimmed for the last, slow dance, the spinning glitter ball casting its shards of light at the dancers' feet. From the stage the singer crooned, *I'll be seeing you, in all those old familiar places ...'* Nina closed her eyes, remembering that this was one of Bobby's favourite

272

songs, that one September evening in 1940 she'd noticed him leave a dance as the band began on its opening bars. Outside a bright, full moon hung low in a troubled sky, and she'd watched him gaze at the racing clouds as the music played on without them. Years later he told her that fear would charge at him out of the blue, a huge monster of a feeling that left him feeling flattened and useless. That night he'd turned to her and smiled, his eyes dark with exhaustion. 'Sad songs,' he said. 'Shouldn't be allowed.'

In the Empire the singer drew breath for the last verse. Soon the lights would come up and she would be revealed, smudged and dishevelled in the merciless brightness designed to discourage lingering. She couldn't allow Hugh Morgan to see her like that and so she stepped away from him, smiling fleetingly at his questioning face. Opening her bag she took out the cloakroom ticket and held it up in explanation. 'Shall we avoid the queue?'

'May I see you home?'

As the hat-girl handed them their coats, Nina glanced at Hugh. Thinking about Bobby had made her feel as vulnerable as he was – as though she wasn't wearing knickers and everyone could see through the flimsy fabric of her dress. She put her coat on quickly, bowing her head to fasten its buttons. When she looked up again he was watching her, a good-looking, wholesome man, certain of sex. In the dance hall, she'd noticed other women casting sly glances over the shoulders of less glamorous men, their eyes lingering on his face. Nina could tell what they were thinking from their smiles: too handsome. Such good looks were almost preposterous.

She turned up her astrakhan collar. 'It's only a short walk,' she said. 'Not far.'

Hugh Morgan was tall as well as handsome, broad and muscular as a navvy, his skin tanned. She'd always imagined sailors as small and lithe. She supposed she'd seen too many films in which agile boys climbed the rigging of sailing ships, quick as monkeys. But the navy didn't have sails any more, just

273

the industrial metal of battleships. In the newsreels the ships were vast and slow and looked invincible. Lieutenant Hugh Morgan would be at home on such a deck.

In her bed he slept on his back, a sheet gathered at his groin. On his left arm, close to his shoulder, a Chinese dragon roared fire, its eyes bulging malice, its tail twisting to a devil's point. He'd smiled as she'd traced her finger over it. 'I was drunk. I wanted an anchor.'

'Too dull.' She drew her hand away, sitting back on her heels.

He'd reached up to cup her face in his palm. After a moment he asked, 'Why did you come to Dad's party?'

'I wanted to meet him. Ever since I first read his poetry –'

He laughed, shutting her up. Fumbling on the bedside table for his cigarettes, he'd glanced at her. 'Have you read the new book?'

'Of course.'

'I haven't. Not a single line.'

Still sleeping on his back he snored, a noise that broke into garbled speech. She sat up, taking care not to wake him, and shrugged on the silk robe with its pattern of Japanese gardens. In the corner of her bed-sit she set the kettle on the single gas ring and stood over it, ready to turn off the heat as soon as its whistle sounded. Above the sink her window looked out over the huddled rooftops of slums, the crooked line broken where bombs had dropped. She could see the dome of St Paul's in the near distance, so unaffected by the surrounding destruction that there was talk of divine intervention. Such talk made her feel weary. She rubbed at a sticky spot on the glass; a few days ago she'd removed the strips of tape a previous tenant had criss-crossed over the pane, the process a chore rather than the ritualistic celebration of the war's end she'd imagined it would be. In the end, there had seemed nothing to celebrate.

For the whole of VE Day she had stayed in her room. Below her window crowds sang and cheered and she imagined strangers embracing on the street. Later a fight had broken out, American voices cursing like film gangsters, a lone police whistle sounding frantic, foolishly impotent. There was a noise

274

like a gunshot, a car backfiring or a firework kept safe for the duration, exploding for the victors. All the same, in the morning she'd expected to see a body sprawled on the pavement, blood thick as tar in the gutter. She'd kept the blackout curtain closed tight, keeping the revelry at bay, and thought about Bobby enduring yet another operation on his hands. She hoped that the streets around the hospital were quiet, that someone would explain to him when he woke from the anaesthetic what all the fuss was about. After an operation he was confused and anxious and she'd wished desperately to be at his bedside, at the same time guiltily relieved that she wasn't.

The kettle whistled shrilly and the stranger in her bed garbled a command from his sleep. Turning off the gas, she stayed very still, watching to make sure he slept on. At last, reassured, she made weak, black tea, sweetening it with the last of her sugar ration before taking *Dawn Song* from her bag. Curling up in the room's only armchair she began to read.

The Boy I Love

In Marion Husband's highly acclaimed debut novel, the first of the trilogy completed by *All the Beauty of the Sun* and *Paper Moon,* war hero Paul Harris returns from the trenches and finds himself torn between desire and duty. His secret lover Adam is waiting for him but so too is Margot, the pregnant fiancée of his dead brother.

Set in a time when homosexuality was 'the love that dare not speak its name' Paul must decide where his loyalty and his heart lie.

ISBN 9781908262721   £7.99

Paper Moon

The passionate love affair between Spitfire pilot Bobby Harris and photographer's model Nina Tate lasts through the turmoil of World War Two, only to be tested when Bobby is disfigured after being shot down. Wanting to hide from the world, Bobby retreats from Bohemian Soho to the empty house his grandfather has left him, a house haunted by the secrets of Bobby's childhood. Here the mysteries of his past are gradually unravelled.

Following on from *The Boy I Love*, Marion Husband's highly acclaimed debut novel, and *All the Beauty of the Sun*, *Paper Moon* explores the complexities of love and loyalty against a backdrop of a world transformed by war.

ISBN 9781908262745   £7.99

Á

Accent Press Ltd

Please visit our website
www.accentpress.co.uk
for our latest title information,
to write reviews and
leave feedback.

We'd love to hear from you!